Sue,

The Tantalizing Tale of a Bitter Sweetheart

Champagne Wishes and Cupcake Dreams

Never stop dreaming.

Jessica Ashley Dafoe

Jessica Ashley Dafoe

Produced by:

FriesenPress
Suite 300 – 852 Fort Street
Victoria, BC, Canada V8W 1H8

www.friesenpress.com

Distributed to the trade by The Ingram Book Company

TABLE OF CONTENTS

ACKNOWLEDGEMENTS

Firstly, I'd like to give thanks to my wonderful mom and dad who are constant encouragers, motivators and systems of support in all that I set my sights on. I am truly blessed to have you for my wonderful and loving parents.

I would also like to thank the two best big brothers a girl could ask for. Along with their lovely wives and adorable children, they always manage to bring laughter and joy to my days.

To my girls, Lynda, Cheryl, Jackie, Veronika, Cynthia, Alicia and Julie, I hope you know all of the ways you have brightened my life since I made the transition to Toronto. I appreciate you all and I hope you each see how different facets of your unique personalities and lovely natures have found their way into creating the vivacious group of girls in my novel (minus Liv and Angelica).

To Chantal and Sara, who have remained dear friends and confidants even though distance separates us.

To Jayson, for encouraging me to write and instilling a "go get it" attitude, as well as for simply being the remarkable and hilarious individual that you are.

To John, for advising me in regards to the steps to take during the publishing process.

To my editor, Alethea, for all of the hard work put in while editing my manuscript.

Much thanks to all. You all played a pertinent role in my debut novel coming to fruition.

CHAPTER 1

He gazed deeply, longingly, lovingly into my eyes. There was an uncontrollable force that was perpetuating our forbidden tension. Every breath I exhaled was filled with a yearning for him. Every breath I inhaled was inflating me with more passion, more need, more animalistic lust.

The scene was all so perfect, with the meadow surrounding us, the waves rippling up over the rocks in the distance, even the brilliant sunset; it was one like I had never seen before, saturated with every warm hue imaginable. Every fleck of colour in that far off fire ball will forever be engrained in my memory as a reflection of my heated ecstasy at that moment felt for this man who sat embracing me and who was, himself, perfection personified ten-fold.

He tenderly kissed my neck as he ran his fingertips along the small of my back and pulled me in tightly to then meet his soft lips with mine. My whole body seemed to be melting in his embrace while he caressed my mouth with his own. It was a kiss so unimaginable I could have sat there forever needing nothing more.

As his lips left mine after what seemed like an eternity, he gently stroked my cheek and reached into his pocket with his remaining strong and nimble hand. I felt as though my body had been transported to the heavens while this dashing and debonair man kneeled before me with a recognizable Tiffany jewellery box in hand. I gasped for air and felt numb. My life would be forever changed because of this moment. My own Harlequin romance made real.

I watched as he flipped the box open to display the most gorgeous diamond inlayed ring. Two and a half karats gleamed up at me, beckoning me home to this wonderful man's heart. While he removed the ring, I saw his lips move as if to say *marry me, marry me.* However, all I really hear is a faint ringing and repetitious sound……

"Portia, Portia, Portia."

The words that are suddenly harassing my ears become louder and louder; the image of my picture-perfect proposal fades into a swirling-sketch and then to nothing.

"Get up! Wakey, wakey, Portia!"

Oh damn it all to hell. Of course it was just a dream!

CHAPTER 2

"Portia! Portia! Get up already! You're about a zillion minutes late for your first day. Come on, you lazy imp!"

Oh, I hate being torn out of a lovely slumber when I'm in the middle of the most wonderful dream, and woken up by the horrendous bellowing of my meddling, unbearable roommate, Minnie. The dream was perfection, and waking to a reality that can only be described as the opposite of perfection, is highly undesirable, yet this similar feeling each morning as I come to, has been my lot in life.

I slowly open one eye to see a familiar, thin, curly haired red-head glaring at me from my bedroom doorway. I quickly shut it and feign being back in a deep sleep.

Why, oh why, can't I wake up to a dark haired, charming and handsome man as opposed to this?

"I saw that, Portia Delaney!" she sounds frustrated. "Not only are you late, but you're making me late too, because I'm doing *my* duty as *your* friend and roommate to be sure that you don't screw this one up! Now get on with it! Up, up, up!"

At this point, she has found her way to the bottom of my bed and is now dragging me by my perfectly pedicured feet, because you never know when you may end up on a date with a gentleman who is won over by a well-cared for set of tootsies, (although I haven't been on a date with a "gentleman" in over six months).

"Okay! Okay! You maniac! I'm up and I can be ready in five minutes flat, so get your skinny rear out of my room and let me get myself together. Thank you, and please be on your way now." I quickly jump to my feet after Minnie unhands them, and sternly guide her out into the hall, slamming the door behind her.

"Have a lovely day!" I manage to say in a sharp and clearly irritated voice.

Minnie is a workaholic, freakishly organized, highly paid executive at an ad agency. Why she still wants or needs a roommate is beyond me. I suppose it's because work is her life and any ounce of energy she has, she wants to be poured into her career, not her home life or even love life for that matter. Minnie is the power-hungry career-oriented woman who honestly, no word of a lie, could not give a damn whether she ever marries or has a family of her own. Sometimes I wish I had that mindset, because I, Portia Delaney, am ever hopelessly focused on finding that one soul mate.

Now what? Dressed, yes I must choose an outfit for the first day at yet another mind-numbing, low paying office job at yet another medical office. I really want to be styling the rich and famous, and designing clothes intended to be strutted down the runways of Paris and Milan, *not* stuck in a dead end job that has me working for pompous and self-absorbed doctors, who get to drive off in their luxury cars and head home to their glamorous trophy wives, not to mention who give absolutely no notice of the front desk help.

Why didn't I listen to my heart instead of my nagging parents?

All right, outfit, yes outfit. Well, this is the most inexcusable tidbit of all. I'm here selecting an outfit for a first day at a job where my only selection can be from an assortment of various coloured scrubs, when I want to be making a selection between Gucci and Versace. *Lavender it is, I suppose.*

With that disgruntled decision made, I reach for my terribly ordinary lavender scrubs, pull them on, jet into the bathroom and whisk a brush through my hair while applying a pinch of foundation and blush. A bit of tinted lip gloss and a quick once over with the toothbrush and I'm set to go. Yes, to go to my …well…bore of a career. Pay increase or not, just the thought of getting compensated to give up my dreams on a daily basis makes my stomach turn, and anxiety take over.

"But enough of this negativity, Portia Delaney," I say out loud to my reflection in the hall mirror. "You are a successful, adorable, intelligent, creative, and inspirational woman with amazing potential. For you, nothing is impossible!" Okay, so do I actually believe this bunk? Not a word. My shrink surely is trying to make me think I do, but, let's face it, I'm at rock bottom with S.O.S. carved in the sand and flare guns blazing.

I suppose, however, there is nowhere to go but up. Work is blah, love life is blah, family life is…well, is what it is. My friends are mostly amazing, but sometimes having great friends who seem to have it all together, just helps highlight everything lacking in your own life. With that summation of my view on my life circumstance, I slip on my god awful, yet comfy Crocs, grab my Marc Jacobs purse, because I must still demonstrate *some* good taste in my daily wardrobe, and strut out the door while working those lavender scrubs to the max.

As the doors open to the elevator my heart skips a beat. That intriguingly mysterious and dashing man from the lobby I crossed paths with the other day is standing opposite me taking in my attire from head to toe. I've secretly been scouting this guy out for months now, but it wasn't until last week that we had our first verbal interaction. We were both checking our mail and he had accidentally received my cable bill in his mailbox. I acted all aloof, because an acquaintance of mine, Lucia, told me aloof is attractive to men. She has been with a gorgeous anchorman for three years, so she *must* know a thing or two about this stuff.

I then tried to converse about how little I watched television due to having so many hobbies. He then asked about my hobbies and I froze. I froze! I couldn't think of one! I couldn't even *make* one up because the idea of "having a hobby" was so foreign to me. I just stood there, eyes wide like a deer in the headlights, attempting to conjure up some interest, then I got thinking about how sad it was that I didn't have a hobby, and by that point he was so uncomfortable, rightly so, that he simply said, "Well, enjoy your afternoon," and walked away scratching his head.

Immediately after I went straight up to the apartment, flipped on the television, and attempted to create a list of actual hobbies that I have, just in case I ever meet him again and have the opportunity to redeem myself. After scribbling *television, wine,* and *baths* on a notepad, I then decided to make a list of fake hobbies. That list included: horseback riding (never ridden one in my life), baking (hahahaha), gardening (well, I did manage to keep all my neighbours plants alive when asked to water twice weekly while she was away on business), fashion (yes, I *do* have an interest and want to make this more than a hobby, but I now realize it is not *even* a hobby). With that I concluded that this must change! I then wrote "GET A HOBBY!!" to finish off the list.

Anyway, back to reality and the present circumstance. This unbelievably gorgeous man who I made undeniably uncomfortable days ago is now standing two feet from me, a half worried, half sincere smile on his face, dark tousled hair, so perfectly out of place, pin striped suit and checked tie. Professional, dapper, yet still somewhat misplaced, as though the clothing doesn't belong on him. He's like a woodsman playing dress up. He's, in short, the picture of my perfect man.

At first glance, he looks like he has it all together, but underneath, he's a little awkward and rough around the edges. Kind of like me. Well, I suppose at this exact moment, I'm a bit more obviously rough around the edges as I haven't had the motivation to shave my extremities for days. However, one good thing about scrubs is they mask all that prickliness wonderfully.

"Good morning," the gentleman says when I enter the elevator.

"Oh, hi there," I manage while feeling my skin get a bit hot. I then become terribly aware that this means I'm beginning to get those red blotchy marks on my neck that result when I'm a bit embarrassed.

Oh why didn't I wear that patterned scarf I had intended to? That would have hidden this mess!

Too late, the embarrassment and frustration feels as though it is producing a bright red blotchy neck and there is nothing I can do about it. I notice the dark-haired gentleman (I think I'll name him Lucas; he looks like a Lucas) glimpsing at my neck. His mouth is beginning to gape a bit in surprise at the noticeable and sudden change in my colouring. "So, watch any good shows on the tele lately?" He asks with a bit of a sly chuckle following.

"Ha ha, oh, well, yes, I do enjoy a show or two every now and then, but as I said, the other day when we met, I really do have numerous other interests that keep me quite occupied."

"Riiight," he responds with a rumple of his eyebrow. At that point I'm getting up the nerve to share my fake hobbies with him, when we suddenly reach ground level and the doors open. With that, my stomach clunks out of my throat and back down where it belongs.

"Enjoy your day," he mutters as he heads swiftly for the exit. Perhaps he's late for work as well.

I'm late for work!

I regain my focus then bolt as rapidly as my Crocs will let me motor to Dundas West Subway Station. While on the subway, I find myself analyzing my interactions with "Lucas".

"Why do I always feel so awkward when interacting with drop dead gorgeous men?" I mean, throw a completely hideous man in front of me and I'll have him entranced and asking for my number. *Just* what I want (insert sarcastic tone). Yet, if a real looker is in my presence, I get all blotchy and tongue-tied, not to mention my inability to make eye contact. Sheeeesh! And when it comes down to it, I think I'm quite a catch, myself.

I mean, I don't know where I sit on a scale from one to ten or anything, but I'm content when I look in the mirror and see my olive complexion, due to my mom's Greek lineage, my prominent, yet not overly prominent, nose, my dark eyes that are nicely framed by a thick set of luscious lashes (for real, I don't even need mascara), my curvy size six bod (Okay, Okay, I know six is apparently the new eight, but I'm proud of my size), and all five feet six inches of me is topped off with a mane of chestnut, all natural, coloured hair. Sometimes I'm actually quite smitten with myself. I'm not about to drown in my own reflection or anything, but why is it that I feel like Medusa the awkward Gorgon when a man I'm truly into, comes along. For someone looking for her soul mate, I sure need a boatload of help unless I want to find myself forever waking to curly cue Minnie for life.

The subway ride to my new gig is quite short, and before I know it I'm squeezing my way past pillars of people who seem to be making it their duty to block me from exiting before they witness me make a complete ass of myself. I bounce off a tall lanky man only to get the strap of my bag caught around an impatient looking woman's push buggy. She gives a sigh and rolls her eyes at me, as if I'm attempting to ruin her day by getting on with mine. I carefully unhook the strap, duck under the arm of a man who has his other arm wrapped around his lady friend while making out as if they're on a sinking ship, and I finally slip shakily onto the platform. I dash up the stairs, dodging loads of manic Monday pedestrians, and finally find myself outside *it*, my new dungeon; I mean…my new place of work.

Here we go again.

I take a deep breath, hold my head high, shoulders back, and walk as confidently as I can into the low-rise office building located on the North side of King Street, right in the heart of the concrete business jungle of Toronto. Just the look of it seems cold and unwelcoming. It's all glass exterior and full concrete lobby make me imagine prison bars immediately.

This is not where I'm meant to be. This CAN'T be my destiny.

This same uneasy feeling has followed me to every work placement I have maintained while in the medical administration field. My heart starts to race as the severe looking security guard nods me through to the waiting room. The sliding glass doors close behind me and I feel a gust of wind that makes me shiver and the unshaven hairs on my legs stand on end.

A friendly enough looking woman, with blonde hair slicked back into a tight bun on the top of her head, smiles and makes her way towards me. *God she seems so peppy.* From what it appears she will be my right hand girl in this office. I see my empty chair just off to the left behind the cold, hard, marble desk.

"Welcome!" she says, "You must be Portia! I've heard all about you and we here at Hopewell Clinic are so excited to have you on board. However, do make punctuality the norm, please."

"Oh my, well, I do apologize sincerely. You see, I was actually set to be here early, however the elevator in my condo building got stuck with me on it (lie #1), and then after thirty minutes they *finally* were able to fix the issue (lie #2). Thank you so very much for the warm welcome," I reply, forcing as much cheer as I can muster. "I look forward to learning the ropes and imparting all my expertise to those that I have the pleasure to manage here at the clinic, (lie #3)."

"Pleasure" and "management" really do not go together, in my world anyhow. I have quite a *laissez faire* management style as I completely dislike and flee from confrontation. I suppose that's the reason I've had five different places of work in the past two years. If there were a *Guinness Book of Records* for the most job placement switches by a medical office administrator, I would have the title, hands down.

I left my last job after one of the doctors asked me to take disciplinary action when it was discovered that a nurse, who had been employed by the office for fifteen years, had been swiping medication to give to her OxyContin-addicted boyfriend. I tried to reason with them and suggested she *was* a nurse and perhaps her boyfriend really was in need of the meds. Who better to receive addictive substances from than a qualified nurse, after all?

The doctor was not impressed and we came to a mutual decision that I find employment elsewhere. So the past two months I've been pounding the pavement, visiting employment offices and websites. This job seemed like my only option if I didn't want to be out on my behind from an inability to pay rent. So here I am!

"Oh dear, I have yet to introduce myself. Silly me! I'm Tricia. I'm the office assistant and have been here for seven years, so if you have any questions relating to the office workings, team members, doctors, patients and so on, just ask." She smiles showing all her clearly veneered perfectly gleaming white teeth. "And I'm up on all the inner office gossip too," she says behind her hand with a little snicker trailing her words. "It's like *Days of Our Lives* in this office! Just wait and see. It's pure entertainment!"

Hm, if it's that exciting around here, I mean come on, *Days of Our Lives* is the longest running soap opera on television for a reason, then I may stick around a while. I DO love a bit of real world entertainment after all.

Tricia spends the next hour welcoming patients while squeezing in time to give me an office tour and introduce me to "the team" as they call it. "The team" consists of four doctors, all male, three nurses, one male and two female, two errand girls and Tricia. Of course I'm the newest member of the crew and am feeling like quite the odd one out. They are all so together and perfectly neat with such professional demeanours.

My scrubs are mildly wrinkled, and in certain light I see a hint of a mustard stain that must have embedded itself even after being run through the wash. Oh well, isn't that the story of my life? At least if these people have the drama-filled lives that Tricia promises, then perhaps I will redeem myself by being drama-free. I'm seriously *completely* drama-free. I suppose that's what happens when life is a snore.

When it comes time for me to take my place at my post (the swivel chair to the left) I realize that there is one team member I haven't yet had a chance to meet. He's sitting in a little room off the main reception area, head buried behind a magazine with the landline phone receiver to his ear.

"Who's that?" I whisper curiously to Tricia.

"Oh, ...that?" she says, with a subtle nod towards the rusty haired mystery man, "That's Darryl. He handles the appointment bookings for the patients.

He's the incompetent son of Dr. Langley. Thirty-six years old, still lives at home, can't even remember to take a shower or wipe his own ass without a reminder."

I'm surprised by Tricia's harsh words. She's actually quite the feisty critic behind that angelic grin. "Thank goodness he has that little office to himself, because I don't even want to know what sort of toxic emissions he releases on a daily basis, if you know what I mean. And my nose certainly doesn't want to have to find out." She adds a little disgusted look and eye-roll then immediately gets back to calling on patients and taking paper work with the perma-smile plastered to her face.

Aside from the critical remarks passed by Tricia, this *Darryl* character, from what I can make of him, has a very nice build and if he's got a face that even comes close to matching that bod, then this just might be an incentive to spruce myself up a bit on a daily basis. At this point, a daddy's boy doesn't bother me one bit. If he can tie his shoes and get me out of my current dating/ relationship/ perpetual state of boredom, then sign me up!

While these thoughts are flooding my mind, Darryl spins suddenly on his swivel chair and begins walking in my direction. I get a good look at his exterior and am pleasantly surprised. I notice a strong jaw, flawless complexion, and beautiful blue eyes. Cha-ching! I'm brimming with excitement. As he traipses past, I also get a decent view of his posterior.

My, oh my, we have a winner. Sold, to the insecure, mid 30's gal at the front desk.

It being my first day at a new job, I decide to put the inner office attempt at romance on the back burner until at least the second day. The remainder of the morning and afternoon pass by successfully, and I feel content about the new work situation, although I'm far from thrilled seeing as for the majority of my day I will be chained to the marble slab at which I'm seated. But as long as I have some incentive to get to work each day, in this case the "Darryl Project" as I've now titled it, I'm motivated enough to continue on in this monotonous career- at least until I'm rescued by my Prince Charming, or die of boredom.

There is this feeling deep within my spirit that keeps urging me, as if it's saying, *"Change things up you lazy sod. This career path isn't for you."* And with that, I make a decision to make it my *"laissez faire" p*light to go ahead and do just that.

CHAPTER 3

As I head out of Dundas West Station after my sombre commute home and begin my trek back to the condo, I start contemplating which of my invented hobbies I will make a reality this evening.

Horseback riding? Maybe another Monday night. Gardening? Well if I didn't live on the 11th floor of a concrete condo building with absolutely no outdoor living space, perhaps. Baking? Yes! I will head home and bake some... some banana muffins! I KNOW I have some overly ripe bananas on the counter and I'm sure the rest of the ingredients are available. I'll just search up a recipe online, make the most delicious batch of banana muffins and move "baking" onto a new list, the "Actual Hobbies" list.

When I walk through the door to the condo, I notice that Minnie's black Prada pumps are lined up perfectly against the wall, but they are surrounded by a pair of leather loafers, BCBG ballet flats, and a knee high pair of Steve Madden leather burgundy boots (too warm for those, but to each their own). None of these are Minnie's or mine so I draw one conclusion.... This MUST be a work meeting because Minnie does not have a social life and can't have real life, actual friends other than the ones she has met when I have thrown get-togethers. I say that she "can't" not because she is not allowed to, but simply because she has a less active social life than a sloth. I suppose work friends can still be considered real friends. I, however, don't think Tricia and

I will be spending time together during off work hours any time soon. Darryl, on the other hand, now he may be another story.

As I add my Crocs to the stylish footwear in the front hallway, I do hear scattered laughter and chatter coming from the kitchen. After hanging my purse on the coat rack I shuffle towards the kitchen in my stocking feet, feeling rather curious and excited to uncover who owns the mystery footwear. I round the corner and am thrown into the middle of an unexpected conundrum.

Angelica? Daniel? Nina? What are they all doing here?

Just as this question finishes formulating in my psyche it hits me. *The intervention! Shit.* I had totally forgotten I had planned a get-together with my friend Nina and Angelica, and Angelica has of course brought along her attached-at-the-hip boyfriend, Daniel because they can't do ANYTHING without one another.

The intervention is for our mutual gal pal Charlie who is a hopeless gamer addict. She shamelessly spends all of her time in front of a screen and owns every type of game console that a person could purchase in today's gamer market. The other day I was at my sister's house babysitting my brat of a niece, Lydia, and she insisted on playing Club Penguin, which is a game site for children. Lydia showed me that she had to create an account. Well, she finally got to the game she most wanted to play which puts you in a virtual room where you play against other Club Penguin members and was doing quite well until a player by the name of Charlie1975 annihilated her. I knew immediately it was my Charlie and I hung my head in grief.

That very moment I sent Charlie a text that read *"Club Penguin, Charlie! Really?"* She responded to my text with, *"It's completely stellar! There are so many games to choose from. You should sign up and verse me!"* Right then I knew something needed to be done. So I called Nina, then Nina called Angelica, who of course recounted the whole situation to her "other half", as they term it, Daniel, and we all decided on tonight for a rendezvous-intervention.

How did this slip my mind? Well too late to prepare now, because here we all are, and Charlie will most likely be here momentarily as well. No doubt she will walk through the door playing Angry Birds on her iPhone or some other ridiculously pointless game. I simply just don't understand the gamer addict world.

"Portia, babe! We've been wondering what's been keeping you!" My enigmatic and bubbly friend Nina shouts excitedly. As she does so, she pounces on me to give me one of her bear hugs. The type of bear hug your uncle gives you at holiday time after not having seen you for a whole year. Nina and I, however, meet up at least three times a week. She's forever attempting to involve me in her fly-by-night interest of the moment. Yes, unlike me, Nina has so many interests that she can only pursue them for a week at a time, but I go along with them all to be a supportive, or perhaps submissive, spineless friend.

Last week it was yoga on the water. We were left stranded out in the middle of Lake Ontario with a surfboard and were expected to perform all of the common yoga poses on the board. I can barely perform them on dry land! Needless to say, I spent most of my time in or under the water, gasping for air and chasing after my board. At one point that hunk of junk felt like my enemy as it flipped and on its way down whacked me on the head. Nina had to yield the attention of the lifeguard at Cherry Beach (a piece of eye candy if I ever saw one). He dragged me out of the water as if I were a beached seal, bandaged my head (not the look I was going for), and determined I had a mild concussion. Then he suggested I see a doctor and went on his way. It's the story of my life. The hot ones always leave me with wounds and scurry off.

Nina, herself is a spunky, self-employed entrepreneur. What it is she actually makes money at is a mystery to me. Her work focus, much like her personal interest focus, changes on the regular. Last thing I heard, she had opened a baking studio called *Baking with Nina*. I remember helping to distribute flyers to local coffee shops and community centres to help drum up business, and on them she had included a picture of an elderly Italian lady. This pretty well indicated that this woman *was* Nina. I knew this was a bit misleading seeing as Nina is a petit, blonde firecracker who has barely spent more than an hour in her entire life, baking.

After the distribution storm, I never heard another word about *Baking with Nina*, which kind of ticks me off as I spent hours printing and handing out those flyers. I got the worst sunburn while distributing them and that night I had a blind date. He took one look at my deep- fried epidermis, muttered some excuse about an emergency situation then flew out the door.

"Nina! Angelica! I'm so sorry to keep you waiting! I stopped at the market to pick up some food, but then figured, why not order in? Mondays always make young, hardworking professionals deserving of pizza or Chinese, or both!" I've been lying a little too well today. I'm beginning to frighten myself.

"Right on, Portia!" Daniel says in his irritating, mushball-for-a-mind, voice.

"Yes, pizza would be lovely, Port." Angelica joins in, "Preferably, gluten free, vegan with lots of spinach." Nina and I look at one another, and giggle.

"Well, *you* girls order what *you* want then. Don't let my concern for all of our well-being get in the way!" Angelica huffs away and drops on the couch in a sulky manner, while Daniel follows like a puppy dog.

"Oh, Ange" Nina blurts out, "Stop being so sensitive! We understand your need to feel healthy and be a good influence on us, but babe, after a shit Monday, we all just want some nice grease in our belly. Join us just this once. Plus we do want Charlie to have reason to stick around when we call her out on her gaming B.S."

Angelica is definitely an oversensitive, spoiled, health nut. I adore her and despise her all at once. She has always gotten whatever she has wanted in life and still manages to make others feel badly about insignificant items, such as pizza toppings. She lives off Daddy and even though she has never expressed any interest or talent for fashion, had her father foot the bill to start up a handbag line. She does nothing aside from hire the designers who create the bags. Then she has the audacity to stamp her name on the designs.

The *Angelica* Line is doing remarkably well all over the country and may even crack the U.S. market. I was livid when she didn't even consider me for the design team. I would, however, prefer to gain full recognition for my designs and not be the mystery designer behind such a brat. Additionally, I suppose I should actually get down to designing something more than the pieces I threw together during my early post-secondary education years. That was ten years ago and fashions have certainly changed.

As for Daniel, well there really isn't much to say about him. He has little substance. He is all beefcake, no brains. Apparently he has a degree in fine arts however I have yet to see any artistic ability or an appreciation for anything art related. About three months ago, Nina and I purposely invited Daniel and Angelica to our "art day outing", as Nina termed it. Art was Nina's interest of the week and we both thought it was the perfect opportunity to see Daniel shine in his element, and maybe give us reason to respect and accept him. He showed up and literally complained, lounged on benches and displayed zero knowledge or interest in any of the art. We were at the AGO for god sake! The most impressive art you can find hangs in that place. I'm under the impression that Daniel is ever the wandering dependent as well. He lives off Angelica's success, or her Daddy's, I should say. It pains me to even attempt to understand him.

"So, cheese, pepperoni, bacon and tomatoes! That's what I'm ordering. Take it or leave it." I announce. I see Angelica with arms crossed looking rather pissed, but she nods in compliance. Daniel wraps his arm around her to console her "wounded ego". *Oh please.*

"So here's how we're going to do this, Charlie will show up and let's make it really fun for her, as if it's not an intervention, but sort of a surprise party. It's like we're celebrating her new life, void of gaming influences!"

"Great idea, Port!" Nina interjects, "Remember I had that party planning business for a couple of months last year? I threw *the* best surprise party and the guest of honour could not stop raving about how perfect the décor and the actual moment of surprise was. Let's all hide in the kitchen. Minnie, you be a dear and open the door when she comes up. Lead her in but pretend that we all forgot and aren't here. Walk her in to have a chat. We will all yell 'New year, new rear!' then throw confetti."

"Why 'New year, new rear?'" I inquire. "And where is this confetti, you're talking about?"

"It's like a new year because the new Charlie is starting right here, right now. And rear is a part of her anatomy that rhymes with year! I have confetti baggies in my purse at all times, Port! Life should be celebrated always and confetti makes life a constant party. It makes every situation fun and happily messy! The best kind of messy!" Nina explodes with unparalleled enthusiasm.

"Good lord, Nina! You have such a zest for life, it sickens me and intrigues me all at once" I reply bluntly. To be honest, I kind of envy Nina's vivacious ways. She keeps her head held high and skips through life, making even the dullest of moments exciting. She doesn't have a boyfriend, yet gets asked out for dates constantly. She gets so many requests that she can actually be picky! I sometimes enjoy living vicariously through her and almost find myself more excited for her dates than for my own. Weird, I know. She always texts me as soon as the date ends and recaps the entire course of events.

Her last date was a setup by a friend of her mother. It turned out that the guy was the grandson of the woman and he still lived at home at the age of thirty-five. He had *never* been independent. Nina said he was so awkward and nervous that his upper lip quivered throughout the entire date and that he spilled hot coffee all down his navy blue knit sweater, which Nina said had clearly been chosen by his grandmother. Lord her stories are entertaining as hell! I have to say, that I've experienced numerous awkward dates but usually I'm the nervous wreck, spilling beverages down my attire.

"Port, your sickness is my joy!" Nina responds as wittily as possible. "Now let's get this pizza ordered, the streamers up, and this confetti ready to be tossed!"

Nina begins rooting through my "craft closet" which consists of old gift bags and tissue paper. She grabs a wad of purple tissue paper and a pair of dull scissors from the kitchen drawer, then she begins cutting strips so vigorously that she looks like one of those angry holiday time gift wrappers you see at the mall. You know the ones who look like they would rather be walking across hot coals than wrapping other people's gifts for minimum wage over holiday time. Nina, however, has a look of pleasure on her face. She's in her element and obviously loving this little project.

When she finishes cutting what seems like ninety-five strips of tissue, she begins fastening the streamers together with scotch tape and twisting them decoratively around the two pillars that stand in the living room. She then directs Angelica and Daniel to get off their rumps and to make themselves useful by looking for candles for a more soothing atmosphere. The two jump up off the couch like they're cadets in the military being given orders by the general.

"I found a load of scented ones!" Angelica shouts from the bathroom.

"Perfect! Bring them here, Ange," Nina replies gleefully. Angelica hands the candles over and Nina already has the match lit ready to set each one of them alight. She then takes four of the six candles and creates a fascinating centrepiece on the coffee table amongst glistening confetti and some white lilies, which were taken from the vase in the entrance corridor. The other two candles are set strategically on the windowsill amongst more spar-kling confetti.

"The pizza will be here in ten and Charlie just texted me to say she will be here in fifteen. She's apparently running late due to subway issues, which I think decoded means 'getting to the next level in *Candy Crush Saga*'", I inform the others with a slight hint of sarcasm in my voice. "Wow! Great job Nina! Looks fab!"

I glance around to detect that Angelica and Daniel have firmly planted themselves back on the couch, next to Minnie, who is trying to no avail to complete the final chapter of her book. The poor dear has been inching away from the incessant couple who keep sprawling even more as Minnie attempts to leave space between herself and the two.

"Angelica! Daniel! Come over to the kitchen and help with the drinks as we decide on who will do the majority of the speaking to Charlie."

"Well, naturally you should, Port!" Angelica retorts. "You know Charlie the best. We all were first introduced to her through you."

"That sounds about right Port," Nina interjects. "I hadn't the slightest clue that Charlie had a gamer addiction until you brought it to my attention when we were all getting pedicures and you called her out. Granted she was so entranced in the game that she wasn't even enjoying the pedi, which had me speechless! I think I remember her even telling the woman who was giving the pedi to stop the service for a moment while she attempted to combat the next villain! I suppose I can remind her of the craziness of that event?"

"Yes, please tell her," I respond, "I'll definitely lead the intervention if you girls (totally disregarding Daniel's being present), would remind her of moments that she has missed due to her fixation on her games."

It was true that I had introduced Charlie to the group. About seven years ago I met Charlie while bowling with my work colleagues at the time. It was some lame attempt at boosting morale in what was a graveyard of a work placement. Charlie was manning the shoe counter and I asked her for a size eight. She casually slid a pair my way, and whispered, "I wouldn't put these shoes on if *you* paid *me* to! I mean, think of all the diseased feet that have been in there."

I was so disgusted by her comments that I slid the shoes back to her and said with a giggle, "Thanks! I think I'll pass."

Needless to say I did not join in on the bowling. Instead, I sat by the shoe counter, keeping Charlie company and seeing how many people she could turn off from bowling that evening with her shoe comments. A total of nineteen bailed on bowling. Unfortunately, but for completely legitimate reasons, Charlie did not last long at that job, but she gained a forever friend (or so I hope) from the experience. Charlie is now between jobs, which I'm positive has to do with her gaming obsession. It's just so depressing.

About a year later I met Nina, also at a work function where she was trying her hand at motivational speaking to inspire individuals to become fearless entrepreneurs. We kept in touch and I introduced the two a few months later. Finally, Angelica joined the mix when I met her at *Fitness First*, a local gym

I joined when they had a promotion for half price memberships. We almost died of exhaustion in Ms. Fitastic Frieda's spin class. And the rest is history.

Just then the buzzer sounds and I run for it, "Papa Joe's, delivery," a husky voice growls before I can even inquire as to who it may be.

"Come on up!" I respond as I flick the button to allow entrance. "That was fast!"

As Papa Joe's delivery man, goes on his way, I feel a grumbling in my belly that is making me want to attack that pizza like a rabid vulture. If I was alone, I would have inhaled three giant slices without a second thought, but whenever others are around, surprisingly enough, I have wonderful will power and can appear to be quite refined.

Just at the moment I'm trying to hold myself back from tearing a slice and devouring it, Angelica saunters over, opens the lid to the pizza box takes one glance and contorts her face to display the most disgusted look. "Yuuuuuck!" she adds, "I'd rather starve. You girls enjoy because Daniel and I are not partaking in consuming that fat filled mess that YOU call dinner."

"Fine by me!" Nina bursts into the kitchen, "The more for us fat-loving beasts."

Lord, do I ever love Nina. She always says the things that are foremost on my mind, which I'm too nervous to say because I'm too concerned I may inadvertently offend people. Most of the time she's bang on, and there are rarely repercussions suffered. My therapist, Dr. Lola Richardson, says that Nina has become somewhat of a mentor to me and that I should pick all of the facets of her personality, which I envy, and emulate them. In short, stop living vicariously through Nina, and start making fearlessness my goal. I haven't yet set the wheels in motion on this plan; I suppose I'm, ironically enough, too afraid.

"Okay, ladies. Take these baggies from me. Everyone gets her own. Sorry Daniel "Nina glances over at Daniel, "There are only enough baggies for four people and Minnie needs to let loose a bit. Let her hair down, so to speak. So you can just perhaps wiggle your hips a bit and holler."

I glance over at Nina, and see a smirk on her face. Here's my chance to join in on her silliness, "Yes! Shimmy and shake, Daniel! Come on let's all practice pretending to throw the confetti while Daniel practices his primo dance moves." Angelica looks at Daniel and shrugs with a look of "I suppose this is alright".

Just then Nina selects *Groove is in the Heart* on her phone, "Alright, Daniel, let's see those welcoming moves!" she bellows.

Daniel begins shuffling shyly from side to side, with blushed cheeks while awkwardly looking at the floor. "Shake it!" I yell, "Yeah you shake what your mamma gave ya, you delicious hunk of man meat!" Maybe he majored in the fine art of dance and had been concealing it all this time!

This tactic actually worked! Daniel went from side shuffling awkwardly initially but with every coaxing cat call he began contorting his body to the most original positions. It was sort of like yoga and weight training set to music, with a hint of ballroom thrown in as he would incorporate a jazz slide intermittently. Nina gives me the thumbs up and sends a wink my way, while Angelica's expression is one of horror. Daniel, meanwhile, continues to perform as if in a dance trance.

My favourite move he did was when he squatted as deeply as he could and then shot up in the air where he performed an attempted scissor kick. There was little to no extension on the kick and he landed on one foot, lost his balance, teetered into the curtain, became somewhat entangled, yet continued to shimmy and dance his way along the curtain until he became untangled, as if it was all a part of the act.

The song finally ends, and Daniel comes to, only to slink back into his shy and awkward manner of being. He seems a tad bit embarrassed but simply saunters into the living area and slumps back on the sofa as if nothing at all had taken place. Angelica, still somewhat aghast at what had just transpired, looks over at Nina, Minnie and I, gives a nervous, embarrassed half grin, and follows Daniel to the sofa. They begin having a 'whisper chat', which looks quite intense. I, on the other hand, am feeling quite proud of myself for joining in on what resulted in becoming a hysterical situation. Dr. Lola would be proud I've let loose a bit and joined in on Nina's wackiness. Lola is like the older model of Nina. I keep meaning to introduce the two because I truly believe they'd be like two peas in an eccentric pod.

Just as I'm analyzing the similarities between the two, my phone beeps, "It's Charlie, everyone! She's just down the street and will be here in two minutes! Take your positions'.

"Yes, yes, but Daniel, dear, you're excused from dance duties," Nina begs, "Please join in on our well wishes and be of moral support. We really don't want to send Charlie running scared, and unfortunately, I fear that your *dance moves* would have her do just that."

Daniel simply shrugs his shoulders in complete compliance. I take it Angelica "whisper chatted" similar words in his ear earlier.

Immediately following Nina's suggestions the buzzer sounds and we all have excited smiles on our faces as if we're about to jump on one giant slip and slide all at once. I send Minnie to the receiver to pretend to inquire as to who is visiting, Up until this point I have been unresponsive to all of Charlie's texts as our plan is to pretend we all forgot, in order to add to the element of surprise. "Hello. How can I help you?" Minnie asks.

"Minnie, it's Charlie! Portia's expecting me. Ring me through please."

"Huh?" Minnie replies, "Okay, but she's not here at the moment. Come on up and you can wait here for her."

"Oh please, Minnie. Portia *must* be there. Where on earth would *she* be on a Monday night? The girl is a homebody if I ever knew one, aside from when Nina or I force her out of her nest."

At these words I feel mortified and look around to see sympathetic eyes directed my way. I suddenly find myself the subject of an unspoken intervention. I shrug it off, (seemingly, although inside my mind is churning at the idea that my boring life is that obvious to others around me).

"Well, she's, she's not here, Charlie," Minnie stutters, "Come on up or suit yourself and wait outside. It's your call." With that Minnie presses the button to allow entrance, and we all hear the click of the door, meaning that Charlie has let herself in.

We quickly grab our confetti, Nina dims the lights, and Minnie guards the door for the grand entrance. A *rat a tat tat* knock on the door leads Minnie to count down on her fingers then she casually opens the door with a nonchalant welcoming smile on her face. "Hi there, Charlie! Come on in and have a drink with me while we wait."

"What do you mean *wait?* Portia told me to be here, no excuses. So I AM. And you're telling me she's not even here?" Charlie replies, clearly irritated, "I skipped a retro Zelda gaming convention to be here tonight." I giggle quietly then cover my mouth with my hand to disallow any noises to be audible. Charlie's reasoning for her disgruntlement helps me to realize that this intervention is beyond necessary.

"Come on in, Charlie, and have a drink. It'll take the edge off." As Minnie says this we hear her footsteps followed by heavier footsteps, and know that it's time. Minnie rounds the corner soon followed by a tattered, ratty-haired Charlie. I point to Nina to hit the light. We all grab a handful of confetti then yell, "New Year! New Rear! New Year! New Rear! New Year! New Rear!"

We continue to chant as we disperse the confetti all over Charlie's knotted mane. Minnie gets a blast of confetti and a few pieces are left dangling from her eyebrow and lodged in her curls. Nina grabs Charlie by the shoulders which becomes the beginnings of a conga line that we all join (aside from Angelica, although Daniel jumps right on board) and continue chanting and conga dancing to the beat of the chant. Charlie looks not only irritated, but mortified at the same time. She's being pushed through the living room around the pillars in a figure eight pattern, over and over while the chant continues.

Finally, Charlie halts the motion of the conga line and yells, "Enough! Enough! I get it! Angelica, you must be the one who put everyone up to this. You, over there on your high and healthy horse. I get it! I'm a fat slob and need to lose a few pounds. Stop the badgering chant! I'll do it in MY time you horrible, horrible people. Oh, and I see you're really serious about this seeing as you ordered pizza of all things, and are serving calorie infested alcoholic beverages." She adds sarcastically, "Sure seems like you want me to lose weight with these healthy options."

Angelica gives a sly sideways glance as if to say, "I told you so."

"Wait, no Charlie!" I interject, "This has nothing to do with weight or weight loss! That slogan just rhymed really well. We want a new year for you in other ways, sweetheart. You have a beautiful figure, really."

"In what ways do I need to make a new year for myself? I don't get it. What is this crap? Candles, confetti, conga lines. It's not New Year's Eve, for crying out loud. Someone please explain," Charlie pleads.

"Charlie, babe, have a slice and a pint, then we'll all sit down and have a nice chat about it. We love you doll." Nina casually takes a slice and hands it to Charlie, then grabs one for herself to demonstrate a silent form of support. She nods to the living room and we all follow suit.

I'm so entirely ready for a slice, I can already taste the deliciousness of that pizza before I tear into it. As we all gather in the living room and take a seat, Nina begins a casual shallow discussion about weather, and what we all have planned for the summer. After hearing about intentions to go cottaging, on road trips and to loads of movies, I step up and step in by mentioning the topic we are all gathered to discuss.

"Charlie, you know I love you and we've been friends for years. We've been through ups and downs and have enjoyed amazing times together. I'm worried about you though." Charlie's eyes are glaring at me as if she feels completely outted and humiliated but has no idea what it's all about. Her dagger eyes make me realize that I perhaps planned this all wrong. If I truly love and care for her, I wouldn't be going about this in a manner that she is clearly not enjoying.

At that moment, I turn to the group and say, "Excuse me, everyone. Please continue enjoying, or NOT enjoying the delicious pizza and beer." I take Charlie's hand and lead her to my room, close the door, flick on the lights and we both sit on the edge of the bed. For a moment we sit there in silence. I gather my thoughts and nerves begin to cause butterflies in my stomach. Charlie continues to glare at me in solemn anticipation of what I am about to share.

"Hun, I'm worried about all of this gamer stuff you're involved in. You don't even look like you anymore." I gently reach out and turn her head to direct her eyes to the mirror. "Have you seen yourself recently? You used to be so well kept and, and clean! You look as though you haven't washed your hair in weeks, and I think I see a piece of biscuit in your hair.

Perhaps some confetti as well.

"This hobby is taking over your life and not in a good way! You seem so irritable and grumpy, anti-social and testy. I know I don't have it all together and I don't pretend to, but babe this is extreme. We brought you here because we all care and want the old Charlie back. Why don't you and I explore some hobbies together. Maybe Nina can suggest something." I plead with Charlie and feel that this may all be impacting her in what may bring a positive result.

Just as I think Charlie is warming to the idea I'm offering up, she lashes out in a manner that I am completely not expecting.

"You care about me. Well, if you cared you wouldn't have run your mouth to nosy Nina and stick up her ass Angelica. You even involved Minnie in this! I am completely fine and proud of who I am in the now. Looks and appearance isn't everything you know! So how about you take a look in the mirror yourself before pointing your manly finger at me! *Ouch!* You are no friend of mine. You've embarrassed, offended, and angered me to a point that…that I don't think this can be fixed, so adios, Portia Delaney."

With that Charlie quickly rises and storms not only out of the room but the condo entirely. I, on the other hand, sheepishly head back into the living room. Where I feel four sets of eyes burning into me and it's so quiet that I could hear a pin drop if it had.

"It looks like things went well," Daniel blurts out, after what seems like an eternity of awkward silence, "I bet my dance moves would have helped the situation."

"Shut up, Daniel," Angelica says sharply.

With that, I slump down on the area rug and am joined by all, but Angelica in finishing the pizza in silence while Nina puts her arm around me. I splurge as a means of consoling myself after possibly losing a friend and swallow the usual three slices, followed by a few beers.

I'm certainly going to feel that at work tomorrow.

As Angelica and Daniel finally make their exit after Angelica sends a fake goodbye air kiss to each of us, I turn to Nina and say, "What could I have done differently? Am I really a bad friend?"

"You're an amazing friend, Port. With this sort of thing she just needs to get there on her own. Unfortunately sometimes it means excluding all the people that love her to see what her life has truly become. Just be there for her when she's ready, sweetie." Why do I pay a therapist one-hundred and fifty dollars an hour when Nina gives the clearest and most pertinent advice?

"Thanks, Nina. Love ya"

"You too, babe. Now get your drunk behind to bed so you can have an amazing day at work tomorrow, you hear!"

Nina grabs a final slice, her Kate Spade bag and makes her way out the door. I slink off to bed with a heavy heart and loads on my mind but know that tomorrow is a new day, and Darryl the office Daddy's boy is awaiting me.

CHAPTER 4

As I wake to a new day, I hear birds chirping and the sun is shining through my teeny tiny bedroom window, ricocheting off the mirror. At this realization my heart sinks just a touch when I flash back to last night's interaction with Charlie, in front of that very mirror. *She became so irate!* I'm still astonished by her reaction. But Nina is right. She'll come around in her own time. Charlie, as I now contemplate things, really is the type that never owns up to anything in the moment, but does come around to an accurate realization eventually.

Like, for instance, when we were all at a house warming party in The Beach, a beautiful neighbourhood just east of Toronto's downtown core. A group of twenty or so were gathered around a bonfire in our mutual acquaintance, Paulo's, backyard and he was giving a speech to thank everyone for coming. Charlie decided to pick up one of the unlit tikki torches and light it on the bonfire. I think she was a bit drunk because she just stood there holding it tightly, yet no matter how tight her grip, her wobbly legs indicated that disastrous circumstances were imminent. In the moment it did cross my mind to steady her and casually remove the torch from her hands.

I, however, did not want to be rude and make rustling or cause a scene during Paulo's speech, so I just hoped and prayed for the best. My prayers went unheard because about three seconds later, Charlie began teetering and tottering back and forth like a cattail in the marsh. This cattail had weight, and after five teeter totters side to side, she fell to the deck with a tremendous thud. The tikki torch made immediate contact with the cedar wood that the brand new lavish deck was constructed out of, and the deck soon was set ablaze.

Guests were running in every direction, some to escape having legs, and designer apparel scorched, others trying to find a water source to douse the flames. Paulo had a look of horror on his face as if he could not quite believe what was happening. He started screeching and literally running in circles trying to make a decision as to what to do to save his newly built gem of a deck. Finally, Paulo's friend Travis had the sense to unwind the garden hose, crank the nozzle to the highest power, and blanket the fire in a heartbeat. Had Travis not enjoyed the company of men over that of women, I would have jumped into his arms immediately and insist we ride off into the sunset.

Honestly, all the good men are gay in this city! It just isn't fair.

The next morning, Charlie denied it all when recapping the evening with me over the phone, and said that she saw the torch was just set alight off to the side, that she had no part in lighting it, and was worried it would fall to produce the very outcome that resulted. Her explanation was that she saw it teeter in the breeze and went to catch the torch before it fell, yet her attempts were too late. I couldn't believe my ears, as I was sure that I was not the only one who saw Charlie light and hold the culprit of a torch. Well, she denied this for three weeks, but when Paulo called her to ask for an amount to cover the cost of the deck and indicated that he had previously installed security cameras in the back yard, therefore meaning he had the entire debacle on tape, Charlie finally owned up. Paulo and Charlie made amends, two thousand dollars later, and the ban on her visiting was lifted.

Anyhow, it's all neither here nor there in this moment, as Charlie has "permanently" excused herself from our friendship. I'm more than certain after all is said and done that "temporarily" is the better adverb to use. *Fingers crossed.* Is it wrong to want to keep a friend close who has similar trials, insecurities, fears and issues and who sets out in life with a, somewhat, bitter attitude such as I do? I just enjoy having a friend who doesn't cause a flood of envious emotion to take over me whenever we spend time.

When I'm with Nina, I constantly feel in awe and almost jealous of the manner in which she cheerfully frolics through life. When I'm with Angelica, aside from wanting to take a pair of scissors and chop off her perfectly maintained honey blonde hair, well, no, I guess that's it.

When I met Angelica, she had just moved from Edmonton, Alberta. Yes, her father is a gazillionaire mainly because he's the CEO of some oil refining business up in Fort McMurray. Angelica was, therefore, fresh off the oil sands and although a beauty, hadn't the slightest idea about high fashion or even the going trends. She had moved here for an adventure, on daddy's tab, and made it her home quickly. It wasn't until I brought her along to a show at Toronto Fashion Week, that she began to take note and step up her own style. She went from thinking GAP was couture to making Prada, Gucci and Dior the norm in her wardrobe. I suppose if I ever do want to crack the fashion industry, I should keep on relatively even keel terms with Angelica as she could have some excellent connections for me.

I jump to my feet...okay slump to my feet...and the topic of mind suddenly turns to Darryl. I catch a glimpse of my reflection in the mirror and notice a smile slowly revealing itself like a fan opening on a hot day.

"Let the games begin"! I say out loud, perhaps a little more loudly than intended, because just then Minnie creaks my door open. "What games, Port? Are there office Olympics at your work as well?"

"Uh, no," I respond, a bit bashfully, and confusedly. "I was giving myself a bit of a pep talk, is all."

"Ah I see. That's great, Port! I'm so happy to see such a positive change in your attitude. You normally would have booted me right out of your room just now, and you didn't! Not only that, you're actually talking to me in a normal tone. It's not even nine a.m. yet! Right on!"

Okay, so she's right. I'm not a morning person. If I'm generally a bitter person in my day to day, in the morning I'm downright wretched. I suppose this whole "Darryl Project" and the slight success last night, wherein I fearlessly led Daniel to demonstrate his passion for creative contortion and movement has got me feeling a tad bit more motivated, and less irritated by people in general. Let's see what the remainder of the day has in store for me.

"Well, Minnie, I know I'm sometimes hard on you, but I want you to know that you are a pretty great roomie to have. I do need to get ready for work though so I'll see you tonight, okee dokee?"

"Sure thing! Have a good one." With that she exits and I enter my walk in closet to make the dreaded work wear decision. Perhaps I'll spice things up a bit and go with leopard print scrubs today!

I grab the scrubs race to the bathroom and have a quicker than quick shower, tidy my wet hair into a French twist. Nina taught me how to execute this style when she had started a door-to-door hairdressing business. It lasted one week as people preferred to make appointments as opposed to being pressured into a new hairstyle at their front door. I brush my teeth, put on more makeup than usual then head for the door. While there I decide on Minnie's Toms for footwear, cram my size eight feet into her seven and a half sized shoes, grab my handbag and rush toward the elevator.

"Good morning, Tricia!" I say with a zesty tone as I approach the marble desk I will be chained to for the next eight hours.

"Hi, Portia! You look smashing this morning," she replies.

I can't help a little smile in response to this, because I know it's the truth as I catch a glimpse of myself in the sliding glass door. "So just to let you know Dr. Brown and Dr. Langley need you to review the order that has just come in and ensure that everything is there. The previous manager submitted the orders regularly but also made regular mess ups."

"I suppose that's why she's no longer here?" I say with an heir of assumption.

"I guess you could say that." Tricia giggles. "Or perhaps it had to do with the fact that she was having a passionate affair with Dr. Markson, and Markson's wife caught wind of the affair, confronted the mistress and vowed to make her life a living hell if she didn't resign and keep her paws off the said Markson. So needless to say, Dr. Markson is off limits!"

"Okay! Thanks for the heads up!" I reply amusedly. "I'm off to check the order."

Wow this place really is like a soap opera. What else will be revealed to me over the next few weeks? Is Dr. Langley secretly a Mafia member and Darryl's in on it, which is the reason he's got a private office of his own? Perhaps he spends his time in that tiny room, laundering money for his dad, or ordering hits on people!

My mind starts swirling with numerous scandals that I imagine to be happening within these walls, when finally I'm brought to my senses by the sight of Darryl trudging into the office. He's got a Jays cap on backwards that is forcing the sides of his lengthy hair to wisp outward as if he has little wings attached to his ears. He's wearing a yellow Nike golf shirt and a pair of cargo shorts, finished off with black converse sneakers and a backpack to add to his student-like appearance. He's definitely a diamond in the rough with that face, those eyes and that physique.

"Hi there!" I manage to squeak out awkwardly

"Hi," Darryl replies sharply as he continues walking directly into his mini office.

All right, baby steps I suppose. Perhaps he's not a morning person either. Maybe I'll give a conversation a try at coffee break time. Yes, he'll be awake and more chipper by then, I'm sure of it!

I spend the remainder of the early part of the day, checking off the supply order and placing new orders that the doctors had submitted for me to look over. With every order item, I find my mind wandering and imagining that the supplies being ordered are for the allocated doctor's personal, private life.

These latex gloves must be for Dr. Colton's drug ring so they can handle the narcotics without a trace. These needles are for Dr. Brown's heroine addicted wife or mistress! Portia, Portia, get your head out of the gutter. All right, think of Darryl. Yes, Darryl. How am I going to strike up a conversation with him? What should I say? I could be generic and talk about the weather. We did have some horrible storms recently. Don't be stupid you complete bore! The news! I'll casually mention the article that I had read recently about the health benefits of coffee and red wine each day! On the other hand what if he doesn't drink coffee and prefers beer? Or worse yet, what if he's a recovering alcoholic and I totally offend him? Ugggg.

I wish conversing with the straight, attractive masses of the opposite sex came easier to me. If I could only pretend that he's not attractive and focus on his flaws, such as his fashion sense, maybe, just maybe I'll have a shot at a fantastic first impression.

After I finish checking the supplies and calling the suppliers with the new list of needed items, I glance at the clock to realize that it's time for a coffee break. I peak into Darryl's office and notice that he is M.I.A. which means he must also have decided to take his morning break. I casually walk toward the break room with the intention of using one of the cappuccino Keurig singles in the office Keurig machine. Perhaps my opening line can be "single for a single?" followed by a flirtatious giggle. I'd probably say it with every intention to sound seductive and instead it would exit my mouth all croaky and crackly as if I were a prepubescent boy.

As I walk into the cramped little room off the waiting area I see Darryl lounging peacefully on the sofa with his feet up on the plush ottoman. His baseball cap is now on forwards and tilted downwards over his eyes so that he can attempt to catch a few winks, I assume. Although I don't want to disturb his slumber, this really is the best chance I'll have to make an impression on him.

I head to the Keurig machine, and clear my throat, trying to make it sound natural and not as if I'm insisting that he notice me. I glance over at him, and I suppose the throat clear was a little too natural because he doesn't even flinch. I begin going about making my coffee, but I have never before used a Keurig machine so am a bit confused by the process to achieve that perfect cup of cappuccino the ads promise. I suppose I need to add water somewhere. I search for the water basin in the machine, identify it and begin filling the machine with the indicated amount. I close the basin, set the cup in the depository and place a mug under the filter. I switch the on button and I hear a gurgling and sizzling sound which I'm sure means all is working as it should.

Momentarily, however, scalding water starts spewing out the top of the machine. I know that it's scalding because a stream of it catches me on the neck.

"Shit!" I scream without realizing how loud or how vulgar I sound. "Bloody hell, this bitch of an apparatus!" I step away from the machine as it continues to spray, and realize just how loudly I was screaming and what a scene I've created as Tricia and Dr. Brown come frantically running into the room. Not only that, but Darryl is sitting bolt upright on the sofa now with an irritated look of confusion on his face.

"Portia! I hope you're alright, but just to let you know the waiting room is exactly adjacent to this room and the walls are quite thin so you must watch your language," Tricia pleads in a quiet yet stern voice.

Dr. Brown gives a glance that needs no words at all. He's clearly annoyed, rolls his eyes and heads back out of the room.

"I'm so sorry, Tricia! Can you please help me get this machine under control?" I beg. Immediately Tricia briskly rushes over and simply flips the off switch, opens the water basin, jiggles it so that it is sitting flush with the filter and turns the machine back on. The cappuccino begins running out into the mug smoothly as if there wasn't any mishap.

"Thank you so much," I say with a whiny appreciative tone. Tricia nods her head and ambles back out to the front desk.

All the while Darryl has been witnessing the situation and shoots me a disdainful look. "It's the first time I've used one of these things. Ha ha," I manage nervously while I feel the colour in my cheeks turn.

"Well, that machine sure got you good," he replies in a monotone and disgruntled voice.

"You've got a mark on your neck that looks like a giant gave you a hickey."

"How embarrassing!" As I utter these words I glance at my reflection in the stainless steel toaster, placed next to the Keurig machine and gasp in mortification. "Portia! You absolute tragic human being!" I blurt out in disgust at the appalling look of the mark the water has left.

"Are you talking to yourself? Why are you talking to yourself? You know I'm sitting here, right?"

"Oh, ha, ha. Yes, yes. I just sometimes have to remind myself of my utter stupidity by speaking to myself out loud. Don't you ever talk to yourself, Darryl?"

"Nope!" he responds, and with total disregard for me, and no intention of carrying on a conversation, he stands up swiftly and strides out of the room.

And that's that! I suppose it was a first impression, just not the one that I had in mind. *Crap...* My mood remains sombre and unmotivated for the remainder of the morning and on into the afternoon. I head out of the office shortly after five and reflect on the situation with Darryl. Well, let's evaluate: I had the confidence to attempt to initiate a successful conversation. It just didn't go as planned.

Darryl remained in his closet of an office for the entirety of the day aside from when he stepped out for what I assume was his lunch break. As he walked past I attempted to make eye contact. He noticed this attempt and his eyes awkwardly and intentionally darted in every direction he could cause them to in order to avoid an eye lock. I suppose that's definitely not a good sign.

Oh well, his loss! Tricia made him sound like he had a load of issues and indigestion IBS problems, so perhaps I'm really not missing out on anything.

Here I go, through the motions of making myself feel better about what is clearly rejection in its most raw form. Girl attempts to get guy's attention, girl gives herself a hickey burn in the process, guy gives disdainful look and avoids girl at all costs. Cut and dried, no question, the definition of rejection.

Shit! The hickey burn!

This thing is going to stick around for at least a week and I'm going to get all sorts of glances from strangers and questions about it from Nina and Minnie, not to mention my parents! For the girls, maybe I can invent some inner office love story. Make it seem like my lover at my new job pulled me into the copy room and the result was the baseball sized wound on my neck.

I guess I'll have to just tell the honest truth to my parents, however, I know they will think the worst and assume it's from some random dude I met but couldn't manage to keep around as a boyfriend. So be it. I'll have to own the bruise with confidence. Nina wouldn't cover it up or hide it, or even be embarrassed by it. She'd brag about it like it was a wound she acquired defending our country in battle. I intend to consider it an accessory and let people think and imagine what they want. Give them something to talk about. I won't be boring old Portia anymore, at least.

At exactly 5:51 p.m. I enter my condo lobby and whisk over to check the mailbox just around the corner. As I open my silver mail slot to find more bills to be paid, I glance out of the corner of my eye a dark-haired gentleman, seated near the elevator. Oh… It's "Lucas" and I'm not prepared for this at all. I can only handle so much rejection in one day.

Perhaps I can take the stairs. Who am I kidding? There's no way I'm walking 11 flights. Maybe he won't recognize me, and if I just ensure that I don't catch his eye, it won't be awkward.

I gently close and lock the mailbox and begin, what I think to be, inconspicuously, making my way toward the elevator, keeping my head cranked fully to the right in order to avoid locking eyes with "Lucas" who is on my left. I must look like a complete horse's ass right now. I'm starting to get a kink in my neck I've cranked it around so hard.

Just as I reach the elevators and press the up button I hear, "Oh Hi P. Delaney!"

Crap. He's spotted me.

I pretend I have a full neck injury and swivel my whole body around while keeping my head positioned to the right.

"Oh, hello! You know my name? I didn't think I ever imparted that information. I surely don't know yours, Lucas" I respond casually although I know I look absolutely ridiculous and having not even realized I added my fictitious name for him to my greeting.

"Huh?... um, anyway, I accidentally received your mail, remember? I only know your first initial of your name, however. What does the P. stand for, and more importantly, are you alright?"

"Well, the P is for Portia, and yes I'm fine. I've just hurt my neck muscles by...by...umm." Before I can think of a believable story, "Lucas" jumps in with,

"Oh I think that hickey on your neck gives me a good idea about the cause of the injury, Portia."

He adds a sly wink.

This damn hickey! Just my luck to run into "Lucas" with this fresh vampire stamp on my neck. He'll for sure think I'm taken or a bit of a tramp, for that matter.

"Ha ha, oh that. Long story! I didn't happen to catch your name yet." I dodge going into detail or inventing some cover up story about my wound and feigned injury. I figure we'll let sleeping dogs lie and let him think what he will. My mind hurts from attempting to be clever and conjure up fictitious accounts of my life for this man. It's exhausting.

"Randall," he replies while advancing towards my right side, with an outstretched hand in preparation to shake mine. I meet his advance with an open palm and feel his strong hand wrapped around mine. Just rough enough to conclude that he's a real man, but not so rough that callouses are chaffing my soft, well-manicured palms.

"I apologize for not being more conversational during recent meetings. Work's a bit hectic and other things have been on my mind, so I'm occasionally not in the mood to chitchat. You have unfortunately bumped into me on those occasions."

Hm, Randall? I like that even more than "Lucas" for him! It suits him just right.

"Well," I say a bit caught off guard by his sociable manner and willingness to not only engage in conversation, but to give reason for his seemingly cold or indifferent behaviour in the past, "no worries. I could tell you were in a bit of a rush both times we crossed each other's path, and I must say that I'm not always the most sociable, depending on the day. No hard feelings whatsoever. It's a pleasure to finally properly meet you, Randall."

Is this really happening? A beyond gorgeous man who I have been distantly smitten with for the past two months has approached me? Okay, now Portia, it's not like he's asking for your hand in marriage. He's simply being a friendly and courteous neighbour. If there's one thing I've learned over the years, it's to keep your expectations low in these situations. I always had the habit of immediately imagining myself married to the man of the hour with his last name as my own even before a date or a second conversation, at that.

My therapist has broken me of this and told me to simply enjoy men's conversation and appreciate them in the now as opposed to building a fantasy in mind for what may come in the future. This way dreams are not crushed. She never says not to imagine, dream and goal set, simply not to pin those fantasies on a specific individual until it's logical. Like say after a fourth or fifth date.

"One thing I wanted to mention to you," Randall says with an heir of concern. "I was in the elevator last evening, on my way to meet friends for a late dinner and a woman, who looked rather a wreck, stepped on with tears streaming down her face."

Oh god. He means Charlie! She probably told him all sorts of horrible things about me and now he wants to tell me how highly inappropriate I was to have pulled something like that last night. Just breathe, Portia, maybe she didn't say anything, maybe it isn't even her he's talking about.

"I'm never one to simply turn my back on a fragile woman who is clearly in distress, so I appealed for her to tell me why she was crying and if she needed me to call somebody for her. Then she sort of unloaded a ton of information that had me a bit baffled. She said that her so called "best friend," he gestures using air quotes to emphasize this, "gathered all her friends to gang up on her to tell her to get her to stop being such a mess.

After she unloaded this information I gently asked her in what ways her friends felt that she should make changes in her life, and I was surprised to hear that she enjoys gaming quite a bit. It's rare to find a woman who appears to be in her thirties that is addicted to video games, but without her even admitting it, I could tell she most definitely does have a problem by how much detail and to what extent she talked about her favoured games and all the conventions she attends. I was surprised when she was at the full height of unleashing all of her emotions that she stated, 'Little Ms. Perfect Delaney! My ass! Some friend! She's the one who has no life and just because I'm enjoying mine, she has to try to take away what is making me happy.' "

With this last addition to his story, I feel the colour change in my cheeks, not because he now knows that I'm the "horrible friend," but because Charlie has outed me as a complete bore.

"Well, you see, Charlie has changed so much since this gaming addiction has gotten a hold of her. I was so worried that I tried to make my concerns known. You must think I'm horrible. Thank you for telling me about your chat with her." I then realize the elevator has long come and gone and I go to press the up button again.

"No, no, you've misunderstood me. I think you're an amazing friend to have gone to such trouble. Not only did you have the integrity to reach out to

Charlie, but you wanted to make it something you thought she might enjoy in the process. So many simply turn their head the other way, no pun intended," he kids, "because they are too worried about a backlash. I applaud you, Portia. It made me re-evaluate my opinion of you completely."

"Your opinion?"

"Yes, well, I suppose, as I said, it had to do with my mood at the moments we had our previous meetings, but I kind of thought you were a bit careless and shallow."

Ouch! Shallow?

"I know that it was wrong of me to peg you as that type, but see, I've dated women who are the definition of those adjectives and I tend to steer clear of them at all costs. You clearly have dimensions to your makeup and seeing how intent you are to support your friends, you're clearly a caring woman. "

As he finishes, I have forgotten any hint of his initial gauge on my personality and am in a tingly daze. My legs feel numb. Did he, Lucas, I mean this stud Randall, just compliment me? I feel as though I'm melting right through this ceramic tile on which I've been firmly planted. I still have enough body control to maintain my stiff neck appearance so I inch my body around to the point that my eyes meet his gaze. His emerald green eyes meet mine, a handsome, full smile on his face.

"Thank you, Randall. That's very sweet of...." As I'm preparing a similar compliment-filled response for him, he becomes entirely distracted and his attention is set on a woman who seems to be giving him dagger eyes from outside. It is quite dark so I am hopelessly unable to get a true glimpse of her, but I can gather that she has mile long legs and a figure to die for with flowing auburn hair, no maybe she's a brunette. Either way she appears to be a stunner.

"Um, is something the matter, Randall?" I ask softly.

"Oh, no, no. That's just my fiancée, Penelope. I was waiting for her to get here. We've got an event to be at shortly," he says dryly as if he'd rather be walking across glass than heading to whatever event was awaiting him. "Well, Portia, it was wonderful to have this chat. I better get going. I don't want to get the Missus in a huff, you know!"

He leaves me with a wink and then vanishes out the door and into the waiting car.

What in the hell just happened here? I was ready to let Randall take me in his arms and he has a bloody fiancée? What a day, what a day. All I need is a couple dozen cats and to take up needlepoint now I suppose.

Just then I remember that tomorrow I have an appointment with Dr. Richardson, not that she at all resembles a cat lady, it just always crosses my mind that without her guidance, that future for me is certainly inevitable. I have a heck of a load to discuss with her. From Charlie, to Darryl, to Angelica to Randall, this appointment could not come at a better time. I finally push the up button and step on the elevator still in a daze about the most recent interaction of the day and think, "It can only get better.

It will only get better."

CHAPTER 5

The next day at the office passes smoothly with only the slightest hiccup along the way, that being when Dr. Markson's wife prowled into the waiting area. She sidled up next to me and demanded I introduce my relationship status and myself. I mean I really don't think revealing my current sex life to the family members of my superiors was in the job description, she however gave me such an intimidating glare, that I felt entirely obligated to disclose every boyfriend, fling, and crush I have ever had and as to whether any of those were "happily" married men whom I was the little dish on the side for.

"If you knew the history of the bull shit that has occurred in this office, previous to your employment began, you would indulge me, ease my mind, and then I'll be on my way," Mrs. Markson whispers sharply into my ear. "I notice you have evidence of a little romp. It's written all over the right side of your neck!"

I see Tricia give me a look of pity followed by a nod, which I suppose translated would mean, "Just give her what she wants already."

"Um, I'm sorry, Mrs. Markson, I really don't have anything interesting going on in my romantic life, absolutely nothing to speak of. The hickey mark is not a hickey! It's a burn that the out of control Keurig machine gave me in the break room yesterday." I respond to her whisper in a nervous tone, which actually causes my voice to go up an octave and exit my mouth as if I'm performing the lead in a Broadway musical.

Needless to say, I've said these words quite loudly and not only Mrs. Markson hears them, but it is clear that Tricia and the entire waiting room have as well because I have at least nine sets of sympathetic eyes on me. Mrs. Markson is a little taken aback by my willingness to admit how sad my current situation is and seems a bit remorseful yet satisfied with the response, all the same.

"Thank you, dear," she says in my ear. As she says these words I feel her breath on my cheek and it makes me shudder. "You keep up the good work."

The miserable woman then casually removes herself from behind the desk and slithers into Dr. Markson's office, no doubt to berate him for selecting a career, which allows him to have his hands on women regularly. I'm sure the poor woman is fed up with his unfaithful ways, but her approach really does not help matters.

After work I'm on my way to Dr. Richardson's office, which is located only five blocks east of my workplace. As I'm strolling along, collecting my thoughts about what I would like the focus of the session to be during this appointment, I see an unkempt, rusty- haired man, resembling Darryl ambling down the opposite side of the street. When I look with a little bit more focus and intent, I determine that it is Darryl, and he's not alone. A tall, slender well-dressed red head is next to him and he has got his arm wrapped loosely around her shoulders. The sun is shining in just a way now that I can't quite capture a glimpse of the woman's face, but she does look familiar.

That aside, I'm taken aback that Darryl seems to have a significant other, and one that is clearly a stunner! Perhaps, Tricia and I have underestimated him in his ability to be attractive to single women who aren't completely hopeless members of the dating pool. A part of me is happy for Darryl and more aware as to why he is so closed off from my attempted advances. Part of me is however even more depressed about my own situation. I am one of those hopeless fish, bug-eyed constantly searching for its dream line to hook it up and out of the murky, slime-bag infested dating pool waters.

I decide that the self-chosen topic to be discussed with Dr. Richardson this evening will be just that, how depressing it is to feel so helpless in the murky, confusing dating world.

The final three blocks of what should be a five minute walk, extends into a twenty minute leisurely stroll, disrupted by frequent stops outside of various businesses including jewellery stores, where I begin to envision being a customer next to my ruggedly handsome fiancé while we carefully select our matrimonial bands. I also find myself perusing the real estate listings out front of a real estate office. My heart sinks thinking about how far in the future it will most likely be before I am able to afford one of these stunning lofts that I've always pictured myself owning. Earning my measly single income causes me to place that dream on the extreme back burner of the proverbial stove of priorities.

I also pass by travel agencies, which have cheap deals of the month with all the packages and flight prices listed in plain view.

Well, if my dreams of having a ruggedly handsome fiancé and the necessary income to afford that swanky loft are currently unattainable, at least my dream of travelling on a budget is not.

I've always wanted to see the entirety of Europe but on the forefront of my wish list is a trip to Paris, Florence and of course Milan. I begin searching the deals for cheap flights to either or all of these cities and see an out- of-this-world bargain on a five night stay in Paris with an included flight all for $1375! I look closely at the fixed dates for the trip and notice the departure dates range between the current week and a month from now. I begin to feel an excitement rising within me. I'm overly aware that the goal of saving and embarking on a journey to the City of Light, in the given timeframe is definitely achievable.

Maybe Nina will kick her entrepreneurial duties to the side for a week and tag along.

It's so strange to think of Nina as a tag along anything though. She'd probably start a touring service on the side while there and make money off the locals. She really is that convincing!

"Well, hello, Portia!" Dr. Richardson greets me as I enter her therapy session room. "I am so very happy to see you and I was thinking about you quite regularly this past week, wondering how you were doing with the homework tasks I assigned you."

Dr. Richardson believes fully in applying what has been discussed at each session into everyday life so that the benefits of her words can be made real to her patients. She therefore gives homework each week and asks that I write down my successes in a journal. I suppose I've slipped on recording my successes but they're all saved on my frazzled and confused hard drive, located underneath my unfortunate frazzled and frizzy mane of curls. It's humid as hell today!

I take my usual place in her office on a low- set plaid fabric, armchair which feels like I've been swallowed up by marshmallows when I sink into it.

"Well, I have had a reasonably successful week, Dr. Richardson. I mean, I know the task was to stop living vicariously through Nina, and to become the characteristics I envy in her. Today I booked a trip to Paris for five days (a bit of a fib, but I intend to, I swear!) and I'm inviting HER to come along with ME. I never take the lead and make the plans because I'm always worried the plans will turn out to be absolutely horrible, and nothing will go right! I guess it's really the tour company that organizes the main details of this trip, but hey, it's a step in the right direction, ain't it?"

"Certainly it is!" Dr. Richardson replies. "Any other news of the week in this area, Portia?"

"Well, I also had decided to have an intervention for a girlfriend who is struggling with a gaming addiction. It was held at my condo on Monday. Although, I mentioned the idea, Nina really did take control of the logistics of the intervention. I did my part to liven things up and impart our concern for our friend by having a heartfelt conversation. Oh, and I've been a little bit more confident when it comes to drumming up conversations with random attractive men. I'm still as awkward as ever when doing so, but that's the topic of discussion for today. Okay Doc?"

Dr. Richardson believes it should be the patient who focuses the session and determines the area of his or her life that is in most need of support. After my encounters and mishaps during the past few days with Darryl and Lucas, I mean…. Randall, I know I could use a lot of help and gain some perspective as to the signals I'm giving off.

"What a wonderful choice, Portia," Dr. Richardson responds.

I love how she makes me feel as though I'm talking to my grandmother. She's only about fifty-five, yet she just has this warm gentle way with me that causes me the sensation that I'm reminiscing with someone who I trust with every part of my being. She's extremely non-judgemental and shows full concern and attention. I suppose I would too if I was making one fifty an hour for it, but somehow I'm lead to believe it's about more than the money for her. She genuinely wants to see me take the steps that will bring happiness to my life.

On the flip side, she's also like talking to a friend who you can share your raunchiest details with, including all the nitty-gritty aspects of life. Everything from drunken one night stands gone wrong to how to spice things up in the bedroom with a current flame. I often feel as though I'm on an episode of *Sex with Sue* in these circumstances. My love life has been so inexcusably dormant for such a long spell, that such conversations have been few and very far between.

My last "flame" was a financial analyst for Brant Energy, one of the most hated energy companies in the country due to their poor marketing and sales ploys. When my parents, who are always overly interested about my advancements in settling down and finding Mr. Wonderful, discovered he worked for this company, they demanded I break it off immediately. It turns out Brant Energy ensnared my folks in a scam that lead to lawsuits and legal talk for months. I had no reason to end the relationship on those terms, as there were additional overly adequate reasons to send him packing.

Everything began relatively smoothly with a first date to a beautiful Italian restaurant in Yorkville, followed by martini and dancing at The Reservoir Lounge, one of the city's most posh jazz clubs. I was too intoxicated after the two shared bottles of red wine at the restaurant and the three martinis, I'd consumed at the jazz club to even realize that he had coaxed me into paying for the drinks at the lounge. I suppose that should have been my first clue that this was going to be an interesting courtship.

It was into our second week of dating that I realized his career as an analyst pored over into all aspects of his life. I was lead to this discovery during one of our lengthy evening phone conversations, which Connor insisted was the key to a prosperous relationship. I didn't want to point out that I thought lengthy conversations only lead to prosperity if they weren't so boring that I had to finish off half a bottle of wine while having them so that I could at least feel a pleasant numb sensation as opposed to the numbness that was brought on by hours of chatting, or I suppose, listening to him chat about logistics and statistics and analyses that he had been able to note about countless boring, god so help me, I don't even know, subjects. And I would just sit there listening and silent and he would push on.

Half the time I would walk away from the phone to go wash dishes or use the bathroom (number one only) and would come back to the phone realizing he hadn't even the slightest clue that I had ever walked away. Connor made me feel better about myself because he was without a doubt the most boring person I had ever known. So at least I discovered that I don't hold the title in that category.

Not only was Connor boring but his obsession with spreadsheets, the Excel programme to be more exact, was freaking me right the hell out. He finally, on occasion would get around to asking me about my day and on one of those occasions I mentioned that, although my job at the time was hectic, it was nice to be able to head to Starbucks next door for a muffin and a mochacchino each day.

I suppose due to being worried for my health, or as attempt to avoid pursuing a relationship with a woman who would transform into a hefty, sizable lady, he appealed for me to stop this midday routine as it was not financially wise or healthy for my waistline. I grumbled a bit and found a way to end the conversation, but at two in the morning I was awakened by a beep on my phone, indicating a text had been received. It was from Connor and it read, *"I told you so"* with an attached excel document tab directly below.

I clicked the link only to be redirected to, of course, two Excel spreadsheets. One of which was entitled, *Money wasted, in daily, weekly, monthly and yearly earnings on Starbucks addiction.* The second spreadsheet was entitled, *Incremental Fat intake and caloric intake over 1 week, 1 month and 1 year due to Starbucks addiction.* This analytical freak had been working on determining these numbers for hours in order to prove that I needed to kick this habit to the curb, but all this made me gather enough sense to do was kick him to the curb.

Directly after, I decided to allow him one more opportunity to redeem himself, as if I expected him to all of a sudden sweep me off my feet and take me on some exciting, adventurous getaway, where he would turn his analytical speak into love sonnets and limericks. Well, it only took forty-eight hours for my hopes of his redemption to be dashed. On a Tuesday evening, while trying to enjoy a cup of tea and an oatcake I heard yet another beep from my phone, indicating I had received a text. When I saw that it was from Connor with an Excel attachment, I almost choked on my bite of oatcake

"What in god's name has he got to analyze and conduct research about, now?" I literally hollered out loud to myself. Once again, Minnie was in earshot and came running just as I opened the attachment and she must have seen a horrific look on my face because she pleaded with me to tell her why I was so pale and if she could get me a glass of water. She also asked if she could grab me a towel for the perspiration that was forming above my upper lip due to pure anxiety and embarrassment that this nut job was causing me.

This sweat, colourless complexion and the utter transformation of not only my mood but also my appearance was all due to the, *Sexual positions that will cause back injury and health concern over one month, one year, five years, ten years and twenty years* spreadsheet. Beneath the main title was a subtitle that read, *Honey, Let's be careful.*

I was livid! This absolute robot of a human being was turning, what should be a beautiful, carefree, act of romance, by which we display love and affection towards one another into a mathematical, worrisome formula that would, without a doubt make for the most wretched and unsatisfying love-making. Oh, I was beyond finished at that point. No more. Good riddance Connor! Once I brought the entire account to Dr. Richardson's attention, she was appalled that I had continued in such a mechanical, unfeeling relationship for the two months that I had.

On this meeting with Doctor Richardson, I was prepared to move ahead with the plan to avoid finding another Connor (perhaps stay away from the veggie section at the supermarket where I met him) and find a dreamboat of a man, who is available, willing and able to sweep me away into the sunset. Okay so at this point I'd just be satisfied with a little witty banter and a romantic walk down Dufferin Street at rush hour.

"So, Portia, I see that you must have gotten a wee bit of action judging by the rather massive love bite on your neck. Come come now. Do tell old Lola the tale."

"Oh my!" I grab my neck. "No Dr. Richardson. You've got it all wrong. This is simply a wound given me by an out of control espresso machine. It sprayed my neck. I completely wish it was a love bite. Believe me. It's been waaayyy too long."

"Ah I see," she responds sounding a little disappointed by the explanation. "Well onward with our little chat then, dear. So tell me, how do you react when a man you are attracted to, or feel that you may have a mutual attraction with, approaches you?" Dr. Richardson inquires, as if she already knows the pathetic reality lying ahead in my response.

"I get all flustered and blotchy, Doc! My neck breaks into hives, my mouth gets dry so that any words that I do manage to formulate and force out of my mouth do so in a high pitched and cracked tone that does not even remotely resemble my normal voice. And as if that's not bad enough, I avoid eye contact at all costs as if I will catch some deadly plague by meeting the said man's gaze. Dr. Richardson, it's dreadful! Please help."

"Dear, the first step is being able to pin point the parts of your interactions that are harming your success in engaging a good man. So we're half way there! Then we just work on perfecting and altering them in just a way that they will go from awkward and off putting, to sweet, endearing and attractive. Believe me, you are a catch and a half and you're doing yourself an enormous disservice by not believing it! The more you have negative inner self- talk and think that you will mess up an interaction, the more certain it is that messing up will be the unfortunate outcome," Dr. Richardson says with a wise and sweet tone.

"So we're going to take this in mini stages, because it sounds like there are a number of nervous characteristics that are triggered in these circumstances. We will work on eradicating one awkward tendency per week. I want you to instigate interactions with men who you would not usually have the confidence to approach, and I don't want your focus to be on engaging them to the point of a date or exchanging numbers. I want you to think in small terms, such as, 'At one point in this conversation I am going to hold eye contact for more than five seconds without diverting my gaze elsewhere without worrying about whether he's fully interested or not.' Yes, let's start with eye contact this week! It is the most simple tendency to correct and will ease you into this activity."

With that, Dr. Richardson rises from her leather armchair and heads out to her office waiting room as I remain seated and a little unsure as to what exactly is happening. A moment passes and she returns with an incredibly attractive young man that I have never met before in my life.

"Portia, let's get started right here and now! This is Angelo. He's a technician from my medical laboratory next door and has kindly offered to take part in starting you on your way to finding confidence and assuredness in your interactions with men."

Angelo does not look as though he has the slightest idea as to what is happening and I can only gather from his stunned expression that he neither offered nor feels obligated to be the pawn in some poor girl's journey through her struggle with inner confidence. However, just as I humoured Mrs.

Markson earlier today, Angelo seems willing no matter how much eagerness is certainly lacking.

I'm feeling slightly flustered but know that Angelo is also feeling awkward so am able to at least keep the neck hive attack at bay, but, today of all days, I would welcome the hives in order to mask the unsightly hickey-like stamp on my neck.

"Portia, I want you to remain seated. First time through Angelo will approach you and I don't want you to divert your gaze. I want you to become comfortable locking eyes with an attractive man. No matter how uncomfortable or awkward it may feel initially, I want you to fight through those tendencies to look away. Think of the staring contests you had as a child (Nina and I had one last week, actually). Use that same approach with Angelo."

As Angelo approached me I opened my eyes as wide as I could, thinking of this as a competitive staring contest. It actually helped me feel less awkward, but I guarantee the scene from the outside looking in must have seemed unbelievably strange. We locked eyes so hard that I could distinctively account for every fleck of bluey-green colour in the man's eyes. We were practically nose to nose and just as I felt an overwhelming sense of embarrassment I imagined it was Nina whose eyes I was examining with the intention to be victorious in a non-sensical game.

I was opening my eyes so wide and with such vigor that they started to well up with tears due to the highly ventilated room and the constant breeze, which was caressing my eyeballs. As the welling of liquid began, Angelo gave an unsure glance over to Lola and then back to me. A look of confusion and a furrowing of the brow alarmed me to the fact that the tears were now streaming down my cheeks as if I was somehow overcome by emotion. Angelo, not knowing what to do, but also being a sensitive gentleman, carefully reached up and wiped my tears tenderly from my cheek.

"There, there, bella. You will find a man. All hope is not lost. Stop crying," he whispered tenderly.

Even though the tears had nothing to do with sadness, I was enjoying the sentiment and being doted on by such a hunk. I eagerly went along with the activity feigning that the tears were emotionally produced. I even added a heaving sob, that came out sounding more like a cow in labour, which unfortunately caused both Angelo and Dr. Richardson to flinch and take a step back in surprise.

Dr. Richardson quickly steps in to change the scene. "Portia, run and get a quick drink of water from the cooler in the waiting area to settle yourself and we'll start fresh with you approaching Angelo when you return. Excellent, maintained eye contact!" she says glowingly.

I suppose I did need a bit of a refresher and a moment to halt my tear ducts. I saunter by Angelo, who gives me two thumbs up and a big, full-toothed grin. I can tell he has me all figured out, perhaps due to what he overheard Dr. Richardson explaining, but also simply because of the way that I carried myself. My insecurities were as evident as a slap in the head to a man who has so much charisma and confidence. I suddenly gain a great appreciation for Angelo in this moment.

I return from my mini-break, ready for more instruction and to be in the presence of such a hunk as Angelo. The remainder of the session involving Angelo actually allows me to learn some techniques in my approach. Angelo is quick to point out some of my mannerisms, such as twirling my hair, biting my inner cheek and fidgeting with my hands that scream, "I'm a nervous wreck!"

At one point I am so into the interaction that I step in extremely close to Angelo so that his dark shoulder length hair grazes my cheek. I do my best not to fidget or lose control of my nerve-filled body by say stepping too far in with aggression that I accidentally knee him in his groin, so the interaction goes relatively smoothly.

I turn my head slightly to the left and look deeply into his eyes once again while paying him generic compliments. In response, this Mediterranean romantic, wraps his arm tightly around my waist and surprisingly dips me so that my fuzzy mane hangs just about an inch from the floor. As he carefully and so protectively pulls me back up, my legs go completely weak, my knees buckle and I fall to the floor with a far less graceful thud. This time, my fuzz makes full contact. As I roll over and glance up extremely slowly to buy more time before full mortification sets in; I finally have Dr. Richardson and Angelo in full view. They are staring down at me like two biologists who have just discovered an unknown species. I close my eyes tightly, then open them hoping this really isn't happening, but as I open them, to my horror, the scene is unchanged.

"Oh, Portia!" Dr. Richardson says with a concerned voice. "You were doing so smashingly well! What in heaven's name happened?"

I can barely gather my thoughts to explain so I don't. I simply laugh. I laugh and laugh until the tears are streaming down my cheeks once again, and by that time Angelo and Doc are laughing along with me.

Angelo bends down to lift me to my feet, however he's learned his lesson this time and continues to hold me steady until I give a little hand gesture that I'm fine.

"Alright,.. Angelo. Well, thank you for your assistance today. I know Portia has already begun to make progress. You're free to go back to the lab. We may be involving you in upcoming sessions over the course of the month, so be prepared."

Angelo gives a little nod and a sly grin then heads back to his day-to-day.

"Portia, well done! As I said before that delectable creature joined us, throughout the rest of the week I want you to make a point to approach men who you know you would normally avoid due to fear of nervousness and awkwardness. Who knows, maybe with your recently demonstrated confidence, you'll have them approaching you! One a day," she adds with a wink. "But do not under any circumstances allow any of them to dip you."

She begins giggling intermittently while she continues to assign my weekly task. "And remember to always make use of only positive self-talk. There is no room for negativity, nothing ever comes from it."

As she is saying these final words of encouragement, Dr. Richardson advances and embraces me in a Nina style bear hug that makes me feel all warm and tingly. She really is like a third grandmother. I think I have a mild crush on Dr. Lola Richardson and perhaps Angelo as well.

CHAPTER 6

The rest of the work week seems to fly by and before I know it, while filing Dr. Langley's patient forms, I glance up to see that it's not just five o'clock somewhere, it's five o'clock right here right now. Not only that, it's Friday night!

I'm brimming with pride while realizing that I've made it through my entire first week with only two horrendous experiences. Okay maybe three if you count Thursday afternoon when I forgot to lock the bathroom door to the unisex washroom and Dr. Brown walked in on me, pants around my ankles deep in thought on the porcelain throne. I would have quickly covered up but I was mid-stream and completely in shock so instead I just sat there and managed to quietly say, "Sorry Dr. Brown. I'll be done in a sec, sir."

"Oh dear god," he blurted. "There is a lock on the door for a reason. Shall we give you a lesson on the mechanics of door locks as well as Keurig machines?"

"No, sir. Sorry, sir," I replied sheepishly. With that Dr. Brown huffed away. He did look unusually tense so perhaps he had been holding his business a while and I took his golden opportunity away from him. I can understand his abrupt nature. I mean it's the absolute worst when that happens.

"Tricia! Have a wonderful weekend. It's been a great week, don't you think?" I brim with joy more so because it is the weekend and I'm heading to a patio with the girls to waste away in Margaritaville, and not so much due to a successful week.

"Oh, Portia, it really has been. You've impressed the doctors and me with your thoroughness.

I'm not so sure Dr. Brown would have the same opinion.

"It's so nice to have an office manager who is focused on managing and not on getting in the doctors pants," Tricia says.

Wow, Tricia actually appreciates my management style! It must have been horrible here before I arrived for her to regard me in such high esteem. Or maybe I have stepped it up and am just not giving myself and my improvements enough credit? Either way, I'm satisfied as I head out the door and into the late afternoon sunshine. Luckily I had the sense this morning to pack a patio time outfit so I don't have to be the dowdy office manager in pink scrubs and Crocs amongst the fashionably forward patrons crowding the patios of King Street West. My transformation will have to wait until I reach Kinko's.

On my walk to the summertime patio my girls and I have deemed our post-work haven, I once again spot Darryl, who happened to have not shown up for work at all today. He called in sick! I know this because I took the call directly from him in which he gave an overly roundabout story that had him telling me details that made me almost want to hang up the phone in disgust. I really don't need to know about the liquids seeping from all parts of a colleague's body that are incapacitating him and making him dependent on a fully functional and private toilet. He, quite obviously, lied about sickness, as I can see he is perfectly lively and able-bodied, reason being, he's got his hands all over that familiar statuesque red-head. This time I have to pin point from where in the world I know this girl.

I've seen her, I know it. I've maybe even had a conversation with her or possibly just saw her in passing, but she is definitely familiar to me from somewhere.

I quickly pull my sunglasses down to the point that they're sitting loosely at the tip of my nose so that I can glare through the shadows to the corner in which the two are groping. I've got to make it my mission to get a closer look at this woman or maybe if I hear her voice, it'll ring a bell.

With this new-found need for adventure urging me on, I attempt to inconspicuously and subtly inch my way down the sidewalk. I casually side- shuffle along in a direct and steadfast line, all the while maintaining intense focus on the two from fear that they may suddenly change the location of their grope fest. I accidentally bump people and am annoying numerous pedestrians. I, however, remain intent to stay the course.

I finally find myself standing directly across the busy, traffic jammed street from the two. I look down and am reminded that I am still dressed in my bright pink office garb, which I suppose causes me to stand out as opposed to blend in while I'm carrying out my Nancy Drew style inspection. This doesn't deter me one bit from uncovering the identity of the mystery groper.

A rush of fearlessness takes over me. I look left and right to ensure that the traffic is at a stand-still and that the subjects of my investigation are too entangled in each other to notice or recognize the pink, frumpy shape creeping towards them through rush hour traffic. I must be staring too intently at the objects of my investigation because as I'm about three feet from the curb and almost at the perfect destination to get a full glimpse, I fail to notice the cyclist barreling along at full speed in the open bike lane, nearest the curb.

I hear a bell in the distance ringing incessantly as if a cyclist is mighty pissed at someone or something that is obstructing his passage, but have absolutely not a clue that I'm the obstruction. All too quickly, my investigation turns into an out-and- out spectacle when I hear, "You moron! Get out of the waaaaaay!!!"

To my dismay I glance to the right just in time or I suppose just a mite too late, to see the cyclist veer up onto the curb to avoid crashing into me. He hits the curb at such an angle and with such force that he loses control and is sent flying off of the bike and stopped only by the hood of a neighbouring vehicle, which is luckily at a standstill amongst the other traffic jammed cars. I gasp and shriek in surprise and concern for the man's well-being and rush to determine whether he has been seriously injured. The owner of the silver Jetta on which the cyclist has landed, jumps out to do the same.

The man is clenching his left leg and groaning in pain, which alarms me to the fact that he needs an ambulance. I dial 911 and get the operator on the line to send an ambulance to the scene. The man is clearly in shock and unable to truly focus on my words, but I'm apologizing over and over and pleading with him to tell me his name so I can send him an apology gift.

The ambulance arrives and has to drive half on the side-walk and half in the bike lane to make its way to the injured cyclist. When the handsome paramedic asks for an account of what happened, I explain that it was my fault. He looks at me with narrowed eyes.

"You're lucky all these cars were in gridlock, otherwise he would have landed on a moving car and possibly lost his life. Please use appropriate intersections and crosswalks, madam, as opposed to weaving through traffic."

I hang my head in shame and apologize. "Please, can you tell me which hospital he will be taken to so I can drop off an apology note and gift?"

Unfortunately, the paramedic seems to have gotten a sight at the hickey mark on my neck and is distracted with a sort of unimpressed look on his face. "Sir, excuse me sir," I repeat while covering the wound with one hand to regain his attention.

"Oh, yes, he'll be at St. Vincent's and from what it looks like, he'll most likely need surgery on that leg so will be there for a while."

"Thank you, for your...your...assistance," I say appreciatively and am tempted to ask for the victim's name but just don't feel it's proper in the moment.

I'll have to do some detective work to track him down at the hospital. Detective work!

With all the commotion I've forgotten about Darryl and his mystery woman, but I suppose ensuring an injured individual is taken care of is more important than determining the connection between me and a work colleague's flame of the hour.

I spin around in hopes that they have simply been unaware of the event that has transpired and are still tightly in each other's grip, but am disappointed to find that the two have moved on. I can't see them anywhere along the street or amongst the commotion. I turn on the spot in a circle a full three times taking in the panoramic view and all angles of their possible getaway, as if I'm tracking bank robbers running from a job gone bad. They're nowhere in sight, and my eager attempts to make the intended discovery, come to an end.

I glance down at my watch. It's half past five. The girls will be waiting and wondering what's keeping me, but I'm sure will be understanding after learning of the events that have kept me from being punctual. I glance at the emergency situation of which I'm the unfortunate cause and assess that all is taken care of. I determine it's time to enjoy the rest of the evening without allowing the recent events to cloud my mind with negativity.

I turn my back, physically on the situation and continue to bustle along towards Kinko's. As I'm approaching the lively patio I suddenly hear a boomingly familiar voice.

"Portia, babe! Get your sexy self in here! You've just made my day with that delicious cotton candy-like getup! I want to devour you right now!"

The booming voice is clearly Nina's and she has quite obviously been here for some time, she is three sheets to the wind. I mean, sober Nina is lively enough. Give her a few margaritas and she's likely to start dancing on the tables and asking patrons for tips! I tell you, even when intoxicated, the girl knows how to make a dime!

I wave and am a little bit embarrassed as her bellowing has attracted the attention of four or five tables around the one at which she is seated. A crowd of people is studying the situation and watching me as I approach the bar. At this point, I'm entirely annoyed with myself that I hadn't changed at work before heading out. These scrubs and Crocs are causing me unnecessary humiliation I know, but what if some well-known individual of the fashion industry was on that patio, and this is my one chance to make that first impression that will get me the styling contract I'm desperate for? Being so busy with my day-to-day at work, these are the moments that matter in the networking world.

I breeze by the patio and head straight for the washroom knowing that Nina is fully occupied in some sing song she's just begun with the table to her left. I head to an open stall and begin slipping my scrubs off without remembering to remove my Crocs. Instead, of having the sense to simply stop shimmying the scrubs down and take the Crocs off first, I continue right along with what I'm doing until I realize the feet holes on the scrubs are too narrow to fit over these tremendously wide set pair of hideous shoes. I struggle a while longer and clumsily lose my balance ending up flat on my back with my bare legs, rumpled scrubs and Crocs darting out and under the door to the stall. "Are you okay, in there?" I hear a voice inquire. "Should I call the paramedics?"

"I…I'm fine, thanks," I manage to say. "I just lost my balance, is all."

As I'm responding I glance beneath the stall to see that this concerned stranger has got a fierce pair of T-strapped Ferragamo pumps on. This anonymous individual knows her fashion, or at least her designer footwear.

I shuffle my Crocs back under the stall and awkwardly bring myself to the standing position. Hurriedly, I begin properly removing the footwear and scrubs in the manner I should have from the beginning. The cramped stall is disallowing me the comfort and freedom I need in order to get clothed and get the heck out of these quarters before I cause myself any further embarrassment.

After what seems like an eternity of struggling to clothe myself with the chosen post-work attire I packed, I'm finally ready to add the finishing touches. A pinch of powder, a bit of shimmer, and a quick application of very berry lip gloss. I then determine it best to use some of my heavy duty concealer on the sizable bruise which has gained the attention of so many this week. I finish applying the concealer, then I grab my bag and head out to no doubt find a surely concerned Nina.

I approach the table on the expansive patio to which Nina has now managed to attract a group of five complete unknowns. I casually saunter over and drag an empty chair to the table joining the party of six. Nina's clearly owning the conversation and orchestrating what seems to be a game of Truth or Dare. Bloody hell, I arrived at the absolute worst time because as Nina senses my presence, she spins 'round to meet my gaze with her own.

"Portia! Where in the hell have you been and where did that delectable uniform get to? You look absolutely divine, but I wanted to get a chance to nuzzle up to you in your work frock, doll. Never mind that, though. You're just in time to be our next subject of study!"

"Um, study?" I ask.

"Yes, doll. I have a list of questions that I threw together as an experiment for my next endeavour. The questions cause you to delve into the innermost portions of your being and the results will allow me to coach you along the appropriate path of life."

"Let me guess, Nina, you're becoming a life coach of some sort?" I respond amusedly.

"Not just a life coach, Port. A 'Perfect Your Pathway' life coach! That's what I'm naming the organization. What do you think?"

What I really think is how unbelievably ironic it is Nina is planning to perfect others' pathways, while her own is one big chaotic jumble. I am sure, however, that the unfocused zig-zagging, criss-crossing trail that Nina calls her pathway, is absolute perfection in her own eyes. She doesn't need direction because she enjoys every minute of her days. She doesn't need the approval of others or the recognition of a job well done. She just does and is and smiles through it all. She's the fearless risk taker who can always take a moment to encourage, and surprisingly enough, guide others to achieve their own potential.

"Neen." I look at her softly. "You'd make the perfect life coach." I give a wink and can see that Nina is touched by my response.

She mouths the words "thank you" and then turns her attention back to the table. My supportive words must have distracted her just enough so not to continue on with her plight to make me the subject of her study. She instead begins firing questions at the strangers who have joined the table. I breathe a sigh of relief and order a house red to sip while enjoying the entertainment of it all.

Angelica soon strides in, looking a touch bedraggled and irritated. Always the needy and self-centred type, she seems to think if someone does not show immediate interest by asking about her day and her goings on, that they must have hard feelings towards her, or jealousy for that matter. The last thing I want Angelica to know or feel is that I'm jealous of her. Jealousy, envy, annoyance, these are a pertinent list of adjectives I would use to describe the wish-wash of emotions I feel whenever I am in Angelica's presence.

Tonight I was set on using Angelica's undeserving success to my advantage. I was finally going to have the gall to converse with her about the possibility of me climbing aboard the design team at the *Angelica* line. I sip heavily on my wine hoping that this will result in the bravery needed to make my proposal. Nina's questioning a moment earlier in regards to career contentment has got me fired up enough to know that the time is now to turn my dream into a reality.

I begin the conversation in the generic "How was your week? What's new?" kind of way and after Angelica gives a long winded response about how hectic things are at work and how absolutely wretched Daniel has been lately, she doesn't even give a shred of effort towards discovering how my week's been. Not one question is thrown my way! She simply sits there sipping her sangria and awaiting more attention to be given her.

I suppose it's now or never, no matter how irritated she is making me in this moment. "So Angie," I begin, trying to butter her up by using her cutsie nickname. "I know you've just mentioned how ridiculously busy your work has been lately, and I'm sure a business that is becoming so successful could use an extra set of hands to help with designing or even styling and selecting bags for ad campaigns and photo shoots. I really am looking to get into the fashion industry because I am beyond bored with my career and it has always been my dream, and...well... I don't know, I just thought you and I could make a great team, or I could at least assist in some way. I designed a few garments back in uni days, and have always wanted to give handbags a go. I also have great taste and an eye for style!"

I can sense from the scrunched eyebrows and wide eyes that Angelica is against the idea and has no interest in taking me on board.

"To be honest, Port, I am a bit taken aback by your request. *The Angelica* line only employs the most reputable designers and those who have either enormous amounts of experience in garment and accessory design, or have been educated in the field. References and samples of previous work are a must and I know you may have an interest, but that doesn't make you Kate Spade."

She finishes this incredibly offensive statement with an overly exaggerated eye roll that makes me want to take the straws from the two sangrias she has just polished off and shove one up each of her oversized nostrils.

I compose myself and give the most sincere fake smile I can muster and say, "Oh I know how reputable each designer is on your team, and I completely understand, Angelica. It's so wonderful that you're becoming such a success on the backs of all of those talented employees you have so carefully selected."

She smiles nonchalantly evidently not at all aware of the dig I've just directed at her, and then excuses herself from the table to take a call. I'm so tempted to make Nina aware of the entire conversation, or lack thereof, that Angelica and I have just had, but control this urge. I know that heatedly discussing my dislike for Angelica is not how I want to end this evening, so I order another red wine and swallow my pride along with a gulp of the full bodied Shiraz.

When Angelica returns she is frazzled, to say the least. She looks a tad pale and her mascara is smudged as if she has been crying. Nina notices at once and stands to whisper something to her, I can't quite make it out, but am sure involves asking Angelica if everything is all right. Angelica manoeuvres away from Nina, grabs her bag so she can drop a ten dollar bill on the table to cover her Sangrias, which would have cost more like fifteen before tip and tax, and heads for the door. Nina shrugs her shoulders and waves me over to her side of the table to no doubt place bets on reasons for Angelica's speedy exit.

"Portia, babe, what in the world was that all about?" Nina asks as I pull in next to her.

"We were just chatting about our weeks and then she got a call and excused herself to take it. The next thing I knew, she was pale as a ghost and her eye makeup was smudged."

"Hm. We'll have to keep updated somehow. Do you think she'll post to Twitter or Facebook?" Nina continues to attempt to get to the bottom of the surprising turn of events.

"Neen, I doubt she'll use Facebook to announce anything to her 3000 friends and fans if she wouldn't even confide in you," I say.

"True, true, you brilliant creature! Now how about another one before we kick off for the night?"

Nina doesn't even await a reply; instead she waves our brute of a server down to request he bring a round of tequila shots to the table. I plead with her to make mine another red wine as my history with tequila is somewhat nasty and foggy, for that matter. But no matter how strongly I voice my opposition to the order of the dreaded tequila shot, Nina is not taking "no" for an answer. She's one convincing comrade because by night's end "foggy" is the adjective to describe my state.

We settle the tab with the remaining group recruited by Nina. As I'm heading to wave down the server for the purpose of using the machine, I notice that the woman sitting directly across from Nina is the very woman who made sure I was alright in the bathroom when I was flat on my back. There could not very well be two women in one night at this establishment that have such unique and pricey footwear. This woman has those very Ferragamo pumps that I was so fortunate to gaze upon from beneath the stall earlier. They were like a beacon emanating down from the heavenly realm towards the depths of the filthiest place.

Seeing as it's a titch too late to strike up a conversation with her and thank her for her concern earlier, I decide to get the low-down on the mystery woman from Nina and hope that I can offer my appreciation in the future.

Nina wraps her arm snug around my waist and we walk out into the starry night. The sky is so beautiful that I can't help being reminded of a similar beauty which I'm sure to find when I finally head to the City of Light. Nina can see my drunken attachment to the night's sky and starts giggling at me and my fixation. I indulge her as I begin twirling.

People are halting on the sidewalks to take in the scene. It all comes abruptly to an end when my heel catches a sewer drain and I once again find myself flat on my back. All this time spent on my back today is sure making me painfully aware of the fact that I have not been flat on my back for the good reason in far too long.

I join Nina in the giggling just at the thought of the present situation. She sits down next to me on the curb and I blurt, "Nina, come to Paris with me next week! Please come! You're the only person I want with me, unless of course I take on a lover between now and next Saturday." I nudge her jokingly.

"Babe! That sounds fab, but are you sure you can get away having just started at your new job? I'm all in as long as you feel sound with all of it, and as long as I'm as far along with my *Perfect Your Pathway* logistics."

"Nina, I know I need this job for financial reasons, but I also don't feel like it's where I'm supposed to be. I'm entitled to three weeks of vacation and there was no stipulation as to how soon I can take them. I'm willing to take the gamble and experience the city I have always read about and dreamed about since I was a teen. I've been ready for this trip my whole life and want to throw caution to the wind. You can join me if you want, or you can stay here and become taken over by envy while I'm traipsing around the Eiffel Tower and La Louvre, eating baguettes and cheese in a magical ancient courtyard and letting a handsome man in a beret have his way with me."

"Well, this man in a beret, I've got to see! Count me in, you absolute nutter!"

Nina's words are music to my ears and I give her a heartfelt squeeze in appreciation for her support and for all the amazing ways she brightens my life.

"You're the best, Neen; the absolute best."

We sit for another minute taking in the night and then begin our journey to the subway with the excitement of knowing we will journey much further together in just a few short days.

CHAPTER 7

I'm going to Paris! I'm really doing this! This adventure I've been waiting for all these years is finally going to be a reality and I'm taking with me, the most wonderful companion of all. No, she's not six feet with dark features, a chiselled jaw and pectorals that make me feel that I'm in the presence of a Greek god, but she's adventurous, exuberant, and just the person I need with me to truly experience Paris fearlessly.

Nina and I have been in constant contact organizing the details of the trip over this past weekend. We also visited the travel agency where I first saw the steal of a deal a few days earlier.

It's now Monday evening and I've just finished my workday with Hopewell Clinic. I didn't have the nerve to inform them of my need for time off during the following week. Tomorrow is the day for that. Tuesday allows enough time for Tricia to find a temp while I'm gone and is one day past grumpy Monday. I have to admit that the grumpiness factor was on overdrive at work today. Dr. Markson and the Missus must have had one horrendous blow up because he stomped into the office like an angry gorilla, and slammed his operatory door with such force I thought the glass partition in the waiting room would shatter.

Tricia glanced at me and whispered, "Maybe his Viagra wouldn't kick in this weekend. I'd be pissed too."

"Ha ha!" I cannot hold back a full bellied laugh at this remark. Unfortunately my full belly laugh attracted the attention, once again, of Dr. Brown who simply glared as he passed into the break room. His eyes spoke to me as if to say, "Stay out of my washroom, or else."

Not only were the majority of the doctors in negative sorts earlier today, but Darryl, the usual emotionless zombie of a human being, aside from when he's groping mysterious red-heads in the street, arrived late as usual and spoke some harsh words to his father as they met each other in the operatory hallway. I know because I was just finished washing up and disinfecting the doctors' communal workspace and was within earshot of the disturbing, disagreement.

Darryl looked infuriated and persisted in berating his father about his lack of support and being too involved in his life. He told poor Dr. Langley that he regretted having him as a father and told him to take a back seat in his life for good, or to exit it altogether. I couldn't believe my ears! Darryl had his father to thank for his entire livelihood and was now acting like his father didn't provide any support like he wanted him to remove himself from his life completely.

Darryl has swiftly fallen off my list of individuals I hope to pursue romantic interaction with. To be honest, I don't know why I even gave him a second thought after hearing these insensitive and unappreciative words escape his mouth towards a kind man like Dr. Langley.

For the majority of the morning and better part of the afternoon I felt infuriated with Darryl and even tried to trip him up as he was walking by my swivel chair by subtly sticking my foot out as he was heading for his lunch break. I ended up misdirecting my foot and what was meant to result in Darryl tumbling to the floor, instead resulted in my croc getting tangled in his pant leg and brushing his bare calf.

I felt mortified as it ended up appearing as though I was making a pass at him. He was still like a bull seeing red and completely brushed off the unintentional advance, trudging heavily toward the sliding glass doors like he couldn't exit this office quickly enough. So needless to say, informing my work colleagues that I would be away all of next week did not seem like the best decision on this day of high tension and high emotion at Hopewell Clinic.

I exit the clinic that evening with a bounce in my step and the knowledge that I'll be meeting with Nina in a few short minutes to head on a shopping excursion for some fashion forward Parisian worthy outfits and accessories. My absolute, most favourite, way to spend a Monday evening after being draped in shapeless peach coloured scrubs and Crocs all day.

I jet as quickly as I can to the subway station and ensure to take the route that will swiftly transport me to the streets of Yorkville, my therapeutic, waterless oasis in the heart of the city. I feel as though I've arrived amidst the streets of New York when I head to Yorkville. It's like a mini getaway that only requires the cost of whatever gorgeous apparel I decide to purchase. I hop on the northbound train up to Bloor and then head east toward Bay. Within what seems like minutes, I emerge into the bright sunshiny evening and am face to face with Michael Kors. Well the store at least. I enter without the least bit of hesitation and am aware that Nina is most likely already lost in the wondrous avenues of Yorkville herself, but am too transfixed on a pair of tan leather peep toe pumps which are propped in the show window, to bother calling Nina.

They are magnificent and are perfect for a stroll down L'Avenue des Champs Elysées. I enter and immediately attain the attention of the consultant, perhaps due to my surprising attire. I confidently announce, "I'll take those in an eight, please and thank you!"

I point to the fabulous footwear and the consultant heads towards the back room to grab my size. She is back in a jiffy with the magical Michael Kors embellished shoe box which houses the prime piece of shoe-wear that will be cushioning my pristinely cared for feet at the moment I step off the plane. I watch as the assistant carefully unwraps them each from the gold trimmed tissue paper and feel a trickle of wetness drip to the corner of my mouth. I then feel disgusted with myself at the realization that I'm full on drooling, lick my lips and close my mouth to avoid any further embarrassment. I slip my right foot in and then my left, stand and want to dance due to the sheer comfort and joy that I feel. They are perfection in the form of stylish footwear.

"Sold!"

A woman shopping with her daughter jumps in surprise of my sudden outburst. "I'll take them," I say at a more acceptable volume.

"Fantastic." She smiles and leads me to the cash. My knees almost buckle when she rings in the price. I had fallen so in love with them that I hadn't bothered to check how much they would set me back, but two-fifty was well worth it for these show stoppers!

I finish charging the pumps to my card and finally check my phone to see that Nina has attempted to reach me in several different modes. She's called, texted, Facebooked, and even Skyped me. I also see that my voicemail box is full when less than ten minutes ago it was completely void of messages. I do the obvious, skip over listening to the voice messages and call Nina immediately.

"Nina! Where are you, girl? I'm just at Michael Kors and have scored the most fab leather heels."

"Oh you absolute shoe whore, you! I'll pop round the corner then. I've just finished exploring the new Kate Spade summer collection. I'll see you in a sec!" she responds jovially.

"Come on you spunky monkey! Let's continue to browse in the fabulous-ness that is Yorkville," Nina yells as she approaches me from around the corner at Bay and Bloor Street. She pulls me along toward Kenneth Cole.

We enter then emerge a short twenty minutes later, each having purchased a new pair of fabulous sunglasses. The remainder of the shopping experience is spent trying on incredibly expensive ball gowns and evening attire, which neither one of us would ever consider buying but are so completely enter-tained with the development of our outing that we continue this activity for an entire hour. We end the shopping spree at Ralph Lauren where I purchase a bohemian-chic maxi dress designed with a vividly coloured striped pattern and a t-back to show off my sculpted physique and tan. It hugs my curves just perfectly and is absolutely stunning, not to mention wonderfully original.

Nina purchases a beautiful nautical style A-line navy and white striped, high-waisted skirt and pairs it with a collared, midriff baring tank. We each decide to throw in complementary fedoras as a means to complete our unique summery looks. We then head to the pub across the street in celebration of our shopping success and to unwind, gab and of course plan our 5 day wan-derings in Paris.

"How successful was that?" I exclaim once we're seated. "I swear, Nina, I'm on excitement over drive just preparing for this trip! Let's order some champagne."

"You know I'd never pass up champs on any occasion, sweets, especially not when Paris is in the cards! So tell me, have you let your work know at all?" Nina inquires in a motherly sort of way.

"It was such a disastrous day for most of the staff today, that I just simply couldn't do it, Neen. Tomorrow I'll be ready. You can harass me all day until I follow through and bite the bullet."

"Oh, you promise?" Nina asks eagerly and in jest. "Hon, I just want you to be careful. You know it's always a sticky situation when you start in a new work environment and immediately are making demands like asking for time off. So be respectful and give them the necessary notice so that you can hold on to this job as long as you need to. I feel so much that your dream job is in the cards, but don't cut and run from your bread and butter at the moment."

"Thanks, Nina, I know you're only speaking from a place of understanding how imperative it is to have a constant income. Lord knows you have the skills to make some green, girlfriend!" I say appreciatively. "I'm completely grateful for the opportunities I've been given in the field of health care. I really am. I admire everyone who is passionate about my line of work as well, I just don't have that passion that I see in others. My heart and dreams rest far away from the medical environment and life is going to pass me by while I'm stuck in the tedious monotony of my day to day unless I take a leap of faith."

I speak with such integrity that I feel like a life coach myself except the coaching is directed inward. "It starts here and now with this trip, and with requesting the time off. I have to stop being afraid of what people might say or how others may react and I need to finally do what I need to in order to achieve my goals."

"I totally understand, Port. You've hung in there a long while on that unfulfilling career path of yours. I admire you endlessly for that! I mean, hell! Look at me, switching paths constantly. I have to admit though, the exhilaration of knowing something new is on the horizon is the best feeling in the world, good sex aside, and I think I'm addicted to the thrill of it. But let's you and me both decide to do the opposite of the other. I am going to make a go of this *Perfect Your Pathway* life coaching initiative keeping my focus locked on it, and you are going to work towards changing your focus full stop. Let's shake things up a bit!"

"I like your thinking. This will be good for the both of us," I say.

We spend the next hour searching Paris tours on my phone, indulging in the expensive celebratory champagne we've ordered and catching up on our separate interactions with mutual friends.

"Port, this may be like pouring salt on the wound, but have you heard at all from Charlie since the intervention?"

"I haven't heard from her directly but Paulo told me that she's been spotted at the pool hall in The Beach attempting to swindle people out of money by placing bets while pretending to be a rookie and then cleaning up. Paulo himself fell for it one night when he was there with his boyfriend. They were so excited to see her and then she pummeled them in pool, took their money and walked out the door. Nina, it's so sad. I really miss her and hope she'll come to her senses."

"My god! That's pathetic and appalling all at once. Hon, she's got to hit rock bottom eventually if she won't let us be her safety net. But we'll be there to scrape her off the ground when she hits it."

"I suppose. It really saddens me that I can't do anything to help. Hey have you heard anything about Angelica's speedy and flustered exit from Kinko's on Friday night? What was that all about?"

I quickly change the subject, hoping that Nina has answers. "I do remember her saying that Daniel was being a horrible turd as of late, so maybe it had to do with that! Yeah, maybe he called her to break things off over the phone, that arsehole. He'd totally be the spineless sort who wouldn't even have the decency to break up in person. I bet he's even texted to end past relationships."

"I don't know, Port, if it was a breakup, I know Angelica wouldn't react that way. You've witnessed her post breakup. Even when the guy calls it off, she's the picture of calm and actually becomes a less spoiled, annoying, whiny brat to be around. I adore single Angelica! She actually has true conversations and shrugs off the whole damn break up thing. Like when she broke up with Gavin, the musician. He chucked her to the curb like yesterday's trash and she invited me the very next day to meet for tea. I wouldn't have any idea she had even been dumped had she not casually slipped it into conversation that she would be more available to get together seeing as Gavin has moved on. Part of me wishes Angelica was in a perpetual state of post breakup! I swear you'd be bumped to the best friend runner up spot if that was the case."

I laugh at this outlandish "perfect Angelica" state Nina has painted and know that Angelica could never bump me from my podium as Nina's go to gal.

"I guess you're right, but the only other issue may have to do with her business. I'm fully aware about how unprofessionally she runs the company and designers can only work in the shadows for so long before they become fully aware of their talent and potential. They'll all want the limelight soon enough. Maybe her manipulating and deceiving ways are finally biting her on that perfectly shaped rear of hers," I suggest with more conviction than the initial possibility.

"Hm....I think you're on the right track there. I'm not about to pick up the phone and inquire, though. I'm guessing we'll find out if our suspicions are right soon enough."

Our gabbing continues for another quarter hour at which point we become surprisingly aware that it is now past midnight and although neither one of us is set to lose a glass slipper and risk her coach transforming into a pumpkin, we do both have early starts to the day set for tomorrow. We settle the tab and split a cab towards the west end.

It's perhaps due to too much champagne, or because of my constant state of euphoria in regards to the approaching trip of a lifetime, but as I'm entering the doors to the condo complex I swear I see Darryl skulking his way out of the side door and down the street in an easterly direction. I'm too tired to put on my Nancy Drew knickers at this point so simply chalk it up to a possible look alike. I mean, I'm told at least twice weekly that I resemble someone a random passer-by knows. So it's quite likely that Darryl has just as familiar a face and build.

As I enter the condo I hear the sound of Bob Marley's melodious anthem "No Woman No Cry" filling the space and a rather wobbly female voice attempting to sing along intermixed with heaving sobs. I rush in to find Minnie face down on the area rug in the living space, curls strewn every which way, and three empty beer bottles surrounding her.

"Minnie! Sweetheart, what's wrong?" I run to sit by her side and stroke her tangled mane which I now see has morsels of potato chips embedded in it, a clear sign Minnie has indulged in a full on pity party for one, this evening. "Honey, can you sit up and chat with me? What's the matter?"

As I ask this more sobs escape from Minnie and she rolls onto her back to stare up at me. Makeup smudged and rosy cheeked, she slowly slinks to a sitting position and leans against the sofa.

"I...I...just want mooooore!" Minnie manages trailed by another bout of tears and heavy breathing.

"Sweetheart, what do you mean? You have so much! You have an incredible career and the respect of your colleagues and employees. You earn enough to support a small army. Please, Minnie, what do you mean more?"

"I want friends, and...and...looove! I want a...a... social life like you! My career is so demanding and takes everything I have. I come home and go to bed and then go right back to the office. Oh Portia, the money isn't worth it anymore. I, I don't even have the opportunity to spend any of it I work so damn hard. I have nothing but a demanding job, that I do love, but I want balance. I need balance!" Minnie breaks down once again and I pull her towards me while stroking her tangled locks.

"Sweetie, you can have whatever you want. Nobody says you *have* to be an executive in the advertising and marketing industry. Re-evaluate. This is the first step! You love the work, you just don't want so much of it, and you're starting to realize that the big paycheck monthly isn't nearly as rewarding when you don't have time to make use of it. So if you want balance, you'll find it by stepping out of the head honcho role."

I see that Minnie begins to calm down and is listening intently adding an involuntary follow up sob every so often.

"Minnie, let me get you some water and a headache tablet then we'll turn in for the night. You just need a good rest. Please take a day tomorrow for yourself. The agency will be all right without you just this once. You need to do something for yourself for a change, darling."

Minnie lays her head on my shoulder. "Thanks, Portia. You are a great roomie and are my one and only contact outside of work in the city, you know. I consider you a dear friend." She slowly rises and I jump to my feet to grab a glass of water and tablet for her. After I turn Bob Marley off, we hug it out one last time, and each of us heads to bed.

In the morning, I feel as fresh as a daisy although the bags under my eyes are trying to tell me I don't look it. I creep towards Minnie's room like a new mother checking on her infant. She's still sound asleep and looks so peaceful that I let her be and don't bother asking if she's taken the day from work. My nerves become agitated suddenly at the thought of requesting time off, but I fight the agitation with a strong cup of coffee and a raspberry -lemon scone then prepare for my commute to work without a second thought of how the scenario will all play out. I'm sure Tricia will be courteous and understanding. And if she isn't, well I'll…I'll just invent some emergency situation that will involve a week stay in Paris.

No! I can't do that. Honesty is necessary. I turn to the emergency exit excuse far too often. This time I will be upfront and just tell it like it is. The last time I invented some tale which would allow me to be excused from work for a couple of days was when I said I was having a surgical procedure done and would need to be admitted to hospital. The whole lie spiralled out of control when people started calling my parents to check in on me and sending me enormous bouquets of flowers. It was like Kensington Garden in my own damn condo. Poor Minnie couldn't even get to her bedroom due to the jungle all of the 'get better soon' gifts were creating in the hallway. My mom finally had reached her limit and came clean to my supervisor after the seventh time the supervisor had called her to check my status. She's always so moral and upstanding that it was probably keeping her up at night, the poor woman. I conclude that this very situation is exactly what I hope to avoid. I was heavily reprimanded for it and want to avoid this happening again at all cost.

As I'm reliving the whole fake hospital stay scheme, I'm given a sobering reminder of the cyclist I accidentally sent to hospital a few short days ago.

I've got to head to St. Vincent's and discover who he is so that I can leave him a gift!

The dear man, imagine trying to make your way home after a long day at work and being entirely thrown off course, literally and figuratively, thereby winding up in surgery and bedridden for weeks. Horrible!

I arrive at work with a few minutes to spare and decide that I'm best to put off the request involving time off until at least the afternoon coffee break. That way no one's day will be completely menaced by the news and I won't have to feel Dr. Brown's dagger eyes on me for more than two hours or so. Let's face it, Dr. Brown and I really haven't started off on the right foot. Truthfully he has permanent dagger eyes directed at me. Maybe it's just how he always is.

At roughly half past nine, I'm surprised to notice Darryl has not shown up. His phone in his tiny little office is ringing continuously, most likely the calls of patients who are attempting to be booked in for last minute appointments. The doctors won't be pleased if there are holes in their days, which could have been plugged with the inquiries coming in and being missed due to Darryl's absenteeism.

I make the quick decision to field the calls myself for as long as I can until Darryl either arrives, or I'm needed elsewhere. I head into his office and the phone begins ringing immediately. As I lift the receiver I'm disgusted at the condition of the earpiece. It's entirely coated in what appears to be ear guck and wax. Flakes of skin are embedded in the all the crevices and it is all smudgy with what is undoubtedly sweat and filth.

"Uggggg," I say repulsively to myself. What did I ever want with this guy and how is that stunning mysterious red head enamoured with someone who could not only produce such grime, but who doesn't have the sense to wipe it away every once in a while. There's at least a year's worth of build-up on this ear-piece for goodness sake.

Controlling my gag reflex as best as I can and holding the receiver close enough to my ear so that I can hear the individual on the other end but not at all allowing it to make contact, I say, "Hopewell Clinic, Portia speaking. How can I help you?"

"Yes, I'd desperately like to get in to see Dr. Langley this afternoon at some point, please and thank you," a female with a sharp and matter of fact tone insists.

"Well, I'll bring up his schedule to see when he has space to fit you in mam. It'll just be a moment."

"Please do and make it hasty, if you will," the woman says harshly. I quickly locate Dr. Langley's schedule on the set up Excel spreadsheet. A sickening feeling takes me over as this reminds me of Connor and his Excel fetish.

"Okay, let me see here. Dr. Langley has a forty-five minute opening between two and two forty-five this afternoon. Will that suffice?"

"I suppose it will have to, won't it," the testy woman retorts.

"Can I please have your name?"

"Penelope Mason. Be sure I'm not kept waiting. I do expect that two o'clock means two o'clock. If I am kept waiting more than five minutes, I will not hesitate to walk directly into Dr. Langley's operatory regardless of whether he's conducting a prostate exam, pap smear or fondling a bulls testicles. Understood?"

"Well, Mam, bulls would see vets, not Dr. Langley, so that scenario would be unlikely. I will ensure that you are not kept waiting if you would just give your word that you will be respectful." As I complete giving my conditions, I hear a click on the other end. That horrendous woman just hung up on me!

Poor Dr. Langley. I'm sure that's the last thing he wants with all that's happening between him and Darryl, an impatient drama queen as a patient to end a day. Such a witch of a woman, that Penelope. That name is just so original but for some reason I feel like I've been introduced to someone with it, or was having a conversation about a Penelope or a friend was dating a Penelope.

I ponder what in the world my connection is to the name Penelope a moment and then am struck with a realization which dumbfounds me. That's it! Randall's fiancée's name is Penelope and although I saw her from a distance the last day I spoke with him in the lobby, I'm almost positive THAT is why I recognize the red head mystery woman that has been sneaking around with dirty Darryl! It's the same woman! Oh my god is it really her who is coming in to see Dr. Langley today? I don't know if I'll be able to compose myself. What if she recognizes me from the condo building? Oh poor Randall. That horrible woman is cheating on that beyond gorgeous man, with DARRYL. This is too awful to even comprehend.

My mind is spinning. Maybe I'm jumping to conclusions. Perhaps Penelope, Darryl, and Dr. Langley are family. Yes! They're one of those close, European families who kiss each other passionately and show constant affection through embracing and what not. All right, that's the assumption I'm sticking with until proven otherwise.

I finally hang up the gunky receiver and root around Darryl's pigsty of an office to locate a pen and paper so that I can remind myself to remind Dr. Langley of the need to be punctual with Penelope's appointment. As I'm searching I locate both a pen and post it note in his desk drawer. The post it is sitting right in eye view and I can't help reading the words that are scratched all over it as if it were a twelve-year-old girl's diary.

"Be mine forever, forever be mine, be mine forever, forever be mine…" is scrawled on every square inch on the tiny neon yellow post it pad. Wow! Darryl has it bad and if it's not for that witch of a woman I talked to on the phone, it's certainly for somebody who has an astounding resemblance to Randall's fiancée. –Yuck. This situation has my stomach in knots and it really doesn't even involve me.

At that moment, none other than dingy Darryl himself steps into the closet sized office, which makes me feel extremely claustrophobic and uncomfortable, not to mention overcome by a terrible and pungent odour.

"What the hell are you doing in my office?" Darryl spits out angrily.

"Well, you were late and your phone has been ringing non-stop. The doctors need to be booked and I thought it would be best if I field the calls until you arrive."

Darryl glimpses down to see the open desk drawer and immediately changes colour to a pink hue when he sees the love post-it in clear view.

"Oh, and you also thought it was necessary to go through my desk I see! You couldn't walk the ten steps to your own desk to grab the materials needed instead? Get out of my space!" he shouts.

I jump back in such surprise that I actually find myself up against the wall and am physically unable to exit the room seeing as Darryl's large frame is blocking the doorway.

"Darryl, I'd really like to, but you'll have to remove yourself first before I can get back to my duties."

"With pleasure!" he retorts becoming more and more enraged and inching his way backwards out of the room so that I can sneak by.

After making it back to my swivel chair I see Tricia glaring at Darryl. She then slowly turns to make eye contact with me and surprisingly says, "That dolt! He didn't even thank you for doing his job while he was slacking off or should I say jacking off in his father's basement. Excuse me a moment."

Tricia rises and glides into the tiny stench-filled office like a cheetah ready to attack, looking so perfectly lovely as she does so. She closes the door behind her.

Poor woman, how has she not passed out from the smell yet?

All of a sudden I hear muffled angry voices. The heated conversation continues for more than ten minutes and I casually carry on greeting patients and filing forms. After the ten minute berating is finished, Tricia exits the room just as composed as she did when she entered it a few minutes prior. She calmly walks back to her station and carries on pleasantly as if nothing had even occurred.

Darryl trudges by, all red faced with a snarled expression as though he's now out for blood. He barges into the doctor's common area and bellows, "I quit! You can all go straight to hell. Especially you, Langley!"

While saying these words he points his oversized finger at his father and the words are filled with such hatred, that Dr. Langley looks absolutely gutted. I'm gutted for him. Imagine your own son, who you've done so much for, turning on you like that.

What a horrible human being Darryl is. If Penelope and he are having a love affair, they are a perfect match from what I have witnessed today.

I turn and look at Tricia mouthing the words "Oh my god." She whispers, "I told him if he didn't quit immediately, I would make sure that he was reprimanded to the point that he will never be employable elsewhere, ever."

"Can you do that?" I ask

"Nope, but he's dumb as bricks and I'm sick of his B.S. So I don't give a damn. His job is so insignificant that you or I could easily add the duty of fielding calls to our days and would be more successful at it than he ever was. The job was created specifically by Langley to give his freeloader son somewhat of a future."

As she's explaining what transpired, Darryl walks by our desks glaring straight ahead with his middle finger fully up and directed at the both of us behind the marble slab, and then exits for what I'm sure we all hope, is eternity.

Tricia and I smile at one another, both of us beaming with new found freedom from Darryl's negativity and hygiene shortcomings. Fielding a few extra calls a day is doable and welcome if it means not having him around to be so nasty to everyone.

While I'm celebrating inwardly, I quickly remember that I need to inform Dr. Langley about Penelope's appointment. I swivel around and scurry into the common area where I find Dr. Langley head in hands, at the prep counter.

"Sir...umm, Dr. Langley, sir? I just wanted to let you know that your slot at two p.m. has been filled by Penelope Mason, sir. She insists that we be punctual for her. Just thought I'd let you know." I turn to walk back to my station and am startled by his reply,

"Like hell I'll keep that space for her. You can call her back and inform her that we refuse to treat meddling, unfaithful, heartless individuals at this office!"

Oh god, do I respond? He's so upset. I have no idea what to say or how to handle this situation. This sort of scenario was not a part of my medical office management practical exam!

While I'm fretting and standing motionless in the middle of the common area, Tricia appears next to me and carries on handling the situation.

"Sir," she says towards Dr. Langley. "I will phone Penelope and ask her to keep her distance from the office. She is not a patient of yours and has no business being within these walls. I will let her know that the police will be called if she enters the premise."

What a star she is!

"Thank you, Tricia. Carry on now, girls. I'm sure there are newly arrived patients to attend to." Dr. Langley says tenderly and appreciatively.

What a delightful man. How is his son such a jerk?

Tricia telephones Penelope immediately and seems to know her number by heart because she does not even bring up Penelope's file; she dials and begins boldly telling her to keep her distance otherwise legal action will be sought.

The whole time Tricia is the picture of calm and composure while at the same time I can hear screeching coming from the receiver. Clearly, Penelope is not taking the news well. After a few moments of Tricia listening to Penelope's wild ramblings and her complete tirade, she simply hangs up the receiver and does a hand brush action. I can't help giggling.

We continue along with the day as if nothing has happened but my nerves begin to get the best of me as the reality that the day is nearing its end sets in. I must make everyone aware to the fact that I'll be away, but so much craziness has happened this morning that I fear the maximum dose for a day's drama has been reached already.

I've got to do it. I just have to no matter what.

"Portia? Is everything okay?" Tricia asks.

"Oh umm, Tricia, thanks...yes...I...I..." It was now or never. "Tricia I'm going to need next week off," I manage in my squeaky, nerve filled voice. Tricia's perma-smile begins to fade to a barely there grin.

"What's that now?" she says as if she hasn't quite heard me correctly.

"I have an extremely important trip to Paris booked, that I actually had planned and paid for long before I became employed here and the rate was so heavily discounted that there is no backing out without losing the whole amount for hotels and flight."

Okay so I *did* end up fibbing just a tad, but the disgruntled look on Tricia's face warranted a tiny white lie. It's not like she's going to call my booking agent and figure out the date that I actually organized the trip.

Can she do that? Oh god, maybe she will do that.

"Portia, I don't know what to say. I suppose there's not a lot that I can say as it sounds like you're heading overseas whether I protest or not. This won't sit well with the doctors and nurses as they are taking so well to your strategies of management, but I suppose we'll have to cope and bring in a temp for the week. This is somewhat disappointing. I wish you had brought the trip plans to our attention when you were initially hired three weeks ago and that way I could have brought the temp in to shadow you much earlier."

"I'm sorry, Tricia, so sorry. I'll do whatever I can in the next three days to prepare for a temp and allow a day for shadowing." Apologizing emphatically has to at least relieve the sting of my news somewhat. "I'll write an inner office email informing all of the doctors about the situation for the upcoming week as well. This will not fall on your shoulders. Please know that," I add guiltily.

"Please do," is all she says in response.

We then carry on with the day in almost full silence aside from when on calls or discussing upcoming appointments with nurses and doctors. Communication between us is absolutely non-existent and I feel horribly awkward, like I'm spending the day with a quarreling lover who is giving me the silent treatment.

I break the silence when I'm heading out for an afternoon coffee. "Can I get you a tea or coffee, Tricia? It's on me."

"No. I'm fine," she replies coldly, her grin now completely faded. "Let me know when you've found a suitable temp please. You do know that it's your duty to call, interview, and hire the individual for the week, and I'd like to have a name no later than noon tomorrow."

I had no idea that was my duty, but I commit to beginning the process as soon as I return. Feeling a little downtrodden and guilty, my excitement has now been overshadowed.

I return to the office within twenty minutes and make the necessary calls to line up three temp interviews for the following day. By the time I have completed the search as well as all other duties for the day the time is approaching six o'clock. I'm willing to work over time if it means freedom for an entire week.

Just as I'm packing up my things I glance at my phone, which has a new text that reads *"CALL ME! WE NEED TO TALK!"*

CHAPTER 8

Nina is honestly a total drama queen. She's scared me half to death with this seemingly urgent text and when I called her immediately, she said she was entirely too busy to discuss anything, so the urgency really couldn't be all that great, now could it?

It always turns out to be so inconvenient when you're waiting on a call from someone. I swear that each and every time this is the case the call finally comes at the worst possible moment. Today, for instance, I'm waiting to hear what direly important information Nina has for me and find myself locking eyes with a man in the Quickie Mart where I'm browsing the magazines. I could've been home by now but truly didn't want to miss the call, and we all know that signals get lost on the subway trains, so I wait, and wait and read and read.

Finally, as I'm going to pick up the newest edition of *Vogue*, I catch a devilishly handsome man peering at me from behind his *GQ* selection. I give a flirtatious smile, as I've realized that I really haven't been following through on taking risks and maintaining eye contact, *so here goes, Dr. Richardson*. I hold eye contact on and off while pretending to glance down and appear interested in the page on which the magazine is opened to. It's just sitting at an ad for Tampax. He continues to gaze at me and shuffles along the magazine section, eyeing me and the magazine in hand. He finally stops about three feet from me,

"You make those scrubs look sexy."

I immediately feel flushed, but work through it. "Thanks, I try to do what I can when my work attire is so limited. You look very nice yourse…." Right as I'm finishing this bold line my phone begins ringing at full volume, and the name *Nina* of course flashes across the screen.

"Sorry, I'm so sorry, I have to take this."

He gives a nod and carries on with his magazine perusal.

I hope to god that he's still here when I'm finished hearing what the urgent matter is. He's dreamy!

"Nina! What was the text you sent earlier all about?" I try not to sound too demanding, but it better be worth shrugging this dreamboat off for.

"Babe, remember the woman that was sitting across from me at Kinko's the other night?"

I think hard and say, "Oh the one with the beautiful pair of T-strap Ferragamo pumps on?"

"Ummm, ….er. I guess so, if the person wearing those T-strap whatchama-callits was sitting directly across from me." She replies. Nina doesn't really care much about designer shoes. She'd wear H&M or Payless and wouldn't be able to tell the difference if she was handed a Gucci stiletto instead.

"Then yes, I do recall her vaguely. What about her, Neen?" I'm getting restless as I notice the handsome patron is heading to the cash.

"Well, she's my newest sign on to be a client at my *Perfect Your Pathway* life coaching centre. She came in for a consultation and I asked her the regimented introductory questions I created the other day."

"Uh huh." *Can we get to the point?* I'm thinking desperately. The said man has cashed out and is glancing at me. I see him look at his watch. *Please just a while longer, don't go.*

"I got to the question about her career…and… well…"

"Nina! What is it?" I say impatiently as I see him walk out the door. If she just spits this info out, I can hang up on her and chase him down before he gets away.

"Port, she's Victoria Lewis!" *OH MY GOD!* I gasp. I'm trembling and feel all wobbly. The attractive patron suddenly is erased from my mind and I sit down hard, directly in the middle of Quickie Mart aisle number three and don't give a care as to the goings on around me.

"THE Victoria Lewis? The Victoria Lewis who is Editor in Chief at *Crave Magazine*. *Crave Magazine*! One of the most fashion- forward, globally recognized magazines on the stands today?" I turn my head to see the newest edition of *Crave* sitting on the Quickie Mart magazine rack and begin to whimper like a deranged creature in the wild.

"Yes, Port! She's doing work at the *Crave Canada* office here in Toronto. They're revamping things in the stylizing and photography department and she's overseeing it while maintaining her role as editor in chief of the international magazine. I want to try to ease her into my life coaching routine, and then I'll casually suggest that she and I meet you for coffee. It really couldn't hurt, doll. And being her life coach and all, I *do* have some pull!" Nina cackles as if she's an evil sorcerer intending to cast some spell on Victoria.

Oh lord, I've just remembered that my first unintentional meeting with Victoria was when I was flat on my back, pants down around my ankles with my head next to a toilet in the ladies room. She never has to know that was me, though. It will forever be locked in my vault of "never to be revealed embarrassing moments in the life of Portia Delaney."

"Nina! You're the best. You're absolutely brilliant, and I will be your personal slave forevermore if somehow, this casual meeting ends up in me having some sort of career at *Crave Magazine*. At this point, I'd even take an unpaid internship under Victoria's direction."

"Oh babe, we'll do better than that. We'll score you some exclusive position as Director of Handbags just so that we can watch Angelica squirm."

"Ha ha ha. Oh Nina, I somehow don't think that Director of Handbags is an actual position, but I do love your thinking. Speaking of Ange, have you heard anything more about her situation? I feel like I should call, but I know how short she was with you the other night, and can't imagine she would be any more willing to confide in me."

"I haven't, Port, but it'll all blow over I'm sure, or all blow up. We'll have to wait until she's ready to reveal anything. Until then, there's always Paris! I can't wait to have you on my arm while we stroll along all the different rues de whatevers and eat croissants by the Eiffel Tower."

"Me neither, Neenster, me neither. Listen, I'm currently seated in a Quickie Mart aisle, and should be getting to the subway. I promised Minnie we'd spend time together tonight. Oh and I told my work about needing time off. It's all somewhat okay, but I'm so pumped about this whole Victoria Lewis meeting, that Hopewell Clinic is currently the farthest concern from my mind. Thanks again Nina! I owe you one. Let me know about what day is best to meet you and the *Crave* mag star when you decide!"

"Okay babe, toodles!" Nina signs off and I peel myself off the ground. Luckily, only a child and his mother came across me planted in aisle three like a sit in protester and didn't seem to think anything of it.

Before I hit the subway I grab a bottle of wine at my go-to wine boutique and then vow to have a good old girls night with Minnie to get her out of her funk and perhaps get some sense into her about looking for a less demanding job.

I walk into the condo roughly thirty-five minutes later and find it silent, eerily silent. Although Minnie sometimes has late nights, it is unusual that they come this early on in the week, and with all the stress she's been under lately, it would be ludicrous of her to still be giving that place as much of her effort when she should be cutting back her hours; especially when I had suggested she should take the day for herself.

I glance down at my phone just to double check I've not missed a text or important call from Minnie. *Nothing.* I round the corner into the kitchen while feeling sorry for myself, and more than slightly agitated with Minnie for standing me up. I'm horrified to find Minnie out cold on the kitchen floor with a knife next to her.

I feel a coldness grip me and become frantic while the worst thoughts possible begin running through my head. "Minnie! Oh my god Minnie! You didn't! Please tell me you didn't try to take your life! I love you. You have so much to live for. This can't be happening!"

I breathe heavily feeling lightheaded and in a complete state of shock. For a moment I just stand motionless and in a daze without feeling in my hands and legs. Finally, I snap out of it and realize that we can't both be completely out of it if one of us needs saving.

Get it together, Portia!

I bend down to try to check for a pulse and am absolutely clueless on how to do this. I start feeling around on her chest and realize I'm full on groping her boob. I get my ear right down to her face to listen for breath because I *do* remember at least that from taking swimming classes as a youth. I got all the way to Bronze Cross. I knew it would come in handy one day.

Okay I think I feel breath so that's a good sign. It means her heart is working and lungs are working, so it's not too late.

I double check by putting my cheek and ear as close to her mouth and nose as possible and start counting to ten….."

"Ah! What are you, what are you doing!" Minnie shrieks.

I rock back up on my knees so quickly I lose balance and teeter back against the lower cabinet doors. I sit there terrified that her suicide attempt gone wrong will morph into a homicide attempt gone right.

"Minnie, calm down. I…I…was trying to save your life. A bit of stress just isn't worth ending it all, sweetheart," I say in the most nurturing and motherly, concerned tone I can produce.

"End it all? What in the world are…" Minnie glances at the scene and zeroes in on the knife that's lying directly to her right. "Oh, you think…you think that I…that the knife…that I was using that to hurt myself?"

"Well, naturally yes!" I say defensively. "I mean, I walked in to find you barely breathing and motionless on the kitchen floor with a butcher's knife beside you, one day after you were in hysterics about how horrible your life is. So, yes, naturally I thought you tried to do yourself in, Minnie."

"Portia, I came home and was cutting some fruit up. I couldn't find the little paring knife I usually use so I grabbed that big weapon instead, finished cutting, ate the fruit and put everything away. I was taking the knife to the sink to wash it. It slipped from my hand. Stupidly, I don't know perhaps it's just my engrained reflexes from being such a fantastic juggler, I decided to catch it, and of course I caught it all right! I caught the sharpest part of the blade on my pinkie finger." She turns her finger around to show me what looks like a deep enough wound to need stiches."

I cringe a bit at the sight of it. "But, but Minnie, for the love of god, why were you out cold on the floor? You scared me half to death!"

"I…I… have a very weak stomach. The sight of blood makes me woozy and when the blood is coming from me, it makes me faint. Portia! Don't you think if I used that thing to take my own life there would be just a bit more blood? Come on, you know I do everything full out, so if I had chosen a knife to do myself in, believe me, you would have known. I don't think stabbing myself would be the method of choice though maybe I'd…"

"Minnie, please, let's change the subject, I don't want you even thinking like that and I certainly don't want to hear about how you'd kill yourself if you decided to. So...um what's this about juggling?" I ask as a means to divert her thoughts away from suicide.

"Oh yeah! I used to join in on the busking festival and everything! I can juggle anything! Various kinds of fruit, vegetables, keys, bowling pins, even small children! Ha, just kidding on the last one. I stopped a few years ago when I stopped having the time to make it to the various festivals because of, well, my work demands. I really miss it." She heaves a long breath.

"We'll have to get you back into it won't we? I'd cheer you on in any festival or fair you juggle in! Hon, let's have a look at that hand. I think it may need stitches and we should probably head to emergency to have you checked out just in case you hit your head when you fainted."

"Eeek, is it bad? Will I lose my finger? Oh god what would I do without my pinkie! It's my third most useful finger. It's super important for shuffling through documents and ad mock ups! Oh man, you really never know what you have until you lose it! I can't lose it, I can't!"

"Minnie, you need to stop losing it right now! You're not going to lose your pinkie. I'm calling a taxi immediately and we'll go straight to the hospital."

"It's my finger, not yours. When it's yours you can react however you wish!" she retorts obviously quite annoyed that I'm poking fun.

"Okay, Okay, dramatic Debbie. Go and sit on the couch and keep this towel on your finger. Try not to look at the cut, I don't want to find you passed out again after this call." I pick up my phone and dial Clark Taxi. The woman on the other end indicates it will be a quick five minutes so that we should head down to the lobby right away.

"Alright, hon, let's go. The cab will be here any minute!" I help Minnie up and grab my purse as well as hers for identity purposes. We make our way to the elevator. Moments later we exit into the lobby; Minnie's holding her finger up in the air while holding the towel tightly around it and looking away from her injury so to not have another fainting episode. She looks quite ridiculous and I can't help chuckling a little at the sight of her.

We reach the front doors and just as we're exiting, none other than Randall comes blowing past, and this time he's quickly followed by the stunning red head herself. I see clearly now that this is the very same woman who has been spotted with Darryl.

Randall looks furious, so much so that he seems to have blinders on and doesn't even see me, or perhaps is too irritated to acknowledge anyone. The woman, Penelope, is calling his name sharply as she chases him in her thigh high patent leather boots. They reach the elevator and by this point Randall's avoiding her at all costs and seems to even be contemplating taking the stairs just to be away from her. As I'm watching the happenings Minnie alarms me to the fact that the cab has just pulled up. Damn! I really want to hang back to listen to what Randall says or does in this moment, but Minnie's pinkie is paramount at the moment so we exit the condo and hop in the cab.

We arrive in less than ten minutes to our unplanned-for destination on our ladies night. I rustle through my purse, pull out a crisp twenty dollar bill and hand it over hastily.

"Okay Minnster, let's do this!" I rush around and open her door to avoid any use of the injured pinkie. We rush to the front door of the emergency section of the hospital and I glance at the sign directly above the entranceway.

We're at St. Vincent's! The hospital the injured mystery cyclist was taken after the ordeal I caused. It's fate! There has got to be a gift shop in here. I'll sign Minnie in, make sure she's occupied with a magazine or a hot on call doctor, and then start the investigation to track him down.

The new route that this whole situation has now taken has me all giddy with anticipation to finally come face to face with the unfortunate victim of my stupidity last week. Oh he'll be so surprised and grateful for my generosity when I hand over a get-well gift and card that surely he won't hold anything against me. I mean, the effort alone to seek a person out and give condolences in person would be enough to melt my heart if the tables were turned!

"Minnie, go on up to the check in desk. I'm going to head to the ladies for a moment, hon." I instruct, although my ladies room visit will be followed by a thorough Ms. Marple style interrogation at the long term patient welcome desk.

I wander like a clueless lost dog through the stark white hallways of the hospital's east wing, reading the signs and following the arrows that are painted along the floor which are supposedly directing me towards long term care. I meander and finally arrive at a rather quiet section of the hospital where a rigid looking elderly lady greets me from behind a rounded counter.

"How can I help you, mam?" she asks in a monotone voice that makes her sound like the robotic voice that chimes in when checking voicemail.

"Oh, hello there. I hope you're enjoying your evening!" I say trying to soften her up a bit, but I see she's unmoved and her face remains void of any emotion or interest. "Um, I was wondering if you could help me, I was involved in an unfortunate situation last week that concluded in a cyclist suffering a horrible leg injury. I was told he would be brought here and kept in for surgery on the injured leg. I felt horrible about the outcome of the accident and just wanted to give him my condolences and a get well gift as well as to apologize for the harm I caused."

"Not sure how I can help you," she responds coldly. "You got a name?"

"Erm, no I don't, see it all happened so fast and he was incapacitated so I was unable to get his name before he was whisked away to the hospital by the ambulance, but if there is a file involving a leg injury due to cycling accident on that computer of yours, perhaps you could search it up and inform me of his name."

"I'm sorry, but if you don't have a name of the patient, and you're not the police, you best be on your way. I'm not in the business of disclosing personal information of patients to individuals who have caused them extensive harm," she retorts in a much stronger tone than before.

I'm harshly faced with the reality that I'm going to have to be much sneakier about this investigation from this point on. I walk away from the counter giving the appearance that I'm heading down the hallway from which I came. I, however, duck out a side exit off the said hallway and find myself in a dark alley. All right, perhaps that wasn't the cleverest of options, but I gotta work with what I've got.

Half frightened in this deserted, garbage-filled alley I make my way to the nearest accessible entrance along the same wing of the hospital. As long as grumpy Gertrude doesn't see me, I can easily blend in as if I'm a visiting relative.

I walk in the sliding glass doors nearest to the alley and immediately take a quick right turn down the first row of patient rooms. As I walk by each one, I stop and peer in to determine whether it's an individual who has recently had leg surgery. For sure the victim would have his leg elevated in a sling at this point. When I come across closed doors, I subtly push them open and have settled on a plan to respond with a perplexed reaction if the patient in the room becomes irate or questions my intention."

"Oh, pardon me! My father must be in the room next door!" I'll say.

Thus far all doors are open and I witness family members crowding around beds and patients resting peacefully.

What a sombre place a hospital is. It really makes you appreciate your health and physical capabilities.

I'm overcome with guilt at the thought of having landed this perfect stranger in this stark environment for a lengthy stay.

I continue around the corner and peer into a room that has a half-closed doorway and feel a thrilling rush of eager excitement. I can just sense that this is the room I've been waiting to find. I glance in and see a definite leg in a sling with a plaster cast to at least mid- thigh level. It's him!

Okay, so I can't just barge in on him without knowing his name and completely empty handed. I back quietly away from the door and then see a plastic covered document, which I assume is his medical chart. I'm sure it's off limits to the common folk but I'm desperate to know his name. I reach for it and see the words *"Leonard Scott"* labelled on the front. He looks like a Leonard, I conclude. I carefully place the chart back in the pocket I withdrew it from, glance up at the room number, say it aloud, and begin my journey back to find out Minnie's status in emergency.

After following the arrows labelled emergency all the way back to determine Minnie's situation I am surprised to find her at the check in desk holding her injured finger just as it was, however, it looks as though it has a fresh bandage on it. She's been treated and is ready to go from what I gather.

"Minnie! Your finger looks as good as new!" I holler down the hall. She walks towards me looking a bit ticked off but keeps herself composed.

"Portia, they treated me right here. I just needed two stitches, and they checked my head. I'm good to go, but where in the world have you been? Are you having tummy trouble or something?"

I then understand her reasons for such a personal question. I had told her I was heading to the ladies so naturally she assumes I've been there for the three quarters of an hour I've been missing.

"I'm completely fine, Min. I just needed to conference with some nurses about something that I suppose I should fill you in on, because we have an errand to run!"

"Huh? What are you up to now?" she asks warily.

"Just accompany me to the gift shop, would ya?"

"Portia, you have become a bit of an enigma lately. You used to be so transparent! What errand are we running, Port? I really just want to get home and go to sleep. This whole experience has been rather unpleasant for me and,"

Minnie says in a whiny child-like voice and it's getting a bit wobbly like she may start full out crying on me.

"I know, Minnie," I say as I clasp her non-injured hand and hold it to me. "You've been so brave and I promise this will only take a few minutes, and it may take your mind off that little injury of yours. It could be really fun!" I start stroking her hand while leading her down the hallway, which has an arrow with the words "Gift Shop" labelled above it.

"Think of it as a late evening shopping excursion and I'll fill you in as we go."

We wind our way through the various sterile, silent hallways and finally reach a glassed front store that has balloons, teddy bears and ribbons displayed all along the entrance. I feel a smile beam across my face as I can just imagine Leonard's face when I arrive in his room with all of these pleasant goodies. I feel like such a good human being for going to all of this effort. Surely he'll thank me. Maybe I'll even get a forgiving embrace out of him.

"Come on, Min! We're on a mission for a fun get well card, some helium balloons and some sort of trinket or other that a middle aged man would appreciate!"

I pull her in to the store and give her the task of finding the card as I head to find a little gift. I see teddy bear after teddy bear and little snow globes with all sorts of things in them as well as aquarium style globes that are actually quite cool. I don't think it's a gift for Leonard. I all of a sudden realize that I'm thinking of him as if we are somehow better acquaintances than we actually are. I mean, he was either flying through the air or in shock the entire time we were in each other's presence so I can't really even call him an acquaintance.

"Stop putting so much thought into this, Portia! Just pick something!" I say aloud to myself bringing blank stares to both the store clerk and Minnie's faces.

I give a little embarrassed smile and continue rooting through the trinkets. Finally, I see a beautiful soap stone carving that looks like either a shark or dolphin. I'm guessing it's a shark judging by the row of detailed teeth protruding from its mouth, but it's beautiful nonetheless. I snatch it off the shelf and head to the clerk.

"Good evening. Can I please have half a dozen helium balloons? A variety of colours with inspirational messages of all sorts would be prime. Thanks!"

I glance to the back of the store to find Minnie still flipping through the card selection.

Lord she's so indecisive. How does she cut it as an executive at that ad agency if she can't even choose a damn card?

"How we doing, Min? Whatever's in your hand should do, hon."

Minnie quickly makes her way to the cash and the clerk begins ringing us through. Forty-eight dollars later, we're on our journey back to room one fifty-two with half a dozen helium balloons following behind us. God, these things are a bitch to control. I've simultaneously bopped a hot doctor on the head and a wheelchair bound patient as I round the corner to find my grumpy new friend behind the welcome counter right where I left her. I have a name and that's all that matters.

"You again," she states harshly. "I told you, no name, no entrance."

"Well, actually, I do have a name. Mr. Leonard Scott is expecting us in room one fifty-two as a matter of fact!" I retort proudly. She gives a rumpled look of confusion and I continue on past her without feeling any obligation to fill her in on how I determined this information that so short a time ago I was without.

Minnie and I briskly head toward room one fifty-two and I quickly inform her of who this mysterious Leonard Scott is that we're planning to shower with all of these gifts. "Look, Min, The other day I caused this poor man to be hurled from his bike onto a car. He shattered his leg and has been laid up here ever since. It's the least I could do."

"Yeah, I'd say so! The poor guy," Minnie responds as a helium balloon catches her on the nose. Just at this moment it occurs to me that I simply told the clerk to provide balloons with various inspirational messages, but I had never double-checked them to ensure they related to Leonard's situation. Unfortunately, the very balloon that has bounced off Minnie's nose, reads *"Heaven's Gaining an Angel,"* Oh man. I don't have time to look through them all, but it wouldn't make sense to remove any because six look so perfect together. Five is just so sparse looking a bundle. Whether death for this man is imminent or not, the balloon stays. He's probably in too much pain to be able to focus on words anyhow,

We gently push the door open and shuffle in. I can hear the television blaring CNN.

Huh, Minnie would be watching CNN if she were home at this time too.

Wolf is reporting some issue happening in Egypt and I see Minnie bending an ear to listen. I give her a nudge and we continue shuffling around the corner until Leonard is in full view. He's much more handsome than I remember him. I suppose the bike helmet and fanny pack had me categorizing him differently upon our first meeting. He's got lovely blond wavy hair and deep brown eyes. A sun-kissed glow, a few days of accumulated stubble with solid build is definitely doing him justice as well.

"Leonard! How are you feeling?" I say as if we are the best of friends. Leonard is startled out of his attentive concentration on the CNN programming and is quite obviously aghast at the sight, which has just appeared in his serene hospital room.

"I'm sure you're having trouble placing me. I caused you a small misfortune that I dare say left you injured and in need of medical attention. I'm Portia."

"Oh, I sure as hell remember you! You're the pink blob that lodged itself right in my path. I should have just run right over you, and then I wouldn't be in this mess."

He's clearly pissed.

"Um, well, Leonard. I brought you a get-well gift and some balloons. I just, well I wanted to apologize. I can be quite daft sometimes and unaware and it was never my intention to cause you injury." As I'm saying this I shove the shark soapstone at him. "Here, I got this for you. It can sit on your night stand and remind you of your bravery!"

"A shark? You're giving me a shark for my nightstand. The only thing that this shark will remind me about is how my step father lost his life, by a SHARK!"

Oh no. NOOO. Of all the luck, I choose the beautiful soapstone carving of a creature that caused his loved one loss of life. I'm such a nob!

"I'm so sorry, Leonard! I had no idea."

"Clearly not, because you don't know me! You have no business being here. Who let you in here? I'll be having words with the head nurse about this." He goes to reach for the buzzer to ring the nurse.

"No, wait! Please don't. I'm going. I just wanted to say how sorry I am, really. I'm so very sorry. Here we got you some pretty balloons and Minnie here has a card for you. Go on Min, give it." Minnie shyly approaches Leonard's bedside and outstretches her hand with the card in its grasp.

"I'm so sorry for your situation," Minnie utters in a sweet and concerned voice. "I hope this cheers you up."

At the sight of Minnie and at hearing her soft, soothing voice, Leonard's whole attitude seems to shift. I can hardly believe my eyes.

"Well, it's hardly your fault, dear. This has nothing to do with you. I appreciate your kindness," Leonard responds and retrieves the card with one hand while gently caressing Minnie's hand with the other. I see Minnie flinch a bit in surprise and then smile as her cheeks immediately change hue to a rosy red.

Leonard opens the card and reads it aloud while Minnie hovers over his bed.

"*The present may seem grim and skies may seem gray, but ahead of you lies a new day. A day filled with sunshine, glitter and gold. Celebrate and look forward to this future story untold.*"

"What a beautiful card to be given from such a warm and beautiful woman. Thank you." He smiles at Minnie as she turns to walk away. "What's your name, if you don't mind my asking?"

"Not at all, it's Minnie...Minnie Ritchie," she says bashfully, but willingly.

"Minnie, do you have a business card or a preferable way that I can reach you? I'd love to get in touch with you when I'm out of this place. I saw you focused on the news programming just a moment ago. Are you a current events junkie like me?"

"Oh yes! I definitely am! If I were home right now I'd be tuning in to this exact network. I'm so happy you have it on," Minnie replies while handing Leonard her business card

Leonard chuckles, "Whatever have you done to that finger of yours? Are you all right?"

"Oh this. Yes, I'm fine, just a wee cut. It's nothing at all."

Huh! Yeah right, nothing at all that had her out cold for only lord knows how long. She's working it, so I have to give it to her.

"Portia here figured it was best to have it looked at. So here I am!" She's so full of life right now. She has this beautiful glow that I can't help being totally proud of myself for bringing this meeting about.

"Well, Minnie Ritchie. We shall be in touch," Leonard says in a debonair voice that even has me a bit smitten.

"Look what I've brought about! At least you can forgive me now, right, Leonard? I brought you this absolute angel after all," I say hoping for a touch of appreciation.

"It certainly made things a bit brighter around here, but I still think you're a daft, ignorant woman, I'm afraid."

Ouch! I guess I deserve that. Hopefully by the time he and Minnie are official, this will all blow over.

"Well, get better soon. Let's get on out of here, Minnie. You two can catch up after Leonard has recuperated."

I take Minnie by the hand and notice that she and Leonard hold one another's gaze for the length of time it takes us to round the corner and head out into the hallway.

The whole way from the room to the hospital's main exit Minnie is flushed and has a smile from ear to ear. I can't help giggling at her immediate change in mood and present happiness. This is just what she needs, and I love being a part of it.

"What's that little laugh for? Are you having a chuckle at my expense?" Minnie asks in a voice that sounds as though she might break out in song.

"Min, I love seeing you so starry-eyed. You deserve this. You really do. Now let's get you home."

She squeezes my hand and lays her head on my shoulder. I feel her conveying her thanks and appreciation and I realize that even if the appreciation and thanks didn't come from Leonard, it meant a million times more to have unintentionally boosted this woman's self- esteem, when she had just, a short time ago, been at her lowest point.

I could feel the kinship between Minnie and me growing stronger, and I'm quickly realizing that she is no longer just a roommate but a true and loyal friend who I enjoy having in my life. It's been a successful excursion to say the least. Not quite the girls' night I had in mind, but one I'm sure we will both remember far and above any chick flick night we had planned.

CHAPTER 9

PARIS! It is so near I can taste the camembert and *fois gras* already. I do a little twirl on my way to the shower and can't help singing a little Motown throughout the entire cleansing process. While I'm soaping up and rinsing off, nerves well up in my belly when I'm reminded about my meeting with Victoria Lewis this evening. I mean, Nina will be there too, and it's just supposed to be an impromptu meet and greet, but it's VICTORIA LEWIS we're talking about! A meet and greet with her is more like being granted a backstage pass to canoodle with a celebrity.

What will I wear? How should I style my hair? I don't want to look too overdone, but want to be easy breezy fashion forward.

I run through these questions in my mind and become so racked with nervousness that I consider taking a day off work, but then quickly push that idea out of my mind knowing full well that I'd be pushing my luck at Hopewell if I did.

I spent the better portion of Wednesday determining which of the temporary office managers would replace me. It was a tough decision because although they all had the necessary education and experience, each of the three interviewees had odd idiosyncrasies that had me perplexed and not willing to commit immediately to any of them.

The initial interviewee was in her mid-forties and was a rather plump woman with a haughty manner. It almost felt as though she was conducting an interview on me. I could sense she used a more authoritarian strategy when managing which I just don't sense will go over well at Hopewell Clinic.

The next interviewee was fresh out of school with little experience. He was a late twenties effeminate sort, who immediately had eyes for Dr. Markson. Before the interview had even begun I could see how his baby blues were glued to Markson's backside as the doctor was bent over rustling through the file cabinet next to my station. I had to take hold of the young man's hand to regain his focus. He blushed and then nailed the interview. I just don't feel like it would be in the best interest of the office to add another element of drama to the environment and I don't even want to think about what Markson's wife would have to say if she discovered there was yet another young twenty-something who was after her husband and other items on his list to nail other than interviews.

Finally, I interviewed Clarice. She was a breath of fresh air due to her breezy mannerisms and her wealth of experience as a temp in numerous medical offices around the city. I could immediately sense that Clarice had the very work ethic, which would complement Tricia's and keep the doctors feeling at ease with the temporary change. The only downside to hiring Clarice for the week had to do with the obvious hygiene issues that were overwhelming to the eyes and nose. She could most definitely rival Darryl in the horrendous body odour department. So was not as literally a breath of fresh air as she was figuratively. Her hair also looked as though it hadn't been washed in weeks and she didn't wear a stitch of makeup to hide her acne-covered complexion. The final note, I am aware, is an unfortunate problem that the poor dear can't fix; the other two, however, would have to be taken care of before she commences work on Monday,

I did decide to hire Clarice, but I also got the task of asking her to clean up a bit before coming in next week. Lucky me!

After getting washed up and changed, I jet out the door to begin my day training Clarice and giving this thirty-seven-year-old woman a lesson in hygiene.

Maybe I'll lessen the blow by taking her to coffee at the afternoon break time? I consider as I'm walking along Keele Street.

By the time I reach the subway I've not only decided on the tactics and wording I'll use in breaking the news to Clarice about her need for hygienic improvements, but I also have selected my one shoulder, hunter green, slender fit, knee length Cynthia Rowley dress, paired with my yellow Steve Madden peep toe flats and my camel colour Calvin Klein trench (it may rain this afternoon) for my meeting with Victoria Lewis.

All of these garments and accessories paired with a new Betsy Johnson gold chain necklace, embellished with green, yellow and pink rose buds, which I purchased on Wednesday after seeing it featured as a must have accessory on *Crave Magazine's* latest trend watch page, will give the appeal and fuss free appearance I'm desperate to portray at my first meeting (well second, I suppose) with such an editorial star.

The nerves that had arisen at full boil from fear of unpreparedness on both fronts in the Clarice, as well as the Victoria Lewis dilemma, have now settled to a simmer and would most likely dissipate fully once both interactions had been accomplished.

I manage the morning quite well, splitting my time between conducting my duties whilst encouraging and training Clarice to the fullest. She really is like a sponge, not to mention the fact that her knowledge of the computer system and all the tech equipment is astounding. You'd think she had engineered all the gadgets and programmes herself from the astuteness she communicated. My insecurities and worries about leaving everything to her were quickly diminishing and it began to break my heart at the thought of telling her what I most certainly needed to in a few short moments.

All day, while interacting and supporting her orientation to the environment I couldn't help notice her greasy, mangled mane that had clumps of dandruff so large it was as if Nina had tossed white confetti at her and all the pieces attached themselves. Not only that, but in all situations that required her and I to be directly side-by-side my nose would become filled with the most offensive odour that evidently I could only detect to be a mixture of moth balls and B.O. If I could just eradicate the senses of sight and smell, she really is a lovely, intelligent woman.

I look at the clock to see that it is half past three already and motion to Tricia the inner office sign for coffee break. She nods and almost seems to manage a smile, which is an improvement after her cold behaviour towards me throughout the course of the week after I broke the news about my need for adventure. One day, I swear, I saw her give me the middle finger out of the corner of my eye. I simply shrugged it off and carried on with my day.

"Clarice, why don't you join me next door for a coffee break? It's my treat! I can give you some feedback on the day as well," I say cheerfully.

"Oh sure! Thanks, Portia. I never turn down a coffee when offered," she responds as I inspect her clearly coffee stained teeth, then quickly look away as I realize she has caught me fixated on them.

"Great, come along then!"

We enter the Starbucks that sits adjacent to the office and are greeted immediately. At least the smell of coffee is washing out the stench emanating from Clarice. I finally feel as though I can stop purposely breathing through my mouth and take in a big whiff of my surroundings.

"What'll you have, Ms. Clarice?" I ask with a sprightly joyful voice.

"Just a tall bold for me thanks!" she responds smiling to once again reveal her big buck, stained teeth.

I order her bold and my blonde and head to the nearest empty table. "A bold, blonde, ha…just the type of man I would order if they had a service like that!" I say and then immediately realize the corny nature of this line. I'm really just trying to make Clarice laugh and warm up to me before I have to tear her down.

Clarice manages a little giggle in response and says, "So, I sure hope you have a wonderful time on your Parisian holiday, Portia. How amazing. I would love to go there one day, or anywhere outside of Ontario for that matter. I've never been. I simply can't afford it with having to support my ailing mother and all."

Oh, no. That is just the sweetest and saddest thing I've ever heard.

I can't go through with this! This poor girl, single, broke and responsible for her sick mom doesn't deserve to be corrected. Maybe I can just let Tricia deal with it? I consider. *No, no, then Tricia would have even more reason to flip me the bird behind my back.*

I have to realize I'm only helping Clarice out. Maybe no one has ever had the guts to be honest with her for this very same reason. It's doing her such a disservice. She really has the potential to be pretty.

"Clarice, that's unfortunate. With all the work you get as a temp, I'm sure you could manage to set some money aside for a little vacation, even just a weekend in New York or Miami!"

She shrugs her shoulders at my suggestion. "I can't leave Mom behind. She needs me."

I see a pained look in her face and gather that she does not want to be pressed on this subject so decide that it's time; time to unveil my real reason for this chat.

"So, Clarice, we are so excited to have you working temporarily at Hopewell and I'm impressed with your capabilities already. I'm sure Tricia will enjoy working with you immensely!"

Here goes. She's so happy and smiling so widely. This is going to absolutely destroy her.

"We really do have rules that strictly need to be adhered to, such as punctuality, organization, completion of tasks and most importantly hygiene," I add while looking at her intently.

She looks long and hard back at me, "Yes, yes, hygiene of all equipment and workspace is definitely important! I am aware."

"Well *that*, and personal hygiene is also quite imperative, Clarice," I say with a little bit stronger of a tone. "It has come to my attention that there is often an offensive odour and there are always ways to eradicate this."

"I'm, I'm not following. What is it you're trying to say, Portia?"

She frowns a little, but I'm becoming a bit annoyed that she's even questioning and it's obvious that she knows fully well what it is I'm trying to say.

"Clarice, you stink! You need to shower regularly, wash your hair bi-weekly at least, wash those bits and pieces. You understand what I mean?" Clarice looks like a hurt puppy dog and I fear she may simply just forget the temp position altogether.

After a moment, during which Clarice appears to be mulling over my comments and determining the best response she finally retorts with, "I'm sorry to have offended you with my repulsive odour!"

The couple at the table next to us is now staring.

"Maybe I should find temp work elsewhere if I'm not welcome to be myself at Hopewell Clinic! I've never been so offended. Really, Portia, is this what passes for appropriate management?" Clarice begins fussing about and looks as though she's set to leave.

Oh shit. She's going to walk. I can feel it. Think fast, Portia, fast!

I have a wonderful idea flash across my currently frazzled brain. "Clarice! No, darling. I just want you to be at your best! Maybe this will translate into you being hired on full time somewhere. I would be willing to give a wonderful recommendation and I'm certain Tricia would as well! How about this, I'm going to set up an appointment at a stellar spa and salon. It's called Lusk and is in Yorkville. I'll be on my way to Paris tomorrow while you're being pampered and styled by the best in the business. They'll do your hair and your makeup. I'll even ask them to throw in a gift set of the makeup they use on you so that you can carry on the application on your own!"

I can see the suggestion has her nestled back in her seat and listening eagerly. "You'll get star treatment and have the most fashionable look for your week as temp at Hopewell. The doctors will be floored and you'll rival Tricia for neatness of appearance, I'm sure!"

Clarice is biting her lip so to control the smile that is attempting to stretch across her face, as if she wants to be sure that I'm not pulling one over on her before she celebrates. "Um, you'd do that for me? That's really kind. I just don't have money for that though," she says meekly.

"Don't worry about the payment. I've got that covered!" Or at least the office credit card has it covered. It is an office expense after all! I'm improving the image of the workplace with this expenditure. Surely the doctors will understand. "I'll make the appointment promptly and email you the details. Come on now, finish up that cup of Joe and let's get back."

I grab my empty cup to toss in the trash and prepare for the stench that will shortly accost my nostrils.

Breathe through your mouth, Portia. It'll all be over soon.

By the time half past six arrives, I'm heading out of the condo with a little spring in my step feeling truly stunning. It's a great hair day, a fabulous skin day, my makeup went on so perfectly and smoothly that I could rival Giselle for Cover Girl (okay, maybe a bit of a stretch), needless to say I'm feeling absolutely confident and ready to knock 'em dead at this little rendezvous..

I arrive at Chez Amour Bistro (how fitting for the upcoming adventure that we're convening at a French restaurant) with five minutes to spare. As I walk through the beautiful rustic looking doorway, which appears as though it's been flown in from some little town in the south of France, the maître d' greets me warmly and inquires as to which party it is I will be joining. "Ms. Victoria Lewis, thank you." I beam as the words leave my lips.

"Oh! Yes, yes. How fabulous it is that Ms. Lewis will be joining us this evening. I see. Here it is a party of three, no?" He gushes and seems almost more thrilled than I am at the prospect of being in the presence of Ms. Lewis.

"Yes, thank you. That is correct. We should be down for seven o'clock."

"You most certainly are, madam! Please tell me, what is she like? Is she as much of a presence in person and just as stunning?" he inquires.

I can't help being reminded that I was actually in her presence for at least three quarters of an hour without having the slightest clue. I commit myself to behaving as though Victoria is a very near and dear friend. I mean, she did attempt to come to my rescue in the ladies room! I can at least say she's definitely someone you'd be happy to have in your presence if ever trapped in a toilet stall

"Victoria is a gem, an absolute gem!" I exude so much enthusiasm and confidence that I have myself convinced Ms. Lewis and I are well acquainted. "I have to say she is one of my dearest confidants in the business and is a stunning woman both inside and out. I knew she was a star long before she was appointed editor in chief." I ramble and am just so caught up in the fantasy that I can't help continuing this charade. The maître d's expression is priceless as well. His head is propped on his open palm at his little welcome podium and his eyes are so wide in amazement, sort of like you see on the faces of children on Christmas morning.

"She and I became extremely close when working in the London office. I was creative director and she brought so much life to the designs through her rich and vivid wording, that I recommended her to the chief at the time to be promoted. Now look at her shine!"

"You...you discovered Victoria Lewis?" the thin dark haired gentleman asks with a totally stunned expression. "You're the reason that *Crave Magazine* has now climbed to the ultimate peak of recognition and now rivals *Vogue* for top editorial magazine? Oh Madam, you are now a star in my eyes and must be served with equal attention as we here at Chez Amour intend to provide Madam Lewis with. I'll inform the staff at once!"

Oh god. Oh no.

"Your name, please tell me your name. It will forever be inscribed in my mind. The whole fashion world must know."

"Portia, sir, Portia Delaney," I say quietly. It will be all right. I'll meet with Victoria and Nina, have a wonderful chat and then exit this bistro to never return.

The chances of me being found out while in the maître d's presence are minimal.

I calm my nerves, breathe in deeply and then ask to be shown to the table.

"Of course, of course Madam Delaney. I'm so sorry to have made you stand here communicating with me for so long. Right this way." The petite man leads me amongst filled tables of couples and groups of friends and families, laughing and chattering away. Finally, we reach a private corner of the bistro where a table meant for four is awaiting me. A floor to ceiling bay window and twinkling dancing lights, which appear as though they were removed directly from the Eiffel Tower itself, surrounds it.

"Oh my, this is beautiful! Thank you so much," I exclaim as Andre (I happened to finally catch a glimpse of his name tag) pulls out my chair and tucks me in with great attentiveness. "Thank you so very much, Andre. You're such a gentleman that I know Ms. Lewis will be quite happy being in your care this evening. I know I am already."

Andre completes pouring water into three of the four glasses that have been set and lights the pillar candle that sits in the centre. I'm entranced in the glow of the candle when a familiar booming voice jolts me back to reality.

"Portia, darling! We're here, lovely!" I turn to see Nina dressed in a body hugging black off the shoulder three quarter length dress and looking immaculate with her hair swept up in a fish tail braid. I glance to the left; my heart suddenly finds its way up into my throat. My body tenses as I take in the impeccable Ms. Victoria Lewis looking absolutely divine in a fitted knee-length ocean blue, knit dress.

"Nina! It's so wonderful to see you. You look beautiful," I manage to say in quite a normal voice. "And Ms. Lewis, it is such an honour to meet you. You are the voice of true fashion as I know it and I am so overwhelmed with joy to be given such a wonderful opportunity to join you and Nina this evening." Okay, perhaps I laid it on a little thick and as I look beside me I become painfully aware that Andre has overheard my spiel and has a look of confusion on his face.

"Well, I'm happy to be meeting such a dear friend of Nina's. She is my inspiration at present and any friend of hers is a friend of mine," Victoria says in a smooth and even tempered yet melodic voice.

Nina winks subtly at me and I feel a jolt of excitement that Victoria Lewis considers me, Portia Delaney, a friend. I can't help smiling ear to ear at how much this must mean for Nina as well. My dear friend has finally found her calling and I couldn't be happier for her.

Victoria and Nina take their seats at the beautifully arranged table and I find myself becoming more and more at ease in the situation. After a drink or two I'm sure I'll be able to chat to Ms. Lewis as if she's an old friend of mine.

When our waiter arrives to take our drink order I'm determined to follow Victoria's lead. "A Manhattan will do, thank you, and please keep them coming," she adds with a little smirk on her face. "It is Friday evening, is it not?" She chuckles.

Nina and I catch each other's eyes and give a little *"I like this girl"* look to one another.

"I'll have a gin and tonic, doll," Nina says. "And please do keep them coming this way as well."

It seems as though the others are ordering from the hard liquor menu tonight, so I suppose I should follow suit. I'm horribly aware of the fact that for me there is a fine line between pleasantly intoxicated and hard liquor induced raving lunatic so I settle on the sweet and tempting Cosmopolitan for my continuous drink of choice.

"Cosmopolitan it is!" the waiter says and marches away like a man on a mission.

Victoria sends a little nod of approval my way, for what I can only assume is my tasteful drink choice and then she begins a bit of an interrogation.

"So, Portia, I've been informed by Nina that you are currently a medical office administrator with the hopes and dreams of becoming a stylist and designer of couture fashion." I nod and sit up stiffly as if I'm at a job interview.

"Tell me what ever led you to turn your back on the fashion industry in the first place?"

"It's a rather long and boring story, Ms. Lewis," I begin. "I always accessorized and designed outfits for myself as a teen and was accepted to the Couture Styling Academy in Vancouver. I attended for two years and presented garments at a citywide fashion show. I also styled models for various charity fashion shows. I was deterred from continuing in the industry by matter of fact parents who preferred me to have a set career that was dependable financially. They convinced me to set my sights elsewhere. So during what should have been my final year at the fashion institute, I was enrolled in the medical office administration program at the college across the street."

"I see," Ms. Lewis comments and clears her throat almost as a means to dismiss my reasoning as being completely ludicrous. "It is always the case that the toughest roads bring the greatest rewards and if talent is there, and was there, turning away from your passion to head down the easy and *dependable* route is actually quite defeating, now isn't it?"

"I, I guess."

"You completely despise your career, don't you? If you despise your career, something must be done. *Your* mind has got to live and breathe fashion if you are going to make the transition to the fashion industry. There can be no fall-back career. If you have a fall- back career then that leads you to be lack-lustre and on the fence within the fashion world. No editor wants to review a designer who simply designs on the side. Fashion and design must be your focus and your entire life in order to be respected and reputable. You also, of course, must have the talent and a thick skin, yet also a necessary sensitivity to allow you to always be able to produce the most fashion forward pieces and looks."

I feel overwhelmed yet inspired all the same. I'm receiving advice from the head honcho of the fashion world's current leading magazine and quite honestly feel as though I am outside of my body hovering up in the clouds and witnessing this conversation from afar.

"I can be that person, Ms. Lewis, I *am* that person..." I say confidently. "Too long I've dreamed of having this burning desire to jump ship and swim towards my destiny. I can truly say that desire is now fully ignited within. I want this so very badly, Ms. Lewis and I assure you I am talented. I will have some of my garments Fed Exed from the fashion institute. They were award winners ten years ago. I know fashions have changed but at least you will be able to see the assembly and workmanship of the garments. I'll also forward pictures from the fashion shows that I had the pleasure of styling. This is my passion. Fashion *is* my passion."

Victoria is sitting expressionless across from me and Nina's eyes are darting back and forth as if she's watching a thrilling tennis match, awaiting the final result. I'm so worried Victoria will completely overlook me and I cannot, for the life of me, discern where this conversation will go. I'm almost breathless as I await a reply from the ever cool and calm Victoria Lewis.

She breathes deeply, and is about to formulate a response. Just as she draws breath to reply the waiter arrives with our second round of drinks. "On the house Madams," he says. "Compliments of the Maitre d for the fabulous Madam Delaney and equally as wonderful Madame Lewis."

No, he did not utter my name first, followed by Victoria's AND consider me equal to her!

I realize that Andre has likely informed the staff of my fabricated relation to Ms. Lewis. Victoria, clearly caught off guard, turns her head slightly with narrowed eyes and says, "Odd, but thank you for your kindness."

I take a huge gulp of my freshly delivered Cosmo and pray that this is the only time I will be awarded any praise that is on par with the praise which Victoria Lewis is deserving of.

While we all sit sipping away at our alcohol concoctions, I am becoming desperate to regain the focus of Ms. Lewis on the words she was so close to uttering before the interruption by the waiter. My desperation quickly heightens as Nina finds it a necessity to take charge of this portion of the evening by discussing Victoria's personal progress at the Toronto office and various tidbits, which are completely menial to ME in the current situation.

"Look, Vic." Nina speaks with a gentle and life coach style reassuring tone. "I know you've had doubts about the success of the Toronto branch, but you've got capable people running things. You've got to focus more on you and on working out those relationship woes with that husband of yours. It's not good to just bury your head in the sand when you know he's up to no good back in New York."

What is she doing? This is not the time for their therapy sessions! Nina set this meeting up for me and somehow I'm sitting here in silence like the third wheel when mere moments ago Victoria was about to communicate the biggest decision about how she can assist me. I've got to get this back on track.

Come on, Portia, do something!

Instead of action, I choose to withdraw. I excuse myself from the table and head to the ladies room in order to allow them the time they need to come to a decision about Victoria's direction in life in hopes that by the time I return, the topic of conversation will return to *my* direction in life. On my way to the ladies room I'm struck with surprise when I see all the bistro staff members watching my every move. As I walk towards the hallway, which leads to the bathroom one waitress is taking an order and the mere site of me causes her to freeze on the spot and drop her pen.

I bend down to pick the pen up for her and she gasps.

"Oh, Ms. Delaney that was unnecessary, though I appreciate your help greatly. Can I...get you anything, madam?"

"No, no. Just need to visit the ladies' ...you know, to powder this nose of mine." I reply as the commoner I am.

"Right, right. Well, I certainly hope everything is to your satisfaction," she adds.

I nod and continue on my path.

I can certainly get used to this treatment!

There's really nothing like experiencing what being a celebrity feels like, even if it is for such a fleeting amount of time. And how unfortunate it is that *fleeting* is the appropriate adjective to describe my moment in the limelight. As soon as I made my way back to the table, the entire web I weaved began to unravel.

I return with a jovial and light feeling hoping upon hope that Victoria will agree to look over my work and offer me an internship, I come upon an unwanted scene. Andre is deep in conversation with Victoria and Nina. I can see that Nina is laughing hysterically while Victoria looks absolutely appalled.

Oh no! He didn't...he couldn't have...that little French bastard!

I maintain composure, although I'm terrified on the inside. Victoria looks me up and down and glares at me as though I'm some extraterrestrial imposter who produces only one emotion in her, disgust.

"You discovered me? Is this the fantasy you are running around town telling people...hmm? Well, that simply won't do." Victoria Lewis speaks to me in the coldest and most dismissive tone, which I have ever been on the reciprocating end of.

"I...I...just got carried away! It was all a big misunderstanding that all seemed so lovely. I just couldn't bring myself to correct the mistake. I'm terribly sorry. I really do admire you so very much, Ms. Lewis, please, let me..."

As I'm approaching the point at which I plan to throw myself at her feet, her phone begins ringing and she does not give a second thought about answering it. While she gabs away to no doubt an actual creative director, Nina looks at me still smirking but also with compassion.

"Well, ladies, I've been summoned away. I've quite an important event to get to tomorrow and must ensure everything goes off without a hitch. Nina, you and I will meet when you're back and do expect a call every now and then while you're on holiday."

Victoria doesn't even give me a second glance and simply sweeps away into the night leaving me feeling dejected and more uncertain than ever about my future prospects in the fashion industry. I sit hunched back in my chair, not wanting to move, eat or even drink. Nina reads my body language precisely because she simply just lets me be in silence for a few minutes. After I finally look up at her I manage a half smile.

"Nothing gained but nothing lost I suppose," I say trying to see the situation from a more positive light.

"Come on, Portia, drink up and let's get out of here! We've got a plane to catch at seven a.m. and this incident will be the furthest thing from your mind while you're in my care, babe!"

A shrug and a sympathetic embrace, then we make our way out into the open air and onto the next chapter of our adventures together. The Nina and Portia diaries have only just begun.

CHAPTER 10

I'm almost at the point of hysterics the following morning. I'm extremely anxious and fidgety and my nerves have gotten the better of me so that I'm bumping into doors and spilling coffee while I'm racing around the condo attempting to pack any remaining items I have forgotten about until this point.

I dreamed the most horrible dreams all night that have me questioning my future once again and have left me completely unmotivated to even be going to Paris. In the most vivid dream I was swimming under water and couldn't find an escape to the surface. I just kept swimming and swimming, suffocating in the murky depths.

Finally, I looked up to see an escape. I fluttered up as fast as I could manage only to witness Ms. Lewis' face grimacing down at me. She then let out a shrill laugh, which was followed by immediate darkness as I realize she had blocked the passage completely. I woke up gasping for air and dripping with sweat. My mind was racing, recalling the dream and I simply could not go back to sleep for fear that I would revisit the action of the dream exactly where I had left off.

If only Dr. Richardson had early morning hours I would squeeze in that appointment I had intended to make but became too busy to manage. I was so confident and excited all week, but the uncertainty that remains from the conversation with Ms. Lewis has me absolutely distraught and just as in my dream I feel like all escapes from my current career are closing. I'm suffocating in it, need to escape it and the one true hope I had, Victoria Lewis, is seemingly eradicated as that one individual who could help me to do just that.

I'm feeling like a stubborn child who is being forced to go to the doctor's office and is resisting with all her might, except this is a trip that one can only dream of! "What the hell is wrong with me?" I question myself audibly just as Minnie rounds the corner on her way to the bathroom. She gives a bit of a sideways glance, but has learned that these incidents she keeps witnessing are just a part of my nature and that no questions need to be asked; just as bawling to Bob Marley is a part of her nature.

No Marley has been playing within these walls all week though. Minnie has been extremely bubbly and has popped in to see Leonard in the hospital three times since their first meeting. She's undeniably infatuated with the handsome victim of my ludicrousness, and from what I gather he is just as taken with her. She's so cheerful and relaxed lately that I can't help feel over-joyed for her newly- found distraction from her time consuming career.

Leonard apparently is just Minnie's sort. He's a successful graphic designer who began his own company mere months ago. It's doing unbelievably well. He was also working ungodly hours at the firm he was employed by previous to beginning his own business. He finally cut and ran after the CEO began demanding him to give more hours for the same insignificant salary. The fifty-two year old is like a new man!

All of Minnie's recent calmness and zen-like behaviour has me overly aware of my ever-increasing spastic nature, especially after last night's events.

I...I have to call Dr. Lola! I know it's only five a.m. but if I can even leave a message for her so that she can later message me with the guidance I need, I'd feel a whole lot better.

I grab my iPhone and hit call next to Dr. Lola's name.

"Hello?" a jovial voice is heard on the other end.

She's awake? This is so perfect! I just need her reassurance and then I'll be back to being Portia the Parisian obsessed.

"Dr. Richardson, It's Portia. I hope I didn't wake you. I'm just calling for a quick bit of advice. I was hoping to get in to see you before I leave to Paris today, but the week flew by so quickly and now here I am as agitated and worry- filled as ever."

"Portia, what about? Is it still about holding men's attention? You know that only comes with practice and what a perfect place Paris is to do just that. Oh,

I am so envious of you; all the ruggedly handsome men with their euro-fit pants. They'll be reciting love poetry to you in no time!"

"Oh, well, no. That's not why I'm calling. I've had *some* success in that area, Dr. Lola, but I'm really just feeling extremely anxious about my career direction. I had a meeting with a very important woman in the fashion industry last evening and I left feeling entirely hopeless. I just have lost all excitement for this trip because I feel that I should be here doing my best to right the wrongs I've done and really take the transition from my current career to the fashion world more seriously."

"Portia, Portia, Portia. Is it not the fashion industry you wish to transition to? I believe that's what you said?"

"Erm, yes," I say with uncertainty as to where she's going with this.

"The most dedicated action you can take to prove your interest and gain not only an appreciation for, but become inspired by fashion, is to go to that very city. It is fashion central, after all! Visit the design studios while you're there, devote a portion of your days to truly finding your muse and even create sketches based on what you discover are the upcoming trends. Whoever that woman is who made you feel so very disgruntled, I'm sure would have the same advice if she truly is the fashion icon you say she is."

"Well, her advice to me *was* to live and breathe fashion if I want to succeed in it," I reply with a clarified view of the situation. Dr. Lola really has this profound ability to just know exactly what it is I need to hear at any given moment. "Dr. Richardson, you've just calmed my nerves entirely. Thank you so much for answering and chatting with me so early. You really are a talented woman."

"So are you, Portia. And don't you forget it! Now go devour a delicious baguette and a wedge of cheese for me, oh and have a few glasses of Chardonnay on my behalf, not the cheap kind though. Really go big or..."

"Um, Dr. Lola, I will, but I really must be going or I won't make the flight at all," I say with a little giggle added on.

"Yes, yes, get going. We'll discuss it all when you get back. Oh and don't forget to take on a lover while there! Parisian men do make the best temporary lovers, you know." She signs off and as I hang up the phone I realize I'm blushing at the thought of taking on a Parisian lover for five days.

Absolutely a ridiculous thought, but I'm sure it would be a blast for the right type of woman. Maybe Nina will!

A smile has found its way to my face and I'm finally feeling extremely excited again. I decide at the last minute to throw my sketchbook and sketch pencils into my carry on and then call for a taxi. I look at my watch.

Perfect! I can still get there with an hour and a half left to get through customs.

I find myself in the lobby about three minutes later after giving Minnie a big squeeze. The lobby is completely empty aside from a couple that I can hear arguing. They are, however, in a little inlet beside the mailboxes and I can only make out a distinct female and male voice disagreeing about something. Being the nosy type I head over to pretend to be checking my mail. I head smoothly and slyly to the mailbox and turn slightly just to catch a glimpse of the couple. I gasp with the realization that it's Penelope. And although I would have expected Randall, instead I see Darryl looking very hot- headed and distressed.

I stand frozen and awkward for what seems like an eternity.

I can't let them see me, I can't let them see me,

"Portia?" Darryl says huskily and with a little too much aggression for my liking. "Portia, what are you, why are you here? Let me guess my father has you following me, that arse!"

"Darryl, I live here. This is where I've lived for three years. Look, my initials are on my mailbox. Do you really think I would spend my time tailing your ass at five a.m. Please, I have better things to do."

"Who is this, Darryl?" Penelope asks in an agitated voice. "You work for his father and live here where I live?"

"Yes, yes I do," I respond coolly. "And I've had the pleasure of meeting your lovely fiancé on numerous occasions," I throw in as I see her give me dagger eyes in response. "Randall. Yes a wonderful man."

As I'm adding this last detail, which has clearly got Darryl to the point of becoming irate, I see my cab pull up. "That's for me! Got to go. What a pleasure it's been bumping in to you both," I say in the most sarcastic tone imaginable. They both remain silent and simply watch me exit the scene and jump into the cab.

The cab ride only takes twenty minutes and before I know it I'm being greeted by Nina who is completely dolled up with ringlets sporadically distributed throughout her golden mane and a maxi dress patterned with roses. She looks absolutely lovely and I suddenly glance down at my cut off jean shorts and Blue Jays tee feeling a bit understated.

"Oh sweetness! You've finally arrived. I thought I was going to have to seduce the pilot in order to keep the plane grounded until you finally made it!" Nina says as if we've just avoided unparalleled disaster.

"Neen, we still have a full hour and a half before take-off. Stop being so dramatic," I say in a playful tone.

"Babe, either you're on a different flight entirely or can't do your simple addition and subtraction because my boarding pass says we take off at six fifteen and are to begin boarding in twenty minutes."

"That, that can't be. I was sure we had booked the seven a.m. departure time with the agent. We even discussed being ready for our seven o'clock lift-off yesterday! Remember?"

"I completely do, but when I checked in half an hour ago they printed me off a pass for the six fifteen flight. My guess is the agency mucked up, sweet pea. Grab your things and let's motor! We're getting to Paris on the six fifteen flight and that's the end of discussion." She grabs my case, winds her way up to the check in and plops it on the weigh scale for the woman to process.

"You two are cutting it very close." The attendant shakes her head and continues tagging the bags. "Gate twenty-one, customs is that way. Just a little advice to you both, run!"

Without waiting another second, Nina and I hold tight to our carry-on luggage, passports and boarding passes and take off sprinting through the airport towards customs as if our rears were on fire. Nina's ringlets are bouncing up and down with such vigor it looks as if her hair is trying to escape from her head only to be pulled back to its root. I'm finding it quite amusing and keep giggling the entire way. Nina is always amusing even if it's unintentional.

After dodging a few families, security guards, who look at us with complete understanding as we speed by and air traffic controllers who are clearly trying to enjoy a bit of a break, we arrive at customs to find ourselves at the end of what appears to be a never ending line. Everyone in the line looks half asleep and unquestionably miserable, but I can quite honestly say that although Nina and I were breathless and windswept with adrenaline pumping full force, we are the furthest thing from miserable. This was going to be an adventure, no matter what happens, and we're in this together. What's a trip to Paris without a few tiny mishaps on the way? The beauty that awaits us has to be earned somehow.

The line slowly snakes along until we finally arrive at the customs conveyor belts. I always become so nervous at this point. Not that I have anything illegal in my possession, but I remember movies like *Broke Down Palace* when someone slips illegal substances in to Clare Danes' bag and she gets thrown in a foreign prison for years. It's all so horrible.

I step forward to start loading the plastic tray with my belongings and remove my shoes before even needing instruction. I'm quivering involuntarily and can feel eyes on me all the while. Nina has joined a far line and I can see her walking through the detector with ease, wearing a big smile.

A small boy looks up at me with compassion in his eyes as if to say, "Lady, it'll be alright. " He must be able to sense how unsettled I am or see that my boarding pass is fluttering like a leaf in the breeze due to the twitching and convulsing of my nerve- filled hands.

I watch as my belongings edge their way along the conveyor belt and have a checklist forming in my mind of all the potential items within the bag, making certain that nothing is violating any law.

So, *liquids, all less than a hundred ml, no aerosol, no knives, no guns, no bombs. Okay, I think it'll all be fine.*

I head towards the metal detector and body scanner. I always feel so vulnerable at this point. I've often been told to take off loose fitting tops to reveal a barely there tank underneath that is practically belly top sized. At least today my Jays top is rather well fitted and they're out of luck because I'm wearing nothing but undergarments underneath. This is not the time or place for a strip show.

I walk through the detector and body scanner completely without incident and I heave a big sigh of relief. I see Nina standing at the end of the conveyor belt awaiting my success in passing security. She's doing a side-to-side shuffle and her ringlets are bobbing with every step she takes. Oh now she's doing the sprinkler dance move.

What a nut! This is going to be a ball of a trip with her.

I start laughing just as the security posted at the conveyor belt says in a deep serious voice, "Is this your bag, Ms.?" He's a large dark man with the broadest shoulders I have ever seen.

"Yes, sir. It is mine. Is there a problem?" I ask in a submissive tone.

"I'm going to have to search it, ma'am I see a rather sharp knife-like object. This is not allowed."

"A knife-like object! I-I- didn't pack a knife! Someone must have slipped it into my bag, Sir. I assure you it's not mine." I feel myself becoming erratic and my mind is whirling.

I'm never going to make it to Paris, I'll be thrown in the slammer, I'll never fall in love, I'll never become a successful designer. With this on my record, Victoria Lewis will forget she ever met me (she probably already has).

As horrendous thoughts are running through my head and panic takes over my entire body I watch the guard rifle through my carry on with such force that items are being strewn about and some are even sent flying out of the bag. He's on a mission and my bag is the innocent victim in this all. After completely tearing through the main pocket whilst sending V-neck sweaters and pashmina scarfs cascading to the ground, he directs his knife hunt on the side pocket.

I hear the *zzzzziiiipp* sound and see his paws plodding and grasping at my unmentionables. A silk black and pink polka dotted thong flutters on to the conveyor belt and moves along to become jammed in the mechanisms teeth at the end. At this point, people are staring not only due to being held up by this ordeal, but even those who have already been cleared who are awaiting family and friends are quite obviously entertained by the scene they are witnessing. I cringe as it hits me that those were my most favourite pair of Calvin Klein knickers.

Please let this be over. This brute better find something that makes this embarrassment and panty loss all worthwhile.

Suddenly, he pulls out my cosmetic case and holds it up as if he has found his holy grail. He drops it aggressively, opens it and shuffles through the contents. I'm horrified as my recently purchased box of durex condoms is sent tumbling to the floor and a handful scatter along the ground next to the foot of the little boy who showed me so much compassion earlier. "What are those, Mommy?" he asks a prim and proper woman dressed in a lovely pantsuit. She gasps in shock and simply grabs his hand to pull him away as if the condoms were some contagious plague.

Nina catches a glimpse of the condoms and yells, "Oh yeah! Portia, you better get some on this trip. That's right. I expect nothing less!"

I send along a cold intentional stare in her direction to let her know I am not impressed. Sex is the furthest thing from my mind at the moment and at this point I wish I could rewind time and leave the condoms off my packing list so that this whole situation could have been avoided.

I bend down to collect the scattered rubbers and stuff them into my pockets meekly. I feel my skin burning hot. The guard finally seems to locate something because he is acting in a more delicate and precise manner. He delves in one last time to the bottom of the cosmetic bag and pulls out a tiny set of nail clipping scissors. "Aha!" he grunts. "Ma'am, these are not permitted. I will have to confiscate these, and please be more careful next time."

I am gobsmacked. He just tore through all of my personals and unmentionables and made me appear as though I'm a common criminal, all to confiscate a set of teeny tiny scissors? I'm so exasperated that I simply sigh heavily and grab up all my things aside from the mangled and clearly wedged thong.

HE can deal with that!

I make my way towards Nina who is ready with her arms wide open for the purpose of giving me a tight embrace. We hug for a moment and then I pull away as I see the time on a distant clock.

"Nina! It's five past six! We've got to run!" I grab her arm and we run towards gate twenty-one as fast as my ballet flats and her wedge heels will allow us to go. We arrive at the gate totally gasping for air as we see a few straggling passengers making their way past the attendants and down the loading ramp.

We've made it!

Our boarding passes are still in hand along with passports and important items. A total miracle accomplished. Just this feeling of knowing for certain Paris is only a few hours away makes that whole uncomfortable security issue null and void.

Paris! Here we come!

CHAPTER 11

This whole journey keeps improving completely! Although after the start we got off to, there really can only be better circumstances ahead.

Nina and I lucked out and are seated right up at the front of the coach section where we have our own row, plenty of leg room and the big screen immediately in front of us is set to be playing *Eat Pray Love* and *My Life in Ruins*. Two perfect movies for the mid-thirties girl searching for purpose. I'm guessing the men on the plane are a bit less enthused about the features, but I've seen enough of those action packed, blood spilling thrillers that most men go gaga for so they can let the ladies have this one for a change.

I curl up with my provided pillow and blanket, put my feet up on the empty seat to my left and nestle in to Nina as Julia Roberts' enticing and alluring smile takes over the screen. I swear she hasn't aged a day since *Pretty Woman*.

The first half of the plane ride is a sleepy and comatose vegged-out experience a *dolce far niente* if you will. But as the announcements over the speakers from the pilot continue updating us on our proximity to the City of Light I feel a bubbling energy that has me unable to sleep for the remainder of the flight. My mind is spinning with ideas to get the most out of this trip and do Paris in style.

"Nina...psst...Nina" I poke at her with my bony elbow. Even though I'm fully alert, Nina maintains her comatose state and I realize that I am going to have to unleash my energy into something other than an interactive discussion with Nina about how we're going to tear up the town.

Finally, I feel a rush of enthusiasm. A motivation I have been lacking for years due to disgruntlement has me reaching into my carry on for my sketch pencils and sketchpad. At first, I simply sketch geometric shapes and hearts to get my hands warmed up, then I'm reminded of Victoria Lewis' blue knit dress the other night.

That's an easy start. I'll begin with a basic and build on it.

I sketch and I sketch; it's as if my hand has taken on a life of its own and I am simply the vessel for the creativity now flooding out of my fingertips. I feel a familiar fire and passion that has been quenched and dormant for so long that it's almost on par with great sex after a long dry spell of inactivity. I am so at peace and one with the pencil that an entire hour passes by and when I finally take in all that I have created, I am stunned and unbelievably impressed with my work. A flowing multi-layered floor length skirt decorated with a large silk bow at the waistline and a paired midriff bearing boat neck sleeveless blouse decorated with black polka-dots.

Next to this ensemble sits the Victoria Lewis inspired ocean blue knit form-fitting dress, only I have added a wave pattern throughout by using alternate shades of blue. Also I have created a sheer silk knee length button-up over blouse with a jewelled belt to add more movement and maintain a distinct waistline.

I feel a proud smile pasted to my face and have to admit I'm extremely pleased with my creations. I consider nudging Nina awake, but then I think of how incredible of an accomplishment it would be to have developed a whole collection by the end of this trip that I can present her with on our flight home. My heart leaps with excitement and anticipation of all the wonderful designs I have in mind waiting to be sketched.

I notice that Nina is beginning to stir so I slip the sketchbook and pencils away and turn my attention to the *US Weekly* I have stuffed away in my tote.

"Wakey, wakey, sleeping beauty," I say as Nina's eyes begin to open slightly."

"My god, woman! How are you so bloody bright-eyed? Were you not up at the same ungodly hour that I was?" Nina responds trying to feign annoyance, yet I can sense the sweetness behind her tone that reassures me she's winding me up.

The remainder of the flight was spent eating some sort of chicken curry concoction, swigging back a few complimentary merlot and taking our turns meandering up and down the aisles checking for any celebrities or male celebrity look-a-likes who we may be able to tag along with once reaching Paris. What better than to find a dashing Parisian local who could take us each on one arm and lead us through the city streets? Or better yet, introduce us to an equally as handsome friend so we could each have a strong-armed gentleman to ourselves. Maybe a bit of a pipe dream, but certainly one I'm holding on to for at least the remainder of this flight.

We have no luck in the handsome man discovery game but Nina, of course, does strike up a conversation with a group of Parisian hipsters who appear to be no older than twenty-two and who are clearly beyond intoxicated. One lanky man, or boy seems more fitting, has wrapped his long thin arm around Nina's waist and is twirling one of her curly tendrils with his spindly fingers as if totally entranced by its shape and texture.

I find my way over and plop myself into his empty seat. Almost immediately, the lanky boy's equally as quirky looking and equally as intoxicated, scruffy friend leans in to plant a big wet kiss on my freshly rouged cheek. I grimace and pull away in total surprise and partial disgust.

"What do you think you're doing? I haven't said one word to you. You don't even know my name, you animal!" Nina is almost in hysterics laughing and moments later the lanky beast plants an equally sloppy kiss right on Nina's lips.

"Yeeeeoooow!" she screeches in utter surprise yet looks absolutely thrilled by it all. "You boys surely are forward, and I don't mind it one bit!"

"Well, I'm a bit more of a prude I suppose so could you please just keep your distance from my personal space bubble," I say gesturing at the imaginary bubble surrounding me. "Please and thank you?"

"Pardon, mademoiselle. You are magnifique," the scruffy boy to my right mumbles. He sounds so divine that I'm actually the tiniest bit smitten. I smile and giggle, but avoid eye contact at all cost. I can't handle another sloppy kiss from this barely legal Frenchman.

Nina, on the other hand, is eating it up literally. She and the rail are full on in make-out territory and have begun to offend passengers on all sides. I watch as an elderly woman quietly informs the flight attendant of the unnecessary loving that is happening in the aisles. The pursed lip attendant marches straight towards the lip-entwined duo and clears her throat so loudly that I jump at the force.

"Madame et Monsieur, if you please halt this activity whilst in the aircraft. Mesdames, please et merci, return to your places on the aircraft." She directs us with a slight irritation in her voice.

"Sure, sure. Very sorry for the disturbance. Nina, let's go." I immediately tear her away from her feisty "love" and head back to the seats just in time for the announcement from the pilot that we're beginning to descend.

"Nina! We're landing! We're almost in Paris!" I'm nearly shouting and get judgemental stares from all around directed my way. "I'm just so excited," I whisper in Nina's ear.

"Oh, doll, I can see and bloody well hear that! Now, we have to track those lovely youngsters down and attach ourselves to them today, you know, just to become acquainted with our surroundings, and ahem, so I can finish the hanky-panky I had begun," Nina insists.

"Okay, Okay I guess it couldn't hurt to hang with locals who clearly will know where to have a good time in the city, but then we are going to continue our search for age appropriate, hot, Parisian men to escort us around. Those guys are absolutely infantile, Neen!" I say with a whiny voice yet half laughing at the ridiculousness of it all.

"Right, right, whatever. We shall go with the flow and dare to do the unthinkable all week, my pet."

I smile and then begin to feel my ears popping and pressure building, almost reflecting the inner feeling of pressure and excitement building in my soul as we are mere moments from touching down in the magical world that is Paris. Nina grabs my hand and suddenly I feel like we're Thelma and Louise in the suicide scene aside from the whole suicide part.

The final announcement comes over the loud speaker."Ladies and gentle-man, Paris welcomes you. We at Air Plaisance do hope you have had a pleasant travel experience and wish you a wonderful day."

Twenty minutes later we've gathered our belongings, exited the plane and are crossing through customs. At the baggage carousel Nina locks eyes with her young Parisian love and they pick up where they left off while I wrestle down the luggage for the both of us. One bag's zipper becomes jammed in the crack at the base of the carousel and I make a full lap of the carousel pulling and huffing, knocking other passengers out of the way with full determination to loosen the bitch of a bag.

Finally, an airport attendant joins in and unjams the luggage piece. I fall flat on my back once again, with the suitcase flat on top of me. Replace this suitcase with that airport attendant and I'd be in heaven. I utter a thank you and manage my way back to Nina who has separated from the youngster for a moment to reapply some lip gloss.

"Nina, I've got it all. Now, let's grab a cab to the hotel. We'll give these guys our hotel name and number and meet with them later, alright?"

Nina heaves a sigh and her juvenile lover man leans in to give her a final squeeze and a kiss. "Til we meet again, mon amour."

"Oh we will meet again! You and me, her and him will be meeting at our hotel. L'Hotel de Triomph. Right near L'Arc de Triomph. We will certainly have a triumph tonight if you arrive with him." Nina is giving instructions like she is talking to her hard of hearing grandmother and the two Parisians are nodding and following her finger with their eyes as Nina is pointing to me then them then back to me then to her and…finally her honey grabs her finger, pulls her in and whispers, "We'll be there. Eight o'clock, in the lobby."

Nina and I jump in a cab and begin the trip to the hotel with full realization that it is already six o'clock Parisian time. The five hour jump ahead has us all mixed around.

"Less time than I thought to have to wait for my tall, lean apple dumpling!" Nina announces with joy.

I'm taken aback at how in to this guy she is. If we were back in Toronto, she wouldn't give a Canadian with mystery man's build and looks a moment of attention. I guess the accent really does overshadow all the rest. It's bordering magical and spell- binding really. I mean, I'm far from becoming overly lustful for the scruffy counterpart, yet I don't find him nearly as repulsive as he would be if his sweet melodic intonations were replaced with say a Texan twang. It's as if the sweet sounds allowed blinders to fall and for any negative features to become muted and less unattractive.

◇◇◇◇◇◇◇◇

The cab driver pulls up in front of a grand, and lavish looking building decorated with ancient carvings and pillars forming a royal entranceway. I can see there is a massive chandelier dangling in the lobby that looks like something you would see hanging in Marie Antoinette's residence. My heart leaps at the beauty of it all.

A man dressed in a black coat- tailed jacket and top hat with matching black trousers, opens the cab door for us and takes my hand with a twinkle in his eye.

"Bonjour Mesdames. Bienvenue a L'Hotel de Triomphe Paris. Your stay shall be enjoyable."

He helps me from the cab and then runs around to Nina's side and does the same. The cab driver hustles to the trunk and removes all of our bags for the bellboy to collect and puts out his hand. I'm confused and tired so simply shake it, which makes him roll his eyes and utter something in French to the concierge in coat tails.

"Madames. He would like to be paid. Thirty-four euros for the travel."

"Oh right, right," I say completely embarrassed. I hand over forty and gesture to keep the change.

The cab driver nods in appreciation and drives off down the cobble-stone avenue.

"Right this way, Mesdames." The concierge beckons us toward the stately entrance and up to the marble desk behind which a pleasant looking woman and an incredibly handsome man are awaiting us with full-toothed grins.

"Ton nom?" the woman says

I give an, "I have no idea what you're saying. I'm a foreigner, please speak English," gesture.

"Ah…your name please?"

"Portia Delaney and Nina Westin, thank you," I say with confidence.

"I see, yes, yes," she says reassuringly as she searches for our reservation in her computer, however, even though her words are reassuring, her face is giving off a look that screams "Where in the hell are these women's names in this damn computer?"

She turns to her colleague and mutters something in French under her breath so that we can't hear her. Although, it isn't as if we would have the slightest clue what she is actually saying.

The gentleman behind the counter shrugs his shoulder and begins his own computer search. I suddenly feel myself becoming impatient at not knowing the issue and whether or not there even is a reservation for us.

"Pardon me. Is there a problem?" I inquire in my sweetest possible voice.

"Madame, there is no problem. Here is your reservation." The gentleman points at his computer. "We are determining your suite. The suite we had you placed in is experiencing de toilet difficulties and de water is shhhhpeeewww shhhhhpeeeewww over the room," he says as he makes a fountain like gesture with his hands. "The suites at your price are fully booked. We figure something, Mesdames. Not to worry."

"Oh! Just my luck to be booked into a shit covered suite in the city of love."

Nina grabs me by the shoulders at the sounds of my obvious dismay and starts singing *Sweet Caroline* with extra emphasis at the "good times never seemed so good" portion. I immediately start laughing and joining in.

"Babe, it'll work out! They're working it out. They aren't having us stay in *that* room and will find us *something* even if it's a different hotel. They have to. Patience, doll!" Nina reasons.

Nina's positive attitude and pep talk must have worked some sort of magic on the hotel staff and perhaps supernaturally filled their hearts with compassion and kindness because in mere moments they summoned the concierge to summon the bellhop and gave their sincere apologies as we trailed along behind our bags toward the lifts.

The bellhop scurries us on to the lift and presses the appropriate floor number, that which I cannot see as he is standing at an angle to block the buttons. It isn't until the doors open that I glance up to see *PH* lit up on the overhead panel and glance at Nina to see the same surprise and shocked expression consuming her face.

We both practically fight to get off the elevator in pure excitement to see our room and have an undeniably fantastic feeling about being on the Penthouse level at such a prestigious hotel.

"Right this way, Mesdames." We follow the bellhop like lost puppy dogs and he comes to a sudden stop. Nina and I are walking so close behind that he doesn't stand a chance and we both bump full in to him.

"So sorry, sir, please carry on," I say gesturing to the door he was about to open. I do a double take at the plaque on the door, which reads *Executive Suite Présidentielle* and lose my balance falling into the wall, which steadies me. The door is flung open; I gather my composure and flash an excited look to Nina whose jaw has now fallen so far I think I may have to help her lift it off the ground.

"Mesdames, your suite." The bellhop extends his arm to grant us entrance and flips the lights to present a suite like no suite I have ever seen.

Not even in magazines or movies, or television shows that follow the lifestyles of the rich and famous! It was enormous and so lavish that I immediately removed my footwear as to avoid messing up its pure perfection. A gorgeous chandelier cascades in a spiral over the centre of the suite, under which sits a massive chaise lounge patterned in black and white flowers, beside which rests a plush leather sofa I could easily plunge onto and take a lengthy nap. The beautifully patterned area rug looks as though Louis XIV could have owned it, it is so intricate and spectacular.

The most incredible part of the suite is how the old décor and charm is mixed so perfectly with the modern, what looks like a sixty- inch plasma television matched with surround sound. Sleek chrome side tables and a matching side board complements the gathering space just perfectly. White lilies are strewn about in various locations, embedded in magnificent vases.

There's a full bar to the right upon entrance which Nina bolts directly to in order to inspect the goods. She gives two thumbs up and an enormous smile, clearly pleased with what she has found. I give two back. The bellhop then directs us to the balcony, which is a full terrace to be more exact with the description. It's practically the size of my entire condo and from its perch presents the Eiffel Tower and L'Arc de Triomphe in full view. My heart leaps with utter joy and amazement at the sight I'm taking in. I stand for a moment almost feeling as though I'm transcending space and time, entirely weightless in what feels like a dream.

"Port!" I hear Nina bellow. "Portiaaaaa! Get your taut ass in here and look at these rooms!"

I come to and follow the screeching, past the expansive cherry wood dining table, set for eight, past the fully fitted kitchen with stainless steel everything and sleek black slate counter tops to match and on in to where I can see Nina's curls bouncing with extra spring as she herself is springing on a fully white made up king sized bed.

"Look at the size of this thing, Port! We can sleep the entire hotel staff in this bed, and I wouldn't mind getting my hands on that piece of eye candy from the check in desk, so it would all be perfection if we could arrange it!"

"It's pretty impressive, isn't it? I'd suggest not offering your bed to the hotel staff though Neen," I say cheekily; "At least not until the second night."

She smiles and bounces off the bed frolicking towards an open door clearly leading to her en-suite bathroom.

"Good god! I think this Jacuzzi is bigger than the bed." Her voice echoes throughout the suite and I see the bellhop cringe at her behaviour. I shrug my shoulders and give a little she's been drinking sign with my hands while pointing towards the en-suite where Nina is now singing *"That's Amore"* at the top of her lungs.

Wrong language and culture but still fitting I suppose.

While Nina continues her celebratory gallivanting throughout her room I make my way across the living space to the second bedroom where I take in a practically identical room to that of the one Nina has made her own, except my room contains additional Parisian style pink and teal coloured furnishings in place of the chrome and black furnishings in Nina's room. My room is also dressed up with another miniature chandelier dangling majestically over the King sized, four poster bed, completed with cascading canopy. I see that I've landed the more romantic boudoir of the two and am in a totally blissful state while in it.

I throw myself on the bed and stare up into the jewels and sparkling of the chandelier but am immediately stirred out of what I hoped to be a bit of a cat nap when I hear the bellhop clear his throat at my doorway. I look up and see him rubbing two fingers together on one hand, clearly implying that he is awaiting tip and to be given leave.

Lord, I have to get better at this whole "tip everyone who assists" thing.

I rush to get my bag and scrounge up a couple notes for the short, stout and dare I say patient gentleman. I glance at his badge, which reads Louis and attempt in my best French accent, "Merci Louis!" He smiles graciously and goes on his way.

I turn from the doorway and hear a rustling behind the bar then a *pop* sound. At the same moment I see a cork come flying across the suite, ricocheting off the far wall. Nina pops up holding a bottle of, what appears to be, extremely expensive champagne and my immediate thought is, *and so it begins!*

She fills two champagne flutes to the brim and marches one directly to me as though we have to get completely down to some celebratory business.

"Thanks, girlfriend! Let's have a toast to achieving our dreams in the City of Light. Fun, Friendship, Love!"

"Hear, hear, my darling," Nina chimes my glass and then downs her glass of champagne as if it's a glass of water being consumed after an exhausting race. I sip away casually while unpacking my garments and toiletries into my stately en-suite, walk-in dressing room.

As I'm selecting my attire for the evening ahead I glance at the time and am alarmed that we have already arrived at half seven. We have half an hour to get primped and pretty before we have to make our way down to the lobby.

"Nina! It's *operation let's get pretty in thirty minutes* time!" I shout into the living space.

"I'm on it, doll! We're always beauties though, hot stuff!" she replies while bustling to her room to begin the additional beautification process.

After only twenty minutes I'm entirely impressed with the two of us. We are in the final stages of choosing accessories after dry shampooing our hair, having quick washes and styling each other's manes up into matching, neatly gathered buns. Our makeup is demur and natural and we look like true radiant beauties, ready to take Paris by storm. Nina is dressed in her midriff bearing blouse with form fitting black trousers. I'm garbed in a T-backed ruffled, mid-thigh length cherry patterned cocktail dress. It has just enough crinoline beneath it to make it flouncy and is so very Parisian.

We grab our most fabulous heels, our best take-on-the-town bags, the two key cards and head for the door. This is surely to be a night to remember, or not, depending on the quantity of alcohol involved.

The night is both of the above as all that I can remember is purely spectacular. We danced under the Eiffel Tower, drank champagne sitting on the Pont Alexandre III, ate fresh tomatoes, cheese and baguette until I thought I was going to explode, on the patio of a lovely bistro which sat adjacent to La Louvre, and then it all gets a bit fuzzy...

There may or may not have been a streaking incident performed by Pierre and Stefan, which turned out to be the names of our newly found companions for the evening. Stefan was the tall lanky youngster and Pierre was the scruffy and unkempt one. A police officer set out to chase them down only to be completely unsure how to go about detaining the said streakers in the least inappropriate manner without drawing the attention of all the passers-by.

It really was a very busy city at such a late hour. Families were still wandering amongst the lights and beauty of La Seine. The juxtaposition of all that was beautiful on that glorious evening against those pasty, nude Parisians hurdling through the scene was one that could only be imagined, which is perhaps the reason that I have such difficulty determining that it was a factual happening.

It most certainly was proven to be just that as I find myself beginning to sober up at roughly half past four in the morning, in my king sized bed, completely unable to fall asleep due to jet lag. I'm flipping through my camera's pictures and find the evidence of the entire night:

- Nina arm in arm with Stefan

- the four of us cuddled up on La Ponte Alexandre III

- making a toast under L'Arc de Triomphe

- Nina flashing her boobs (nothing new there)

- the said streakers' paler than pale behinds scurrying down the cobblestone

- *and… oh no, no! what the? I didn't!*

At the tail end of the roll of film, the final picture, of which I have absolutely no recollection, is one of myself and Pierre wrapped up in one another's embrace, lip to lip as if we are long lost loves who have gone years without being together and are attempting to consume one another's faces in order to make up for lost time. The sheer shock of this finding sends my mind on such a swivel that I begin contemplating whether I went any further with him.

I jump up and turn on the lights, check under the covers, under the bed, in the washroom, the living area, searching for any evidence of Pierre's presence in the suite. My mind is quickly set at ease when I've completed the search with inconclusive findings and determine that no findings means no drunken sex with a minor. I flop back into my heavenly bedding and finally fall fast asleep.

CHAPTER 12

Waking up a few hours later is somewhat painful and rattled with waves of nausea as well as a pounding head. I sometimes forget the love-hate relationship champagne and I have. This, however, is not going to stop me from taking in as much of this glorious city as I can. I creep into Nina's room, and find her alone and sprawled across her bed, still in a deep Nina style, comatose slumber.

I decide all I need is a large glass of water, two tablets and a strong espresso to get this day started right. I throw on a denim playsuit, pull my hair up into a tidy ponytail, throw on my biggest sunglasses, slip on sandals and a bit of lip gloss. To avoid Nina awaking to believe I have perhaps been abducted I scrawl a quick note *Coffee time, ask the bellhop where*, then I head down to the lobby. I'm on a hunt for espresso, and I know just the place!

As I enter Café Lateral on this majestic Parisian morning I can't help but notice its proximity to L'Arc de Triomph and I resonate on the irony of my current situation and what that monument represents. Sure, I've come a ways in the past few weeks in regards to taking ownership of my path in life and being fearless when it comes to attaining my goals, but triumph? I had not quite reached that level as of yet.

I'm determined, however to remember this moment, the moment I decided my own self-selected destiny would become a reality and that one day I will see that monument as being synonymous with my own situation. I turn my inspired gaze from the view of the landmark and make my way to the counter to order one of those infamous café au laits the hotel bellhop insisted Nina and I make it our duty to try on our first morning in Paris. Seeing as Nina had consumed enough champagne last night to drop a walrus on its back for a day or two, it looks as though I'd be following along with the recommendation on my own.

The shabby and tense looking gentleman behind the counter approaches me with a certain look that seems to imply "Oh another one! I wish you'd all just bugger off," yet I'm sure that's really not what he's thinking at all. Perhaps a beloved pet just passed away or he bought the wrong toilet paper upon use of which has left him with an awful chaffing situation on his backside. Chaffing of any kind is dreadful, and back there is downright torturous. You have to walk like a penguin to keep it from throwing a wrench in your day.

"Bonjour, madame, Que voulez-vous? Dites-moi vite!" the man demands abruptly.

Oh god, I have no idea what he's saying but he's already so irritated I can't just stand here silently. What is the drink again?

"Café…cafe…uno…café au lait por favor?" I say, hoping I have made some kind of sense. The man glares at me as though the sight of me sickens him, and huffs his way to the espresso machine muttering what I'm sure are French obscenities. I'm so worried I'll bring him to the point of rage I decide to have my money in hand and ready to go. He slides the bowl of coffee roughly across to me so that a quarter of its contents slosh over the side. I am not about to complain.

I quickly pay and find a seat nearest to the window, far away from the proprietor and his mutterings. I swear if I were to transform him into a cartoon character there would be scalding steam streaming from both ears.

After the tense ordering situation I find peace by the window, watching the mix of tourists and locals passing by. Children hand in hand with each of their parents, a beautiful woman breezing by on a yellow bicycle carrying groceries in an attached basket, obvious tourists with cameras around their necks snapping pictures of each other on the ancient cobblestone streets; it's all so wonderful. This is why I came, for this peace and the inspiration that can be found in these streets, these cafes, the hidden corridors and landmarks. They all have a story, and I'm here to learn to truly begin to live mine.

As I'm contemplating what the remainder of the week will bring, the entry bell on the doorway jingles and I catch a sight of the most delectable man I have ever encountered in person. He strides past me in a confident and deliberate manner towards the wretched human being behind the counter. To my amazement the ill-tempered attendant greets him with an enormous smile and begins making his order promptly while carrying on what sounds like a jovial and pleasant conversation, although the French being spoken is completely lost on me.

I scan the scene and determine that this gorgeous new arrival is actually quite the regular at Café Lateral and must be one hell of a charmer to transform the mood of that unwelcoming and miserable little man into this exuberant individual I now see before me.

As they continue in their interaction, I cannot help but take in the pure magnificence of the man before me. Clothed in a navy Polo cable knit sweater which fits just right to show off his well-formed chest and strong arms, jeans which sit perfectly, not too loose and not too tight. They adhere so nicely to his backside that I'm fully aware it is remarkably toned and delightful to look at.

Unfortunately, my scanning of his backside has turned into inappropriate ogling and when I eventually divert my eyes back up to his face I see that he has finished his interactions with the café barista and is now giving me a concerned look. A sudden wave of embarrassment begins to take me over but immediately dissipates! Good god this man must be something special because I don't even care that he has caught me glaring at his ass as if it's my prey and I'm the hunter. He is unbelievably handsome and I will glare if I want to.

He saunters over to the side counter where he begins to add what look like vanilla shavings to his cappuccino and I take in everything from the neck up. Smooth caramel coloured skin, a chiseled jaw that even Michelangelo would have had trouble mastering on his portraits, the perfect amount of scruffy yet sexy stubble framing his undeniably delicious lips, and those perfect eyes that are so clear and vibrant, it's as if I'm gazing into the waters of the Caribbean. I breathe it in, all of it and as he glances at me once more with the awareness that I've been checking him out this entire time, he smiles to display a perfect set of teeth and two perfectly positioned dimples, still evident within the scruff. I exhale perhaps a touch too loudly because he lets out a chuckle and makes his way toward me.

"Bonjour, mademoiselle. Je vois le matin vous trouve bien?"

I shrug, uncertain of what he's said other than "Hello Miss" and set my chin in my hands while shaking my head to communicate, "I don't understand a word."

"You, you look well this morning, Mademoiselle," he immediately says in perfectly spoken English with only a hint of a Parisian accent, yet just enough of one that I linger on his words and find myself getting warm. He speaks with such confidence and in such smooth, melodic tones that I feel like the vibrations of his voice are gently caressing my whole body to the core of my soul.

"I can sit? Mademoiselle, can I sit?" he corrects himself and gestures towards the empty chair across from me.

I blush and can't even believe my good fortune. In this moment, while enjoying an espresso coffee in the most romantic setting imaginable, aside from the hostile barista, the most delicious and seemingly charming man is requesting to not only chat but to also share a table with me...ME!

"Please do. I was hoping you would ask me," I say and am amazed at my boldness in uttering this line.

He smiles graciously and sits promptly. For what seems like a full minute or two, we simply sit in silence. He studies my face with such intent focus that I can feel my eyes wandering and darting in various directions to avoid making continuous eye contact as I'm quite certain I would begin full out drooling at the sight of those incredible grayish blue eyes.

At the moment he is gazing at my hands and sees them trembling slightly, he reaches out to calm me, gently placing his strong hands over mine and I am immediately reminded of my objective given to me by Dr. Lola.

Eye contact, Portia, make extended eye contact until it is comfortable.

I lift my gaze from his strong warm hands wrapped comfortingly around my own to his broad and well-defined chest and then finally to his limpid pool-like eyes that are now fixed directly on my own. I'm for a moment uncomfortable, feeling as though I'm back in Dr. Lola's office in an eye-lock resembling more of a staring contest as opposed to one of pure admiration and wonderment. The longer I stare, the more I become transfixed and comfortably lost in the moment, unaware of all that surrounds me, in time and space; unaware of the comings and goings in this little café; simply captivated and held prisoner willingly by this feeling and this perfect being who has somehow wandered into my Parisian morning espresso time. His eyes emanate warmth and comfort that I have never before felt at this capacity.

After what feels like a beautiful eternity he finally says, "Mademoiselle, you are beautiful. You are from America?"

"Thank you, you also are quite beautiful, I mean... handsome," I say, a bit nervously. *He really is beautiful though.* "I am from North America, but from the country of Canada. I live in Toronto."

"Ah yes. My apologies. Your accent is not always decipherable between you and the Americans. I am Guillaume and am delighted to be acquainted with you."

"The feeling is quite mutual, Guillaume," I reply with an increasing confidence. "I'm Portia and it is so wonderful to be able to meet true Parisians while visiting, especially those as friendly as yourself."

"Portia, you are here for the business or the pleasure, here in Paris?" he asks with a sly grin after saying the word *pleasure* and I find my nerves rising again and the colour in my cheeks turning slightly.

"To be honest, it's for a mix of reasons. It's been my dream to spend time in this incredible city and to simply become lost in its beauty. I'm also, in a way, here for business as well because I must regain my motivation and inspiration for sketching and creating garments. I hope to become a designer."

"Remarkable, as are you, Portia. I'm no foreigner to the streets of this city and hope to be involved in both your business and your pleasure while you remain here. I am a model for the magazines and the runway. You will design for me one day, yes?"

As he speaks these words I almost fall clear out of my chair, yet regain composure promptly when I understand the importance and fate involved in crossing paths with this perfect stranger.

Don't mess this up, Portia!

Just as I find myself beginning to feel unwaveringly comfortable gazing into Guillaume's baby blues I glance nonchalantly out the window only to see Nina the tornado blow by the window while holding on to her sizable floppy, yet quite chic hat with one hand and her Coach purse in the other. Sporting a lovely polka dotted sundress she strides clear by. I notice Guillaume's gold Rolex is displaying the time to be half past eleven and am quite impressed with Nina's ability to welcome the day at such an early hour. I casually watch her strut along as though she is on a definite mission.

She passes the café entirely but halts about three doors down to consult with some passers-by. After a brief exchange and gesturing Nina turns on her heel and heads back towards Guillaume and I. I'm suddenly aware that this magical moment is about to come abruptly to an end so breathe Guillaume in peacefully one last time as Nina approaches like an elegant trudging bull.

The door opens, bell chimes and Nina rushes in wide-eyed, looking as though she is filled to the brim with information and needs to share it before she implodes.

"Nina! Over here!" I wave her down after she has rushed passed my handsome companion and me.

"Oh, Port! Thank god I found…." She gazes at Guillaume and looks completely gobsmacked. "Well, hello there. Aren't you a sight for sore and hungover eyes." She approaches Guillaume with hand outstretched. "Nina…and you are?"

Guillaume takes Nina's hand and brings it to his lips. "Mademoiselle, I am Guillaume. It is a pleasure to meet your acquaintance especially since you are a friend of Portia."

I have to say that the lips to Nina's hand initially causes a pang of jealousy to rush through me but his words that follow set me at ease and put me back into an all-consuming trance.

"Well, well, well, Ms. Delaney, you have most definitely been busy this morning. You two are just adorable sitting here drinking your specialty coffee. I'd leave you both to it but Port, I have become aware of such insane news from back home that I just had to hunt you down to tell you!" Nina says in a concerned tone, yet she can't be too overly concerned because she's fighting a smirk that keeps threatening to fully reveal itself.

"Neen, what is it? I knew this was far too early an hour for you to have gotten yourself together by. This must be big! Tell me already," I plead. Guillaume clearly becomes aware that the news he is about to overhear may perhaps be somewhat of a private nature so, being the gentleman that he is, excuses himself from the table only to strike up a conversation with the irritable barista. He does, however, caress my hand as he goes and I feel a rush of excitement surge through my body. I watch him stride away and I guess may be peering a little too long and hard because I suddenly feel a tug on my pony tail and am shocked into redirecting my focus from that beautiful behind back to Nina.

"Good god, woman! Concentrate! I know he is scrumptious, but you really want to hear this."

"Sorry, sweets. Go on. What is it?"

"Portia Delaney, it has happened! The very *it* that you knew would happen. You called it, babe. You really did."

"What? What did I call? Come on, Nina, you can't do this to me! You can't rush in here and separate me from that amazingly delicious man saying that you have news I MUST hear and then give me nothing, tell me tell me tell me!" I say as if I'm Oliver Twist begging for more porridge, except far less worried about getting the strap for it, although Nina is quite unpredictable.

"Port, it's Angelica...she...she's finished! Her company is in shambles. She's been found out. I got an email from Victoria Lewis. We've agreed to keep sessions happening over the course of the week via Skype as she needs them and in her response to what time she prefers to arrange a session she casually mentioned that she needs reassurance about her most recent actions where she took it upon herself to end the existence of a purse line because she gained a first-hand confession from the designer herself, that she was a fraud and hired actual designers to create the designs but was incredibly stingy with pay and took all of the praise herself without even acknowledging that there is behind the scenes help."

"Nina rambles on, spewing this information as if her lips are in some incredible race to achieve a record for most words formed in a minute.

"Angelica had no idea that Victoria Lewis was the woman she confided all this information to the night we all met at Kinko's and she not only disclosed this info, but actually laughed about how completely talentless she actually is in the design and fashion world, yet how incredibly successful she has become due to being the money hungry cold-hearted business woman her father raised her to be. She even likened her designers to a group of feather brained individuals who have impeccable abilities, but who are never lead to believe this as she believes too much confidence would inspire each to step out and become successes on their own. Victoria has spent a number of weeks investigating this matter.

"She even went so far as to visit the headquarters for the *Angelica* line. Angelica did not even recognize her when she walked in so demanded a full introduction. Once Victoria did just this, Angelica had the nerve to request a two page spread of *her* fall collection in the next issue of *Crave*. This made

Victoria's blood curdle and after a number of secretly carried-out meetings between herself and fed up employees, Victoria had enough of a reason to take her findings to the tabloids. She's been outted on the largest scale, Port!"

"Holy hell!" I reply after listening to this full account with my jaw hanging fully open in silence and shock. "If Angelica divulged this information the night at Kinko's but had no idea that the person she was speaking to *was* Victoria, why did she leave so abruptly? She must have become aware or else why the sudden change in mood?"

"Here's the kicker," Nina says as I'm literally on the edge of my seat awaiting what it is she has to say next. "When Victoria finally laid into Angelica about her fraudulent designs and horrendous treatment of her employees, Angelica broke down and rambled on and on about how it didn't even matter at this point that Victoria was ready to do her in because her ex-boyfriend Daniel had already sunk the company financially completely independently of Victoria's design fraud accusations."

I make a gasp sound that is so loud and obnoxious while taking in such a large quantity of air in the process that I feel a little light-headed and woozy. When I regain composure I see Guillaume, the barista and a new couple who have entered the café staring at me confusedly. I suppose the sound was quite atrocious and not in the least lady- like. Guillaume has his hand now under his chin as he's resting the attached remarkably strong looking arm against his chest. He's giving me a quizzical look as if he's attempting to figure me out. I give a little wink and half- smile and he returns the exchange by once again exposing those perfect teeth and letting those dimples make another appearance.

I can't believe the confidence I have right now! It's got to be this city! It must be the magic of this place,

I glance back at Nina promptly, not because I want to break the exchange with Guillaume but because Nina has sat herself on my lap and has blocked my view fully to steal my attention back from that dreamy being.

"Portia! For god's sake, snap out of it for just a second. I'll let you two get back at it in a moment. Just hear me out!" She snaps her fingers in my face as she says these words with a slight desperation in her voice.

"Sorry, Neen. Go on. So Daniel sunk the company financially first? I knew he'd only bring trouble in the end. How did he get access to any of the finances? That's absurd that he was even trusted with such an integral part of the business no matter to what extent he had access!" I say completely dumb-founded by all of this information I'm being given. I don't even know my true feeling about the matter. I mean, on one hand it's awful to know a "friend" has been so negatively affected, but on the other, a part of me feels that Angelica is getting just what she deserves. I'm somewhat torn by it all but must admit that the joyful feeling I'm experiencing as a result of Angelica finally being unmasked is in truth winning over the concerned and sympathetic side.

Am I a horrible person?

Nina quickly makes me feel loads better with her response to follow. "Hell, Port, I don't know why that silly daddy's girl gave him access to such an impor-tant facet of the company, but come on, we saw this coming and I couldn't be happier that she's undone."

I nod overly emphatically to communicate that we are on the same page in this regard and then I buck her off of my lap with one swift knee jerk that sends her stumbling towards the neighbouring couple who block their coffees for fear that she may land directly on their table. She luckily stops short of this outcome transpiring. She gives a little yelp, while smoothing down her hair calmly and returns to the seat on the other side of the table while glaring at me deliberately. The glare quickly turns into a brightened fully delighted gaze when she sees that Guillaume is making his way towards us.

"Mon *chérie*, I must go to the workplace now that I have appointments at this day. You will remember me and we will make the time to see this perfect paradise together, no?" He says while running his hands down my shoulder. I stand to drink in the entirety of his words and to allow for a better chance to receive a mite of physical contact before having to let him out of my sight.

"Guillaume, it would be a dream come true to see this marvellous city with you," I reply, and as I do he pulls me close and fully caresses my body with his own. He wraps his strong arm around me so tenderly yet with just enough strength that I feel completely weak in the knees. He leaves me with a slow and lingering caress of his lips on my cheek then whispers, "I will meet you in the front of your hotel. It must be L'Hotel Triomph, correct?"

I nod while still in his embrace.

"Tonight, beautiful Portia. Nine o'clock. I will be there," he utters and then turns to stride out the door. As he walks away both Nina and I sigh heavily and I let my knees fully give way, falling roughly onto the slightly distressed wooden café chair beneath me.

"I am so unbelievably envious of you right now and was just so entirely turned on by that interaction I just witnessed that I can't even be mad at you! You little minx!" Nina finally breaks the speechless spell Guillaume has just left us both under.

"Nina, I am so completely taken by him, you have no idea. He's so perfect! He really is. And he's going to show ME, Portia Delaney, around my dream city! I'm dreaming. I must be freakin' dreaming and I'm going to wake up completely alone, back in my solitary queen- sized bed in Toronto, under my overly feminine floral duvet because men have been so void in my life that there is no need to have gender neutral décor. Pinch me….please!"

Nina takes the request entirely too literally because a nanosecond later I feel a shooting pain through my left arm that makes me squeal and then laugh harder than I have in a while.

"Not a dream, babe! Not a dream at all" Nina declares between her own full bellied laughter.

We take our time sipping our coffee while I spread a tour map of the city out on the table for the two of us to decide on the sites and shops we most want to see that day. I quickly decide that this day should be all about site seeing and shopping and that my own design studio drop-ins should be left to later in the week. After all, Guillaume must have a few suggestions on this matter so why seek out these landmarks independently, when I could quite possibly be given first class treatment with a handsome fashion insider on my arm?

We complete our selection of must-sees and then the sweet interrogation begins about that rugged newcomer who has wandered fatefully into my life.

"Portia Delaney, I have sat here for a little over an hour while trying to remain respectful of your privacy and await details to come my way about that gorgeous hunk of man! Do you realize that this is completely out of character for me to have waited so long to get info out of you?"

"You've been extremely controlled, Neen! I'm so proud of you for not questioning me about him while he was still sitting across from me. That would've been your usual route. Sweetheart, I'll fill you in later, but come on! We've got Paris awaiting us!"

"You sly tigress! You better fill me in! You're such a tease," she kids. "Come on then, I suppose I'll have to put my patient panties on."

CHAPTER 13

Like starry-eyed children Nina and I begin to take in the city in a completely sober and awestricken state of wonderment and appreciation.

We set off down Champs-Elysees and find our journey resulting in a visit back to the very spot we witnessed the minors bearing it all mere hours before. This time the scene had far greater meaning and inspiration in it. La Seine, a winding body of flowing water making its way through the bustling city, although simply a river, became much more than that to me in the moment. If that river could talk, it would divulge stories as old as the earth upon which it flowed; tales of love, and achievement and those of war and bloodshed. The streets were rich in this history and La Seine had, and will continue to have, a front row seat for it all.

We continue to transfix ourselves in the gurgling movement of the water for a moment then I nudge Nina to join me on the continued journey back to the pinnacle of the Parisian skyline.

We reach the Eiffel Tower in minutes and immediately begin snapping pictures in front of it as though it were a long lost relative we were dying to get a picture with. A gentleman passing by understands that we are in need of a photographer to capture the two of us in a shot together and kindly offers to do just that. Nina pulls me close and we expose the most effortless and lively smiles.

The sun is shining, and there is a gentle breeze enticing us onward toward the tower's base. As we follow the guidance of Mother Nature herself we arrive at the base to find numerous buskers and performers who are complemented by lovely melodies of an elderly, beret capped accordion player off to the left of the scene.

Nina and I are completely entertained and focused on the acrobats who are balancing in such a way that I am fully fearing for the spandex sporting male acrobat on the base of the balancing duo as his manhood is seemingly the main point on which his female counterpart is placing all of her weight. She has one leg straight up over her head and her supporting foot is firmly planted on his private landmark.

"Damn!" Nina has clearly read my mind, "His junk must be getting absolutely mutilated!"

"Maybe he has a jock strap on," I say in hopes that I am correct.

"I know a jock strapped man when I see one, Port, and he is not wearing one. He must have balls of steel! I think I'll get a picture with him after the show and see if I can get the information out of him."

"You're completely going to get a hold of his package, aren't you?" I tease.

"It's all in the works, babe, all in the works," Nina says, staring steadfastly at his central region.

I break away from the performance drawn to the sonata that the elderly accordion player is now piping out of his instrument. My feet feel so light and I'm so inspired after the wonderful morning I've experienced that I begin to twirl with the rhythm. I twirl and twirl and then...

"Tu es cooookooo." I hear spoken in a gruff and gravelly voice. I complete a final twirl and realize the music has stopped due to the accordion player's eyes being transfixed on my twirling.

"Cooooookoooo, jeune fille. Seulement cooookooo," he repeats as he begins to inch his way slowly towards me. The frail man reaches to light the cigarette, protruding from his thin lips.

"I'm sorry to have disturbed your music, sir. Please keep playing. It was lovely."

"Oui, oui. I will begin again in moments, dear girl. Your weeeeeeee," he says as he attempts to imitate me spinning, "is lovely additionally." He then laughs a husky laugh followed by a deep smoker- style cough.

I smile, entertained by his sense of humour and am immediately drawn to converse with him. If La Seine could not tell me the stories I would love to hear, this man can certainly tell a few tales about these streets and days gone by, I'm sure of it. I sit on a rock wall and beckon him over to join me. I glance around quickly to see that Nina is preoccupied with an interrogatory conversation between herself and the man of steel manhood. So I conclude that I have a moment to pry into the elderly man's past.

"Monsieur, you play so beautifully. Tell me all about life in Paris?" I inquire graciously.

"Mademoiselle, Paris is the centre of the universe to me. I lived in this place my whole life. I have never left its streets except to bury mon...my father, as you say, forty years ago in Nice, the town of his birth. I have not only lived in these streets my whole life, but have loved in these streets and warred in these streets. I have experienced the low lows and the high highs but have never turned my back on this place. I will die in these streets beneath that tower of magic and dreams, playing my accordion until the end."

"Have you never wanted to venture away? Perhaps another country? Another continent even?"

"For what reason, dear girl? Every possible need I have is more than fully met within this place. The people flock and fly from thousands of miles away to be here, exactly where I am. Under this beautiful sight, in these ancient streets. To leave is to turn my back on my one true love. I, my dear, am ever committed to my loves as I am committed to serenading the people of these streets. This city has remained faithful throughout the years, caring for me. I have shared love with many, the city of Paris is the only that has never left me."

He says these words with such passion in his husky voice that I'm moved to press further.

"Have you loved women or men from other countries?"

"Oh yes! I have loved many women and more than half have been visiting from other nations. Turkish, Japanese, Australian, British, Ecuadorian. My darling, I can go on and on. Love is a fluid emotion and my love spans this globe."

Although I'm intrigued, his words also slightly revolt me. This frail little man is talking about these women as if they are international conquests, but I suppose he sees this more as reaching out to all corners of the world he has not set out to see. "Have any of those women been North American?" I can't help but ask.

"But of course, mademoiselle! My last visitor whom I kept warm throughout the nights, while she was here discovering this city, was an American; a beautiful New Yorker. She had the fashion, the physique, the sweet voice filled with longing for adventure and escape from her horrid matrimony. Victoria, ah yes! She was a sight for these sore and tired eyes. Her tender touch softened my exhausted and calloused hands. She will always be remembered as my American jewel. I long to caress her ivory face again. Her work is too much to her. She lives for her work. She would not remain for one hour longer than her work had allowed for. Alas she kissed me goodbye and flew back over that sea."

He hangs his head slightly and I sense heartbreak is the term to explain reasons for his defeated body language. That aside, my mind is focused on the fact that the coincidence between the woman's name, her fashion sense, her workaholic tendencies and the city of her origin are so strong and all too perfectly point to the very Victoria Lewis, herself.

I continue to pry more on the subject. "You poor man. I can see you miss her. She sounds beautiful. Was she quite young?"

"She was a seasoned young woman. Her hair was a golden honey colour; her lips so full and inviting. My love for her reaches across the sea. I only hope it is felt by Victoria and that she one day shall return."

Okay so maybe I'm getting ahead of myself with the whole "this must be Victoria Lewis he's talking of" theory, but the actual Victoria Lewis does have honey blonde unnaturally coloured hair. My current tendency to romanticize every aspect of this place is now transferring across the Atlantic and involving the very woman I soon hope to convert from a disinterested acquaintance to an employer and friend. There are, though, millions of Victorias in North America. What are the chances that the said Victoria is the one and only Victoria Lewis of *Crave Magazine*? Slim, but I remain hopeful and continue my gentle interrogation of the matter.

Being unsure what "seasoned young woman" implies in terms of *actual age* I continue with the questioning. "Do you know her last name, sir? Or perhaps you have a picture taken between you both?"

"Victoria is ashamed about the last name she has taken. It's attached to her by her husband, whom she is no longer in love with. She would not say." He sighs and continues, "I do, I do have a photograph. I keep it with me since the day we had it taken on our walk through these streets. It is locked away in my accordion case, my dear. I will reveal it the day you return to visit me here; this way you have a reason to come back to chat with a lonely old accordionist."

"Sir, I would visit you regardless of this enticing offer. I am here for four more days and will visit you at least two more times! You're a great addition to this place. You've improved my day with your accounts of this city and your deep devotion to it. I will be back," I say, as his wrinkled rough hand takes mine and lifts it to those thin and worn lips.

"'Til we meet again, *mademoiselle*. I will unveil my love. You have my word."

"Au revoir! Adios! Arrivederci!" I say while waving as I saunter back over to where Nina is flirtatiously questioning the acrobat while eyeing his centre region. The man is quite a piece of art in that body-clinging leotard. I can make out every indentation and rippling muscle. The man's female counterpart is eyeing Nina with quite the aggressive expression on her face to match and she has me worried that a totally ignorant Nina will soon be her dinner.

I take matters into my own hands, or at least Nina, and lead her over towards the carousel ride pretending that I have a fascination with old merry-go-rounds and want more than anything to get a photo of myself on this particular piece of Parisian history.

The remainder of the afternoon takes the two of us touring beauties to La Louvre where we stand speechless in front of the being of restraint herself; the infamous Mona Lisa whose stoic and ambiguous expression seems to be the very portrait of enigmatic mystery. There's something about the eyes and the subtle smirk that tells me she was a lovely, misunderstood, vivacious woman. We carry on out of her private viewing area, and I see her gaze following me from behind her glass encasement, speaking to my soul almost urging me on as I go.

Finally, during our early evening dining at a lovely, bustling café quite near to the hotel, I impart my possible findings in regards to Victoria Lewis' love affair with the elderly accordion player.

"Nina! I swear it's her! I have to go back to him in the next day or two and find out for sure because it is absolutely torturing me to feel so assured yet so unbelievably unsure all the same!"

"Port, there are about a zillion Americans with the name Victoria. And I'm positive at least half of those have blonde hair and about half of *that* half are seasoned young women! Whatever the hell that means. So, I suppose it *is* a possibility, but come on, Port, do you actually think Victoria Lewis, Editor in Chief at *Crave* would get mixed up in a love affair with an elderly accordion player? Sure, she probably has lovers, but lovers who are corporate like her and get her motor revving. Not a poor sap like the man I saw you speaking with."

"I don't know, Neen. He was quite the gentleman and extremely smooth. This city has a way of making a person forget themselves! I feel it already. I'm a different Portia here. Victoria was probably affected by this place in the same way. It's a city where you escape from your everyday choices and ways. I believe it really *could* be Victoria Lewis that will be the subject in that picture tomorrow."

Nina stirs her butternut squash soup and remains silent for a moment. I can tell she is struggling to be impartial in the matter. Finally she takes a slurp, places her spoon back in the bowl,

"Why does it matter so much to you, Port? I mean, no offense, but it's not like the two of you are close. Well, not yet anyway." She saves my wounded spirit. "So what would you tell her? That you met a friendly old accordion player and spring it on her that you found out she had a passionate affair with him? That could be an awkward convo, and I actually think it would absolutely hurt your chances of moving to her good side. Do you feel that it may give you some sort of personal link to her in a way?" Nina questions.

"I guess, maybe, hell I don't know! If not that, maybe I'd use the findings as leverage or a bribe for a job at *Crave*?" I cringe as I say these words, but am just being honest with my closest friend to whom I feel I can relay any passing thoughts. I am, however, clearly aware that I am out of line with this *particular* thought and see that Nina feels the same as she quickly grasps at her heart and gasps.

"Portia Delaney! That's a horrible, horrible thing to say or even consider. You do know that I am a confidant of Victoria's and look out for her well-being as her life coach? Port, you're my best friend, and never have I ever heard you speak of doing something so cunning and abusive. Shit, Portia, you almost sound like Angelica, spewing ideas out like that."

I immediately regretted the words as they exited my mouth and even the thought of doing such a thing to a client of Nina's who has placed trust in her fully. I suppose it's the pure desperation to work at *Crave* and under Victoria Lewis' direction that is causing my mind to seek out any and all routes to make this dream outcome a reality.

I gather my thoughts and attempt to put my current undeniably apologetic feelings on the figurative table. "I, I know, I just want to work for her so desperately. That was an absolutely disgusting thought and I really don't know where it came from. I know it has to be hard work that gets me into *Crave*, not swindling and scheming. The thought is past, Neen, not even an option. I'm so sorry and do know the confidence Victoria has in you. I'd never get in the way of that continuing. I'd never be the one responsible for taking all that you've worked for away from you."

"Port, there's nothing wrong with making connections to get ahead, and hustling to get what you deserve, but not at the expense of good people who have worked hard to get where *they* are."

She sighs, grabs my hands and finally begins to speak with less of a scolding teacher's voice and more with a compassionate and concerned friend's voice. I finally relax knowing that she's not completely taken me off her *top friends* list altogether.

"I know how badly you want this and you'll get there by being the hardworking, creative and talented person you are. Stop with the stories and the thoughts of scheming to get the prestige. Look where all that crap got Angelica. You're my closest friend and that is not the way I see things happening for you. Trust me, trust your abilities, work hard, you'll get there, love."

"You're so right, Neen. Nina, you've truly found your calling. You're going to be an incredible success in the life coaching business, mark my words."

She smiles and there's an unspoken communication of forgiveness that passes between us. I turn my attention to the waiter passing by and gesture for her to bring our bill as I have glanced at the time and notice that it is now approaching seven o'clock p.m.

I must get back to the hotel in order to be ready for Guillaume. My heart quickly is awakened after my recent disappointment with myself had caused it to completely plummet. I have a thrilling feeling take over my entire body and soul, and just know that this night is going to be one that only dreams are made of.

CHAPTER 14
· ·

I feel my bag slipping slightly from my grasp and am entirely too aware that my nerves are taking hold, causing my palms to become clammy and hands to begin yet again to tremble.

The lobby is bustling with people and the overnight bag is feeling heavier by the second as if it insists on being some laden reminder that I'm about to take off on a getaway while already on a getaway, with a complete, yet beyond sexy, stranger. Why it's a laden reminder, I can't help but be annoyed by. My fearful and negative, self-scrutinizing side is attempting to take over my excitement in the moment, that's why! And I'm fighting it with all I have.

After returning back from the day of sightseeing I was welcomed by a note left by Guillaume, which read:

> *Chérie,*
>
> *I look very much forward to seeing your beautiful face this night. Do pack some belongings. My tour will take us outside the city of Paris tonight, yet we will see more of its offerings tomorrow. I will meet you at 9 o'clock in the lobby.*
>
> *Entirely yours,*
>
> *Guillaume Boisvert*

So here I am with my belongings for a "stay away" and thoughts swirling through my mind such as *Portia this is crazy! You just met him this morning. He's a complete stranger and this is completely uncharacteristic for you. But he is so dreamy and you're already living a complete dream so why not go full out?* What woman doesn't fantasize about this very circumstance? An incredibly gorgeous male model, sweeping her away on a getaway to some adorable cottage, nestled into the French countryside, I mean it's straight off the big screen! What the ending scenario may be, I can't say; I'm hoping that it doesn't ring similar to *Texas Chainsaw Massacre* and steers more along the lines of *Notting Hill.*

Earlier that evening, once the note was handed me by the bellhop and I almost passed out from sheer disbelief of what was being promised to transpire, Nina ripped the note out of my hand and was so excited for me that she danced around me like a hula girl and then consumed an entire bottle of champagne herself back up in our hotel room while believing that she was sharing the bottle with me. I, however, nursed the one glass poured while stressing over outfits to bring and attire to select for tonight.

Once I was fully ready to be swept away in my most chic black ruffled cocktail dress, sling backed pink Gucci pumps, hair twisted half up with lovely curled tendrils falling delicately over my bare shoulders, and my afore mentioned "'getaway tote'" I attempted to find Nina to get a send-off hug, but she was M.I.A. My search took me all over the suite until I noticed the patio door slightly ajar. I stepped out onto the balcony to find Nina passed out on the floral patio chaise lounge. Rooting around for a spare blanket, I located a heavy fleece throw, covered her up, and kissed her forehead.

"Nina, you'll always be my star." I sat for a moment at the end of the lounge stroking her hair while taking in the Parisian night skyline as if taking a photograph with my mind.

I will never forget this moment; I will never forget this place.

Here in the lobby, my nerves are calming slightly after deciding to grab a red wine at the hotel bar. I'm sipping it casually, glancing as if one eye is spastically glued to the grandfather clock above the concierge desk and another eagerly glaring at the entryway in anticipation of Guillaume making his star appearance. He is like a celebrity after all.

After what seems like an eternity, but in actuality only works out to be the length of time it takes to consume a glass and a half of Shiraz, he appears in clear view. He stands outfitted in what appears to be a designer charcoal hued suit, looking so perfectly kempt with just enough stubble to cause me to begin imagining the feeling of its roughness all over my body. A fire rises within me and before he spots me I take one last large gulp of the full bodied Shiraz, rise to my feet as the fire remains stoked within and make my way over to him.

"Guillaume, I'm so happy to finally see you again! It feels like this morning was a lifetime ago!" I say confidently.

He spins around, gazes at me from head to toe, pulls me in and sweetly caresses my ears with his words. "Chérie, you look goddess-like. I am overtaken by your appearance. You are to me divine." He kisses my cheek adoringly and takes me by the hand while grabbing my tote with the other. He then leads me out of the hotel. We hop into a waiting car and he directs the driver saying "Auxerre, monsieur, merci."

Auxerre? I've never heard of it, but it sounds lovely. Anything that comes from the mouth of this gorgeous man sounds lovely and sexy as all hell.

"Portia, are you prepared for an adventure with a true Parisian?" he asks with a cheeky look in his eye and mischievous grin.

"That is one of the main reasons I came to Paris, Guillaume. My answer is of course 'yes'!" I nuzzle up to him and stroke my head against his collar. His arm finds its way around me and I feel so perfectly at ease that I find myself lulling off to sleep for what only feels like a moment.

I suppose the Shiraz has gotten the better of me because when I am stirred awake by what I can only think to be the car swerving around country roads, I view the time on the car's dash to be ten fifteen p.m. and Guillaume smiles down at me longingly. My stomach fills with butterflies at his handsome face and I immediately feel a magnetism drawing us together. His warm full lips finally find mine and we exchange the sweetest and most tender kiss I have ever experienced. His lips linger on mine for just the perfect amount of insatiable time, and then find their way down my neck and back up to my cheek. He sweeps my hair back from my forehead, kisses it and then pulls me close into what feels like a safe cove to be held until we arrive at our destination.

"Chérie, you will adore this place. It is the place of my most enjoyed restaurants and wineries. We will enjoy a delicious late meal on the terrace of *Vieux Port* and reminisce about your day then we will find comfort at a private cottage I have recently purchased for my holidays from the business of Paris."

He strokes my head and once again finds his way to my cheek with his warm lips. I feel as though I'm melting into the warmth of his embrace and right as I have gathered the words to respond to his description of the events that lay ahead, the driver halts the car and swivels around to announce, "Madame, Monsieur, we have arrived at the destination."

"Oh merci, Jacques! We will require your services in two hours," Guillaume replies.

I take in the scene around us as Guillaume helps me out of the car. We have stepped into what appears to be a medieval village, patterned with the most ancient looking cobblestone and quaint little homes, shops and restaurants. Guillaume takes my hand and leads me along towards a stone- covered archway and we pass under it side by side, through a well-kept lavish garden that has been lit up for the evening patrons of the restaurant ahead. The maître d' rushes towards Guillaume with open arms as he catches a glimpse of us approaching.

"Monsieur Boisvert! Mon soir est marveilleuse avec toi ici."

He speaks with such a passion in Guillaume's presence that even though I do not understand most of what he is saying. Guillaume is seemingly extremely well-liked in this place. I feel a little squeeze on my palm and look up at him to meet his warm smile. He leads me along as we follow the maître d' to a private terrace that awaits us at the side of the old stone building. It is lit with twinkling, sporadically placed lights and overlooks a babbling stream, winding its way under a lovely arched pedestrian bridge.

The maître d' helps me with my chair and leaves us with a menu after presenting the delectable sounding specials for the evening. I must admit that although all items listed sound scrumptious, nothing on that menu seems even remotely as delectable as Guillaume looks.

I don't know how I'm going to make it through this dinner! Drink, flirt and enjoy, I suppose.

And that is exactly what I do. We share deep lingering exchanges of the eyes and I find Guillaume reaching for me to engage in slight, soft reassuring grazes over different parts of my exposed arms and legs. We share the adventures experienced throughout the hours we were apart earlier that day. Guillaume recounts how intense his couture and editorial photo shoot was and I find myself hanging on his every word, completely astounded by all that really is involved when it comes to modelling. I mean, three hundred and fifty different poses, seven wardrobe changes, working with countless ill-mannered photographers and clients…it really doesn't sound like the easiest of gigs. He talks with such passion and excitement about his work that it is clear to me that he absolutely loves every minute of the cutthroat modelling world.

After I give a summary of my journey with Nina and laugh about the possibility of becoming a trained acrobat when I return to Toronto, we then continue to disclose what seems like every detail of our lives in that two hour time frame. I tell him of my career woes and difficulties, my insecurities, about my needs to always impress my parents so that I tread too cautiously in almost every facet of life. I express my desire to plunge in fully instead of tiptoeing and that at this very moment I feel I'm acting as impulsively as I have ever done before.

"Guillaume, in these short few hours, you have been such an incredible inspiration for me to take that plunge. I must thank you."

He then tells me of his tragic childhood, about bouncing around from foster home to foster home, never having known his real parents or any kind of loving home life. My heart breaks for him as he reveals accounts of physical abuse and a longing to belong. He divulges that he never felt a part of anything until Marie Solsun, a renowned French agent of the industry, discovered him. She took him in as if her own when he was 15 and became a motherly figure to him from then on. "She saved me, Portia. Individuals, they say that the entertainment business is all bad, but truly, this business and Marie have saved me and renewed my trust in people."

I feel so unquestionably drawn and close to him at this point that it is I who place my hands on his and gently begin to stroke them. I feel a connection forming and my attraction to him is so far beyond the physical that I am lost in this moment, sitting here talking and learning his past and his hopes and his dreams; expressing my own with the knowledge that a caring and supportive man is being attentive to them and to me.

We carry on sipping our Chablis from this very region, its flavour enhancing the sweetness of the moment with every sip. I'm beginning to feel more and more uninhibited and Guillaume demonstrates that the same change is occurring in him as he slides his chair around more closely to mine and strokes my face with his gentle yet manly hands. I take another sip of wine and he removes the glass from my hand then leans in to kiss my lips once more, this time the passion has escalated to an insurmountable point as I now feel drawn to everything about him. The passion is building between us both and it is clear that our dinner is nearing its end not only due to all food and wine finally being consumed, but also due to our desire to consume one another.

We walk out of the restaurant and stroll towards the waiting car hand in hand. After a short ride quite literally down the street and up a narrow paved road leading into a picture perfect landscape of rolling hills, we arrive at an adorable stone cottage, nestled sweetly up on a perch and overlooking the calmly lit town below. I lean over to grab my door handle, but before I can even reach it, my door swings open. Guillaume reaches for my hand, helps me out and then lifts me clear off the ground. He transports me up to the cottage and into the awaiting front room where a fire is alight. The driver has carried our belongings in behind us and swiftly places the luggage then communicates a polite "au revoir, madame, monsieur" and is on his way, closing the door behind him.

While the driver, Jacques, has been arranging luggage and wishing us well, Guillaume's gaze has not left me, nor have his hands. His fingertips are now massaging my back with just enough vigor to stir up my immediate passion to such intensity that I feel I may burst. He pulls me in so closely and tight to him, that I can't help acting on this intensity. I find his lips with my own and his hands find their way up to caress my neck; he kisses me in such a confident and fiery, animalistic -manner that I feel I've not only been transported into the cottage by him, but also into a dream world that could only be imagined and not fully experienced. In this moment, my dream world and reality are converging, and it is beautiful. Life is beautiful.

He grabs me around the waist, lifts me up to allow me to wrap my legs around him, and carries me to the king sized bed awaiting us just off the sitting area. I breathe heavily as he kisses my neck and lays me down upon the lush duvet. He lifts my dress smoothly up and over my thighs to expose my bare midriff. His lips find my navel and work their way down, down, down…

I feel the anticipation building within me as the clothing I'm wearing is lifted presenting my fully vulnerable and writhing naked physique to this man, who is parallel to none. He unbuttons his shirt to expose a perfectly sculpted chest. I can see he is breathing just as heavily as I am. I reach up and pull him tightly down on top of me and we melt into one another fully and repeatedly. Time stands still; my worries, fears, insecurities and inhibitions are forgotten entirely. In that moment I just am.

◇◇◇◇◇◇◇◇

I awake to a lovely stream of sunlight, breaking through the shutters, bathing my face in warmth, adding to warmth felt from the cocooned embrace Guillaume has kept me wrapped in all night. I look over my shoulder and see that he is still fast asleep. I study his face, so perfect, so seemingly unaffected by any negativity or heartache, so at peace; I recall his story from the evening before and I'm overcome with respect and compassion for all he has endured. I lay still, allowing the flashbacks from our intertwined moments of sweet ecstasy to completely take over my thoughts, for what feels like a quarter of an hour longer. I feel Guillaume stir and the sheets rustle above me. He runs a finger down the side of my face, takes my hand, brings it to his ever so talented lips, pulls me back in to wrap me up once again.

"Good morning, beautiful Portia," Guillaume says in a sweet and doting tone.

"Good morning, handsome," I respond, feeling the butterflies again forming deep within. I stroke his back with my finger tips and as the excitement of the past twenty-four hours is taking me over, a bitter feeling seems to be lurking in the distance behind the sweetness. I block it out and don't allow the fear I have of being just a one-time thing to him ruin this moment.

It is so indescribable how comfortable and at peace I feel when with this man. It's as if I go from being this absolute train wreck of a human being, who can't even tie a shoelace without falling ass backwards down a flight of stairs, to a chic, calm and ever so confident woman. Being in his presence, transforms me, all of me! I'm fully committed to keeping this man around; if not as the love of my life, at least as a dear companion and friend. Only time will tell.

I soon realize that my lengthy moments of contemplation have been accompanied by a phone call and Guillaume is now having, what sounds like, a serious conversation. He is flailing his arms around, gesturing as if he's cursing out an ignorant driver who has cut him off. I even think I see a vain throbbing in his forehead. I casually slip on my robe and slink away subtly onto the cottage's back veranda to give him a moment of privacy. It really is sublime in this place. The view, the charm of the streams and these ancient buildings; this place is the perfect escape from an escape.

"Portia, ma belle."

I hear Guillaume's deep and tender voice, and turn to see him standing in the doorway.

"I am so sorry to be like this and do this to you my dear. It is Marie; she insists I arrive back in Paris as soon as is possible for a campaign she says she has involved me in. This is a very important client and, and I don't know what more I can say but…"

"Guillaume, it's all fine. I understand totally. You couldn't have known."

Could he?

My insecurities are creeping in.

Did he plan this all? Was he even talking to Marie just now or is this all an act that he has rehearsed before coming here as a way to make a quick getaway after getting exactly what he wanted?

"Portia, beautiful girl, I will make this all up to you," he says as he approaches me still bare- chested and sporting only a pair of boxer briefs, making me entirely too aware that I may never get to see this piece of complete art in flesh ever again if my worrisome insecurities prove to be accurate. He embraces me and kisses my cheek for a lengthy lingering moment and then frantically rushes in to begin arranging and packing his belongings.

"Portia, you stay, relax. I will call a car to arrive for you around noon so you can enjoy the cottage and some peace here. I would never rush you out of the beauty surrounding us. My dear, I will be in touch with you after this campaign work has finished. I enjoyed every moment with you."

He speaks with such seriousness and conviction that I can do nothing but believe all that he is saying and trust in this moment that this is not our last interaction.

A grey cloud continues to hover dubiously, threatening to release all the stormy negativity that always results after I've felt I've been used and rejected by yet another object of my affection.

"Thank you, Guillaume. I appreciate you're offering me this time here and a car of my own to head back to the city. I hope we can meet again before I leave Paris, but if not, I've loved every minute in your company as well," I manage to say, though my voice has quite a wavering sound due to nerves and a familiar melancholy that is taking over at the thought of never seeing him again.

"Portia," he says while stroking my face, "I promise you. Look at my eyes."

I do. They are intense and look filled with purpose and sincerity.

"I promise I will see you again here in Paris; not only that, I will see you and find you wherever your life takes you. I promise." He kisses me passionately on the lips, gives me one last squeeze and rushes to the door as we both hear the car horn honk. "Au revoir, ma belle."

"Au revoir," I reply.

And just like that, this indescribable moment is over and I find myself alone with the memories, and a promise.

The remainder of the morning is spent dwelling on the possible outcomes involving Guillaume. I try with every ounce of energy to be positive, but my doubts keep creeping in. All other situations like this have only ever ended in my worst fear being realized.

What makes this circumstance any different? He's going to continue on in his lavish and beautiful life, find a new woman to seduce by tomorrow and I'll be yesterday's news.

I attempt to allow myself to see Guillaume in a fully incomparable bubble of his own, but to no avail, I simply sink in sudden bitterness. After an hour of relaxing on the veranda and wallowing in self-pity, I remind myself of my true purpose for coming to Paris, *Design!* I draw my previously begun sketches from my bag and continue to add to the initial designs of the line I have just now decided to title "Fleeting Romanticism."

The earlier sketches coupled with my new ideas of adding a flowing floor length gown with a studded and feathered crisscross back and an empire embellishment of floral print against muted ivory tones is the ultimate garment to portray romance and whimsy. I also begin sketches for a form fitting Chantilly lace dress, intended to be just sheer enough to stir up the feeling of eroticism yet due to the elegance of the lace, maintain the heir of expensive luxury.

My fingers move with nimble motivation and excitement as my newfound inspiration nudges me on. Finally, the uncertainty caused by Guillaume's premature departure has been pushed to the back of my mind; clarity and sanity have found me in the form of couture brainstorming.

Before I know it noon has arrived and I hear a knock at the door. I wave to the driver through the window, throw my robe on the bed replacing it with a pair of jeans and a cotton blouse. *Shades cover all melancholy and angst* I remind myself as I plop my Jackie O inspired sun glasses on the end of my nose and make my way out of the cottage, which now I most certainly feel a bitter sweetness for.

The car ride back is sombre at times yet filled with anticipation to see Nina and to begin discovering the fashion world that is Paris.

God, do I ever need a good laugh right about now. Nina, you better not be off shagging that bean pole juvenile, Stefan.

I smile at the thought.

I am finally dropped at the hotel and see the time is approaching two o'clock in the afternoon. My first desire is to head up to the king sized bed awaiting me in my suite and wallow for the rest of the afternoon among chocolate cake, a bag of potato chips, or crisps or frites or whatever the hell they're called here and finish that junky goodness all off with a bottle of fine merlot. This is, of course, my usual course of action after the realization hits that a man I care for has slipped through my fingers. I decide to defy the old Portia.

I need adventure in a moment like this! You're not the old Portia; you're a new person! Get yourself together.

My inner pep talk has clearly turned into one which has made its way to my lips because I soon become aware that I have been mouthing this internal speech while standing out front of the hotel and the bellhop is staring at me with concern.

"Mademoiselle, is there a person I can call for you? Are you in distress?" he asks with great sympathy in his voice.

I chuckle a nervous and embarrassed laugh, "Oh no no, I am absolutely fine. Merci! I am just heading off for a walk. Please can you watch my bag until I return, monsieur?"

"But, of course, mademoiselle. It would be my pleasure," he says and removes my bag from the entranceway promptly.

"Thank you so much. I shouldn't be more than an hour or so," I say and then begin my greatly anticipated journey back to my accordion-playing friend. The walk makes me feel more awake and more alive than I have all day. The warm breeze gives the sensation as though it's re-energizing and igniting a fire for discovery within me, the temporary bitterness brought on by the day's events is now slowly leaving with the blowing wind.

Beneath the tower I spot my elderly acquaintance and make my way towards him with a lively curiosity to determine who this true love of his is.

"Dear girl! You have returned to me!" he hollers as soon as he sees me approaching across the way. "Come, come I have something to share with you to thank you for keeping your promise."

He wraps his arm around me and I suddenly feel so comforted after the emotional rollercoaster I've experienced over the course of the day. A tear comes to my eye, and I can't even explain why. It's like my grandfather has his arm around me. I always felt so safe and secure in the care of my granddad. He always told me I was the most beautiful girl in the world and inspired nothing but self-confidence and security within. This man suddenly is bringing a wave of that same security and positivity. How could I have ever broken my promise to this gem?

We arrive at his accordion case and he quickly produces a picture for me which is worn and faded, yet still has enough clarity for me to recognize the two people within the picture to be a much younger version of the lovely man whose company I'm now in and what also *does* appear to be a much younger looking Victoria Lewis!

I'm speechless and can't help staring at the two, so endearing and clearly so deeply in love with one another. Victoria is wearing a yellow sundress with a large sunhat that is obviously blowing slightly in the breeze. She's holding it with one hand and laughing as her companion is snuggled up close to her and doting on her much as Guillaume did with me such a short time ago. Her face is so youthful and alive. She can't be more than twenty-five in this photo and he looks much less weathered than he appears now. He looks no more than forty-five. Ruggedly handsome with a Clark Gable appearance and build; it is all becoming clear to me as to why Victoria Lewis engaged in a romantic affair with him. He was to her as Guillaume is (or was) to me.

What went wrong? Why did she never make the trip to see him again?

"You seem very amused by this picture. Is it all that you expected and anticipated? You have become quite silent."

"Yes, well you see, I am acquainted with this woman. I…I thought you said she was your most recent love. This picture is…." Oh god, how do I say this without making him feel old or senile? "Well, it's not new or recent, monsieur."

"I was quite truthful my dear. Victoria was my most recent love. I have waited for her return. She will always remain my most recent love until the day I depart this city for good. She stole my heart, and with her it will be locked until I see her once more or am no more."

My heart goes out to him and I see a pain in his eyes as he describes how endlessly and seemingly hopelessly devoted he is to Victoria. "My friend," I say gently, "I know you've loved Paris and are devoted to this city, but isn't it worthwhile, if not for a sense of adventure, at least for your wounded heart, to travel to North America to see your true love. Even if it's just to confess that you have loved her and thought of her all of these years? "

"Dear girl, that thought has many times crossed my mind. Even if my senses told me to go, I have not the funds to take me there. C'est impossible," he responds in a humbly defeated tone.

"Yes, I suppose that is not the easiest predicament, to be in. Having loved and lost, I know what torture you must be in, especially when you are uncertain as to whether you ever really lost her. Perhaps it is truly only space that is the culprit in this love hiatus and once you close the gap made by the distance between you, the love you both shared will be rekindled. You must try, sir."

This entire conversation is causing me the inability to focus on anything else as I'm still in shock at the discovery that it is THE Victoria Lewis who is the object of his affection.

I've got to tell Nina!

"My friend, I have enjoyed reminiscing with you and promise that I will return again before I leave to head back to Toronto. Please consider my words. You really mustn't give up.""Till we meet again, lovely girl," he utters in his gravelly muted voice.

"Au revoir, for now," I say with a wink and turn to begin the walk back to the hotel.

The streets are, as usual, filled with pedestrians, both tourists and locals, intermingling amongst the beauty surrounding them. I take my time, although excited to confide in Nina about the recent events and discoveries made, I know that appreciating each moment in this place is just as exciting and purposeful. My thoughts once again retreat back to insecurities as to when and whether I will hear from or see Guillaume again. As despair and doubt is managing to once again consume me I hear magical words bellowed in my direction, the very words that every down on her luck, lonely and broken woman yearns to hear.

"Beautiful lady! Excuse moi….toi!" A whistle follows. "You are magnifique, mademoiselle! Ton nomme?"

The words come from across the way, but I spin to see that the man speaking, or should I say hollering them, is undoubtedly directing them at me as I see his eyes focused precisely on me. I smile, knowing that this semi-interaction is just enough to redirect my doubtful thoughts; I carry on contently towards my destination.

My situation only improves upon entering the hotel. I'm greeted by the bellhop who scurries me towards the main desk for what I assume is to collect my stored tote. He ducks behind the check-in desk, I hear him rustling around and within moments he reappears with a cheek-to-cheek grin on his face, holding a bundle. I gasp in glorious shock and delight.

"Pour toi, mademoiselle." He says, quite obviously beyond proud to be playing a part in the moment. "Pour toi. From a Monsieur Guillaume Boisvert." He continues and places a dozen long stemmed roses in my quivering arms.

CHAPTER 15

"He...sent...these....he....for me? From.....Guillaume? "I finally respond in regards to the perfect parcel I have just received. I'm so overcome with emotion I can't even string a full sentence together. I have never been one to enjoy flowers as a romantic gesture, but after all of the second guessing and negative self-talking as to whether Guillaume would be just like all the "others", these roses are just about the sweetest thing I have ever been given.

"Oui, mademoiselle. Pour toi! He has included a message also." He hands over an envelope and I'm surprised to see that it has been opened already. I glance at the bellhop and staff who have gathered around. They all seem far too engaged in the circumstance and I see bashful looks on the majority of their faces coupled with wide-eyed anticipation for me to read and react to the message that each has clearly already had the opportunity to read.

God this must be good.

I remove the letter from the rumpled envelope and find a lobby chair to settle on in order to read its contents while avoiding a nasty fall if I have another weak spell at Guillaume's words.

Beautiful Portia,

You have captured my heart fully. I have thought of only you this entire day and wish to be next to you at this very moment.

If I were there, by your side, my lips they would be serving only you; making you smile with the words they would form for you, making you tingle all over with the sensation they would cause as they caress your swan-like neck, making you yearn for my other parts while they find your tender lips. This will all be real to me once again in mere days. I will come to you.

Until then, please journey to the following locations. They are all establishments of the Parisian fashion industry. All people listed are aware of who you are and are expecting you tomorrow. They are each my dear friends and will treat you, my dear girl, perfectly:

Danielle Parent, Editor in Chief at La Vie Magazine, 75 Avenue Kléber

Michele Gagnon, Couture designer, 1232 Boulevard Barbès

Liv Pickard, Paris Fashion Week coordinator and CEO at Bekta Handbags and Accessories, 504 rue Charlemagne

My darling, I wish you a magnificent time while visiting my friends. I will see you following the close of my client's campaign on Wednesday evening.

Adieu my sweetheart.

Guillaume Boisvert

I've been holding my breath while silently reading this entire letter and once the final words are read I exhale all the worry that has harassed me all day. I sit dumbfounded for a moment and analyze how purely perfect my current situation is. What complete fate to wander into a strange and foreign coffee shop only to meet the man who cannot only be equated to one from my romantic dreams, but who can also play such a critical role in assisting me along my new career path.

The more I analyze the events of the last forty-eight hours, the more in awe I am of how fated this entire trip has proven to be. From Guillaume, to the sketching inspiration, to the sweet elderly lover of Victoria Lewis, it is all so surreal, and something tells me that the best is yet to come.

"Portia, babe! You're back!" I'm suddenly rattled out of my awestricken state by an exuberant welcome from Nina and the man of the moment, Stefan.

"Oh, doll, are those roses for me? You shouldn't have!" Nina adds jokingly. "I can see that Don Juan, Guillaume is holding his status as not only the sexiest man I've ever laid eyes on, but as the most romantic as well." She glances over at Stefan. "Sorry honey, you're a cutie, but Portia's guy is beyond comparison. You can't even hold a candle to him."

Stefan shrugs his shoulders looking a bit disheartened.

"I have to say, Nina, I'm living a bit of a dream at the moment. I need one of your love pinches to make sure this is all real!" I respond fully expecting Nina to pounce on the opportunity to pinch me, but she resists temptation and heads down the *life-coaching* avenue of interacting.

"Love, soak it up and enjoy. It's not a dream, it's the life you've been waiting to live and now you're doing it." She rubs my shoulder.

"You are the happy girl!" Stefan, bless his heart, does his best to join in on the conversation. "I wish you luck. Nina fills me in on all of this excitement you are now part of."

"Yes, he's right, Port! I've filled him in and he's filled me in, if ya know what I'm saying," she adds slyly behind her hand and I can't help but giggle. "Now, let's head upstairs so you can tell me all about your little rendezvous with Guillaume. Don't you dare leave out one detail; I want to hear it all, even the kinky bits."

She gathers my tote and passes it off to Stefan while I cling to my long stemmed roses as if they were a cherished family heirloom. They smell delightful, and from what I can see are thorn- free. This is exactly how I see my companionship with Guillaume blossoming; sweet and gentle to the senses and void of surprising prickles or prick-like behaviour along the way.

What else could a girl ask for?

We arrive back to the suite within minutes where Nina grabs the tote out of Stefan's arms while showing him the door coupled with the explanation, "It's girl talk time, sweetheart. We'll be in touch."

Stefan leans in to kiss Nina and she accepts it on the cheek giving the impression that their fling is now nearing its end. He hangs his head and nods to communicate a "pleased to have met you" message towards us both.

I'm sympathetic and see that he appears a bit hurt by Nina's sudden dismissal.

"So? Tell me everything!" she insists. "Don't spare one detail. I want it all!"

I do just that; I tell her about everything from the magical dinner to the tender, passionate love-making to Guillaume's early departure and my day of self-deprecating analysis of the abandoned experience only to be welcomed by a wonderfully romantic letter and roses to complete the twenty-four hour adventure.

"Man alive! That sounds like the best twenty-four hour soap opera episode ever. You must be reeling with excitement! Damn, if you're not, you clearly don't have a pulse."

"Oh I am, Neen. I most definitely am. Now, how about you and the hipster juvi? What's gone on there? It's clear you've done the nasty from your back-handed comment you shared earlier but what else? Are you two going to carry on something? It did kind of look like an out and out dismissal you gave him just a moment ago."

"I'm....just not sure we really have anything in common."

I could have told her that before she started chatting him up on the plane.

"He's hardly able to speak English and he constantly wanted to ride his skateboard wherever we went today. It was beyond embarrassing trying to speed walk and trot along in my wedge sandals. At one point he asked me, well at least I think he asked me, to jump on! Imagine me, doubling on a skateboard around the streets of Paris. At that exact point I thought to myself 'What in god's name am I doing with this child?"

I want to laugh hysterically at the picture I have in my mind of Nina balancing on an adolescent's skateboard while he embraces her and steers them around Paris, but she looks utterly disgusted with herself and I can't rub salt in this new wound.

Can I? Yes.... I can.

I begin laughing hysterically to the point that tears begin streaming down my face and after a short while, Nina slaps me then joins in laughing heartily at the ridiculousness of her choice of companion.

We laugh and laugh. "So, if you knew you weren't really a match or even in the least bit attracted, when and why did you get it on with him?"

"Oh, babe, that happened last night when I had my champagne goggles on. You left me passed out on the chaise. I woke up still hammered and knew I didn't want to spend the night alone in such a beautiful suite. He'd given me his number the night before so naturally he was my first and only choice in the given circumstance. I don't know, with the view from that terrace and the unlimited booze in that fridge, my eyesight along with my judgement became impaired and we went at each other like animals in the wild. I mean, it wasn't my finest moment, but he was rather talented for being such a young age. He did this thing with his thumb where he…"

"STOP…RIGHT….THERE!" I beg her. "Unlike you, I do not need to know *your* evening's raunchy, kinky details. Save them for your diary boo."

"Hmph, fine by me. Your loss," she says. "It's worth a listen, just saying."

"I think I'll stick with my decision, Neen. So like I said, do you think you'll see him again before we leave and will you keep in touch?"

"Unlikely, babe. I don't see any point in it to be honest."

"But, well, just think about his view point, Neen. I mean, what if you're like his Guillaume? What if the thought of never seeing you again devastates him? Come on, be a bit more compassionate. See him one last time!"

"Port, what's the deal? Two days ago you were cringing at the sight of us tonguing in the lobby and now you're trying to couple us up? You're a big conundrum," Nina says exasperatedly.

"I don't want you or I to cause the heartache that I was feeling earlier today, and have been victim to so often. It's a horrible, horrible feeling and the only thing that would ever make it better is if they had the gall to meet with me and let me down gently as opposed to doing the usual and avoiding me incessantly. Please, Nina, don't break that lanky juvi's heart."

"All right, I suppose it couldn't hurt, but promise you'll be there. We can all go for coffee! You can bring Guillaume so I at least have something to look forward to with this whole scenario," she says with a devilish wink and grin.

"I don't know about that. Like I said, Guillaume has this campaign he's involved in and he won't have a spare moment until it's done which won't be until Wednesday night. So unless we're making a coffee date for Thursday, he won't be able to make an appearance."

"Done! Thursday morning, coffee at Café Lateral. It will give you two a good amount of time for an early morning romp, and maybe even a bit of early afternoon delight afterwards before we board the flight home. Oh I can picture you both now walking into the cafe all dishevelled with that glorious post coital glow! I'll take your first picture as a couple while you're walking through the doors. Candid is best!"

"Nina, slow down, you're going to hyperventilate you're becoming so excited." She's actually out of breath from her rambling.

"Sorry, I'm so excited for you! I'll tone it down until Wednesday's nearer, but what the hell are you going to do while you are waiting for the next moment you get to jump his bod?"

"He sent me a bunch of names and numbers of a few of the most well-known people of the Paris fashion scene and has already informed each that I'll be around to see them tomorrow! Come with me Nina. You're such a social butterfly that I just know you will make me feel more at ease. I get hopelessly awkward when around intimidating and powerful people."

"I'm down for a few go-sees! This could be exhilarating! What if one of them offers you a job on the spot? That would be so fab. Imagine being a permanent resident here and having that hunk of a man-friend indefinitely."

"I don't know if I'm ready for that big of a change yet, Neen. Even though it sounds fascinating it would be extremely impractical. I don't speak more than five words of French, my whole family is in Ontario and I have way too many loose ends to tie up back home. And of course I would miss the crap out of you and Minnie and, well, I guess that's really where my list ends these days. Sad right?"

"Um a bit, but I get your logic, babe, and I would miss you like crazy. Let's see how it all pans out before we go planning your relocation strategy. How about grabbing a bite?"

"Fabulous idea. You read my mind lady-friend."

The remainder of the evening is spent sipping wine, eating gourmet delicacies and meandering through the streets once again. I finally filled Nina in on the left out discovery I had made earlier in the day about Victoria Lewis' Parisian lover. Her reaction was of course one of utter disbelief and needless to say, she demanded that we stop by the Eiffel Tower once more so that she could take a look at the photograph.

"It must be doctored! There is absolutely no way it's her! She's happily married. Okay well contently married....maybe -we'll just leave it at...married. Regardless, she wouldn't have some overseas love affair! I'll believe it when I see it."

We arrive at the base of the tower once more to find the gentlemen laying down on an adjacent grassy knoll to where he usually performs. He seems to be stargazing and after his confession of unending love for Victoria, I imagine he is thinking about her. Where she is, who she is with, whether or not she is thinking about him. Poor lovely soul, he is so committed to her memory and the hope of once again seeing her.

"There he is!" Nina shrieks so loudly that the gentleman is startled out of his obvious thoughtful trance. "Monsieur, we are here to finally settle on a disagreement. Portia here is convinced that your Victoria is the same that is Editor in Chief at *Crave Magazine* and who is happily married."

The ambushed man quickly rises to his feet to receive us cordially even though Nina's approach is far from deserving of such a reception. He scratches his head and stands silent for a moment as if gathering his thoughts fully before formulating a reply to Nina's inquiry,

"Madame, she was a Victoria who did not share with me her last name. Yes. I knew of her marital ties, yet she was unhappy. It's my understanding that she was forced into the marriage at a young age. She was merely eighteen on her wedding day. By the point I found her in my arms she was twenty-five years of age and ready to bid the man adieu. She was working endlessly to become independent with the ability to support her own needs. It was some fashion magazine with whom she had gained employment and was writing the editorials for them. That is the last I know and heard."

"Married at eighteen?" Nina says clearly baffled. "But Victoria confided in me all the details of her marriage. They fell in love when she was twenty-eight after she met Roger in the Virgin Islands snorkelling. It was a passion filled beginning but began to fizzle quickly.

"Well, mademoiselle, here is the photograph. The same that I showed ton ami earlier."

Nina lunges for the photograph as if it were the golden ticket which permits entrance to the Wonka factory, glances at it and I see an immediate softening of her previously business-like demeanour. Suddenly, her need to prove us both wrong means little to nothing and she is simply as endeared by the photo as I was upon my first glimpse.

"She is so lovely. How beautiful," Nina finally utters. "And, sir, you're an absolute heartthrob. It's no wonder Victoria fell for you."

"She is beauty at its rarest and most precious. She will always remain that young and beautiful creature in my mind. But tell me, *chérie*, how is she then? Happy, successful, loved?"

"Sir, she is extremely successful, but struggles to find true love in her marriage. As I said, it cannot be considered a true marriage. They never see each other except to argue over possession of assets gathered."

"My heart sinks to hear that. I'll send a wish into the sky for her and hope it finds her."

"Do you hope to reconnect with her, if you could?" Nina inquires.

"It would be like a dream come true to see her once more after all this time has passed. I would like nothing more," he says with a little more liveliness than before.

"Sir, we will do all we can to make your wish a reality." I finally break in on the interaction.

"Everything we can…everything."

CHAPTER 16

The following morning I am a ball of nerves. "Nina, get up! I want to be at Michele Gagnon's before ten a.m. so that I can have an hour or so at each appointment. Dress to impress too. I mean you always do, but don't choose today to go through a grunge phase, is all I'm saying."

"I'm up, I'm up. Just having a bit of a lay in for a moment. I like to meditate on what happened the day before and apply it to the day that lies ahead. It helps me stay centred."

I stand in Nina's doorway in an astounded state. All these years I thought Nina simply went through life not thinking about the next moment to come, but here she is talking of meditation and reflection as being an integral part of her routine.

Wow, I really don't know Nina at all!

"Sure Nina! I'm just going to pop in the shower but please be up by the time I'm out." I say, still quite perplexed at her reply.

"Okay hon, will do," she replies in a very peaceful and monotone voice that doesn't faintly come close to resembling her normal booming verbal expressions.

Three quarters of an hour later I'm becoming antsy and impatient, pacing back and forth along the expansive marble flooring while Nina is still drying and styling her hair. I keep glancing at my watch seeing that if I want to stay on track with the day, we should be at Michele's studio in ten minutes. It's clearly not going to happen. Suddenly an idea hits me.

I've got to go this one alone. Nina's holding me back. She can't be my crutch forever. "Nina!" I holler, my voice carrying through the vast cathedral ceilinged space, "I'm heading out now. Meet me at the address I told you about when you are *finally* ready."

"Ok, babe, toodles!" Nina says in the most jovial voice, clearly having not one iota of an idea that I'm somewhat pissed off.

I grab my tote with my sketches tucked safely inside along with a good luck charm which is a miniature dream catcher I was given by a street person who claimed that he was the Oracle. Back at that time *The Matrix* was on my top five list for best movies of all time. It really hasn't brought me the best of luck mind you. I feel that luck is turning!

Rushing out the doors of the hotel I am welcomed by another glorious and sunshiny day. I glance down at my letter from Guillaume.

First stop 1232 Boulevard Barbès.

My map indicates that it's not a difficult journey by way of transit and saving a penny or two is a necessity for me at the moment so I head towards the nearest tube stop and jump on the appropriate train. The woman sitting directly across from me nods at me seemingly in approval of my apparel. I have to admit, I don't blame her. I look fierce.

My ensemble is a leather dress with a ballerina skirt. It's edgy with a feminine flare and I feel like an absolute stunner in it. My heels are two- inches and graffiti patterned with sporadic pops of all of the bright colours of the rainbow, to add just a touch more femininity. My tote is a dual toned black and cream leather to complement the outfit fully. With the most remarkable man in my corner, the streets of Paris and this outfit I feel as though nothing can stop me.

Just as these thoughts finish formulating in my mind I hear a loud *screeeeeeeech!* and am suddenly thrown sideways so I am laying on top of the teenage boy sitting to my right. (Nina and I have got to stay away from the minors after this trip). The train has come to a complete halt. The lights then begin to flicker and within moments we are thrown into darkness.

Shit. Nothing can stop me aside from this steal death trap! Okay breathe. Portia, just breathe. No one else is panicking or too shocked. This must be a regular occurrence.

Momentarily screams and gasps begin to come from all areas of the cabin

Okay maybe not. "Zut alors! Sacre bleu. On y va!" I hear from a variety of people surrounding me. I'm listening trying to make out people's conversations but the language barrier is proving to be a bit of a wrench in the attempts.

As I'm leaning to my left to listen to what I think is broken English I gasp at the sensation of what feels like a finger running up my thigh. The sensation continues to creep further and further up my inner leg and toward my lady bits.

I can't believe this is happening! I'm being sexually accosted on a Parisian subway train! Pervert! I bet it's that teen. He clearly thought I was making a move on him and now he's taking full advantage of the situation.

As these thoughts roam around my mind, the sensation finds its way beneath my ballerina ruffled bottom. I can't take it anymore.

"Stop, you dirtball! Don't you dare go any further or I will take my nail clippers from my purse and jab you in the balls so hard that you will wish you were a woman!" I yell as loudly as I can. At that very moment, the lights flicker on for me to see a whole cabin staring at me, and absolutely no one in my vicinity.

The only culprit in the matter is my tote strap that has edged its way onto my thigh and up under my skirt most likely due to my having leaned over to listen for solutions to the predicament. I hang my head and hope that after a moment all of the horrified eyes that are now fixated on me will be diverted elsewhere. It takes longer than expected and after another ten minutes of the train sitting motionless, the confused glares and disgusted sighs dwindle to nothing. The train finally lurches forward and we are on our way again.

The tube incident has set me back another fifteen minutes, but I'm content to finally be off the train and out in the daylight once more when I ascend from the underground. I find myself on the necessary street and walk along gazing up at the addresses as I pass each building. I soon figure that I'm a few addresses away from Michele Gagnon's, and the butterflies take over my insides.

I wish I hadn't become so frustrated with Nina. She would have kept me calm and had me ready to strut into this place like I was CEO of Vogue.

I arrive outside the extremely modern looking building that is landscaped beautifully with gurgling pillar fountains.

This is it, Portia; the start of something sensational.

I strut through the foyer to the front desk, over which reads: *"Michele Gagnon Couture Fashions"* and I smile imagining that one day that will be my name next to *"Couture"*.

"Bonjour, hello. My name is Portia Delaney. I've been informed Monsieur Gagnon is expecting me."

"Ah, oui, oui. He and Nina will be with you promptly," the chicly dressed assistant responds. I find myself choking on my own words. "Ni...Nina?"

"Oui, a friend of yours arrived recently and indicated she is your assistant and likes to be sure that you will be made comfortable with what will take place at your meeting with Monsieur Gagnon. He is touring her around his studio."

Oh no. What is she doing here! She better not mess this up for me.

...I quickly push any negative thoughts from my mind.

"Right, well she does do a thorough job at making me feel prepared and comfortable. She's a wonderful assistant, that Nina!" I regroup and carry on with the façade. I take a seat on a leather armchair and await the duo's arrival still feeling a bit thrown by the scenario.

How in the world did she get here before me? Her hair had her looking like a drowned rat when I left her; it would have taken her at least another twenty minutes to style the true Nina way, and I couldn't have been on the trapped train for more than fifteen. Well I suppose if she cabbed and ran and didn't fully style...

My calculating and pondering of Nina's speedy ability is interrupted by the sound of the studio door whooshing open to reveal an entirely ivory clad Nina with her still dampened hair swept up into her signature French twist. Her pantsuit is unbelievably professional and screams "business woman and right hand girl at her finest." I'm falling even more in love with this best gal pal of mine.

Following Nina from the studio is an unkempt looking gentleman, clothed in a simple black T-shirt and torn denim, paired with combat boots. His hair is untamed and shoulder length. It appears that he hasn't shaven in days. I breathe a sigh of relief at the realization that Michele is a true artist, focused on his work and not on the pretentiousness of the industry. Guillaume couldn't have selected a more down-to-earth looking and welcoming designer to introduce me to. Even in his absence I feel entirely drawn to Guillaume, his sincerity and spot on judgement.

"Bonjour, mademoiselle!" Michele rushes towards me and is quite spastic and jittery in his movements. A true eccentric and somewhat peculiar, I'm immediately set at ease in his presence, as disjointed as that may seem.

"Guillaume has said only the most wonderful things of you! And Nina, she is a thorough assistant who has told me of your talents and intentions to begin a line. You look magnificent, Portia. It is clear to me at this moment that you have the style and sense to assemble couture. Come with me. On y va!"

I give a quick smile to Nina and she returns the gesture then follows me through the whooshing doors to the other side. In that moment I feel a transition take place within me. The journey to the other side of that door and on into that couture design studio is like the transition of myself finally leaving the old disgruntled medical assistant behind and moving into my true calling. Entering the studio, I *am* a designer and I *am* the very picture of myself I have wished to become for years prior to this. Fear restrained me for far too long.

Michele begins by showing us his setup at the studio. He has his sketches and choice of fabrics for given projects hung in the creative section of the space. Next to this is his workspace, where I see every type of sewing apparatus imaginable, and half sewn garments scattered about. Michele is a truly authentic and hands on designer. Clearly, he is a perfectionist and is fully entrenched in his own creations; a true artist in the design industry.

From there Michele leads us to the styling area where his lavish and ground-breaking designs are draped around dress forms and they are in the process of being properly hemmed and paired with appropriate accessories for the purpose of runway opportunities. There's a wall of accessories and shoes that has both Nina and my own jaw gaping wide open. I think I see a touch of drool forming on Nina's lower lip so nudge her to suck it back in. A slurp and an exchange of how clearly impressed we are brings us to Michele's inquiries as to my own stylistic abilities and designs.

I withdraw my sketches from my bag and spread them across his drafting table for him to peruse and to critique. I finish organizing them and take two steps back so I am standing directly next to Nina. She grabs my hand and I feel her give a little squeeze in support of the clearly nerve racking situation. Michele puts a pair of dark framed glasses on and leans in so close to the designs that it seems as though he's attempting to use his sense of taste and smell to make his judgement about the designs.

He peers and wafts in each design for a full minute, inspecting every pattern and detail included. Moving from one to the other, I begin to feel a bit worried when sighs and deep breaths accompany his study. As he makes his way to the final design, peers, groans, and takes a step back, I hold my own breath while waiting for the verdict. Michele spins on his heel to face me, removes his spectacles, hangs his head and I feel a rush of fear.

After what seems like an eternity, Michele looks me in the eye intensely. "Portia, mademoiselle, the designs are, are…intricate, pleasing to the eye. You have a talent. Even more, it is clear to me from your own ensemble and the details you have added to the designs that you are a wonderful stylist and have a talent for bringing the main garment to life with appropriate pieces. Will you please do me the honour, and consider being of help behind the scenes at my fashion show tomorrow evening? You can assist in preparing the models for the runway and selecting complementary accessories."

I feel faint and know that Nina senses my shock at the request as she moves in closer to steady me. "Monsieur Gagnon, it would be a dream come true to be able to assist at your show tomorrow. I would like nothing more than to be involved. You are an artistic genius, and I'm so honoured to even be considered for this opportunity," I say with a wavering in my voice.

"Magnifique!" he replies. "Please, Portia, my name is Michele. Monsieur Gagnon makes me feel ancient and like your father. I'm a friend to you now. It is Michele."

"Of course Michele, as you wish," I reply with a nervous grin.

Holy hell, I'm friends with Michele Gagnon!

"Guillaume will be a model within my show tomorrow so you will have more time with him I have heard your time was cut short last day. He has shared his deep sadness felt because of being apart from you, Portia. You must be a special lady to him," Michele says.

I can't help but feel my heart leap at this last comment. I turn to look at Nina and see the excitement in her expression about the whole exchange. I shake Michele's hands, collect my sketches and determine time and location for the magnificent event. I'm then on my way with my chic assistant at my side.

As we head out of the building to flag down a cab (because I sure as heck am not banking on the tube to promptly get me to the Editor in Chief at *La Vie Magazine*) Nina bursts with excitement.

"God, Portia! What a start to the day! You are going to be styling at a couture designer's fashion show tomorrow night! Unbelievable, un-freaking-believable! I'm in awe, in shock, feel faint.... could vomit....but won't. How are you so composed, so calm? Can I come? Can I watch? Shit! This is my first Parisian fashion show experience ever! Not my first fashion show, but Parisian fashion show, and that's huge! What will I wear? I think we should shop for shoes tonight. My Payless kitten heels won't cut it for tomorrow's event. People would heckle me or hiss me, or do whatever Parisian fashionistas and fashionistos do to indicate they are offended. If we meet your fashion people then head for a quick bite, we can hit the shops by..."

"Nina! Relax. Remember, this isn't for you to stress over. It's my behind that will be slinging accessories for a celebrity designer. This could make or break *me*, not you, honey."

"Babes, I'm just so excited for you and want to be the best side-kick I can! That means having all designer apparel to really look the part, no?"

"You're the best side-kick just as you are." I attempt to console her manic behaviour but am completely sincere.

She settles and smirks then literally puts her best foot forward to hail us a cab.

Within minutes the lunatic cab driver, who is clearly racing against the clock, delivers us to the front door of *La Vie Magazine*. Even though our most recent adventure had me on cloud nine, my nerves are once again taking over and have knocked me back to reality. I breathe in, look up at the four story building before me bearing the words *"La Vie "* inscribed along the front stone work and get a full understanding as to how pertinent this magazine has been and still is to the fashion world and just how important Danielle Parent must be to its success. Not sure exactly what has fully come over me, I turn to Nina with a new determination in my voice.

"Neen, you've been instrumental in helping me with my confidence and I appreciate you so much. You know that, right?"

"Sure, doll," she replies

"And I owe you so much for stepping in to butter up Michele Gagnon when I was an initial no show."

"Don't even mention it, Port." She looks perplexed and is obviously staring at me intently wondering where I'm going with this spiel.

"You were such a great friend through this all, and look at how perfect and professional you look for me today!" I say just to lay it on super thick.

"Well, you deserve it. Everyone needs a great sidekick. What would Batman be without Robin? Or… or…well that's the only duo that I can think of right now! These Payless heels are killing me and mucking up my train of thought!" She groans and I see my moment to relieve her of her duty.

"Nina, I'm giving you a leave of sidekick duty. Go and shop. Buy yourself a gorgeous outfit for tomorrow and some designer pumps. I can go the rest alone."

"Doll, I couldn't abandon you! This is an editor in chief! This is the big time and I know how nervous you get."

"Nina, I need to do this. I've got to get over my nervous tendencies and fears. You're amazing, but I can't use you as my social buffer anymore. I've got my own spunk and need to learn to get in there and sell myself."

"Babe, you're totally right. You can do this. You only think you've needed me all these years. You've got this, Port! Just be sure to sell yourself to deserving prospects. No sketchy men on any street corners, if you know what I'm saying." She giggles at her side comment in true Nina fashion. "Go get 'em girlfriend. I'll be in Le Triangle D'Or if you need me."

"Thanks, Nina. You enjoy the day and we'll meet back at the hotel later. Let's say six or so? I want to get a full fashion show of all you buy." She smiles, nods, then waves her hands as if to say "get your butt in that door."

◇◇◇◇◇◇◇

La Vie Magazine's executive office is beyond impressive and seems to run like a well-oiled machine. Everyone is impossibly polished and carry on smoothly in their daily routine. I'm greeted promptly by a stout moustached gentleman and ushered up to the fourth floor where I'm asked to take a seat on a plush cream-coloured sofa. Individuals I assume to be assistants, copy writers, and junior editors float by me garbed in sleek looking suits and pencil skirts.

After what feels like an eternity due to nerves but in actuality is likely only about forty-five seconds the moustached gentleman returns carrying a tray containing a pot of coffee, one of tea and delicious looking macaroon treats. He balances the tray with great control on one hand while waving me after him with the other.

This is it!

170

I follow the stout man while inhaling the scent of what I determine to be Irish Cream coffee and hope that there's a bit of Bailey's in there to take the edge off. Perhaps being completely blitzed wouldn't be the makings of the best first impression, though being three sheets to wind landed me my first spot on MTV as a guest video jockey.

That's all neither here nor there, because in this situation, full awareness is key. We finally reach a set of oak double doors that the man delicately nudges open. Before me is an enormous and bright room, decorated in all pastel accents. The woman behind a clear table rises to greet me and I can tell by her walk and posture alone that she is a force to be reckoned with. This woman is like Victoria Lewis, Audrey Hepburn, and Madonna, all rolled into one sleek and slender, fashion forward package.

She approaches me, strutting across the office in what looks like a Valentino suit and impressive sling backed peep toes. Her arm, outstretched in my direction, is adorned from wrist to elbow in glimmering bangle bracelets.

"Bonjour, Portia. I am Danielle Parent," she says in such a high-pitched mouse-like voice that I'm taken aback. I also can't believe she feels the need to introduce herself. It's quite obvious who she is. I feel at ease and quickly reach for her outstretched hand.

"Bonjour, Madame Parent. It is such a pleasure to meet you and I am so very thankful that you have taken this time out of your day. I won't take much of it. I'm eager to be part of the fashion world and could use all of the advice I can get. I am a keen stylist, but am also trained to design."

Danielle reaches up and gently holds my chin in her fingers looking me in the eye.

"But of course. That is all you must say. Guillaume has made it all clear to me. Come and sit. We shall have a good chat."

God, I love Guillaume! No way would I be getting this treatment if he hadn't thoroughly worked his magic on these people. I think I just may propose to him when I see him tomorrow night. Screw tradition and the common expectations.

Danielle is the picture of refinery and poise. She answers every question I have about where I might fit in at an established fashion magazine. Her reply astounds me and incites a more favourable view of Victoria Lewis than I initially had on the day we met. It's due to Victoria's harshness that I've sought out to prove I can make it in this industry, so maybe that was her intention all along. Victoria Lewis is as much a part of the success of this trip as any other.

Danielle runs through the magazine's hierarchical system and divulges a description of all positions listed as well as the qualifications needed to hold such a position. She flips through some of her most cherished issues of *La Vie* from over the past twenty years. I hang on her every word as she says,

"Portia, fashion, it is like making love. Each season is like a new lover with whom a glorious connection is made. As each piece is unveiled it is like a caressing of the senses, awakening them once again like an erotic touch. Great, true fashion and styling must create this feeling within, keep you wanting more. It must be insatiable like a lover's first kiss on the cheek and promote yearning to feel more and to go further into the creations of the designer. It is my job, here at *La Vie,* to present the designs to the everyday fashionista and cause this individual to feel as if he or she is a part of the ménage.'

I'm so captivated by this metaphor and by the movement of Danielle's perfectly pouty lips; I'm feeling somewhat attracted to her and am burning up a little. It's not so much that I have an affection for her, but more a result of her talking of two of my favourite things: fashion and sex. She has me wishing Guillaume were waiting for me on the other side of that door.

"Portia, are you able to inspire the sensations resulting from love making with your very own designs? This is the true question to be assured that the fashion world is one for you."

I clear my throat and breathe deeply to attempt to eradicate the aroused sensation that is taking me over. "I do feel my designs can be quite titillating to the senses, Madame Parent. Michele Gagnon has offered to include me in his show tomorrow evening. He viewed my designs and was impressed with them as well as the styling complementing them."

"Marveilleuse! Michele Gagnon inspires such eroticism in me! He's a genius and if it is he that has given you such compliments, I'm not in any place to argue this."

I blush due to flattery and also because I am aware that the lovemaking metaphor has not been put to rest. "Merci, Madame. That means the world to me."

I leave Danielle's office after an exchange of contact information, with my head held high feeling ready to take on the world and like the possibilities are endless, not to mention, still a little hot and bothered.

I find myself connecting with *La Vie Magazine* employees as I make my way out of the building. Casual smiles and nods, exchanged confidently as if I've already made it, give me the motivation to truly do just that.

Avenue Kléber greets me with open arms and I almost feel like skipping toward the taxi stand but don't for fear that I may catch a heel in a sewer drain, once again, with a face plant as an end result. I glance down at Guillaume's letter to read the final destination scheduled for this already life-changing day.

Rue-Charlemagne, number 504.

Although I am flying high, I know it's not time to become over confident and celebrate the success of the day too soon. Liv Pickard, the Paris Fashion Week coordinator and CEO of *Bekta Bags and Accessories,* is awaiting me and I couldn't feel more humble or more appreciative.

The ride is swift and smooth. I hop out of the cab and strut towards the doors, attempting to recreate Danielle Parent's walk. I see that the structures look like a block of row homes that have been converted to office space. I enter with ease to a minimalist lobby area where a thin timid looking woman is seated behind a desk.

"Bonjour, I am Portia Delaney here to see Liv Pickard. Guillaume Boisvert organized an appointment for me today."

"Oui, je sais, I know Liv has told me this. It is nice to see you. Liv is quite busy and unfortunately is not able to see you presently. Please sit. I am happy to answer any questions you may have about the company and the Fashion Week production," the woman says in a soft and wavering voice that tells me she really hasn't the slightest clue about production or about full company details.

Quite confused and a bit disappointed, I humour her anyhow and pull up a chair to at least ask about the business. While leaning in to discuss the company's longevity and the number of years that Liv has organized Paris Fashion Week I glance to an open doorway just off the lobby and see a set of steely eyes peering out at me. I can only make out a partial appearance but see that it is a woman with long wavy hair and a darker complexion. Her face looks tight and clenched as if quite pissed about something.

"The company is thriving and we are so very proud of its success and the appeal it has for young professionals...." Melanie the assistant is saying. She catches on to the fact that I have taken notice of the mysterious woman in the doorway. Her eyes' focus, follow my own. Melanie's voice gets even more pitchy; her nerves are clearly taking over. Her eyes are wide and her posture quite tense.

"Liv is the talent behind the whole success of the company and the world of fashion bows to her. She has friends in this industry who are loyal and recognize her genius as being unmatched," Melanie continues.

Good lord, she's shaking like a leaf and has clearly been ordered to say each word to me. What for?

"I've never worked for a more talented and beautiful woman. She is truly breathtaking and men see this too. They throw themselves at her as she passes through her days."

What in the name of...what is her deal?

The mystery woman, who is quite obviously Liv Pickard, bursts into the lobby and paces towards me with a look of severe irritation. She stops next to me as if on a perch, holds me in her sight for a moment, flips her hair, turns on her heel as if walking the runway and marches back through the doorway.

The catwalk appearance was clearly timed to the compliments about her beauty and men's fascination with her.

What is happening here?

I'm suddenly so completely uncomfortable that I thank Melanie for her time and make my way out of *Bekta* quite perplexed at what has transpired. I'm already finding myself haunted by the hatred that seemed to exist behind that glare.

Why would Guillaume send me to such a lunatic? There's got to be an explanation.

I've settled on the possibility that she's had a horrible day and is simply despising people in general at the moment, but this thought is immediately proven to be wrong as I'm stepping into the cab and my focus zeroes in once more on this seemingly possessed woman standing in the doorway to the building motioning the cut throat symbol with her left hand for none other than me to see.

"Drive, On y va!" I squeal to the driver.

Nope, she's definitely a lunatic!

CHAPTER 17

T he fourth morning of our time in Paris arrives and for the fourth con-
secutive time I awake with an ear-to-ear smile in anticipation of the day.
Not only do I get to see Guillaume again, but I'm able to see him while helping
to style one of the most celebrated couture designer's fashion shows. We'll be
like a fashionista, fashionisto duo. Do our thing for the runway and then take
the "erotic passion" inspired by the designs back to the hotel room. How hot!

I roll out of my king sized bed for, sadly, the second last time and throw
on my robe just as I hear a sounding knock at the door. Making my way out
of my room through the glorious suite I notice that Nina's bedroom door is
still shut. We did have a good night with the champagne while we strutted our
newly purchased clothes down our marble runway as if we were Heidi Klum
and Gisele Bundchen, perhaps with a bit more weight to our stomp.

The knocks get louder and more frequent. I reach for the handle and swing
the door open, ready to receive more roses from Guillaume or a thank you
basket from Michele, for my "willingness" to participate in styling his show
this evening, but am somewhat disappointed to find the empty-handed
bellhop on the other side.

"Mademoiselle, it has come to my attention that we now have your room
available for you, and we are expecting a very important guest who has
reserved this suite for the week. You must pack your things at once and settle
into the room on the sixth floor."

I stand silent for a moment and it is clear that he can read the expression on my face to mean *"You have got to be kidding me!"* Okay, so we did get this amazing suite for a full three days after only paying for whatever awaits us on the sixth floor, but this is supposed to be the most magical day for me. With the fashion show and finally seeing Guillaume again, I don't want to spend our last night here together in a twin bed on the sixth floor.

I want my suite!

So my recent success has turned me into a bit of a diva, but this room change could not have come at a worse time.

Suck it up, Portia. You're still in Paris at a luxury hotel with a gorgeous man awaiting you and a designer itching for your assistance at his couture show. Snap out of it.

"Sir, thank you for the information. I'll wake my friend and we will begin to collect our things. Should we meet you at the front desk for our new key and directions?" I say trying to keep any irritation from becoming obvious in my tone.

"Oui, mademoiselle, please do. If you would please exit this suite no later than ten o'clock this morning, we need to clean it and prepare it for our most honoured guest." He glances around the suite with a look of disgust. I follow his gaze and see that the place is a bit of a disaster. Clothes from our personal fashion show are strewn about and empty champagne bottles are scattered around the sitting area. Open containers of half eaten take-out are emanating a pungent odour that I can tell is harassing the bellhop's senses. His gag reflex is quite controlled as it seems.

"Au revoir, mademoiselle; I will see you in one half hour in the lobby." The bellhop sighs and then retreats to the elevator.

I rush into Nina's room and jump on her bed, bouncing next to her until the movement stirs her awake.

"Port," she finally says. "What the hell are you doing? My head feels like it's getting compressed and mixed in a blender. Why are you torturing me like this?" she says in a sullen and quiet voice.

"Nina, bad news. We have to change rooms and only have a half hour to get out of this suite. Come on, you can pass out when we get to our new room." I pull her by the arms.

"You're joking. This must be a prank. I don't believe you. Please get out of my room, babe."

"Nina, I'm not kidding. Our fairy- tale accommodations are being taken over by someone far more important than you and I, hard to believe I know, but it's true."

"Bullshit. Who could be more important than you or I?"

I giggle then put my arm around her.

"We're stars, Neen, but mostly only in our own eyes, not quite as important in the eyes of the hotel staff."

"Well, they better recognize how fantabulous this girl is. Who gives a half hour notice for two peaches like ourselves? Horrendous, I tell you. That bellhop won't be seeing my ta-ta's again anytime soon, I'll say that much!"

"*Again,* Neen? What do you mean by *again*?" I say in a half laugh, absolutely dying to hear the story.

"It's not what you think, Okay. He came by to deliver some French onion soup and a baguette to me after you sent me packing yesterday. After setting it down he just stood there. He hovered over me without saying a word. I was so hungry I started devouring the soup and just thought he would go on his way. He didn't, Port, he stood there, silently. I finally realized he was waiting for a tip and my usual tip to not eat yellow snow would clearly be lost on him because I don't think they get much of that around here. I had no change on me, but he was like a vulture! I had to give him something for the road, so I did the first thing that came to mind; lifted my shirt for a full ten seconds and by the time I had lowered it down so that I could see again he was gone."

She hangs her head in embarrassment, which is quite uncharacteristic for Nina. After a moment she jerks her head up as if it were attached to a string and gasps. "Port! You don't think that my little ta-ta display is the reason we're getting downgraded, do you?"

"Not a chance, Neen. The day was bound to come when we would be sent to the room we paid for."

Although I half believe my supportive words, I can't say that I fully disbelieve the possibility that Nina's teats have landed us in lower-end accommodations. "Come on, girl. Get your ta-tas dressed and your stuff packed. We've only got twenty-five minutes now."

By ten a.m., Nina and I have managed to chuck all our belongings in random bags with absolutely no consideration for what belongs to who and we are standing as frumpy as can be awaiting our new room key in the lobby.

The bellhop is avoiding Nina's gaze, or perhaps her chest at all cost and is simply engaging me in the directions for finding our new room.

He's not even going to lead the way? This really is a downgrade.

We reach the room and I swing the door open to find a shoebox sized space with two twin beds that have been positioned so to only be separated by the space needed to wedge a one foot by one foot end table snuggly in place. I wince and hear Nina behind me whimper.

"Back to reality, Neen! Welcome to the Paris that we can *truly* afford."

"Babe, shut it. I can't bear it. I'm jumping in that bed that's been constructed for a small child and conking out in hopes that *this* is a dream and I'll wake in a few hours to be back to our previous reality. Step aside, sweets." Nina nudges past and drops on the twin nearest the doorway, nestles into the tightly tucked sheets and I hear her snoring within minutes.

All right, so this is a bit of a crap way to start the day but it can only get better from here. Guillaume, Michele, a true Parisian fashion show, how could anything go wrong from here on in?

It only takes me about thirty-three minutes to determine that it can. Things can go horribly wrong and they do, beginning with yet another *"thud! thud! thud!"* on our hotel room door at exactly 11:07 a.m. Nina is still sawing the metaphorical log and doesn't even flinch at the sound. I, on the other hand, am startled to the point of drawing a line on my eye from eyelid to hair line as opposed to keeping the eyeliner solely on the eye where it belongs.

"Sheeesh!" I bellow, then quickly slap my hand over my mouth for fear that I may have woken Nina. She squirms a bit but fails to open her eyes, then continues on with her heavy, slumber induced breathing. Rushing for the door, I catch my knee so hard on the corner of one of the tiny bedframes that I crumple to the floor in pain. I manage to keep my reaction to the pain at a minimal level and simply silent scream while clenching at my injured limb.

"Thud! thud! thud!"

The knocking continues. *What in god's name is so damn important that it can't be told to me by the room telephone? Damn bellhop!*

I reach the door and with more aggression than intended fling it open so hard that it swings right around to hit the interior wall, but feel little remorse as I see none other than the same bellhop who demanded us to leave our luxury suite, for this bathroom cubicle of a room, where I bump myself with every movement I make.

"What do you want?" I say with a harsh tone to perfectly match the aggression of the door swing.

"Mademoiselle, a letter, it has come for you and I have been instructed to bring it directly to you with haste." The bellhop says this in such a formal and respectful tone that the remorse of the harsh words, door swing and possible hotel room damage is finally felt. I grab the letter between my fingers and the negativity lifts slightly. My heart skips a beat in anticipation of yet another letter from Guillaume.

He's such a sweetheart. He's probably writing me to tell how excited he is to see me tonight at the show. I bet he'll have more roses waiting for me when I arrive!

I politely thank the bellhop and then rip open the envelope as quickly as I can, unfold the note and see writing that does not resemble the writing of the other letters, given me by Guillaume, at all.

To Ms. Portia Delaney,

It has come to my attention that you have decided to make use of something belonging to me and me alone. I do not share. What I earn, I keep and will make miserable any other who tries to make this belonging hers when it is my own blood, sweat and tears that have made it so worthy and valuable. You are an insignificant piece of dust who has now become stuck in my eye. I will flush you out as I flush pieces of excrement down the toilet. Be warned to keep your distance from what is mine. Paris is my city, fashion is my world. Do NOT attempt to enter it.

With most serious regards,

Liv Pickard

I stare at the words while gripping the paper tightly within my sweaty palms. I re-read the letter over and over until my vision becomes blurred and my head feels cloudy. I feel as if my body is absolutely frozen and I want to laugh at the ridiculousness of this woman but the light-heartedness which I would love to view this circumstance with is being hijacked by a chill that keeps running up my spine upon reading and re-reading the words *"You are an insignificant piece of dust"* and *"Be warned"*.

It's clear that the "belonging" she is referring to is none other than Guillaume. He's the one and only "item" that would cause this jackal of a woman to threaten me over. If this is true and he is in some serious relationship with Liv, I'll be devastated and utterly mortified at myself for thinking that *he* would ever choose "an insignificant piece of dust" such as *me* over a powerful and successful figure of the fashion world such as *her.*

I sit on the corner of my twin- sized bed and bury my head in my hands. The insecurities of my past all of a sudden wash over me and before I know it tears of sadness and fear are running down my face. I'm contemplating avoiding Michele's show altogether, running from it all and simply returning to my safe and reliable life.

It's not so bad really. I make a decent living, get to wear pyjama style clothing through the entirety of the work day, get to have evenings and weekends free. It's actually alright and I...I...

Oh, who am I kidding? I would rather eat the excrement flushed down Liv's toilet than return to my simple life I have come here to begin to leave behind. Whether Guillaume has fooled me into believing that I have found a prominent and special place in his heart, or not, Michele Gagnon's opinion of me must be my primary reason to get my butt to that show tonight. Fashion will be *my* world, whether Guillaume chooses to be a part of it or chooses that absolute freak show of a woman as a companion instead. She can most certainly be prepared for me to inhabit *her* world, one way or the other.

The remainder of the morning and early afternoon, the euphoric excitement I initially felt about the day is replaced with a steadfast aggression; a need to succeed no matter who I have in my corner.

I'm no piece of dust, and no man's second option. This is my day to shine and I will not tuck tail and run.

Nina finally joined me in welcoming the day at half past one and by then I had managed to grab my morning espresso, read the updates on Michele Gagnon's website about his new line that I would be styling and popped into the hotel salon for a little extra pizzazz in my previously lifeless mane. I'm on a mission to make this not only my first appearance as a couture stylist, but also the finest it can be.

The two of us, by two p.m., have our makeup done for the show and are selecting our final ensembles to make our grand appearance in. Nina had made her selection easily after the in- room fashion show she put on for me. The yellow leather jacket over sheer Ralph Lauren blouse paired with a sheik and snuggly fitting charcoal pencil skirt is the dead ringer and I told her so without hesitation.

I've chosen an outfit that screams, "Watch out fashion world (and Liv Pickard)! Portia's here and she's here to stay!"

I emerge from the Porta-Potty style bathroom, spinning and pirouetting towards Nina who is hunched at the end of the bed adjusting her Mary Janes. She doesn't see me coming initially but the whoosh of air I'm sure she feels as I come barrelling towards her tickles her senses and she lifts her head as I arrive just under her nose. The expression on her face is all I need to see in order to be convinced that *this* is the outfit for my debut.

"Oh la la, mon *chérie*! Tu es Magnifique!" Nina says giving a little kiss into the air to follow.

"Well done, Neen! You've been picking up a little bit of Parisian speak on this trip!" I reply trying not to maintain all attention on me and how damn gorgeous I look. I am a total stunner though. It has to be said!

"Portia Delaney, you look like you should be on the cover of one of those big time fashion mags you'll soon be styling for!" She remains completely fixated on me and proceeds to accost me by running her hands all over the crinoline and layers of my couture masterpiece. I catch a glimpse of myself in the mirror and admit that I would want to have my way with me too. The emerald green fit and flare gown is so flattering to my bust and waistline with the scooped neckline and the corset style bodice, I look like I'm straight out of *Vanity Fair*, the novel, not the magazine. My hair is now piled in ringlets on my head and bedazzled with pearls. My exposed neck is adorned with a rose gold chain, elegant yet understated with a tiny pearl encased diamond dangling from its end. I've finished this ancient-made-new again look off with my BCBG stilettos and an ear-to-ear fuchsia pink smile.

"Nina, Let's get this," I say while maintaining my plastered grin. Euphoria has gripped me once again.

"Babe, you're going to knock 'em dead. They won't even know what's coming for them." Nina says.

Her saying this reminds me of the unfortunate and disheartening situation that may accompany the evening and the jargon that Nina's spewing starts to take on a whole new meaning to me.

Knock 'em dead? I just might have to in a state of self-defence against the crazy Liv Pickard. God I hope she's not there.

It's crossed my mind to make Nina aware of the letter I received while she was sucking all of the oxygen out of the room in a deep sleep, but I just couldn't see how it would appease the situation any. Knowing Nina, she'd march right up to Liv and rip her extensions clear out of her hair without a second thought, if I enlightened her to the situation. I decide to keep the recent events to myself and carry on in my determination to use success as my weapon of choice.

The early afternoon breezes past and after a quick bite at our best-loved café, most certainly not due to the service although the rigid man seems to be warming to us a bit, we jaunt down the cobblestone towards the hotel taxi stand; my emerald green fit and flare "duds" getting the much wanted and needed attention I expected all the while as we strut it out.

By half past five, Nina and I have arrived at Carrousel du Louvre and I, in true Portia form, feel as though I could vomit everywhere. I feel flushed and like I'm burning up; my head is fuzzy and filled with the usual thoughts my subconscious likes to attack me with at a moment when survival of the fittest instincts are necessary. I generally cave to them and become devoured by my own fear and insecurity.

Not this time! Vomit, if need be, and get over it, Portia.

The venue is sparkling with what appears to be waterfalls of white twinkle lights, pouring from all sides. As I peer up through the triangular shaped glass roof, dusk is setting in and the faint appearance of stars in the sky are peeking through to become the natural backdrop of this fateful event. Suddenly, Michele Gagnon catches my eye. He's no longer the casually-garbed character I met yesterday; he has traded in his T-shirt and ripped jeans for a three-piece suit with coat tails and a top hat to suit. My matching eighteenth century inspired ensemble and his choice of wear settles my nerves because it is clear that this night is truly meant to be. We're a dynamic duo, prepared to take on the catwalk.

Gagnon takes notice of me and swiftly walks towards me, his arms outstretched as he approaches.

"Portia! You are perfection; a true complement to my collection and the season." He wraps me in his affectionate embrace and I can't help wanting to pat myself on the back for taking the time to learn about his new line.

"Come, come. I will show you around the location and then we will begin to make the most magnificent show. You will be my behind-the-scenes-star."

We amble through the venue where I see all the stark white seats set in stringent rows, so orderly and perfect awaiting Paris' who's who of fashion. My stomach does a little flip and I take a deep breath to inhale the calmness of the space at this moment. We continue through to the backstage area and I am completely taken aback by the scene. "Calmness" is definitely not the word to describe it. Models are scurrying all over the place, half dressed with rollers in their hair. Hair and makeup stylists are applying powder and hairspray with such thoroughness that there is a cloud caused by the mixture of beautifying products hovering over the whole area. At this moment I see only female models and begin to wonder at what point I will be able to see Guillaume.

I'm thrust out of this train of thought as Michele takes my hand and rushes me into a curtained off area, just next to the runway. An overwhelming sensation at what I behold consumes me. Before me stands what I would equate to be on par with the holy grail of a runway stylist's career. Three full walls of the most lavish jewellery are glimmering and shimmering like the stars above. Diamonds, emeralds and pearls as far as the eye can see; gold, brushed silver, rose gold, and every type of additional gem stone one could possibly fathom embedded in the necklaces, bracelets and rings from which I will be selecting.

This is a dream; I'm living a truly magnificent dream.

I casually turn to Michele and say, "It will do. I can work with this."

"Very well, very well. Please come this way now, Portia."

He takes my hand once more to lead me through to a coupled sectioned off area and am once again dumbstruck at yet another wall of every form of heel in every hue imaginable. Each pair is set on its own showcase with the associated designer's name stitched into a fabric insignia. Manolo Blahnik, Gucci, Prada, Dolce and Gabbana, Coach, Louis Vuitton, Michael Kors, and loads more surrounding me and calling to me. They almost have voices that say *Pick us, Portia, pick us. We'll make it together. You make me the star of the show, we'll do the same.*

Michele brushes my shoulder and glances at me in concern as I must have an unnecessarily awestruck expression on my face at this point. Talking shoes? How could I not?

"Mademoiselle, you are prepared for the task ahead?" he asks in a soothing tone.

"I am, Michele. I was born ready for this. I'm just taking it all in."

"You will be wondrous, Portia. I have every confidence in you."

I see the separating curtain rustle and a figure of a woman silhouetted on the other side.

"Portia, you remain here and make yourself familiar with the items. Here's the list of designs, their order to be walked on the catwalk and the sizes of the models who will display them. Study the photographs carefully, choose wisely and be confident." He smiles and walks through to the other side, leaving me alone in my dream world.

I stand for a moment feeling exhilarated and more than prepared for the task ahead. I then begin pulling pieces to match each look and have just about made my way through half of the list of Michele's designs when the mysterious silhouetted figure which appeared before, returns, only this time continues to pass through the curtain. My blood runs cold when I see that it is none other than Liv Pickard, garbed entirely in a black feathered knee length, strapless, sweetheart dress, with a matching feather adorned fascinator nestled on her bristly looking extensions.

She marches towards me and I try my hardest to remain steadfast in my assigned role without letting this freak show bring me down. My hands soon give me away as I notice the papers in my hand begin to flutter at ultra-speed.

"You did not get my letter, I see. I demanded that you stay out of my world. Yet you are here! Do you not speak English? I wrote that letter in the North American language but you foolish, foolish girl, are clearly stupid!"

A morsel of her spit hits me on the cheek. I wipe it in disgust. Now I'm irritated. A fire is rising within me.

Who does this woman think she is?

I take a step towards her. "I understood your letter perfectly, but I'm afraid that I don't respond well to, nor do I make a point of following orders from, a crazy person. Please keep your saliva to yourself and in your filthy mouth. I don't want to catch your crazy."

She gasps and her fierce expression becomes even more intense. I see her chest heaving and her brows furrow. I brace myself for the worst.

"I'm *not* crazy! You and all others who say that are wrong. It was *you* who put that idea in Guillaume's head, wasn't it? He was infatuated with *me*, loved me endlessly and then *you* pried our love apart! I knew it!"

"Oh my, you are so out of your head," I say aghast at her speculations. "I'd never even heard of you until after Guillaume and I began our involvement a short time ago. You must have shown him your crazy all by yourself. I *knew* this had to do with Guillaume. You're a nightmare."

"No, no! I don't believe you! He sent you to me as a mocking act! You are in this together. You're trying to enter my world and take it over and take my love away. You are a horrible person and I know Guillaume will choose me again. You will not remain in my world," she says as she pokes me hard in the sternum.

"Well, you see that curtain? That curtain represents the border that YOU have crossed into MY world at the moment. Now get the hell out of it you lunatic," I say as I march towards her with such fierceness that she backs up by at least five steps where I draw the curtain in her face. "Don't make me call security on your behind. Be crazy elsewhere." I hear her let out a low growl and see her heels beneath the curtain stomp away.

What an absolute nutcase. Guillaume better explain himself. I did not sign up for this.

I continue to arrange the accessories and place them neatly next to each model tag and design sketch to which it will be delegated. My heart is beating with an alarming force and as I try to calm myself by breathing deeply and focusing on the task literally at hand, I feel it beat more and more ferociously.

Is this a reaction to the event and my role in it? Is it because of the visitation from that wretched woman? Maybe it's because of my uncertainties stirred up about Guillaume.

I quickly come to the conclusion that this horrible sensation is a result of all three. Overwhelming angst, excitement and nervousness is the mixture of emotions pulsing through this heart of mine and my flight as opposed to fight inclination is urging me to run. I slink to the floor, head in hands scattering the designs of Michele Gagnon as I fall. I'm surrounded by his greatness, and the opportunity he has offered me and I'm frozen, in....in fear. Once again fear is winning.

I feel immobile and stuck to the hard tiled floor beneath me. I feel destitute. A rustle once more, the curtains flutter and my heart jumps into my throat as the pounding continues, in fear that it is once again Liv, back for another round. The curtains part, opening this claustrophobic circumstance to the open air of the venue and the sight before me halts the pounding, settles my nerves and calms my anxieties. Dressed in a recognizable ensemble, straight from Michele's sketches, stands Guillaume with a concerned yet warm expression on his face

"*Chérie*, I sought you out for a lengthy time here. I am so happy to find you but not with such sadness on your face. What is it beautiful Portia? What has happened?" he inquires as he approaches me and crouches down by my side with his hands to my face. "Tell me, love, what is troubling you? Michele adores you and your designs. Surely this must make your heart leap and bring a smile."

I raise my eyes to meet his compassionate gaze. "Guillaume, it has been a mixture of reasons that I feel troubled at this moment. Michele is remarkable and so accepting of me. He's giving me this amazing chance even though I'm a nobody. It's making me quite nervous and fearful that he'll be disappointed with me and regret his choice. I know I can do this, but my insecurities are taking over."

"Portia, is it just this? That is silly to think so little of yourself. You *are* remarkable. I know this is a moment Michele will never regret." He continues to stroke my hair and my face then draws me in to an embrace.

"Guillaume, there's more. You sent me to a woman named Liv Pickard. She…well she has been awful toward me. Tell me, Guillaume…" I pause and am silent for a moment worried to mention her and question him for fear that I may offend him and lose him indefinitely.

"Portia, continue, please. I have a horrible feeling I know what it is you may say next."

"Guillaume, is she…is Liv Pickard… your, well your significant other? Are you two in a committed relationship?" I ask meekly. "She was horrible to me at her office and then sent a threatening letter to my hotel room and then moments before you walked in here, she was here trying to make sure I keep my distance from you. I didn't ask for this, Guillaume. I don't want to be involved in some dramatic love triangle in which I play the lesser role. It's not my style and I deserve better." I feel his embrace become more intense.

"Portia, Liv and I did have a romance. It was a furious love that involved much trouble. She has not let go and I am moving on while attempting to remain compassionate to her feelings. How she discovered our involvement I'm unaware, but please believe when I say that a relationship with her is not something I wish to revisit. I sent you to her thinking that Liv had no understanding of you and me and our connection. When discussing Liv's abilities in the fashion world, I have only good to say about her, but clearly personal emotions were ignited in her upon discovering our bond. For this, I apologize. Please accept and give me a chance to right this all. I have missed you so much these past days, after such an incredible experience in the country."

I hang my head and then nestle against his broad chest enjoying every fleeting moment spent in his warm embrace. He kisses my head and the insecurities begin to wash away. A mere moment later I glance at my watch and am alarmed by the time.

"Guillaume! The show is starting in thirty minutes! I have more accessories to pull and must meet the remaining models. Good luck, handsome! I can't wait to see you strut your stuff!"

"Portia, I wish you the best luck of all. Enjoy the moment, *chérie*. My thoughts will be on you and my heart will beat for you the entire show until I can reunite with you afterwards. You will be flawless tonight my girl." He speaks with such sweetness that I hang on his words as he turns and strides out of the space.

I collect all the scattered design sketches and model photographs with sizes attached to continue matching the remaining looks with appropriate accessories. I finally complete the process and make my way out of the accessories section feeling re-energized and untouchable after Guillaume's pep talk. He is a magician for my soul.

I bustle towards the styling area where I can see from a distance, models lining up for final pinning sessions, hair primping and makeup touch-ups. I feel as though everything is happening in slow motion as I'm making my way, head held high toward my post for the show; hair piled high to match. A blonde curly haired model brushes by me and I teeter on my stilettos but maintain my composure and then suddenly Guillaume is in full view, so debonair and dashing. I ensure my walk is as sexy and confident as can be as I saunter toward him, but suddenly the unimaginable happens. I pause in my stride, gasp, and clench my chest in shock.

No! it can't be! Not after his words to me.
My heart sinks. I'm undone.

CHAPTER 18

I want to…I want to rip that feather fascinator off her head and stomp on it like I were a two year old. Then I want to pluck every feather out of that ridiculous dress she is gallivanting around in and cram them up her nose.

Who does she think she is, pouncing on Guillaume like that right in plain sight for all to see?

She's got her arms wrapped fully around him and one leg up in the air while clearly shoving her tongue into his mouth. And him! He's hardly even fighting her off. He's almost enjoying it. I want to vomit, I want to cry, I want to run! But I won't, I can't.

Michele approaches me looking a bit frazzled and I try my best to put what I have just witnessed to the back of my mind.

"Portia," Michele says in a bit of a distressed manner. "You have the selections complete?"

"Yes, Michele, they're all laid out and prepared. I'm just on my way to arrange them for the models. Each look is dazzling with your fascinating designs," I say with full truth behind the words. His designs are beyond spectacular.

"Perfection!" he replies, looking relieved and more assured that the show will be a success. "I will see you in moments once all models are ready for their initial walk."

He clenches my hands between his own. "Thank you, Portia. Be brave and be your wonderful self! This will be a magnificent show."

I smile in appreciation of his kind words but the smile is subdued as I see Guillaume and Liv continuing in their exchange. Models are ducking around them to get to their positions before the show and the two are oblivious. Liv is now whispering something in Guillaume's ear and I see a hand working its way down his chest to his inner thigh.

Bitch! I can't take it anymore!

I march straight towards the entangled pair with a fierce vigor. The pulsing I now feel is like a whole new beast. I'm out for blood. My emerald green gown swooshes with every step; my stilettos clickity- clacking along the tiled floor all the while. I march…march…march right up to them but do not halt. I've become like a ferocious bull and am charging with all that I have after seeing the colour red in the form of Liv's hands on Guillaume's junk.

I lumber heavily towards the intertwined duo. As I find myself adjacent with the unaware pair, my shoulder catches Liv precisely in the right location to send her wobbling over on her heels and tumbling to the ground. I stride right on by, dismissing her devilish gaze and Guillaume's surprised look of guilt and sorrow at the scene I have witnessed. I carry on, quite pleased with the take down.

In one smooth motion, requiring no words at all, I've dismantled a toxic interaction, cued the models to line up in their appropriate order and distributed all accessories to each. I am primed, they are primed and Liv is livid. She remains skulking in the curtains of the runway wings. I place my headset over my ears and whisper, "Code intruder. Looks like a chicken. Totally draped in black feathers with a pissed look on her face."

I see two gentlemen entirely cloaked in black, lead Liv out of the backstage area. She's giving them a piece of her mind from what I can tell. French is spewing from her mouth and the two men are not even taking notice.

What a wretch!

I see Michele cue the music and kiss the gold cross hanging around his neck.

Here we go!

I begin cuing the girls one at a time to make their way in sequential order onto the runway, leaving a fifteen second pause between each one. I hear gasps of delight come from the crowd and see flashes of light filtering and reflecting off the triangular glassed roof above.

They love it! They love the designs! How could they not?

The stylist for the male models has the men arranged and ready to walk for the second half of the show on the opposite side of the stage. I see Guillaume leading the crew and I look away knowing that my focus must be on distributing the accessories for the second round of looks. I'm rushing to collect accessories, dress models to distribute the new round of accessories and shoes. I fling designs while continuing to cue the girls for their next walk.

I turn to grasp a forgotten necklace and pivot back to see Guillaume surprisingly in front of me with an apologetic expression. I divert my eyes and push on with the task, which seems to be passing at a lightning-fast pace. All the while the thoughts *"How could he? How could I have been so stupid?"* are racing through my head. But the thoughts that are clearly lined with a fiery and passionate rage are causing me to be so on point with the rhythm of the show that I almost feel I should thank the horrible pair for angering me in such a manner. I'm giving commands like a drill sergeant would and pulling garments like I designed them myself. The intensity of my emotions is allowing me to ensure this show goes off without a hitch and I feel amazing.

"Zu are bery good at dis!" a dark haired Russian bombshell whispers as I complete adjusting her in her second look.

"Zank zu," I reply without thinking and with little control over the incorrect words that have left my mouth. Luckily, the gorgeous gal does not seem to mind and simply continues on toward the wing for her second walk down the catwalk. Flushed cheeks and all, I carry on doing what I apparently do well.

The music changes as the men begin their first walk down the runway and I recognize the song as being Nine Inch Nails' song about inappropriate animal loving. The beat is as intense as the emotions coursing through my body. I see Guillaume take to the stage and walk with such confident and smoldering movements that I almost am able to forget what I so recently witnessed.

I glance out to the crowd and see Liv in the front row glaring at him the way I had the day he strutted by me at Café Lateral. Her animalistic gaze and facial expression goes perfectly with the words to the song. She looks as though she is about to leap on him from the crowd and have her way with him like she were an animal from the wild.

He poses for a moment at the runway's end then makes his way back, maintaining focus and not giving Liv any notice. While he arrives at the wings and passes by me his hand gently grazes my own. I feel a shudder of excitement but quickly supress it as the hurtful scene from moments ago replays in my mind.

The remainder of the show continues to be flawless and dazzling, peppered with dabs of edgy music as well as romantic orchestral compositions. The women's second round on the runway is even more majestic than the first with garments breezing and flowing romantically, complemented by the music, wonderfully displaying the elegance of the designs that are draped over the bevelled beauties whom I had the pleasure of bevelling.

For the first time I'm truly able to take in the scene before me. My styling task is complete, this is the female models' final walk and I simply relax and gaze in amazement at the magic of the moment. So much beauty, both natural and created, all intermingling under the starlit sky that is blanketing the City of Light. I'm awestruck. Then as quickly as the show began, it is over. My heart rate slows and I exhale for what seems like the first time since the show began.

Michele comes bursting through the curtain next to me, lifts me off the floor and spins me around,

"It was magnificent, Portia! Incroyable, you talented girl! You made my show as perfect as it could have been. Come with me. Come on the stage and we will bow at once. Your name will be mentioned, I will make sure of it!"

Almost immediately Michele's name is announced by the show's emcee. He grabs my hand and rushes me on to the stage. We make our way to the middle of the runway and bow in unison after which Michele races to the side of the emcee, whispers something to the perplexed man and scurries back to me just in time for the emcee to add, "Merci beaucoup to the debut styling of Ms. Portia Delaney. Michele speaks highly of you."

I curtsy gracefully feeling numb all over while the crowd, who have already risen to their feet in honour of Michele's masterpieces, continue their applause for little old me. Tears form in my eyes and a single tear finds its way down my left cheek. I have chills, but not the kind experienced at the sight of Liv's letter to me, the kind you feel when your joy is so overwhelming that it can't be expressed, like fireworks bouncing around inside that can't find an escape. In short it is the most exhilarating and welcomed feeling I have ever experienced.

I take in the scene once more and scan the crowd attempting to make eye contact and smile in appreciation to individual spectators. As I'm doing so, I notice an empty chair.

Liv's chair. She's left!

Initially pleased at the realization I feel perfect and exit the runway with Michele, totally confident and proud of my efforts. Shortly after I step behind the scenes worry sets in.

Did Liv leave the audience to seek out Guillaume once more? Are they continuing their grope-fest elsewhere?

Once again my heart plummets, but I carry on putting on a celebratory face, sharing champagne with the models and Michele. I chug the glass of champagne that is poured for me so fast that a few of the models and stylists pause in their own enjoyment of the delicious bubbly and stare at me aghast. I smile and continue to indulge in a chocolate covered strawberry that comes by on a platter. Savouring every juicy morsel I turn to request a champagne refill and stop in my tracks. Guillaume has joined the celebration, Liv - free and focused on me and me alone. A single lily is in his left hand that I assume he plucked from the venue's entranceway bouquet. Our eyes meet and he gives a "what do you say? Forgiven?" gesture.

I'm not sure how to feel. Excitement has returned but is muddled with panic.

Can I trust him? I barely even know him and even so it's like I've been on an emotional rollercoaster continually.

I breathe deeply and walk toward him, heart guarded and ready to bail on this whole confusing mess of a romance but open to possibilities.

"Portia, you were wonderful. Your composure after viewing the interaction between Liv and I, it was very professional of you. I know the charge you put on us was deserved and I am very sorry."

"Guillaume," I say in a sombre tone, one that doesn't at all reflect the emotion I was feeling moments earlier. "I'm so confused by you. How is it that just before I saw Liv with her tongue down your throat you were telling me that you and her were not an item in any way and that I was the one you wanted?"

"Portia, it is a very tricky and confusing circumstance, one that I'm not sure you will understand as a new comer to the fashion industry. Liv, she is very powerful on the Parisian fashion scene. Angering her could bring my career to a full stop. I've tried to break ties with her once before and she made it her duty to contact all clients she knew so to take work from me. My manager finally pleaded with me to attempt to make some sort of companionship work with Liv to avoid being shunned by the industry here. I am trapped."

As he says this he truly has a tortured expression on his face and I suddenly feel sorry for him.

"Guillaume, that's outrageous! She can't manipulate you like that! Doesn't she realize how desperate that makes her look?"

"What Liv wants, she gets. Once she has set her mind on something and is determined it is hers she digs in her fingernails and does not remove them. She pounced on me, Portia. That is what you saw. In front of other well- known models and designers, I am being forced to appear as though I am still her lover and companion. I do not have the choice to break this façade. It makes me feel as sick as can be, but I do not know what other possibilities I have. I must play the game or lose all I've worked for."

I grab his face with both hands and stare in to his sparkling greyish-blue eyes, feeling his stubble under my fingertips. "You have to stand up for your-self, Guillaume. Whatever may be will be, but this is not right. Your manager, the one you confided to me is like a mother to you, she needs to let you free from this if she is as caring as you said."

He looks away and sighs. I get the sense he believes me to be too naïve to be giving advice about the predicament. He leans in and kisses me softly on the cheek. "Portia, I will try." He breaks away from our embrace and disap-pears through the curtained wing.

Have I upset him? Have I made everything worse by insisting? Maybe I've been too pushy. I don't want to lose him! Shit! Who am I to give him advice after what he's been dealing with?

I decide to search for him to apologize and to…to…shut my big yapper. As I'm making my way out of the wings to the open space of the venue, Michele gently grabs my arm.

"Portia! I'm to give a toast. You cannot leave me yet. *You* will be honoured in the speech. Stay, please."

My heart is telling me to find Guillaume, to chase him and embrace him; to let him know I understand. My head is telling me to put my career first and do all I can to demonstrate to Michele that I am beyond grateful for this opportunity.

I stay. My stomach churns throughout the entirety of the speech when I should be beaming and bursting with pride and excitement. Michele's words are those of adoration and appreciation for me. I hear each compliment he pays me but the true message is not fully resonating as I'm completely focused on finding Guillaume as soon as Michele's speech ends. The only thought running through my mind is *"Stop talking! Finish this endless speech already!"* while my face has a pasted appreciative yet insincere smile across it.

"...and she will one day, in the near future be a celebrated designer and stylist who I will be assisting to repay her for such tremendous efforts this evening."

Is he done? Oh thank god he is!

I continue smiling and nod appreciatively to the applauding models and stylists. I race up to Michele and give him a hug to reinforce my appreciation.

"Portia, we will be in touch. I will find you in Toronto one day and we shall collaborate. Be well, dear girl." He kisses me gingerly on both cheeks. I blush and nod in agreement.

Once the chatter and champagne consuming continues I subtly back my way out of the wings and find myself in the auditorium. Rows and rows of empty chairs peer back at me. Emptiness is consuming me at the thought of losing Guillaume to that witch, Liv. I walk as quickly as can be through the entirety of the venue. I finally find myself in the lobby next to the elegant bouquet from which Guillaume stole a lily for me. He never did give it to me though in his disgruntlement caused by our recent conversation. I pluck one for myself, imagining he gave it to me. I inhale its fragrance and sit on a stone bench nearby.

A moment of reflection brings me to the realization that I've seen the good and the bad of this industry in one fell swoop. Are people really so manipulative and conniving that they will cause suffering of others to get what they feel they deserve? I don't think I can or will ever be like that and I never want to be under the thumb of such a powerful nutcase as Liv Pickard. I breathe deeply and decide to be naïve and vulnerable in the moment.

My journey will be different. Surely, there are more good and honest people than terrible, carnivorous gluttons such as Liv, in this world.

I stand to search for Nina, as I realize she's been waiting for me since the show's end, and hear footsteps behind me. I turn to see Guillaume and feel a fully sincere smile take over my face. I run to him and pull him into an embrace, which is more than reciprocated as I sense that he intends to do more than embrace. He kisses me passionately on the lips. I break away panting slightly, trying to catch my breath due to the pure passion of the moment.

"Guillaume, I'm so sorry about trying to tell you what to do. I had no right. It must be a horribly difficult situation, but I know that moments like what I saw before the show are not frequent between you two. I know you care about me and want to be with me. She has to let go." I revisit the stubble on his face, running my fingertips along his jaw line to his enticing lips. He kisses them as I do so.

"Portia, it is not that easy. Liv and I, we have a history. She is a strong woman and one who can be sharp and forceful, yet I still care for her all the same. My heart is with you, but a piece must remain with Liv. In honesty, Liv does not always have to force my affection out of me. I do care for her. The feelings I have for you are fresh and passionate. I wish to explore you more and explore our connection more, but Liv will remain in my life indefinitely."

"But, but….earlier you told me you were just playing the game and this was all forced on you! I don't understand, Guillaume. Please don't toy with my emotions anymore. I don't know how things are done here in France, but back home love triangles don't ever work, and I don't want to be a part of one if it means sharing you with that horrible woman. She threatened me, Guillaume! If you cared for me at all, you wouldn't allow that. You would turn on her for attacking me like that."

"I'm sorry for the manner she chose to show her feelings. She is a passionate woman…"

"You mean psychotic!"

"Portia, please, this is not easy. Please do not become upset with me. The relationship with Liv has been forced in a way, but over time, I have grown to appreciate her strength and have found a glimmer of the good in her."

I'm shaking and my head is spinning. I don't know what to believe from this man anymore. My eyes avoid his gaze upon me. I divert my view to the floor then the stars above. They sparkle and shimmer over us and I wish I could see the fate of Guillaume and I and love in them, but a haze is forming.

I look back to Guillaume's chest and take it in for what I feel may be the final time, my gaze creeps back up toward his handsome face but is halted by the sight of a fresh red lipstick stain on his white collared shirt; a stain which matches Liv's choice of lip colour for the evening's event perfectly, a stain that was not there during our discussion backstage mere minutes ago. I'm all too aware of our fate in that moment.

"Guillaume, I can't... I can't be a part of this. No matter what the relationship is with Liv and you, I can't share you. I won't. It will break my heart. This is already breaking my heart and if Liv won't let go, then I need to." My eyes fill with tears. "Guillaume, the call, the call you received in the morning at Auxerre, that was her, wasn't it? She was ordering you back to her like you're her servant. Don't you see! She has your nuts in a vise and you're letting her squeeze and squeeze until you have no balls left. Is that what you want? No balls! I have to...I'm going. I wish you well, Guillaume, but I can't be anything to you if I can't be everything to you. I deserve to be someone's everything. Thank you for what we had."

I race away tripping slightly and then recovering my footing as I go. My humiliation is over shadowed by pure disdain for the entire situation. Disdain for Liv, a sudden disdain even for Guillaume, the man whom twenty-four hours ago I thought could do me no wrong, no harm. Disdain for my stupidity in believing I could be his everything.

On my way to the exit of the venue I catch sight of Liv Pickard chatting with Michele and I see a white lily in her left hand. The tears stream down my face. I let the lily in my grasp slip to the floor and I continue running before she spots me and sees that she has won.

CHAPTER 19

I arrive back to the hotel after walking aimlessly for well over twenty blocks through the hauntingly familiar streets, which I had walked days earlier in a wonderfully blissful state; happiness that was caused by the seeming perfection of things. Guillaume was a part of that perfect picture, but how mere hours can change a person's perception of their circumstance.

Nina rushes to me, seeing I'm distressed and tear stained. I'm sure mascara is streaming down my face along with the tears that have been trickling on and off like a faucet as the evening's events replay in my mind.

"Port! Babe, what's the matter? You were fabulous tonight! I gave you a standing O when the emcee announced your name! Are you upset that the magical moment is over? You know you'll have loads more nights like tonight. Don't be daft!"

I sputter words out as sobs intermittently interrupt my syntax to make what I'm saying like some sort of broken English. "It's…n…ot th….at, Neeeeeeeen."

I bawl at the thought of saying Guillaume's name. "It's….Guil…..auuuuuume."

His name lingers on my tongue and I can't bare it. I rush into the bathroom, an unwillingness to say anything more. I figure if I keep the nightmare circumstance locked up inside, perhaps I'll wake tomorrow to find that it truly is only that, a meaningless nightmare that never took place.

Nina knocks lightly on the door, but I don't respond. I turn on the tap and douse my mascara- covered face with cold water and stare at myself in the mirror. I look like the bride of Frankenstein's monster in this turn of the nineteenth century style gown and my hair in ringlets set against this mess of a melted off face. I wipe away at it, but my mind cannot turn off the frustration and confusion brought on by the evening, and the wiping turns into forceful scrubbing to match the mix of emotions rising within me. Anger, frustration, irritation, and pain swirl around inside; the tears continue, as do the sobs.

"Portia, please let me in. You don't have to talk, or tell me a thing. Just let me in, doll," Nina says calmly from the other side of the door. I turn to unlatch the door and let her in. She immediately envelopes me in a Nina style hug. I must say it is exactly what I need. We sink down to the floor and Nina continues to cradle me in her arms. She strokes my hair the way my mom used to when I had a bad day at school.

"Port," Nina finally says. "You were incredible tonight. I'm so proud to be your friend and to be able to say that I know you. I'm not just saying that either. I actually turned to random people around me in the crowd and screeched 'I know her! She's my best friend!' I don't think any of those stuffy Parisians had a clue about what I was saying, but I didn't care. I'd shout how proud I am of you from the rooftops! From the top of the Eiffel Tower even! Let's go there, I mean it! I'll prove it! I will scale that structure that to me resembles a man's erection and shout your name from the tip!"

My sobs finally calm down to casual spastic deep breaths while I crack a smile at the thought of Nina yelling that she knows me to a crowd of posh Parisians.

"Thanks Neen," I manage to say. She kisses my forehead and helps me off the bathroom floor. "Why did you lee….ave before I fini….shed backstage?" I ask, realizing that I was only about fifteen minutes back there.

"Oh, sweets, I'm so sorry that I forgot to tell you! You remember I said Victoria Lewis wanted to continue life-coaching sessions even while I'm here? Well, we had planned a session for two p.m. Toronto time, so when the show concluded at seven thirty, I had to motor my ass out of there to get back in time. Vicky is a stickler for time so if I want to keep her as a client, I have to be punctual."

"Ah, well I think she could be as good for you as you are for her. Lord knows you need a kick in the pants to get your butt to places on time! So if it takes

Victoria Lewis to get you to be on punctual for once, then I suppose she can't be all bad," I reply, finally feeling pulled together and like myself again.

"She's a great woman, Port. I can't share details because of the whole 'client confidentiality' thing," she says with air quotes. "But I can say that she's having a shit time in her marriage. She's miserable and heartbroken and I've finally gotten her to a place of vulnerability. I see the scared and insecure little girl beneath the seemingly cold, business-like exterior."

"I'm sure she has a kind heart, and that is so sad to hear. You're probably doing her a world of good, Neen. I know that even if you and I weren't friends, and I didn't get your therapeutic talks for free, I'd pay you to coach me too," I say.

"Well, I may have to start charging you at the rate things are going!" She nudges me and I laugh heartily. "I'm not going to pry about what happened, babe, but you better tell me soon or I'll have to track down Guillaume myself and get it out of him one way or another." She winks and then heads to begin organizing her belongings. "We have to leave quite early tomorrow. They need us out by ten a.m. so let's pack tonight so then we're ready to head to meet Stefan like you had suggested. I can be the kind-hearted person who lets him down easy."

"Neen, I think I'll pass. You go on your own. You don't need me there and I'd be too sad. The café is where I met Guillaume and I had planned for him to be with me now and on through the morning tomorrow. I'll hang around here until you get back."

With that I unbutton my gown, slip it off and heave it over the dressing table that is wedged into the corner. I slip on my nightie and slink under my covers in hopes that a good sleep will renew my view on my current situation.

My sleep is riddled with harassing dreams much like those, which disturbed my sleep on the evening before departing for this city. Visions of Liv smiling mischievously from the ground waving at me as I take flight back across the Atlantic, followed by Guillaume's sudden appearance by her side, arm around her and joining in on waving me good-bye, has me wake with a sullen and heavy heart.

The morning sunshine peaks through our sliver sized hotel room window and I hear a rustling coming from the bathroom.

Nina's up before me! Maybe she really is smitten with Stefan after all if she's this eager to get to him.

I roll onto my side and flashbacks of last night's events flood my mind. I can't shake the disappointment of it all, but manage to get to my feet to begin to gather my things for our lengthy trip home.

I arrange my couture outfit from last night neatly in the bottom of my suitcase and begin folding and placing other items on top as I find them around the miniature room. I grab the black cocktail dress I wore on the evening I spent with Guillaume in Auxerre, and I feel a hot sensation accost my eyes; tears are forming. I bring it to my nose and breathe it in. Guillaume's scent is still present in the fabric.

"Port, doll! You're up! Are you sure you don't want to join me this morning? I'm heading out in a few and will roll my case down to the lobby on my way so no need to worry about looking after things if you're not, but I wish you would change your mind," Nina says sweetly.

"Thanks, Neen. I'm going to take things easy this morning. After I pack I may go for a walk in the area, but nothing more. I'll see you back here at noon," I reply in a quiet and sombre tone.

"Ciao, babe. Turn that frown upside down by the time I get back, ya hear?"

I smile attempting to display an intention to comply with her request. The door closes behind her and I'm left to my thoughts and raw emotions.

By half past nine I'm in the lobby after throwing on jeans and a T-shirt along with my navy Keds. The bellhop approaches me to ask to assist in watching my bags while I enjoy the city for one last time. I nod and hand over my case, but don't venture out. Instead, I find myself at the lobby bar where I order a mimosa and a cheese plate as I plan to drown my sorrows in pricey champagne and fatty Gouda. I remember the nerves that overtook me while I sat in this very spot awaiting Guillaume to sweep me away to the countryside.

It seems like a lifetime ago.

"Ahem, mademoiselle. Is it you, this Portia Delaney?" a gentleman asks who appears to be part of the wait staff. He is holding a package in his arms with an envelope attached.

"Yes, I'm Portia Delaney," I say with nervousness behind each word.

"For you, mademoiselle. It was sent by courier a moment ago." The gentleman passes the package to me. I'm unsure what to do. My first feeling is that it's from Guillaume, an apology, a change of heart perhaps.

But what if it's from Liv, a threatening letter with some harmful device like a
bomb or something? I get the feeling she's capable of anything; even taking out a
hotel and everything surrounding it within a ten-kilometre radius.

Knowing I will have to open it at some point, I close my eyes tightly and rip
away at the wrapping while listening carefully for any kind of ticking sound.
Once I feel the unwrapped weighted object in my grasp, I open my eyes to see
what looks like a piece of stone work resembling the same ancient form of stone
I walked along in the streets of Auxerre, while arm in arm with Guillaume.
The heart that has been carved into the centre solidifies my assumption as fact.
Tears spring from my eyes and suddenly I'm a sniffling mess. The bartender
rushes to grab me a tissue and gazes at me sympathetically.

"Madame, you will be alright. Whatever it is that has made you so *malheu-*
reuse, all gets better with the passing of time. Smile, *beau fille*. You are a beauty
in my eyes."

The tears stream more steadily at the sound of these sweet words and I
begin tearing open the letter that has come with the parcel. Through flooded
eyes, I read what may be the final words I ever receive from Guillaume.

Beautiful Portia,

I am so very regretful for the manner in which we left one
another last night. It saddened me beyond words when you left
after saying you would not be a part of my life anymore. You to
me are a glorious ray of light streaming into my life, offering such
promise, happiness and excitement. I intended us to become so
much more. My ties to Liv hold me back. They restrain me I am
aware, yet it is a vicious cycle of knowing her power in this indus-
try and a feeling of security when I have her on my good side. An
appreciation has grown in me for her and I cannot upheave this
companionship with her yet, my love.

I have removed this stone from the walkway we treaded upon
when finding our way to the restaurant in Auxerre. I brought
it back to Paris with me after our night together with all inten-
tion to give it to you last evening. That night in Auxerre is one
I will never forget. A part of my heart will for always remain in

that place, with you. Now a symbol of my heart will go with you wherever you may find yourself. Be well my love. I will think of you evermore.

Yours always,

Guillaume

I hold the stone to my chest and am reminded of the moments lying in his arms listening to the sound of his heart against me. This cold slab is so meaningful yet not even close to representing the pure warmth, which I felt and was comforted by. As much as I should be a wreck of tears after reading such a touching letter, something disallows the tears to continue. This stone, this note, this romantic gesture, it's all simply symbolic without the substance and as I think back on interactions with Guillaume over the past week, I begin to believe that it all lacked substance and was mere show; pretentiousness at its best.

He should be here! Not this cold stone or the roses he had sent... He should have chased after me last night if it was so heart wrenching for him!

In a passionate moment brought on by indescribable clarity, I take the note between my fingers and rip it to bits. I dump it, along with his earlier letter to me, in the bar's garbage.

"If he wants to leave me final words, he can tell them to me in person himself! That Liv really has ripped his balls clean off!" I say aloud, forgetting where I am and that there are a number of couples and families trying to enjoy a lovely Parisian breakfast. Who needs ball talk with their croissant? I peer around and mouth the words *I'm sorry.* A few people look at me in disgust and then continue their morning rendezvous.

I stay at the bar for the entirety of the morning, downing mimosas as if they were a miracle cure for a broken heart, so by the time Nina finds me at noon, I am... well...I think I'm extremely intoxicated. If a slight breeze were to be blowing in that lobby bar, it would most certainly have sent me tumbling off that bar stool which I now feel an absolute connection with, and it's not just because my butt cheeks have likely left a permanent imprint in the leather cushion.

"Port, here you are! Are you ready for our trek back to the Americas?" Nina asks exuberantly.

After accidentally and uninhibitedly letting a foul sounding burp fly, I manage to say, "Ah, Neenster! You do not know the fun you have missed hurrrr. Francois and I have had a wonderful morning together! Haven't we Frank?" I turn to the perplexed bartender and he nods compliantly. "But Neen! What'd'ya mean *trek*? No way in hell I'm walking back to Toronto!"

She smiles and giggles emphatically. "Oh bloody hell, Port, let's get going. I suppose I have to be the responsible one for this trip home."

She grabs my arm and helps me off the stool ensuring that my tab is settled. I turn to take one more look at the stone slab sent by Guillaume, but the thoughts *I deserve more than a piece of rock as a memento*, creep through my mind. I turn on the gift leaving it for the bartender to dispose of. It would actually make a nice decorative hanging, to be honest. Surely they can make use of it somewhere in the hotel. And with that I turn my back on Guillaume and I march on to becoming more than an option to somebody out there.

The journey home is uneventful. We make our flight with loads of time and I sleep the majority of it, attempting to avoid feeling the onset of hangover. When we finally land in Toronto the symptoms are full blown and I am forced to down three tablets to relieve the pounding headache the countless champagne drinks have brought on. Reality is setting in; the fairy tale is over.

Did it even happen?

I dread the thought of working on Monday, but at least it's only Thursday. With a few days to recover and regain composure, by re-evaluating my plan of attack to transition out of my office job into the fashion world, I will feel primed to face all on dreaded Monday.

I enter the condo at half past four in the afternoon. The concrete walls almost speak to me as if excited for my return like they haven't seen activity in days. Everything is so orderly and neat, almost exactly as it was when I left last Saturday. I peer into Minnie's room, which is *House and Home*, photo shoot neat.

Minnie hardly ever makes her bed in the morning on a weekday. She mustn't be staying here much. Leonard has really won her heart like a champ! God I'm a great matchmaker! I better get mentioned in the wedding toast.

I can hear it now:

"Portia Delaney, you're the reason that this flower in full blossom has found her way into my once romantically barren life. By becoming a roadblock to my bicycle, thereby flipping me onto the hood of a nearby car where I lay with a fractured leg, you somehow paved the way to true love. Thank you from the bottom of my heart."

I sigh at the thought and continue puttering around and settling back into life in Toronto. I gasp realizing I never turned my phone back on when we landed and probably have about a zillion messages waiting for me. Okay maybe that's an overstatement, but I'm sure I have at least one or two. I cross my fingers in hopes of a few message notifications popping up on my phone. I swear, when that automated female voice tells me "You have no new messages" it's like she's mocking me, as if she's saying, "You absolute loser. Please get some friends."

I'm adamant that this will not be the case today.

I switch the phone on and wait…and wait….and wait….

Maybe it's just taking a while to find service.

At last I see the missed call with 1 new voicemail notification pop up and a beaming smile arises on my face. That is until I see that the one call missed is from work.

Uggggg! They know I've been in Paris! What in the world do they want?

I press the check voicemail button and type the code in somewhat fiercely then listen for the verdict and intention behind the call. I recognize the voice in the message immediately.

"Portia, hi there. It's Tricia from work. I know you're not back until Thursday, but there is an urgent matter that the doctors must discuss with you as soon as you return. Please come by the office Friday morning at eight-thirty, thank you."

I have to go in to speak with the doctors before working hours? An urgent matter? What can be so urgent that I have to pry my jet lagged butt out of my bed to go in to the clinic? It must be for a raise or something wonderful, like that. I have put in a hearty effort over the two weeks I've worked!

I alleviate any stress by believing this positive nonsense and spend the remainder of the afternoon and evening lounging on the sofa, watching numerous chick flicks and resting off this hang over that is plaguing me. By nine p.m. I am zonked and there's still no sign of Minnie. I complete my ablutions and keep my mind from racing about all things from Guillaume to tomorrow's meeting by popping a sleeping pill and a half that Nina gave me when we parted earlier in the day at the point she could sense I may have a sleepless night otherwise.

A pill and a half. I'm pretty sure that's the dosage she suggested,

Before I can complete that thought I've sunk in to a dream state. Dreams of lollipops and Ferris wheels, roller-skating derbies and pumpkin pie, Gucci shoes, and mimosa's fill my mind.

◇◇◇◇◇◇◇◇

I awake the following morning with a mouth so dry it feels like it's filled with cotton balls and woodchips. I glance at the time and am horrified at the sight I find.

8:15! I'll never make it in time! Damn sleeping pills made me oversleep and all the dreams that they caused have me craving all types of pie!

Quite breathless a mere thirty-five minutes later, I arrive at the office at ten minutes to nine and sigh hoping this meeting was one that they can wrap up in the time remaining. Breezing into the office, I attempt to present myself as a new woman, a woman who is now well travelled and cultured after a five day stay in Europe. I keep my glasses on, feigning that it is to demonstrate my stylishness, and not to cover the dark circles beneath my eyes.

"Hi,Tricia. I got your message and I'm sorry I'm a bit late. Jet lag is a bit of a bitch, you know! She gets me every time I return from exotic far off locales," I say nonchalantly with a slight chuckle to follow.

"Right, well, Portia, the doctors are waiting in the boardroom. Just go down the hall, all the way to the end then take the door on the left," Tricia replies in an awkward manner involving very little eye contact, which is extremely uncharacteristic for her.

"Oh, well, okay...thanks, Tricia. It's great to see you!" I say and head down the seemingly endless corridor towards the unknown. I rap lightly on the solid door that has *boardroom* inscribed on it and gulp down the fear that is threatening to take me over.

"Come in," a deep, booming voice sounds from the other side. I recognize it as Doctor Brown's voice and immediately have a flashback to being caught with my trousers down around my ankles, exposed fully for Brown to see. I cringe at the thought of having to sit across a boardroom table from him.

What if he brings that instance up? Oh god how humiliating it would be!

"Portia, is that you out there? Please come in. The doctors have all been waiting a lengthy time."

I grasp the handle and make my way in bashfully. "I'm here. It is me and I'm so very sorry for the tardiness. You see, I just flew in from Paris last night and am entirely jet lagged. I overslept and, well, that's my story and I'm sticking to it!" I add a smile and an awkward snort-laugh, which seems to make the entire panel of doctors quite uncomfortable. I take in the sight of the disgruntled looking row of elderly men, garbed in white and I seat myself sheepishly across from them.

"Ms. Delaney, please take off those sunglasses as there is not even a natural ray of light in here," Dr. Langley says.

I comply and prepare myself for what I'm beginning to think will be an out and out scolding.

"Let's make this quick, shall we? You've taken up enough of our time as it is!" Dr. Brown begins.

Oh god, this can't be good if they're letting him start off this whole inquisition style meet and greet.

I'm completely out of luck as Brown immediately begins to ramble on roughly, spit flying as he pronounces each syllable precisely.

"It has come to our attention that not only did you jet off to Paris after only your second week of work here at Hopewell Clinic, but in your place you found a woman, who is extremely proficient and fastidious in her work, but whom you also felt needed a head-to-toe makeover, on us! Here in my hands I have an invoice from one Lusk Salon for a Ms. Clarice Dawson for over four hundred dollars!"

Shit!

"Now, I'm not any regular at the spa, Ms. Delaney, but that amount for any number of treatments on our dime is four hundred dollars too much! We are not in the business of makeovers and escapades to European cities. We are in the business of medicine and healthcare, and being here in Toronto is how we maintain our clinic. We need a manager who is reliable and takes her job seriously. *You*, Ms. Delaney, quite evidently do not. The woman you hired to replace you *temporarily* has picked up your slack impeccably. For this reason, we are relieving you of your duties at Hopewell Clinic and we wish you good luck in your future endeavours."

And therein lies the not so subtle and oh so familiar medical office employer message set to the tune of, 'Portia, get the hell out.' I suppose it could have been worse. I mean, they could have asked me to pay the amount for the treatments. These stiffs do have hearts, I suppose.

"And, Ms. Delaney, we will be sure to deduct the spa amount from your final pay. That will be all."

Damn it!

CHAPTER 28

After the unfortunate incident that resulted in me getting the boot from a job that, although I was dreading returning to, I was kind of starting to view with a positive light as a temporary money maker, my spirits are low.

I amble back out to the waiting area of the clinic where Tricia, who clearly was made aware of the intention of the doctors, is ready with sympathetic words.

"Portia, I know this must be a shock to you after a week away. It was probably an incredible trip and this must be beyond shitty for you to return to. Please, can we meet at some point today for a coffee and a chat? I hate to see you go so suddenly, and I really do want to share some details with you that may be of interest. I take my morning coffee break in an hour or so. You could do some therapeutic shopping and then meet me next door for a latte around ten fifteen?"

Tricia talks in a sweet tone, but part of me feels uncertain as to whether I can take her kindness sincerely. She may even be the one behind all of this. She did, after all, despise me for jetting off on my trip to Paris.

I bet she orchestrated this whole thing.

"Fine, Tricia. That sounds just swell. There are some matters I wish to discuss with you as well, so ten fifteen sharp will work for me. The sooner I have clarity and answers on the issue, the better."

"Perfect! I'll see you then. Please don't let this ruin your morning or your day. We'll have a good chat."

I smile tensely and make my way out of the office after pausing to reflect as to whether or not I have any belongings to remove from my space.

Nope. Not a one!

As usual, when I'm sacked or I quit a job, there's not one item at my work space that belongs to me, and I suddenly see that I'm the office temp, and no long- term medical office manager at all.

On to the next one.

My hour spent waiting and reflecting causes me to boil over in frustration at all that has gone on since my final full day in Paris. Yes, the trip was an incredible experience; yes, the city and the culture was all I had envisioned in my mind, and, yes, I made leaps and bounds by making my name known and heard for a moment at a celebrity designer's show, but the truly magnificent moments are so fettered with the stubbornly looming cloud of heartbreak so that the whole trip is left on my mind as being one of disappointment. Even the happiness and successes of that trip feel temporary.

I'm a temp at life itself. I'm the disappointment, not the trip.

I'm feeling so down in the dumps that I'm hopelessly aware there's only one individual who has the charisma and blunt nature to get me out of this sudden spiral downwards. I take out my phone seeing that it's only half past nine. I sit on a nearby park bench as the bustling swarms of suits scatter along the sidewalks of the business district in the city's downtown core.

They're all permanent in their goals and careers. Look at me, caught up in a mess of indecision and uncertainty.

I scroll to Dr. Lola's name, breathe deeply, and hit the "call button.

"Helloooo? Dr. Lola Richardson here! How can I help you?" Never one to let a call go to an assistant, Dr. Lola is the ever-reliable therapist that I'm so happy to have found.

"Oh, hi, hi there, Dr. Lola. It's me, Portia. I…"

"Portia Delaney! I've missed that lovely voice of yours since our early morning chat on Saturday! I've thought about you each and every day. How did everything go? Please tell me you did as I said and immersed yourself in the culture and the fashion, and…" She pauses and changes her tone to one of a sultry and seductive nature. "The men."

After giggling slightly, I take a moment and reflect on her questions realizing that if I measured the success of my trip based on what Dr. Lola's instructions were for me then I did indeed have one triumph of an adventure.

"Well, I have to say that I accomplished all you instructed me to, Dr. Lola. I started a new line of sketches and met a celebrity designer who allowed me to assist at his show. I met the celebrity designer through an incredibly handsome gentleman who swept me off my feet but then sure enough broke my heart in the end. So, all in all, it was a success in your books."

"Marvellous! That's what I like to hear! I'll let you tell me about how incredible the sex was with this Parisian lover of yours later on, but do tell about what impact the connections with this said designer now has on you igniting your career in fashion." She sounds as if she's bursting with enthusiasm.

"Well, that's…that's the problem. See, I thought I could continue at my medical office job and slowly transition over to my dream job as opportunities present themselves, but I had a rude awakening this morning, Doc. I've been canned. I'm miserable! Even though I despised that career, I need the paycheck. To make matters worse, I'm so distraught and wishing the romance in Paris never took place so that he isn't on my mind so much because it's driving me crazy!"

"Portia, first of all, never regret the experience of taking on a lover for a short time, because although you may feel sad and destitute now, at one precise moment he was exactly who and what you needed. Now on to discussing the professional progress you have most certainly made. Remember what that woman, you know, the one you are determined to believe is so horrible, had said to you about making it in fashion?" Dr. Lola says, her voice quiet with a compassionate tone.

"You mean Victoria Lewis, the woman who didn't give me the time of day to speak my case before she chided me and walked out? Meeting her was my dream and she pretty well squashed my hopes before they were even substantial."

"I suppose that's her, yes! That woman, whether you see it or not, has given you the best possible advice. It's sometimes through the people we have an initial feeling of intimidation and resentment towards that we receive the most pertinent words for our success. You just need to want to hear the words."

"I'm not quite sure what you mean," I say, attempting to recall any useful advice given before Victoria hurriedly left Nina and me.

"If I'm remembering correctly," Dr. Lola says, "the morning you called me before you took off on your trip, you were distraught about your meeting with Ms. Lewis because she left you rashly, but you did pass on a piece of advice she gave. You told me Victoria said 'in order to make it in fashion you have to live and breathe fashion.' So, Portia, I see it as a blessing in disguise that you've been shaken out of your current job, because it has absolutely nothing to do with fashion! You must spread your wings and flutter to the tree top of your desire."

I consider Dr. Lola's words and recall Victoria's utterings to me as I hung on them in a trance brought on by fear and inspiration.

"I do…I do recall it now. Thank you, Dr. Lola, for reminding me of the critical words Victoria shared. It just all seems so daunting to live and breathe fashion without the stability of a paying job."

"But, Portia, I know you all too well. You, my girl, need to have a rug ripped out from under you before you take action. I believe that if you remained at that job, you'd get in to your monotonous routine, complain of already having too much to take care of, and you'd *never* get on with the career you truly are meant for! Face it, Portia, sometimes you get in your own way and are your own worst enemy."

She continues with an increasingly fiery tone. "Forget Victoria Lewis or whoever else you may think is out to get you. It is *you* who is treading on your own dreams by fearfully returning to your life of routine! Stability isn't all it's cracked up to be. Look at me! I'm completely unstable and loving life! Join me in instability, my dear. I assure you that you'll blossom and flourish. You simply must create, create, create!"

For a moment I'm astounded at the harsh words, Dr. Lola has fired at me, but then I'm reminded that it *is* Dr. Lola and subtlety or indirectness is *definitely* not her approach. I suppose that's why I trust her so fully. She tells it like it is, a motherly Nina I can depend on no matter how unstable she claims to be.

"I'm just, well, I'm scared, Dr. Lola. I'm afraid I won't be able to pay the bills and support myself before I make it."

"There's no shame in admitting that, but I'm sure a wonderful woman such as yourself has an infinite number of helpful friends and family members that will see you through your transition. We're not islands, Portia. Today you need support and they will help you, just as you will help them in times of need."

I consider her words thoughtfully, ticking through the list of people in my life and mentally crossing out the ones that aren't candidates to be my life system for a time like this. The list is far from "infinite". I mentally discard of Angelica because the unstable should not support the unstable and I'm quite sure we would end up in full out cat fights daily if I was forced to be put up by her.

I decide against appealing to Mom and Dad, as they've been entirely too generous to the point that I would be ridden with guilt, not to mention just the idea of crawling back to them for more after they believed me to be a true success in my "selected" medical office career would be a horrendous blow. I'm already viewed as the awkward and odd duck at family gatherings. Throwing in unemployed spinster to that is highly undesirable.

So that leaves Nina and Charlie, but Charlie has been completely M.I.A. due to her rage towards me, which never makes for a healthy support system. Nina has been so wonderful already and she is flourishing incredibly in her new career that I fear I would be a distraction.

I couldn't do that to her.

I conclude that my less than infinite list of supporters has dwindled to zero. I hang my head at the depressing reality.

Pride is such a bitch. I have to let her win.

"Well, Dr. Lola, you've certainly been of help this morning," I say in a rather disheartened tone. "I'll keep you updated and let you know how I'm getting on."

"Wonderful, Portia, please do. Over the next few days also do me a favor," she says eager to assign me my bit of homework for the week ahead. "Let your guard down. Be vulnerable to those who truly do care. Put your pride aside and you will climb farther and faster than you can imagine."

"Will do. Thanks, Dr. Lola. You're one talented lunatic," I say appreciatively with a light laugh. She chuckles heartily on the other end of the line. "Adios, Portia." And then I hear a click.

Glancing down at my watch I see that it is just past ten. I rise from the bench to begin my walk back to the coffee shop to meet Tricia for the purpose of hashing out the "real reasons" for my termination.

Striding into Starbucks I find Tricia already there still wearing that sympathetic smile which makes me want to scream, turn, and stomp right out. I don't. I humour her need to console me, and take a seat opposite her in the bustling and rather noisy space.

"Portia, thank you so much for joining me!" Tricia has to practically yell in order to make her voice heard over the enthusiastic table of businessmen to our left.

God they look so happy and successful. It makes me sick.

"Hi, Tricia. I really had nothing else to do seeing as I'm unemployed," I say in a very negative and sarcastic tone.

"Portia, you have to know that I had *nothing* to do with your termination. I truly didn't. Clarice is wonderful, but I consider you to be remarkable because although you may not be quite as organized and meticulous as her, at least you brought a sense of normalcy to the workplace. You did the job and I felt like you were a person I could chat with outside of the clinic. It's been so hard through the years, not having someone to identify with and shoot the shit with."

She sounds dismayed and quite sincere. As she rambles, my perspective of her and the cause of my termination is altered a touch.

"Well, I had no idea you felt that way, Tricia. I thought you despised me, especially when I flew off to Paris," I say much more pleasantly than my previous contribution to the conversation.

"I did despise you because I was jealous and knew that the office would go back to being the robotic factory riddled with some annoying Ms. Markson drama. My fear was that I would want to pluck out my own eyeballs due to boredom and monotony and then where would that leave me? Eyeless, lonely, and despising my job."

I'm stunned at Tricia's confession.

She was envious of me? But she always seems so pulled together and like her social and home life must be fab.

"Well, jeepers, Tricia, I had no idea you felt that way. You always seemed so posh and demure, like you had too much excitement already to have time for little old me. I could always use another gal pal, though. Look, we'll stay in touch and give each other a heads up about any social events and *you* must promise to keep me up to date on the soap opera type shenanigans that continue on at Hopewell," I say much more enthusiastically with a beaming smile.

"Oh! About that…so there's something you must know. It may come as a shock to you, because I absolutely detest him now, but dreadful Darryl and

I used to be an item." Tricia looks as though she could vomit when she says "Darryl" and "item" in the same sentence. I'm dumbstruck at the new bit of juicy info.

"He was awful to me, though, because that horrendous woman, Penelope, who already had a hotter than hot fiancé to call her own, weaseled her way between us. I know he was consorting and carrying on with her the entire time."

"Why is this Penelope chick so hung up on a greasy loser like Darryl? I don't get it!" I reply.

"They go way back, Portia, to high school, even. They were king and queen at the prom, voted most likely to marry and blah…blah. She's the type who wants to live up to that expectation of all who declared it. She lives in the past and has her hooks in him. Unfortunately, for her, Dr. Langley never approved of her way. He's always communicated with me, even when Darryl and I were dating, that he would never allow them to be together indefinitely. He says she's manipulative and a money grubber."

"But Darryl has nothing!" I chime in.

"Yes, but Dr. Langley does! That woman, Penelope, has freak accident attached to full inheritance, written all over her. She's wicked and Langley knows it. Unfortunately, the blow up and the surmounting tension that the relationship is causing between Darryl and his dad, has Dr. Langley wanting to patch things up and do whatever necessary to make things less dramatic between them. Langley is now letting Darryl call the shots, and Darryl's taking full advantage."

She pauses and looks down at the table while running her finger along her cup nervously. She looks up seemingly hesitant and a bit timidly about the next words she has to say, "Portia, it's because of Darryl that you were terminated so quickly. He used his dad's sudden understanding nature as a means to make you go away. Langley complied and did all he could to dig up alternative reasons for your termination, which included the spa treatment and the trip to Paris."

"Oh that dirt-ball! He disgusts me! I knew that incident in his office infuriated him. I can't believe I ever thought he would make a suitable candidate to get me out of my dating dry spell!"

"I can't believe I *actually* dated him for two years!"

"Good lord, Tricia! Two years? What in god's name made you stick around so long? He must be a star in bed or something."

"No, not at all! To be honest, it was the convenience of having him around. Little effort was needed. We would ignore each other at work all day and then join up in the lobby and head off together. I suppose it also had to do with my competitive nature. Once I understood the hold Penelope had on him, it made me want to win and I set out to dig in just as hard as she was. I came to my senses when she and I had a full blow out with hair pulling, pinching, and clawing right in the middle of the office reception area." She winces at the memory and then gives a bashful half smile.

I'm in stiches laughing by this point and can't believe that such a lazy low life has inspired such heated passion in two gorgeous and accomplished women.

"Tricia, this little chat has brightened my day, and if I can take anything away from the experience, it will most certainly be the image of you and Penelope hauling off on each other, while those dinosaur-like doctors watched in horror."

As I'm sipping away on the frothy latte Tricia kindly ordered me, while still grinning like a fool at Tricia's latest gossip, a text comes through on my phone. *Charlie!* The text is short and concise, yet makes my heart leap with excitement: *Port, I miss you. Let's get together soon. Xo*

The moment I thought would never come, the moment I believed was simply wishful thinking at its most desperate and insane, has arrived. My expression has clearly changed from one of a light-hearted nature to one of pure joy and triumph because Tricia immediately inquires as to what the message is about.

"Oh, Tricia, it's silly, but a friend I thought I'd lost forever, just let me know we're all good. Forgiveness is a wonderful thing, especially when it's coming from someone who means the world to you," I say.

"That is certainly wonderful news. I'm so happy to hear that. Listen, I have to jet back to the office and sure wish you were coming too but add me to your contacts, and don't leave me out of any of your girl time chats and events! I want to see more of you." Tricia lists off her digits as I type them into my rather light contact list.

"Toodles, Tricia! I'll be in touch, you can bet your teeny tiny booty on it," I add, feeling comfortable using casual speak now that we're not colleagues in a stingy tight-assed clinic.

Tricia looks a bit taken aback at my boisterous and complimentary comment but then seems quite pleased with herself as she struts out of the shop quite obviously clenching her butt while she does so. I carry on attempting to formulate the perfect text to send Charlie in response to her pleasant message to me.

Charlie, I'm so happy to hear from you…

No…

Hey, Charlie! I'm ecstatic to hear from you! I've been waiting for this moment for weeks now and have missed you so much. Please, whenever you're free today, let's chat. Call me, girlfriend!

Hardly one minute passes and I hear the sweet sound of Patsy Cline's "*Crazy*" sounding from my phone. Yes, that's the ring I selected for Charlie because she's been an absolute nut job lately. I don't think she would appreciate the humour, though.

Note to self: Change Charlie's ring tone before seeing her in person.

"Charlie!" I bellow having not a care in the world as to whose coffee talk I am disturbing around me. "How are you? What have you been up to? Fill me in, sweetheart."

"Hi, Portia," Charlie says in a less energetic tone, yet for Charlie enthusiasm is saved for pinball and Golden Tee, so I smile to myself just at the thought that we're even chatting. "I've missed you. I want to hear all about what you and the girls have been up to as well. Can we do drinks tonight?"

"Of course! I know I'm free, and I'll get in touch with Neen and Ange to see if they can swing it."

"Perfect, thanks, Portia. Let me know where is best for you all to meet and when. Can't wait to see you," she replies, still in a monotone voice, but the words used are out of character for Charlie so I can tell she's on the upswing.

"Great, Charlie! Will do!" I sign off and then clench my phone feeling like my mood of the day has definitely turned a corner.

Job loss to friend reclaim. Perfect!

"You would not believe how awful she was to me! She treated me like some low-life nobody when I am the head of the *Angelica* design team. Who does she think she is, Nina? Really? She's ruined me not only to my company, but to the whole industry!"

"Ange, you know this day would come. Whether it was Victoria Lewis who ratted you out, or your very own design team, it doesn't matter. What you were doing was wrong. You had to be stopped. Claiming you're the lead designer when you don't have the first clue as to how to assemble a bag, or much less work a sewing machine to begin with, is downright immoral."

Have I said how much I adore Nina for her curtness?

I'm fully smiling on the inside. Angelica looks as though her head is about to pop clear off. She is absolutely steaming mad at Nina. I'm ready to duck and cover in case she blows.

The waiter of the restaurant approaches to take our order, and I do all I can to signal that it's best if he returns later. I wave my hands in a "no, no, no... don't come any closer" manner, but he doesn't clue in.

Poor sap doesn't know what he's in for.

"Ladies, are we ready to order?" he says cheerfully.

"Leave us be!" Angelica hollers. "Nina, you put Victoria up to this, didn't you? And you, little miss fashion wannabe over there, looking all innocent." She spits her words in my direction. "I bet you had a part in this all too! I knew when I rejected your proposal about working for me you'd be irate. I didn't think you'd stoop this low. You were both always jealous and believe it when I say you haven't heard the last of me. I'll come back from this and be even more successful than prissy Victoria Lewis herself!"

I clear my throat in attempt to hide a giggle. Nina has been stirring her tea nonchalantly as if she's not even paying attention to one word the entire time Angelica has been on her rant which I'm sure has enraged her even more."

"Does that mean you ladies need a few minutes longer?" the now timid waiter asks.

"Of course it does, you idiot! Leave us be!" Angelica yells and then continues on her rampage. "You can both say good bye to my friendship, because I don't maintain a relationship with backstabbing bitches like yourselves. You wait and see, both of you will end up penniless nobodies and I will make it bigger than I already had. Take your two bit ideas and your hopeless dreams and stay out of my life!"

She rises from the table, still burning red, grabs her bag, accidentally, or perhaps intentionally, toppling her chair over while she goes. The waiter ducks into an empty booth to clear the path for her to trudge by. Then as if the whole ordeal never occurred, there is pleasant quiet, and witty, easy conversation to follow.

Nina and I arranged to meet in order to hear the real details of Angelica's recent hardships. When Angelica appealed to Nina to cease in her life coaching of Victoria Lewis, Nina wouldn't budge, which transformed Angelica into a raving lunatic.

"Well, I'm sure pleased she took her misery out of here before Charlie arrived!" Nina remarks. "That woman needs a getaway, maybe even a forever getaway so she keeps her crazy rage away from you and me."

"I feel sorry for her, but then I remember how horribly dismissive she was of me and my talent as a designer and all of a sudden I couldn't care less. She really did make her own bed and, although I may have lost a friend, I can't say I believe she really ever *was* a true friend to begin with."

"My feeling exactly, Port. And isn't it ironic that on the day Angelica high tails it out of our supportive circle, Charlie makes her way back in?" She pauses and glances at the door. "And speaking of the hotter than hot, Ms. Charlotte Channing herself, look who it is!"

"Charlie!" I welcome her warmly. "I'm so happy to see you, sweetheart. You look amazing!" And I wasn't just saying that. Her previously drab and dead looking hair was now glossy and lustrous, flowing beautifully into natural ringlets at its ends. A glow to her complexion and her sparkling clear eyes tell me she has come a long way from the screen- addicted homebody we had approached mere weeks earlier.

"Thanks, Portia. You're just saying that," Charlie says humbly and bashfully. "I do feel like a new person. I'm proud to say, and I know you two will like that I have not played one game, computer, casino or pool hall based, in over a week. I'm really trying to take a new direction in life."

"That's fab, babe!" Nina says. "What was it that finally kicked you in the ass? Was it our attempt at an intervention?"

"Not exactly," Charlie giggles slightly. "I mean, that whole intervention thing did get me thinking, as angry as I seemed, it was helpful and opened my eyes. Really, I guess it was when I went to take out twenty dollars to buy subway tokens and the machine heckled me with a message of 'insufficient funds.' I had no job, no savings, and couldn't even get around the city with ease, unless you consider hiking from Yorkdale to Dundas St. 'easy'."

"God no!" I respond. "So what did you do?"

"Even after I took him for all he was worth at the pool hall, Paulo took pity on me. He gave me a place to stay when I couldn't pay my rent anymore. I'm with him and his boyfriend in The Beach now, and even though I appreciate their kindness, I'm working like a fool to get a job somewhere so I can give them their space back. They've been so amazing to me though."

"Fantastic news, Charlie. I'm so happy to hear that," I remark.

"Paulo even took me to his stylist and paid for me to get my hair done for the first time in over a year! I feel like a new woman and really don't want to go back to being drab old Charlie."

"So, doll, you're saying you don't have work at the moment, is that right?" Nina asks.

"I'm working as hard as I can to find something. I've been on every job site and gone into all the businesses in The Beach trying to sell them on my skills, although customer service hasn't been my strong point in the past," she says and I give her a little wink in remembrance of the bowling alley gig shenanigans. "I feel there's something on the horizon. I'm even thinking about going back to school part time! Maybe I'll take design!"

"Perfect!" Nina says. "I'm asking, hon, because this past week I've recruited a handful of new clients at my life coaching centre, thanks to the referrals given by Victoria Lewis, and I can sense I'm going to need a hand in the office. It's simply reception type work, but I'll pay you a decent salary, and I know the hours would allow for you to take courses easily. So what do you say, will you assist me?"

"Nina, do you even have to ask? I'm in! Thank you so much. I won't let you down!" Charlie is bursting. I don't think I've ever witnessed such excitement in her.

"I know you won't, babe, as long as there's no more gaming bullshit that I have to put up with, you will make the perfect assistant to me. Start on Monday, nine a.m. sharp. I've leased an office on King and Church. I'll text the address and info."

"Amazing!" I say on the fate that has rekindled our true group of friends and given Charlie the break she needs. I can't help thinking of my own situation. This whole time I've kept my recent news to myself. It does sting to know Nina had an opening for an assistant and I missed my opportunity to communicate my need for the position, but I'm so happy for Charlie that I keep quiet and trust my break will come soon enough.

"I think this calls for a celebration! What do you girls think? Party at my place, tomorrow night. I'll send an e-invite out when I get home."

"Fabulous! Yes, that's such a fantastic idea, Port. Sort of a 'Charlie's back' soiree," Nina says enthusiastically.

"Well, you both know I'm not a fan of being the centre of attention, but, I guess I'll be all right with it just this once," Charlie says.

"Then it's on!" I announce. "Party at my place, eight thirty; Put on your dancing shoes and your party hats, ladies! It's going to be one for the books."

CHAPTER 21

"Port, you'll never guess the news I just came across! Go to *City Rhapsody's* online magazine and check out the main page!"

Nina has been calling me incessantly for a good hour. I attempted to ignore her and switched my phone to vibrate even, but the lunatic just wouldn't let up.

"Nina, this better be good. I was having such a fantastic morning sleep in. It's only nine a.m.!"

"Stop bloody complaining and just do what I'm telling you!" she replies in near hysteria.

I switch on my laptop and type *"City Rhapsody"* into the search engine. In seconds the main page pops up and in clear view is the heading *"Angelica Preedom left penniless pauper."*

"Oh my god is that?"

"Daniel? Yes, yes it is!" Nina almost sounds delighted, which is somewhat sick, but the same emotion is attempting to overtake me in the place of the emotions I should be feeling: concern and pity.

The accompanying pictures include a collage of Daniel escorting some modelesque looking woman, tall, blonde, enormous breasts, wearing clothing so tight that it almost looks as though they've been painted on. The descriptive captions include:

Trusted companion of Angelica Preedom romances super model on The Angelica Line's tab.

The article explaining the alarming photos unveil that Daniel, who had been given control over the company finances, had been skimming off the top for years in order to support his gambling addiction as well as his flame on the side, Ms. Perpetua Dryden.

> *Perpetua Dryden, an Irish born supermodel, is said to have met Daniel in Las Vegas two years ago, over a game of Black Jack. The two have been consorting and indulging in their habit together regularly, all on the dime of Angelica Preedom's formerly successful handbag line. It just keeps getting worse for Preedom. This news of her companion's infidelity and money grubbing comes mere days after her company had been ruined by the who's who of fashion, Ms. Victoria Lewis. Lewis alleged that Angelica was posing as a designer and becoming wealthy off the hardworking talented designers who worked on her handbags behind the scenes. These designers were supposedly not compensated more than minimum wage and were kept anonymous so Angelica could reap all of the benefits. Angelica herself, in the words of Ms. Lewis is 'an imposter with absolutely no design abilities of her own.' The Angelica Line is now a fractured mess.*

I sit in silence while reading the details listed and almost forget that I'm still on my call with Nina.

"Port! Did you see it? Did you read it? I knew that Daniel flake was good for nothing."

"Poor Angelica," I say. "I feel so badly for her, Neen. Sure, she's been a horrible friend and an enormous bitch lately, but she must be heartbroken and feeling so alone right now."

"I know. She's just so prickly though, that it's impossible to step in to comfort her. Maybe throw an invite to the party tonight her way and see if she bites. As long as that bite is left at home and she doesn't unleash her fury on me while I'm turning your living space into my own personal dance floor, I'd be happy with her being there."

Nina is one to make a dance floor wherever she's inspired to do so.

"I'll invite her, I guess. I just want the night to be about Charlie, so if Angelica shows up and starts raving about her own personal drama, I'm sending her packing," I respond.

"I'm with you on that. Charlie is our blossoming star of the evening. We'll make sure the whole night is for her. Listen, hon, I'm heading into the subway now, but have a good read and let me know if you find out any more juicy details. Also, I'll bring some treats for this evening. My *Baking with Nina* days did have some benefit!"

"I can't wait to sample some. See you tonight!" I say jovially and with urgency to get Nina off the phone so I can go back to perusing the alleged details about Angelica.

I spend another half hour clicking through the information on the Internet and find that the story has grown legs, making it to all the Toronto based magazines.

Poor Angelica.

I really do feel for her, and as I'm contemplating how broken-hearted she must feel and how blindsided she must have been from hearing the facts about her wretch of a boyfriend, my mind wanders and I begin to relive the heartbreak that overtook me on my final day in Paris. Regardless of how horrible Angelica has been lately, I feel compassionate and sympathetic for her situation all the same. Being made to feel second rate and like you're just not enough to a man you have such affection and attraction for can pretty well be equated to having your heart ripped full out of your chest and thrown down a garbage chute.

Memories and moments spent gazing into Guillaume's iridescent and welcoming eyes, being wrapped up in his embrace and feeling his hand around mine as we strolled through Auxerre are flooding my mind. Memories so sweet and dream-like yet so unquestionably painful to recall given the way things ended. He'd been perfection. My one hope is for Guillaume to encapsulate all that I believed him to be when we met on my first morning in Paris.

Could that good, kind and generous, concerned man, really be underneath the confusing mess that I was left with? No one is ever as good as they seem.

My mind wanders while I continue to peruse various online magazines for more *Angelica Line* news. As I'm scanning through the headlines, a subtitle roughly a quarter of the way down the page catches my eye: *The Best Way to Predict the Future is to Create it!*

I recall Dr. Lola's words, "Create, create, create!" and I'm all too aware that creating the perfect man is beyond my skill level, but there are numerous design ideas awaiting my creative action. I have no control over the circumstance that binds Guillaume to Liv, but I have the power to leave it all behind by doing what I was born for.

I head to the door, throw on a jean jacket over my T-shirt paired with joggers, stuff my feet into my Van sneakers, grab my bag and keys and rush out the door. But to where? Well, off to purchase some fabric for my designs, of course!

Enthusiasm has gripped me. I feel a confidence resurfacing as I recall a memory that has only a delightful place in my heart. That being the moment that Michele Gagnon admired my designs. I hold on to this recollection and head into the two-for-one fabric store on the corner of Dundas and Keele. The colours and vibrant prints that welcome me tickle my senses. I dive in and start swimming through the rolls of material truly feeling a surge of excitement and rebirth.

A woman in a flannel shirt, with her hair in a high ponytail, rushes to be of assistance and just as she gets near enough, I start pulling and piling fabric rolls in her arms until the stack is up to her chin.

"Will that be all?" she finally asks after I've placed a lovely zebra print atop the mountain.

"I believe so, yes," I say. "Throw in some thread, white and black, to the purchase. Thanks a bunch!"

I settle at the cash register, assist in bagging the yards of fabric, then grasp each sack in my hands and stride back to the condo feeling as though I've hit the jackpot.

Create, create, CREATE!

I spend the majority of the late morning and early afternoon turning the living space into my own personal work studio. Swatches of fabric are strewn about, my sketches are scattered strategically next to selected fabric I've decided on for each, and a single dress form is set, awaiting my pinning and pinching. The ancient sewing machine I've yanked out of the storage locker sits on my bedroom desk, which I've dragged out into the open space.

By the end of the afternoon I'm mesmerized by what I've accomplished. Fabric for three of my designs has been cut and pinned in a way that will result in three showstopper looks. I've also begun sewing two of the three. The looks are taking form, and I can imagine them coming to life, flowing and breezing down the runway and later down the city streets. My heart is racing and I almost want to continue on like this through the night, yet I'm well aware that the invites have gone out and the party will be happening shortly. Being the host means having some sort of party-like atmosphere set up so I tidy up by heaving everything into Minnie's room.

She's never here anyhow.

An hour later, the condo living space is spic and span, the bar is arranged with every essential alcohol in order to create a multitude of mixes; glasses are set out, cheeses, fruit and mini pastries are arranged just adjacent to these. I hop in the shower for a quick cleanse, and throw on my black ruffled cocktail dress; the same, which I wore when romanced by Guillaume. Memories harass me for a moment. I quickly brush them aside with a pass of a comb through my hair. 'Revelry' is the word of the night and Guillaume will not put a damper on the excitement I feel for Charlie and my accomplishments of the day.

I finish dressing and beautifying while going through the checklist in my mind of what I want to achieve and what I have achieved in preparation for the party.

Damn! The cake!

I had meant to attempt baking a cake, but with all the excitement of the day *that* clearly did not happen. I regroup and make a plan to head to the grocery store at the corner, garbed in my fanciest attire and all.

On my way through the lobby, I meet Randall head on. He enters with a tightened and tense expression.

"Hiya, Randall! It's been a while. How are you keeping?" I ask, but am all too aware of how he's been keeping. It's written all over his face that he has perhaps discovered the cheating ways of his fiancée.

"Oh, hi, Portia. Yes, I'm all right. You've been well?"

"I have! I'm just rushing out for a cake. I'm throwing a party for that friend of mine you met in the elevator the night I tried to intervene in her gaming antics. She's turned a corner so we thought we'd have a celebration. Hey, if you're not busy, you should pop by! I have a feeling that whatever you said to her in the elevator had some sort of impression on her."

Randall hesitates a moment and then I see a sudden warmth take over that previously deadened expression.

"I think I might. Where are you in the building again?" he asks seeming more cheerful.

"Eleven zero six. The party starts at eight thirty, but come by whenever you can! I'm so happy you'll pop by," I say. "Ciao! See you shortly." I race out the door and half strut half jog to the corner for what I hope turns out to be a decadent and aesthetically pleasing gateaux.

After begging the attendant in the grocery store bakery to write "New Year New Rear" on a selected vanilla bean cake, she finally obliges. She, however, holds firm and declines to use extra icing to mold two perfectly shaped butt cheeks in the centre. I suppose I understand her lack of enthusiasm to humour me in my request. She's old enough to be my mother, but so is Dr. Lola and I guarantee that Lola would be all over decorating a cake with a variety of saucy and scandalous creations. Perhaps I'll have her make the cake for Minnie's inevitable bachelorette.

I finally get back to the condo just in time to fire on the oven and pop additional appetizers in for warming.

Thirty minutes to spare! Damn I'm good!

I light a few candles, throw on some background music, and enjoy a pre-party glass of wine with a read through of the August issue of *Crave*.

My heart lurches as I flip my way to the haute-couture section and see none other than Liv Pickard in a group shot. Victoria Lewis' magazine's coverage of Paris Fashion Week and multiple images of the queen of the event herself is a slap in the face. It's like the two most heartless women are teaming up to harass me with reminders of my insignificant status and the absence of Guillaume in my life. I breathe a deep breath and sigh.

Guillaume.

I'm stirred out of my nostalgia by a loud thud at the door. I meander over trying to pull myself together as I go, feeling it may very well be Randall, or even his cheater of a fiancée here to ream me out. I look through the peep-hole, ensuring it's not some Freddy Kreuger looking character. No hostess wants to be murdered right before guests begin to arrive, what an embarrassment that would be, and highly unpleasant to have caution tape and blood splatter welcoming Charlie on her big day.

I exhale happily when I see it's just Nina with a tower of containers in her arms.

"Hey, Neen!" I swing the door open and unload her scrumptious looking baked goods. "Did someone let you in?"

"Totally. Well I kind of wandered in with a pleasant Asian family. They took pity on me seeing I was loaded down with these delicacies."

"Thank you so much, sweetheart. These look delicious. Can I sample one?" I say referring to the appealing looking fudge brownies that are staring me in the face.

"Of course, doll! Be my slender little guinea pig."

I dive in before she even completes her sentence, grabbing a substantial corner piece. I hold it gently in my hands, preparing for the flavour that is soon to be delighting my taste buds.

Self- control, Portia. Nina's here. No closet eating behaviour.

My inner self-talk doesn't work because my love for chocolate automatically sends a message to my fingers to stuff the entire hunk in my mouth to the point that bits are protruding out and settling on my moistened lips.

Unfortunately, the moistness of my lips is unmatched by that of the brownie, and I find myself choking on the dried texture that has found its way to the back of my throat. Not only that, but the flavour is far from delightful. I keep tasting chunks of unmixed baking soda.

Anxiety is taking over as the brownie is sitting wedged in my mouth with no hope of disintegrating. My options are to spit it out, but that would offend Nina horribly, or somehow get around her to subtly pour some water and wash this unpleasantness down. She hasn't spotted my distressed state yet.

I must look like a beast!

Beads of sweat are forming on my forehead and strands of my hair have gotten stuffed in my mouth with the brownie.

Water! Water!

After thirty seconds in awkward agony and distress, I'm finally over feeling worried about potentially hurting Nina's feelings. I rush to the sink, knocking into Nina as I do, in turn causing the tray of baked goods she's assembling to go flying into the living area. I stick my head under the faucet and soak the dry heap of sawdust in my mouth.

"Good god, Portia! What the hell is wrong?" Nina says.

I'm unable to speak and focus on washing the morsels down my throat. After a minute I've finally emptied the majority of the brownie and feel like my heart rate is slowing to a normal pace. Finishing off the rest with an actual glass of water, I turn to Nina and say, "Good brownies, Neen! Too bad *Baking with Nina* never caught on."

She stares at me for a moment, walks over to the tray of brownies, opens the garbage can and dumps the whole lot of them into it. We look at each other for a moment attempting to read the other's expression and suddenly start laughing uncontrollably.

"Babe, you'd never make it on Broadway. You can't act or tell a lie if your life depended on it. Were they that bad?"

"Awful," I respond holding nothing back.

We giggle a touch more and then hear the buzzer ring. I rush to the speaker. "Hellooo?"

"Hey, Portia, it's me! Charlie! Paulo and Travis are with me too."

"Excellent! Come on up," I exclaim as I hit the entrance button.

As the party gets underway, guests stream in steadily, and even Minnie makes an appearance with Leonard in tow. Remarkably enough she's not the slightest bit irritated that I've overtaken her boudoir with my designs and fabrics. She beams at the sight of it all and gives me an enormous hug.

"Portia, you're fabulous and I'm so happy you're finally doing your thing and what makes you happy."

I feel tears well in my eyes at her words, but fight them off.

"Thanks, Minnie. I'm delighted for you too! You're so calm, and obviously you and Leonard are picture perfect for one another. Don't be a stranger, though. This *is* still your place too. Just give the word and all that shit I've piled in your room will be removed."

"Don't even worry about it, Portia. I'm comfortable with Leonard, and my work is perfect. Leonard set me up with a job at his work as the in-house advertising and marketing expert. He pulled some strings from the comfort of his hospital bed. Just like that my hours are nine to five and I leave work without a second thought about it. No more wallowing to Bob Marley, face down in the middle of the living room floor." She winks and grabs a hold of Leonard's arm. "And his leg is almost as good as new. Just in a cast for a few more weeks, but he's totally mobile and able to get around. You know what that means?" she adds in a giddy voice.

I have no idea what *that* means, but I suppose it's an attempt at letting me know she's getting laid on the regular.

"That's all so amazing, Minnie! You see how things can change in an instant with a bit of positive energy and a kick in the pants?" I wrap an arm around her and give her a squeeze. "Have a cocktail. I think that untouchable hunk, Travis, has taken over bar duty so give him your request."

She ambles over toward the bar with Leonard hobbling along beside.

I glance around the room and see everyone chatting, laughter and gleeful expressions in every corner, especially on the face of the guest of honour herself. Charlie is eating a slice of the "New Year New Rear" cake, which was an absolute hit and made her giggle ecstatically when remembering the occasion that brought that slogan to life. I'm so happy for her and to truly have my friend back.

As I'm taking in the delightful scene surrounding me and humming along to the sweet melodies of TLC's throwback album, I see none other than Angelica walk in dressed completely in black leather from head to toe.

Sure it's trendy at the moment, but that's cow overload right there.

I catch sight of Nina. She turns to check if I've noticed who's joined the festivities and rolls her eyes when she's aware that I've most definitely taken in the new arrival. Following immediately behind her, but clearly not with her, as he breezes past towards the bar, is none other than Randall. He's hell bent on downing a stiff drink. I see Travis pour him a straight up scotch and he throws it back without hesitation.

Poor sap.

He immediately requests another, downs that, and then makes his way over.

"Randall! You made it. I see you found the bar all right. Care for some cake?" I welcome him and attempt to help him soak up some of that scotch.

"Hey, Portia. No cake for me, I'm cutting out the sweets. Great turn out! Thanks for the invite."

"Happy to have you here, Randall. I've been meaning to ask if everything is okay. You seemed tense earlier." I try to tip toe around the sensitive fiancée drama.

"Huh. Well, it's funny you should ask. If you consider finding your fiancée with her tongue crammed down the throat of a ragged slob in the parking garage being okay, then hell, I'm friggin' fantastic! She's such a witch. To be honest, I'm glad I saw what I saw. It makes me realize I'm too good for her. If she wants a hobo, he's exactly who she deserves."

"Oh, Randall, I'm so sorry to hear that. You're too good for her if she can't see how wonderful you are." I put a hand on his shoulder. He looks up to the ceiling as if searching for relief from his angst in the stippling.

"I don't know if I ever really loved her, to be honest. It's interesting that what's causing me the most anxiety is the thought of having to break the news to Mom and Dad. They were so thrilled for me. I'm their only child and they have such high hopes for grand kids and for me to have a family of my own. I guess I was sort of forcing something that wasn't even there to begin with. Excuse me Portia, I'm just going to grab another drink."

"Of course, Randall, remember that there are tons of great women out there who are better suited for you than that horrific ex fiancée of yours. I hope you don't mind me saying."

"Not at all. Thanks, Portia." He hangs his head and walks back towards Travis.

As he does so, I catch sight of Charlie and her gaze is following along with Randall's motion.

What's this? A bit of a match- making opportunity? Well, if I can't be lucky in love myself, I might as well be of assistance to those who have a hope in hell of finding it.

I stride over to Charlie and take her by the arm, pulling her along towards the bar in a steadfast manner.

"Port, what are you…where are you…." She pauses in her attempt at questioning when I plant her directly next to Randall, who has lined up three more drinks and looks as though he's contemplating death by scotching.

"Oh, well hi, Randall," Charlie manages to say. "Is one of those for me? I simply love a good scotch."

I hang back and watch these seemingly unimportant words capture Randall's attention. At least they've got an appreciation for a good scotch in common. It's a start. I back away and let the magic of the union unfold. Sitting on the sofa next to Angelica, not by choice but simply because it is the only free seat in the house, I turn to make nice.

"Hi Angelica. I'm happy you got the invite and came along even after yesterday's incident. You look fab!"

"Spare me, Portia. I'm only here because I thought that bitch, Victoria Lewis, would be here so I could give her a piece of my mind. I think while I'm here I'll alert you to the fact that I now hate you even more than I did yesterday. How is it that you're throwing a party for Charlie after she was so dismissive of us? You've given no support to me in my horrible situation. I deserve a party! Not her! ME. I'm a wreck and you've ignored that fact and moved on with your life like I'm yesterday's news."

The room has become quiet and the music playing is a soft and slow tempo song that I can't quite make out over Angelica's accusations.

"Angelica, that really isn't fair." I attempt to calm her as I see people staring and can tell they are listening in. "Nina and I wanted to support you yesterday and you turned on us ferociously. How can I lend support to someone who called me a 'backstabbing bitch' when I had nothing to do with what has happened?"

"You must have! You're all liars. I bet you're all in on this with Daniel and that tramp, Perpetua. She makes me sick, and so do you!" Angelica hollers causing all remaining guests who were unaware of her ranting to take notice. The room is silent and all eyes are on Angelica.

"Angelica, I'm going to have to ask you to leave. You're causing a scene and this is Charlie's special night," I say calmly and take her gently by the arm.

"Forget Charlie! What a loser she is. You support her over me? Throw her some pathetic excuse for a party for what, for putting down the Game Boy for a minute? Bullshit. And let go of my arm!"

She wiggles her arm away in a huff and rises to leave, stumbling on her stiletto leather boots as she goes.

The room remains silent for a moment until the sweet sounds of Pharrel start blasting through the condo, courtesy of Nina who has now cleared a space to unleash her dance moves. She always knows how to make awkward moments entertaining.

The party resumes, and I breathe a sigh of relief at the thought that Charlie's party has gone off almost entirely drama free.

Charlie! Where is Charlie?

I search the living space and kitchen. Maybe she stepped out for some air.

I shall find her after I relieve all of the wine I have stored up.

I rush to the bathroom, pushing the door open in distress but quickly feel the urge pass as I am pleasantly welcomed by a certainly high school style scene. Randall and Charlie, in each other's grip, making out like teenage lovers.

"I knew you'd hit it off!" I bellow

"Oh, Port, hi. We were just, you know...well...."

"Charlie, no explanation necessary. You two go on. I'll use Minnie's bathroom"

I close the door on their romantic moment in hopes that one has been opened for a new love to blossom.

I really should start a matchmaking business! Damn, I'm good.

CHAPTER 22

. . . .

I wake Sunday morning with not the slightest hangover and eager to get back to designing. Pirouetting through my bedroom singing "I'm Every Woman" at the top of my lungs, making my way into the living area I find myself faced with the disaster that the ever so successful celebration for Charlie caused.

Half-filled cocktail glasses are set in random locations all around the room. Half eaten appetizers and pieces of cake cover the surface of the counter and table. Pillows and the cushions from the couch somehow found their way into the hallway. I have no idea why.

Oh...actually yes I remember!

Nina began rounds of "trust falls." I think she was trying to use her life coaching strategies on the party guests in hopes that it would evolve her business. She sure has a skill for promoting.

I crank up Whitney Houston's greatest hits album and begin to shimmy and shake while I get the space back into shape. The sweet melodies and rhythm of "I Wanna Dance With Somebody" has me cleaning the place at double pace. I heave the rest of Nina's "treats" into the trash-can, gagging as I do so in remembrance of how awful those brownies were. I refuse to ever sample another baked good made by Nina.

I make my way towards the hallway to begin tidying the mess of cushions and place them back on the sofa. A number of glasses placed on the entryway table distract me from completing the intended act of collecting the cushions.

Grabbing them, hoping no stains have been left on Minnie's expensive furniture, I catch sight of a piece of paper, one that I don't remember placing there. I put the glasses down and take the familiar looking paper in my hands.

Guillaume. Where did it…how did it get there?

It's the letter from Guillaume with the list of contacts he provided for me including their information.

I didn't even know I still had it! I know I didn't place it on that table.

I put the mystery of the appearing letter to the back of my mind and am jolted back to that happy day that I received it, so thrilled that the man of my dreams was reciprocating my affection and doing all he could to help me.

I scan the list of contacts, cringing at the sight of Liv Pickard's name. Just seeing it underlined as if she's someone important, makes me want to rip the paper to shreds, but I don't. I see Michele's name, along with Danielle's, and I'm well aware that this piece of paper has more meaning than just being a reminder of a love lost. It holds a connection to my past and future career success.

I dwell momentarily as to what should be my next step. Yes, I'm designing and creating, but I can't leave the contacts gained during my time in Paris in the past. I must keep in touch and remind them of my talent and intention to make it known to the world.

Should I? Could I? Would he? Would Michele answer if I called his office? Would he give me the time of day even though I'm thousands of miles away? It's Sunday, I could leave a message.

I take the phone in my hand and dial the country code for France followed by the number on the paper. My hands are trembling as thoughts about what I should say storm through my mind. Before I have a clear verbal plan of attack, I hear, "Bonjour! L'office de Michele Gagnon."

"Oh, hi there, bonjour, hello. I'm not quite sure if you remember me, but I was in to tour Mr. Gagnon's studio last week. My name is Portia De…."

"Oui! Yes, I do! Michele will be thrilled to talk with you. He was most impressed with your gift for the styling. I will tell him you are calling. One moment, mademoiselle."

I breathe a sigh of relief and feel a confidence returning. This was a fantastic decision, a wonderful decision, a…

"Portia? Is that you? I am so happy you are calling. My mind was just thinking of you while I was preparing garments you helped me style, for shipment to various boutiques. Tell me, are you well?"

"I'm doing all right, Michele. No experience can match the one I had while assisting at your show so it is hard for me to respond with enthusiasm about being back in Canada. I suppose it all feels like it was a dream. I wished for a version of that very experience all of my life and to have to return to normalcy in Toronto, after being on such a high in Paris, is a tough pill to swallow."

"Portia, why must that thrill that you experienced here at my show end? The door is now open to many opportunities. How can you be so saddened and uninspired after seeing your name alongside mine in all of the fashion reviews? I am not sparing any flattery of you in the promotion of your name!"

He pauses, as does my heart, uncertain that I've heard correctly. I'm speechless and feel numb for a moment, so much so that the phone slips clear out of my hands, falling with a thud to the hardwood floor. I grab the phone, regain composure and stutter into it with nervous excitement.

"Michele, I think I may have misunderstood you. Did you say my name is mentioned in the Parisian fashion reviews covering your show?"

"But of course! You were a star. I insisted that your name be mentioned. I even threatened to withhold interviews unless the magazines and newspapers agreed."

"Michele, I don't… I don't know what to…"

"Guillaume fought along with me to make sure you got the credit you deserve. He sat in on every interview I gave and at times even elaborated on my mention of you by adding his own opinion. I do think the reporters began to suspect a romantic connection. Is this true, Portia? Is there a romance between you two? I would be so thrilled to hear this. I am a romantic to the core."

I'm still in a daze at hearing the news that not only have I been mentioned in top magazines and newspapers, but that Guillaume has been partnering with Michele to make it all happen.

"Michele, I had hoped there might have been a romance that would continue between the two of us, but it really just is business as I soon discovered on my final night in Paris. I'm so grateful to you for your kind words and for all you have offered me. How can I ever make it all up to you?" I divert the conversation away from the mention of Guillaume. I can't bear the thought of reliving or recounting the events that unfolded on the day of Michele's show.

"Returning of the favor is not necessary because it was not a favor. I believe every word I shared with the media. It was truth. I would be honoured... if there is one thing you do as an unnecessary repayment, for you to please one day partner with me on a collection. I would like very much to work with you."

He proposes this in such a humble manner as if he is an insignificant beginner like me.

"You do not even have to ask, Michele. It would be a dream for me to work alongside you again in anyway. To design and create with you would be surreal."

"Very well, it is done then! We will be in touch and bring our creativity together very soon! Portia, I must go. My studio has suddenly filled up with visitors. Before I say au revoir, please read the columns in *La Vie, Rouge* and *Reveillon* magazine. You will get a taste of how your styling was viewed by some of the top critics of Paris fashion."

"Thank you Michele! I will have a look as soon as I'm off the phone. You've just given me such a boost once again. Goodbye. We'll be in touch."

My heart still in my throat after hearing of my new-found, yet surely only fifteen minutes of fame, I scurry to assemble the condo to a respectable state and then plop down in front of my laptop for a bit of Parisian fashion site scouring. I type in "La Vie" and within seconds an image of me with a beaming smile across my face, standing shoulder to shoulder with Michele Gagnon appears. The headline reads something in French, but I can only assume it praises Michele's show and my own efforts in its making. I continue to click through the entire issue and then turn my attention to the other magazines suggested by Michele. They each have a similar picture simply from various angles, but the same dumbfounded smile paired with the appearance of tears welling in my eyes is the image displayed.

As I'm glancing through the final article's associative images I glimpse one that is intended as a sweeping view of the venue. I catch sight of a group of male models organized and ready for the runway and see Guillaume with a pained expression on his face. An expression I had never, in the short time I knew him, seen. I dwell on whether or not the picture was snapped before I came across Liv and him snogging, or after. I suppose it doesn't matter.

Guillaume, whether helpful or hurtful, must be absent from my mind if I want to move forward without a haunting reminder of experienced heartbreak.

My face is all over top Parisian fashion magazines for god sakes! A step in the right direction if I do say so myself!

◇◇◇◇◇◇◇◇

"Nina! You must have been behind it! It had to have been you. How else did a letter, which only you and I knew about, end up laid out in plain sight for me to come across? You probably got too blitzed last night to remember taking it out of your bag or you're just attempting to pull one over on me. Come on Neen! Fess up to at least one of the two options. This is driving me bananas!"

"Babe, I swear I never even laid eyes on that note. You only told me about it. Then I have no idea what you did with it after the day you used it as a reference to whisk around to the different appointments. I'd tell you if I had some sort of responsibility in its sudden appearance. You know I love taking full credit when I deserve it, but I don't deserve it in this case. That note never found its way into these hands."

"I'm positive I threw it out on my final morning in Paris though, Neen! It just doesn't make sense that it ended up here in Toronto when I have a clear picture of me discarding of it in the hotel lobby's wastebasket. I mean, I was horribly intoxicated at the time, but I know I'm not imagining it."

Discovering the initial letter from Guillaume has plagued my thoughts since my morning attempts to get on with more designing. I finally caved to the pressing confused thoughts and called Nina for answers. She's been unable to offer any. I get a tone indicating a call coming through and quickly dismiss Nina.

"Hello, Portia speaking," I answer the second call cheerfully.

"Ms. Delaney? Oh, hello there. My name is Mireille Beaudoin. I'm the chief editor at *The Stiletto Press* here in Toronto. It is my understanding that you made quite a mark on Danielle Parent and she raves about your work on Michele Gagnon's masterpiece of a collection. *The Stiletto Press* is a Canadian branch of *La Vie Magazine,* and Danielle has insisted that we take you on board in our styling and accessories department. You can assist our lead stylists by selecting appropriate pieces for the various editorials. How do you feel about this opportunity Mme. Parent has offered?"

How do I…how do I feel? So beyond excited and overwhelmingly pleased that I can't even string a sentence together to express my gratitude.

"I…I…am feeling, well…happy and pleased, no thrilled to be offered this chance. I'm so surprised by this offer and I have to tell you it comes at the most opportune time! I want so badly to continue on in the field of fashion and styling. I won't let you down, no matter what the position entails. This is my dream, my passion and even though my resume is a bit light on fashion experience, I assure you that I'm the one for the job."

"Yes, well you already have the…."

"And I'm also designing a collection that will keep me looking ahead to the budding trends, which will greatly add to my understanding as how to accessorize and pull garments and…"

"You don't really need to tell me…"

"I really would be honoured to have a chance." I suppose stringing together words was not as big of a problem after all.

"Ms. Delaney! You already have the job. You have more than a chance because I've already given you the job. You really needn't continue on promoting yourself. This isn't an interview. You have the position as junior stylist for our weekly "What to Wear" pieces." She says this in a slightly irritated voice, and I feel a bit silly for my ramblings.

"My apologies. See, I had to work so hard and interview at so many places in order to land all of my medical office jobs so forgive me for being a bit taken aback at how simple this process is."

"Enjoy it, darling. This doesn't happen often, so Danielle must have been extremely impressed by your work."

"Thank you so much, really. I'll have to give Danielle a call personally to thank her as well. This means…"

"No, no! You don't need to personally thank Mme. Parent. I have already thanked her and she is a very busy woman," Mireille interjects.

"Okay. This all means the world to me! Is there a time you need me to pop in tomorrow?"

"Tomorrow, come by in the afternoon. We'll be busy with layout meetings in the morning so I won't be available until around one o'clock. I look forward to making your acquaintance then. We're at one fifteen Jarvis Street, main floor. See you then and there, Ms. Delaney."

"Yes, I'm looking forward to it. Good-bye."

I end the call and sit in a daze for a moment, waiting to see if this is some glorious dream that I will find myself shaken awake from. Being laid off, put aside, and I suppose the less than perfect departure from Paris, I feel weightless and exuberant, so full of life. It's like the curtains are drawing open and the action of my life is truly beginning.

◇◇◇◇◇◇◇◇

"Port! That's totally fab! How in the hell did this all come together so perfectly? You landing a job in your dream career, me finally finding my calling and actually becoming quite successful at it, we deserve it, babe!"

"I'm so unbelievably ecstatic about this all, Neen. I mean, after getting laid off I thought I'd spiral into some depressed lump, stop washing my hair, start packing in four thousand calories a day, and then before you know it I'd need everyone to make house calls because I'd be unable to get my enormous backside off the couch. This has been the best turn of events imaginable and I owe it all to Paris and, interestingly enough, that letter from Guillaume. Which I'm still so completely confused about! How did it get here?"

"A little angel must have transported it and left it as a reminder of your talent and how desired you are by perfect Parisian male models."

"Thanks, Neen, but I'm sure it was a much less supernatural means. I suppose I have more pressing matters to attend to though, like deciding on an outfit for my first day at *The Stiletto Press!*"

"You enjoy, babe. I'm off to see Vicky! She's quickly becoming the Cuba Gooding to my Tom Cruise. She pays me enough to be my one and only client, but I'm still working like a dog to bring in new clients. Spread the word!"

"That sounds like a great plan. Please tell me you're softening her up a bit. That woman needs something to make her crack a smile every once in a while."

"I'm working on it. I had thought of setting her up on a date or two then I thought it might look as though I'm running an escort service so reneged on the idea. Ciao, babe!"

"Bye, Neen."

I put my phone down and check the time. I realize that between the calls to Michele and those from Nina and Ms. Beaudoin, I've spent the better part of the morning on the phone. I pry myself off the sofa and get out for some air to perhaps find a *Stiletto Press* worthy ensemble for my first day.

Champagne wishes and cupcake dreams made real!

CHAPTER 23
· ·

My first day in my true career, a career that makes me excited to be alive and thrilled to wake up this late morning.

I throw open my wardrobe door and an ear to ear smile encompasses my face as I roughly push the scrubs aside and go directly for the DKNY pant suit I purchased yesterday while on a fashion high. I hang it in the bathroom and jump in the shower, humming all the while.

Forty- five minutes later I'm skipping out of the condo, Marc Jacobs bag in hand, and Gucci stilettos strapped to my lighter than air feet. I'd dance all the way to my new office if it wouldn't result in confused and concerned stares.

Maybe tomorrow.

I arrive outside of the modern and stately all glass office and am aware that my smile is still as wide as it was when I had flung open my closet doors an hour or so earlier. Little to no nervousness to be found in me, I stride confidently through the glass doors. A rather warm looking gentleman is on a call so I take a seat so to not hover and annoy the assistant on my first day.

"Good afternoon! How can I help you?" he inquires charmingly, after he has completed his call.

"Hi there, I'm Portia Delaney. Mireille Beaudoin called yesterday to offer me a position as a junior stylist. I was so thrilled when I got the news. I've never simply been handed a job that I didn't even know existed. It's all so perfect." As I'm speaking I see his warm and welcoming manner mutate into a different animal. His smile and brightly welcoming eyes morph into a tense tight grimace that has a scowling undertone to it.

"Yes, so I've heard. Follow me," he says curtly.

"So seeing as we'll be colleagues, what's your name?" I continue to attempt to butter him up even though it's obvious he wants nothing to do with me.

"I don't feel sharing personal details is always necessary in the workplace. I'm a private person."

"Too private to even share your name? What will I call you then?" I say perplexedly.

"Nothing," he spits, obviously becoming more and more annoyed by my pleasant manner.

"All right, so *nothing* it is," I reply with a little giggle. He rolls his eyes and begins walking at double the speed towards a room marked "Editor in Chief, Ms. Mireille Beaudoin" on the door's plaque.

"Portia Delaney, here to see you for her 'assignment.'" He adds little air quotes while spewing the word "assignment," which has me even more confused.

"Oh, well thank you Kevin. I will have a word with you in a moment about the purchases for that Fall/Winter spread you will need to make."

"Kevin! Ha, I found you out!" I squeal, causing both Mireille and Kevin to stare blankly for a moment and then carry on as though I'm non-existent.

"Portia, please come in and sit down. I'm so happy you could make it to us this afternoon." Mireille's words are saying "welcome" and "nice to meet you," but her eyes are glowering and giving me an unsettled feeling. She takes me in from head to toe and I become tense.

What in the hell is happening here? They asked me here. I didn't beg or plead for this job! They're treating me like I'm some leach here to suck the life out of them.

Mireille rises and towers over me, garbed in a black blazer and skin-tight leather leggings. Hm, *she and Angelica would get on well.*

"Portia, this is how things will work. You will answer to Kevin. He will give you direction and you are to comply and complete each task he assigns you. Although Mme. Parent speaks highly of you and is the reason we have offered you this opportunity, it is highly unprofessional for me to simply go on her words alone before seeing your full talent with my own eyes."

I nod, wide-eyed and surprised by how altered her tone is towards me presently from the peppy, cheerful voice she used on the phone yesterday.

"You may dislike some tasks that you are asked to undertake, but I assure you that if completed well, you will take steps forward to entering into the role of a true stylist."

"I assure you I'm equipped and ready to take on any tasks you are ready to assign me. I have to say that I woke this morning so excited to be a part of what goes on here at *The Stiletto Press*. I researched your history and became familiar with your contributions to the print world. I am very excited to help in any way that I can." I ramble in hopes that Mireille will take to me a little more. She appears unmoved, and seeing as I don't believe her harshness can become much harsher, I decide to inquire about a specific detail I was unable to find during my research, a detail that she had mentioned more than once in our conversation.

"Ms. Beaudoin, on a bit of a side note, I hope you don't mind me asking, but you had indicated that *The Stiletto Press* is a branch of *La Vie*. I did not find any connection between the two magazines at all. In fact, *La Vie* stands alone and is not affiliated with any other magazine. I did find a connection between your magazine and a Parisian magazine called *La Coeur*. I hope you don't mind me saying."

Mireille's lips purse, and she looks as though she's ready to spit fire at my inquiry.

"Ms. Delaney, are you attempting to undermine me and my experience here as the chief editor? Do you think me to be an imbecile? That I do not know the affiliations between my magazine and others? If I say that we are affiliated with *La Vie*, then we are affiliated with *La Vie,* and by you going on your little Internet search, you are demonstrating a lack of respect for authority. Not a good start, Ms. Delaney! I do hope this will not continue on."

She sits and spins around in her chair to gaze out the window. There is silence for a moment. Then she spins back around to scribble a note on a pad of paper.

"Please seek out Kevin. He will be ready to instruct you on your initial duties for the afternoon. And, Ms. Delaney, Donna Karan pantsuits will be unnecessary for the work you will be starting with here. Jeans and a T-shirt will be acceptable for your tasks," she adds with a slight smirk on her face. "You are excused."

"Thank you, Ms. Beaudoin," I say humbly.

Jeans and a T-shirt? I didn't get rid of my scrub attire to graduate to jeans and T-shirts!

By three o'clock I'm well aware of the reason that designer attire is undesirable for my work at this hellhole. Kevin had me begin by scrubbing the toilets, changing the light bulbs, and mopping the entryway. I've pretty much been demoted from office administrator to custodial staff and cannot take another moment of this.

This isn't right!

Danielle Parent is quickly losing my respect with every dust bunny I sweep up and by the time five rolls around I'm steaming mad literally and figuratively seeing as my final task was to steam clean all of the carpets.

At precisely 5:15 p.m. I march into Mireille's office, ready to unleash my fury, but compose myself and hold in my rage, even though my chic DKNY garment is stained with dirt and grime, my hair is a tangled and sweaty mess, and one of my Gucci heels has cracked after it got jammed in the vacuum's on switch. Yes, I should have taken the heel off my foot and wiggled the shoe out gently, but impulse took over so I yanked with all my might, leaving a portion of the shoe behind.

Just my luck.

"Ms. Beaudoin! What a wonderful first day I had!" I manage to elevate my voice to a seemingly cheerful level. I show all my teeth in a forced grin. "I'll see you bright and early tomorrow morning!" I turn to walk out the door.

"Just one moment, Portia. You are telling me this work is something you enjoy and you mean to stay on longer?"

"Well, yes! This is my dream career! I'm taking those steps towards becoming a true stylist, just like you said."

"But you are aware that becoming a stylist may take months, even years. You wish to continue in this position until you are promoted from scrubbing and cleaning?"

"I do," I say with as much convincing force as I can muster.

"I admire your tenacity and will see you tomorrow," she replies, scribbles yet another note on her pad of paper and spins to gaze out her window once more.

I breeze, well maybe limp due to the mangled heel on my shoe, out of the office, hair scraggly and flying, still dripping of sweat. Kevin grins as I limp by, yet his expression is altered as I add in a "See you tomorrow, Kevin!" He looks aghast and immediately rises to consort with Mireille.

Now I know I have to figure out what the hell this is all about. I'm being made to look like a fool, and Danielle Parent must have an explanation for it all.

Although it is already approaching midnight in Paris, I cannot put my need to discover what, or who, is behind the events of the day aside.

After arriving home to the condo, I dial the number for Danielle and know I will likely get a machine, but am prepared with an appropriate message to leave. Just as I thought, I hear a machine pick up giving instructions in French. I wait for the beep then leave an entire account of my day, the circumstance that brought me to Mireille Beaudoin, and beg Danielle to return my call at her earliest convenience. Then I run a hot bath and sink in to wash off the stink and memory of my day as *The Stiletto Press* workhorse.

◇◇◇◇◇◇◇◇

The following morning I arrive at the office fifteen minutes early just to let them know I mean business and that I'm not going to throw in the towel until I discover the reasons behind Mireille's motivation to offer me a position. I hang up my bag and wipe at the muffin crumbs that have stuck to my oversized T that has "No Fear" printed across the front. I bought it with my babysitting money when I was in junior high, but am not one bit embarrassed to sport it at this place. I'm also quite content with the fact that it still fits me. I want the "No Fear" message to stare Mireille and Kevin in the face all day while they have me completing god-knows-what tasks.

A moment later, after I've arranged my belongings and have mentally prepared for the events of the day, my phone rings at full blast. I look at the caller ID screen and see that it's a Parisian number.

Danielle!

"Hello, Portia Delaney speaking," I say in an even keel manner so to not alarm her to my true state of desperation for a chat.

"Portia, bonjour. This is Danielle Parent. I recently listened to your message and sensed the urgency in your voice. I knew I must contact you at once with a reply."

"Thank you for your promptness, Mme Parent. Can you fill me in and enlighten me as to why you suggested Mireille hire me at her office? I appreciate it, but in all honesty, it is not the work I had in mind."

"Portia, that message you left me was surprising for me to hear. I assure you that I have no contact with Mireille Beaudoin. Her French magazine, *La*

Coeur was at one time a main competitor of *La Vie*. It has not done as well since Mireille left Paris to begin her North American magazine. She has been scheming to find a way back into the spotlight and I am so furious to hear that she has included you in her scheming. I do not see the purpose in it all."

"Neither do I. I was so excited when I thought you had pulled some strings to allow me my first experience as an employed stylist," I say in somewhat of a deflated tone.

"Please realize, Portia, I do speak highly of you, but it is very difficult to simply hand someone a job as a stylist at a large magazine without the true experience. I have hundreds of interns working under me. Some offer their time without pay and some are compensated a quarter of what a fully employed stylist receives. They all have hopes of climbing the ladder, but it takes time. It is not as simple as what Mireille has convinced you of. You must leave them at once and not give another thought to the whole circumstance. Work hard and your break will come, one which does not involve scrubbing of latrines." She sighs in a disgusted manner after speaking these last words.

"I understand, Mme. Parent. Even though I was beyond appreciative when I believed you had managed to find me a job all the way over here in Toronto, and this is a bit disappointing to hear, I'm more than indebted to you for your time, advice, and honesty with me. Thank you so much. I won't involve you in the outcome and my investigation of this matter. I know you're quite busy."

"Portia, have faith in yourself and chase your dreams fully. As for the situation with Mireille, I intend to make it my duty to find out why she is attaching my name to such hideous activity as deceiving a lovely girl like you. It smears my name as well as yours with a bad paint. Don't hold back when you quit today. You let them know that I am aware of what they have been up to and I do not take it lightly. Good luck, Portia. Your success is my wish."

"Thank you. Goodbye Mme. Parent." I hang up the phone and see Kevin enter with about a thousand garment bags piled in his arms.

"Well, don't just stand there!" he hollers in my direction. "Help me out here."

"I'd like to, Kevin. I just can't," I reply cheekily.

"What the hell are you talking about? You're not crippled! Get over here."

"This just seems like a personal and private task that has been delegated for you only. I'd hate to cross privacy boundaries and make you uncomfortable."

He manages to reach the front desk with difficulty and heaves the pile atop all of his files. "You are on thin ice, missy! I don't like your attitude at all, and as your superior, I will have to reprimand you for your disobedience."

"Go right ahead. You're all a bunch of slimy, shady wannabes at this second rate magazine. You only wish you were on par with *La Vie*. You all thought I was so ignorant that I wouldn't figure out your scheme. I mean, I haven't fully figured out why you all went to such trouble yet, but I intend to. Good riddance you horrible, and dare I say, fashion-challenged attendant. I mean, look at yourself! What are you wearing?"

He gasps and checks himself in the mirror. "What are you implying? These terry towel shirts are very trendy. I have them in four colours, and these painter pants are so comfortable and have so much give for those days when I'm a bit bloated. I, I...well I don't need to defend my fashion sense to you! You're a nobody and that's far worse than a somewhat successful wannabe."

"Right, well enjoy that status because I will be a somebody one day and you will wish you'd never crossed me." I say these words with such conviction that I spit them and a morsel lands on his cheek.

"What is going on here?" Mireille enters, hair streaming behind her.

"I was just leaving!" I say, still worked up from the confrontation with Kevin. "I've chatted with Danielle Parent. I know your little secret and want nothing more to do with you or this poor excuse for a magazine. Good day!" I strut past her and catch sight of "RAEF ON" as I walk by the entranceway mirror. "RAEF ON!" I holler as I go.

Mireille lunges to keep me from exiting, but I easily slip past and leave her teetering on her Jimmy Choos. "What are you saying?" Mireille inquires. "And who do you think you are? You will regret your behaviour, Ms. Delaney. Mark my words that this little incident will be your demise."

"So be it!" I say as I make my way out the welcoming exit. "I have enough dirt on you to do some damage as well. Good bye and God Speed."

I hear Mireille grunt as I go, but it has no effect on me. I march on like a trumpeter in the Thanksgiving Day parade.

Once again, jobless, wandering and feeling a bit dejected, I find myself steered towards Nina's new office.

I might as well pop in and pay the girls a visit if I'm unemployed once more. Perhaps Nina has some more Dr. Lola style advice for me.

"Babe! I wasn't expecting you! Have you come to gloat about your prestigious position at your new gig? Charlie, get in here! Port has popped by." Nina flings herself across her waiting area sofa. Luckily, there are no clients in need of a place to sit.

"Oh hey, Portia! So I heard about your new magazine position. What fantastic news!" Charlie beams. I hate to tell either one of them about the shit circumstance I've just walked away from. I mean, this is the first time in months Charlie has shown any interest in anything other than her top score. I'd hate to ruin this milestone with the reality of my situation.

"Hey, Charlie! Yeah it's everything I could have hoped for and more! I'm just free right now because my work day doesn't start until eleven"

And Nina said I can't tell a lie. They both ate that up like a piece of banana cream pie!

"So tell me Charlie, how are things with a certain someone I saw you groping in my bathroom?" I ask adding in a slight giggle.

Charlie blushes and giddily replies, "I think I'm gaga, Port. I mean, I'm not sure if I'm the rebound girl or what, but I'm enjoying whatever it is we are. He's such a sweet man." She says it in such a tone it's like she's singing the words.

"I'm happy for you, Char. You deserve all the best," I reply and give her a little squeeze then I turn my sights to Nina who is still strewn across her sofa as if she's the Queen of Sheba.

"You look like you're totally in your element you graceful goddess!" I joke.

"You know it, babe. Oh!" She springs up to a sitting position. "I meant to tell you, Port, that I got the strangest call on Saturday morning. With the party and the drinking and the dancing, well…you know…it just slipped my mind. At first the call was all about Victoria Lewis and her involvement with my business. I thought they were doing a write up on *Perfect Your Pathway* and the clients that it draws in. Vicky is quite open about her time spent here, which I love! It's because of her that I've become so well known in the city. I swear I may need to hire a few more assistants! All that aside, this woman quickly shifted the conversation from the success I've achieved, to then asking about Angelica and her affiliation to you. She bridged the two together by asking about how Vicky played a role in the downfall of Angelica's line, which I suppose makes sense. It was just so strange that what she seemed most interested in was you and your situation."

"Situation? What do you mean by that?" I ask quite perplexed by the news. "What was this woman's name?"

"'Situation' meaning what you're up to in the city and what your relationship status is and so on. She said her name was Valentina or something. She sounded so reputable with a thick French accent. I just went with it and didn't give it a second thought. I kept thinking how great it could be for news of my company to go global. It's my dream, Port, but it was only after that I realized it could have been a bit too personal to involve you in the conversation the way that I did." She hangs her head and I feel my stomach knotting tighter and tighter with every passing silent moment.

"Neeen? What exactly did you confide in this absolute stranger?" I cringe while waiting for her to work up the nerve to tell me all the details.

"I guess I sort of...kind of...told her you despise your medical job, which is true! Then she asked about your work in fashion. I'm not sure how she knew you wanted a career in fashion, but I told her you're planning a shift to a career in fashion and that you sometimes take a bit longer to become...well...you know you always need a good kick in the ass to get moving!"

I sit down on the sofa in silence and gesture for Nina to continue. She does.

"Then she asked about your love life and I suppose I laughed a bit. But you laugh all the time at yourself, Port, so please don't be offended! I basically told her that you don't have a love life in the city and that the only romance you've had in the past year was a two day fling in Paris, which caused you a lot of heartache and to have a couple meltdowns while overseas. I think that...no I know that is all I said."

"I suppose it could have been worse, but did you have to make me sound so pathetic? I mean, I don't know what this woman wants, but it must be related to the exposure I'm getting since working on Michele Gagnon's show. I want them to think I'm fabulous, Neen, even if I'm not quite there yet."

"You're beyond fabulous already and you better start thinking it! Just because you've been in a bit of a rut does not take away from how completely incredibly talented, beautiful, and intelligent you are. Fabulousness is not measured by circumstance but character, and you, my dear girlfriend, have got it!"

Nina speaks with such conviction that I have a hard time disbelieving what she's saying. The trouble is that when you've viewed yourself negatively for so long and have had a string of mess ups and bad relationships with hopes being dashed in all categories of life, it's hard to tell yourself that none of it matters and that under it all you're still fabulous. I'm getting there, but it'll take a few more wins beforehand.

"So that's it? That's all she said and all she asked? I'm so confused by all of this especially with this whole job mess!" *Oops...*

"What 'job mess'? Your new job? It's amazing that you landed it!" Charlie chimes in.

"Yes, completely and I love it so much. It's as if the position was made specifically for me."

Well, at least that last bit wasn't a lie. I mean, it was created just for me. It's just that scrubbing shitters isn't what I had planned for my big career move.

"I mean that it's all so out-of the-blue and I don't understand why anyone wants anything to do with little old me, way over here in Toronto. I only styled one fashion show, for god sakes! It doesn't make sense that this woman would want to know so much about me. Why didn't that woman, that Valentina lady, why didn't she approach *me*? It's all doing my head in. I need a drink."

"Babe, it's only nine thirty a.m. and don't you have to be at work in a bit?" Nina inquires earnestly.

Crap.

"Yes, you're right. I wouldn't want to start off at this job on the wrong foot by walking in blasted."

Good response, quick thinking.

"Neen, I better jet, but if you get any more calls from people wanting to know information about me please please pleeeaase tell whoever it is to talk to *me*."

"No need to ask twice. I'm sorry I said as much as I did. You know me, so impulsive and hair-brained sometimes... "Nina replies with obvious remorse in her voice.

"I know, Neen. You meant well. You always do. No worries." I give her a kiss on the cheek and wave to Charlie, making my way to the door while I do so.

My journey home is quite interesting. I reach the subway station and make my way down the platform. I suddenly sense I have an admirer, a man, who'd been walking directly behind me the entire way from Nina's office is now standing directly next to me on the platform. My personal space is being completely infringed upon and I'm uneasy about the situation. I want to turn and give him a piece of my mind, shoo him away, even mace him, but I don't. I stand there sandwiched between this stranger, who wreaks of cheap cologne, and a pillar to my right.

I step onto the subway train and walk to the furthest point of the car, finding an empty seat near the door, in case I must make a quick exit. The said culprit follows me and sits directly across from me. So now I'm caught in one of these uncomfortable "where the hell should I look so to not make eye-contact?" moments. I mean, I know Dr. Lola wants me to practice maintaining eye-contact, but not with mysterious and forceful, stalkerish men like this guy.

Sheeeesh!

I pretend to nap and pray that he doesn't attempt to take advantage of the situation. I hear stop after stop being called. This is borderline torturous, and I've never felt more excited to hear the chime for my stop. I race to the door, turn to the gentleman and spit the words.

"Don't you even think about following me from here you greasy, stinky, pervert!"

Okay, so maybe that was a bit over the top.

The thought of this strange imposter following me to my home is causing an extreme sense of anxiety. I exit the subway and breathe a sigh of relief when he does not follow.

Still shaken and taken aback by the entire course of events that have transpired over the past twenty-four hours, I amble along deep in thought, attempting to unscramble who is behind this entire mess. From the magically appearing letter to the nightmare job offer; from this Ms. Valentina to the creep following me home. I'm in a state of complete and utter confusion.

"Someone give me some answers!" I say out loud while desperately reaching up to the sky, giving little concern to who witnesses. Then as if out of thin air, I hear in a terribly thick French accent, "Answers? You wish for answer? I am the one who deserves the answers!"

I peer straight ahead in the direction of the voice. Fiery eyes glare back at me. Voice quivering, knees trembling.

"What are you doing here? How...why are you...."

"Shut up and listen to these words, you disgrace of a woman!"

CHAPTER 24

"You're a nobody and a little pebble in my shoe who continues to annoy and not understand my clearly communicated message!"

"Liv, I....I...."

"What is it, you incompetent girl? What is it you want to tell me? Go on and spit it out, you foolish insignificant female."

Liv has appeared like a nemesis out of thin air, robed in a boob exposing, hip hugging yellow wrap dress, standing like Wonder Woman with her hands planted firmly on her hips. Her heels are so high they make her legs seem to be a million miles long and she's towering over me in my scraggly denim and "No Fear" T. I want to cower and run, but I stand frozen, staring up at, well, more so at her enormous chest than her face.

God those things are massive!

"Liv," I manage to say once more. "I don't know what you mean. I left Paris and Guillaume behind. What could you possibly mean by me annoying you and not heeding your message?"

"Stupid girl! You think I don't know how you bewitched my Guillaume? I saw that note he left you, the one that included not only information to find me and other members of the industry, but his confession of his feelings for you. I saw it!"

"But how...how did you find it when I clearly remember disposing of it at the hotel?"

"Oh yes! Yes you did dispose of it! You tried to discard of it so that I would never catch on to your exchanges…"

"Um, to be honest it had more to do with my own emotions than you, Liv. You really have no bearing on my actions. I think you're a bit…"

"And I, being clever and having people on my side to get things done, recovered the letter from the trash!" she continues as if she's cured some terrible plague with her scheming. "You think you deserve his attention and his love? That you can steal him away to North America after all the history he and I have enjoyed? I will not allow it! I will stop it and ruin you and all your little dreams in the process."

"Hold on just a minute, back this up just a bit. The letter, are you saying that the letter appeared in my apartment because of your doing? Liv, tell me you didn't break into my condo and plant that letter there. I will have you detained immediately!" I begin finding my confidence in confronting this absolute lunatic.

"I would not stoop so low as to even step foot in your rat infested apartment!" she spews roughly.

"Actually, it's quite lovely, really. It's got a great view and is all modern in finishes and…" I realize these details are insignificant in the moment.

"I have my sources and, as I said, people who have been investigating your pathetic little life. I know all about your friends and your dormant love life aside from what you began with my Guillaume! Your friend Angelica and I have enjoyed a number of good chats. She happily dropped that note to you the other night. I wanted to remind you of who and what you will never have! That note is temporary! You may have been romanced by Guillaume and enjoyed some success while in Paris, but this will never be something that is constant in your life!"

"Was the whole *Stiletto Press* position your doing as well? I knew it made little sense and that seems to be the best way to describe you!" I say getting my own jab in proudly.

"Of course it was all orchestrated by me! Mireille wants nothing more than to see Danielle Parent fall so when I suggested she attach Danielle's name to you, and ensure that you fail at the tasks she set out for you, she could have an article about Danielle's lack of good judgement in regards to stylists and future successes in the industry!

You fell into my little trap with your display today. You acted horrendously and right this moment Mireille's editors are preparing to print an article sharing your unprofessionalism and Danielle's poor judgement. Mireille and I both win this way. I'm so clever that at times I astound myself! Even the inappropriate words you directed towards my confidant on the subway train will get back to Mireille and she will report just how wretchedly you behave in public."

I gasp in horror. "You can't do that! It's all false and it will all be proven untrue! You had that man follow me and I was worried for my safety! I will make sure the truth comes out."

"Maybe months from now, but by then the harmful seed will have already been planted. Danielle's image will be tarnished and you will never be given a chance from a reputable magazine. The truth is not as interesting as rumours and gossip! You'll learn that when you finally enter the true fashion world. But I doubt this will ever happen, thanks to me!"

"Why are you so...so...wicked? I haven't intentionally done anything to harm you! Why are you putting so much effort into hurting me! I didn't ask for Guillaume to give me his time and attention and I assure you I walked away from him. It's not my doing that he's continuing to attempt to promote me in Paris! I didn't ask for this, Liv! You have to stop this and ask Mireille not to print that article. I'm begging you, please." I'm on the verge of tears. My voice is wavering and I'm at the point of groveling in hopes that she will have the tiniest morsel of sympathy for me.

"You! You pretend to be all innocent! I know it's because of you that he's leaving me heartbroken in Paris! I despise you for this!"

I begin to see tears welling in her eyes at the utterance of these words. "What are you talking about? Where's he going? I don't know what you mean! Liv, please believe me." I inch closer to try to gain her trust while looking into her clearly devastated eyes.

"He's going to New York! New York of all places! He never displayed any intention to go there until after he met you. You must have had some doing in this, and I will get to the bottom of it." She turns away, head in hands. For the first time I see a more human side to the raging beast that is Liv Pickard. I feel an uncertain connection to her in this fleeting moment. I am well aware of the undeniable urges Guillaume magically produces, the yearning he implants in a vulnerable woman's heart. Regardless of her sternness and her intimidating tactics, Liv is merely a woman like me who has lost someone she longs to be with.

I sigh and place my hand on her shoulder. "Liv, he's just a man and you have a whole city of wonderful companions to choose from. You…"

Liv spins so quickly I stumble back in surprise. She steps towards me, holds her arm back, and open hand slaps me so hard across the face that I am sent tumbling to the ground. I grab my face in agony. "Why would you do that?" I bellow in pain. "I was trying to be kind! I was trying to show you compassion and let you know I understand your heartache because I feel it too! What is wrong with you? No wonder Guillaume wants to get away from you! I had nothing to do with his choice to move to New York. *This* isn't New York you psychopath!"

She steps in and puts her teal coloured pump on my chest to keep me down on the ground.

"Stay down where you belong, you dog! You won't have much choice after that magazine article is printed. I will get him back and you will continue to be just as you are; you helpless piece of dirt." She removes her pump from atop the "No" on my T-shirt, spins and strides away. I must say I have never been happier to be left alone in my entire life.

I sit a moment longer while Liv's negative words are burrowing into the core of my being as if trying to deter me from surging ahead with my plan to reinvent myself. I refuse to let her defeat me! I'm not helpless; I'm not dirt; I'm not the groveling, nobody she transformed me into!

She won't win like she's planned! Not like this!

I brush myself off and am aware that a few passers-by are watching me rise after what was an alarming scene. A woman rushes over to me to inquire if I'm all right and communicates that she was on the verge of calling police, but was relieved when the woman dressed in the Big Bird getup took off and left me seemingly unharmed.

"I'm fine, thanks. Aside from the stinging in my right cheek and my temporarily wounded pride, I'll be A-OK." I smile and she pats my back then scurries back across the street to man the counter at her fruit stand.

My initial urge is to call Nina to unload the drama of the morning on her, but I fully recall that she has no idea about the history I have with Liv. I decide to once again keep these unfortunate discoveries to myself and take the heat of whatever may come from it discretely. I suppose it's been less of a discovery and more like Liv has dumped an enormous pile of shit on my head. *Lovely.* The stench of it all is making my stomach turn.

◇◇◇◇◇◇◇◇

Three days have come and gone since the unfortunate circumstance where I found myself quite literally under the heel of the maniac fashionista. How she's managed to rise to such a prestigious and influential position in life is beyond me, yet I am all too aware that sometimes it is the bitchiest and most cut-throat women who claim the best of the best, even when it comes to men.

It's for this reason, and this reason alone, that I refuse to let Liv win. The only problem is that I don't have much experience in stopping cunning and malevolent iconic figures from taking me down. I need to keep my head on straight and not allow myself to be yanked down to Liv's level. No matter what her status appears to be, I know the truth. She's merely an insecure, power-hungry female who will one day simply self-destruct with little to no help from me.

My mind is finally taken off the happenstance. This relief comes in the form of a call from Charlie to meet with the girls and I for some chit chat and catch ups. Although I've spent a good deal of time on my designs and am unbelievably proud of the masterpieces I've created, I've had little to appease my mind in regards to the accusatory article looming overhead.

I've thought long and hard about how to stop the inevitable from happening, but so far have only come up with the idea of hiring a hit man to off Liv and Mireille. That's clearly not my style. So I've remained inactive and tortured with imagined scenarios as to how everything will play out. For this reason alone I'm fervently pleased to have a night out to forget my woes and focus on the phenomenal group of ladies I have for support in any and all situations.

"Hey girls!" I cheerfully say as I enter the 8th Street Bistro with Minnie on one arm and Tricia on the other. "I brought in the reinforcements in case Angelica caught wind of our little rendezvous and we need back up. Tricia, meet Nina and Charlie. They're a couple firecrackers but are just about the sweetest friends a girl could ask for."

"Welcome, ladies!" Nina says as she rises to greet us. "Tricia! I'm so happy Portia brought you along. I've heard the absolute best things about you! With your sharp tongue and that quick wit of yours you and I will get on remarkably well. I just know it!"

"Well, Nina, I've heard many interesting facts about you and would like to think the same," Tricia responds, clearly amused by Nina's forward greeting.

"I told you she's a bit nutty," I say to Tricia giving a little wink to Nina.

"Hi, girls, come and have a seat," Charlie says, clearly eager to get into the drinks and the gossip that's been simmering since our last chat.

"Charlie, you're a vision! Your face is beaming and I can't get over how wonderful and healthy you look these days," I remark.

"That's what regular romps with Randall do for her," Nina chimes in. We gaze at Charlie and then simultaneously sigh at the thought of how incredible a night in the sack with Randall would be.

"Oh you girls, stop!" She pauses, but I can sense she is in total agreement and continues. "I mean it's true. He's amazing! The best I've ever been with. We're so in tune with one another's bodies. It's as if he's inside my head and aware of everything I want him to do without even needing me to say a word. And he's so sweet too. He leaves me little notes all over his place in the morning and sends me cute little gifts and messages all day long. I can't get enough. Apparently, neither can he because…well…he's already been talking about a walk down the aisle with ME!"

She says this final word in a manner that sounds like she can't even believe it and is responding to someone else's news of possible matrimonial bliss. I almost fall out of my chair upon hearing the announcement. She's beaming and so clearly in love that I can't help shrieking with joy for her.

"So this is why you gathered us all so zealously!" I finally am able to formulate words again.

"I guess it was partially the reason. But I also lost out on so much time with you girls in the past year that I really want to make these get-togethers happen more often!"

"Well, babe, we're so happy to have the true Charlie back and better than ever!" Nina announces.

"Penelope has looked absolutely devastated whenever I've seen her lurking around Hopewell Clinic waiting for Darryl," Tricia adds. "I think she finally sees what a horrible choice she's made. I can't believe she keeps choosing that cheese-dick of a man for a companion over such a lovely man as Randall."

"Tricia, I think you're running a tight race with the others to become my new best girlfriend!" Nina says in awe of Tricia's sweet-mannered dig at Darryl's expense. Tricia smiles her perfect smile and takes another sip of her Caesar.

"Okay, so your turn, Min! What's the deal with you and Leonard? I mean, you are never at the condo so you two are practically living together. Is he the one? Huh? Huh?" I pry jokingly with a little nudge.

She blushes and wisps the hair out of her eyes. "He's my soul mate. I can feel it. We are so comfortable with each other it's almost like we're the same person. It kind of freaks me out a bit, but exhilarates me all the same."

"Hm, so it's like you're dating you!" Nina concludes. "I would love to date me! I'm such a catch and would make myself the happiest girl in the world."

We all laugh at the thought of Nina romancing herself. It's not too far off from her reality as it turns out. She pampers herself with every chance she gets.

"That's wonderful, Min!" I add after the laughter has died down. "Should I completely transform your room into my studio then?"

"About that, I'll probably be ending my lease at the condo at the end of next month. Leonard and I are pretty sure things are progressing well enough that I'll be fully moving in to his place. I'll help you find someone else though, Portia!" she says almost apologetically.

Although I'm surprised at how quickly the two lovebirds have made a nest together, I can't be upset at her decision to leave me. If I found Mr. Wonderful, I'd do the exact same thing.

I just need to find Mr. Wonderful. Damn it, that's the toughest part!

"So, Port, how's the rest of the week been at that new posh gig of yours. What's the magazine called again? The Shoe Press?" Charlie asks, most likely to change the subject from what she senses to be a difficult subject for me. Little does she know that the topic of my career is even less desirable for me to be discussing in the moment.

"Oh, well, no it's called *The Stiletto Press*. There's a bit of a learning curve at the magazine, but I'm becoming more comfortable now that I have a week under my belt there." I continue on with the fibbing. "I'm really more excited about creating my designs!"

"Great to hear, Portia!" Tricia says. "It's so incredible that you've moved on so seamlessly to the career you prefer!"

Yeah, "seamlessly" my tush! If by "seamless" she means being slapped, heartbroken, and made to scrub the crap off of the said Magazine's office floor.

"Isn't it great!" I reply emphatically. Perhaps a little too emphatically because I sense that Nina is picking up on the fact that my words are unmatched by my clearly awkward and squirmy body language. She stares at me with a concerned look and I inadvertently make eye -contact, holding her gaze for a moment and then looking down at my drink evasively. I can tell from how intently Nina is staring at me that I will soon have a load of questions fired my way as soon as she can get me all to herself.

My suspicions are soon proven to be correct. The girls' night comes to an end a mere three hours later. Nina grabs me by the hand to walk with me to the subway. At first, we saunter silently swinging our arms as we go. Just as I believe I've avoided the questioning firing squad, it begins.

"Port, is everything okay, babe? I saw those pearly whites you were exposing all night and especially when you were discussing your new job, but the expression you had pasted to your face was obviously a big old cover up! Is work stressful? Are they treating you well? Do you need me to set that Mireille woman straight?"

Dear god please do!

"I'm fine, Neen, it's just…"

It's just that I'm absolutely jobless, heartbroken, roommateless, and soon to have my character smeared by Mireille, herself!

"I didn't expect the fashion industry to involve…well…I… I'm trying to find my feet, but I feel as though I'm getting knocked down at every step." I leave it at that, and see that Nina is done pressing for details as she draws me in for a shoulder-to-shoulder compassionate squeeze.

"No need to say more, doll. It must be difficult. You'll find your footing. We'll chat tomorrow, but you go home and get some beauty sleep. I don't think you can get anymore radiant though, but try! Prove me wrong!" she says light-heartedly as a Nina style attempt to lift my quickly plummeting spirits. Tomorrow may be my doomsday after all.

We part and the entire subway ride home I remain fixated on the matter of the article. After Liv exposed all of her wicked intentions I did extensive research on the print cycles of *The Stiletto Press* and discovered that press day would have been today, meaning the new issue would find its way to retail outlets and magazine stands all over the country a few hours from now.

My heart is beating rapidly as I have visions of me wandering the streets searching for employment and being rejected at every turn because businesses of all sorts have come across the inaccurate account that has painted me as if I'm some ill-tempered employee with a horrendous work ethic and a bad attitude.

I bet Michele won't even want to work with me! I'll be finished! And Danielle Parent will never speak to me again after bringing her into this whole mess and allowing those bitches to drag her name through the mud.

I sigh heavily and begin my walk to the condo, completely wide-eyed while I do so for fear that Liv will jump out from a hidden corridor or alley way and assault me once more.

If only I had more of a mean -streak, I would attempt to unveil all of the horrible facets of her character, but I just have no reputation to stand on in the eyes of the print world. No one would listen to little old me.

My mind drifts to deep thoughts about Guillaume and his role in everything. Anger rises within me at the sudden assumption that he planned this whole mess! Introducing me to that wicked woman is what has caused this all! He just washes his hands of it all and jets off to New York? I wanted to believe he had no intention of harming me, but I'm suddenly characterizing him as the true schemer in this whole nasty scenario and seeing him in a new and unflattering light.

He never truly wanted me to succeed! This was all in his little plan. He wanted to see two women go at each other over him and that's exactly what he got! If he cared, why isn't he here helping me and defending me against Liv the lunatic? I hate him, I hate him,

"I HATE HIM!" I scream at the top of my lungs as I enter my condo lobby. A woman with her children jumps in surprise at my rancorous bellowing and then scoots them into the elevator. I wouldn't want to be around me either, I suppose. I'm just a failure in all areas of life and come tomorrow will most likely have to move back in with my parents.

I take a long hot bath, and crawl into bed attempting to sleep off the anxiety that has haunted me tirelessly for the past three days. The sweet slumber I had hoped to find is instead disturbed with nightmarish dreams and visions of me as a withered up old woman, begging for money on the street-corner. The only somewhat positive part of the dream I suppose is that I'm still sporting my most current jeans and the "No Fear" T-shirt.

They still fit!

CHAPTER 25

I rise bright and early the following morning but do not feel eager to begin my day. The anxiety from last night is gripping me even tighter and my stomach is in knots at the thought of the countless copies of current *Stiletto Press* magazines that are primed and ready for sale.

The usual urge to spend the morning working on my designs is absent. My ravenous need to relieve my stress with food is instead taking over.

I need fresh air to clear my head.

This thought leads me out the door after throwing on some joggers a hoodie and some sneakers. I walk to Bloor Street as if I have some destination in mind, but am simply allowing my feet to guide me.

I wander down Bloor Street, although on a semi-intent hunt for delicious eats of any sort. I'm drawn into a bakery café that has an enormous cut out of a scrumptious looking cupcake outside.

I could down a cupcake that size in a heartbeat.

Whenever I'm feeling low, my locked away tendencies to over eat pastries and sweets of all kinds are suddenly unleashed. This situation has me on melt down mode and cupcakes of any and all sorts are the medicine in order, even at nine fifteen in the morning. I quickly order a six pack of a mouth-watering cupcake medley; red velvet, vanilla bean, mocha, lemon merengue, Oreo cream and hazelnut, then I find a seat nearest the window and within minutes consume three of the six in the daintiest manner possible. The woman behind the counter looks a touch concerned, but smiles warmly and compassionately.

"Everything Okay today?" the attendant inquires. "I can see you're enjoying my cupcakes, but at the rate you're downing them there must be some asshole out there who's just run off with your heart."

Hell, is it that obvious that I'm in heartbreak recuperation mode?

"I'm all right. I just had a rough week at work and yes, I guess there is an asshole man involved," I say humbly.

"Darling, there's always an asshole man involved when it comes to over eating. From your slim physique I can tell this isn't normal for you. Do yourself a favour and forget him if he's forgotten you. It's only fair." The trouble is, he hasn't forgotten me, apparently, but I'm not about to unload my whole present circumstance on this stranger. That's what Nina and Lola are for.

"Thanks for the advice. I…" As I'm preparing to change the subject and avoiding unnecessary sharing of my depressing situation, I catch a glimpse of the word "Stiletto" in a reflecting mirror.

She has a copy of The Stiletto Press on her back table! Oh god, is it the current edition? I'm going to vomit or poop or….

"Is that the newest issue of *The Stiletto Press* I see on your back table?" I ask in the calmest way, although sweat is forming heavily on my upper lip.

"Yeah, it is! I just grabbed it on my way in this morning. I don't normally buy that one. I find it a bit uninteresting and like they just rip off ideas from the good magazines, but it's the cheapest and my hubby has me on a budget."

"Could I have a look, if you don't mind? Please?" I say in a pathetic manner.

"Oh, well sure!" She slides the magazine across the counter like a bartender sending me a shot of tequila. I wish what I'm about to read would have the numbing effects of tequila, but am painfully aware it will wrench me into my fully unwelcoming reality.

I grab the magazine and rush back to my table where I begin rifling through its pages. I can't flip them fast enough. I'm a complete ball of nerves.

What section would an article totally ending a desperate woman's career before it even starts be in? City Life? Do's and Don'ts? Diamonds and Duds? God I can't take it!

I pop another cupcake in my mouth and munch away, smearing the vanilla bean icing on my lip corners as I do so. Swallowing hard I see *it*. In the section titled "Fashion Forward," a heading that reads *"Portia Delaney, Hot in Paris, turned Not in T.O."*

I wipe my face clean as I begin reading. My neck is burning up and the heat is rising with every bit of text I scan. My heart drops at the portion that reads:

> *"Portia Delaney begged to be a part of our family and then behaved as if she was too good for our establishment. Her fiery disposition enticed us to write this summation as a warning to respectable editors NOT to hire her for your team. Instant star on the Parisian fashion scene or not, work ethic, and apprecia-tion for employers is a must. Unfortunately, Portia Delaney has neither of the two."*

I'm distraught and utterly undone. I lay my head on my arms and tears stream down my face. They even brought the experience at Hopewell into the article.

I bet it was that jerk Darryl who blabbed!

My one saving grace is that Danielle Parent is not mentioned. I have no idea why, but at least that is a small victory in this hopeless situation. I continue to sob for a few moments, completely aware that the sweet woman behind the counter is witnessing my reaction.

Finally somewhat composed, I rise from the table and make my way back to the counter where I slide the magazine to the attendant. She sees the fresh tears on my cheeks and immediately tosses the magazine into the garbage behind her.

"Darling, anything in here that caused you to become this upset is not worth my time. I knew that magazine was junk!"

I manage a half smile and say, "Thanks for that."

"You do know that those words in there will be forgotten in days. Trash will always be trash. That magazine is right where it belongs."

"I guess I do."

"Good, now save those last two cupcakes for a couple pals, remember to tell your friends about us!"

I turn to gather my things. "I will be sure to. Thanks for your kind words and delicious cupcakes this morning." I make my way out the door somewhat determined to not let that trashy article in that trashy magazine, ruin my day.

Clouds hover low in the sky as I step back out onto Bloor Street, but I glimpse a ray of light seeping through from behind the cloud cover and decide that perhaps this day can only get better in more than one sense of the word. Upon completing that thought my phone begins blaring out Nina's ring tone, Spice Girls "Wannabe." I answer before the girls can get too far along in the addictive ditty.

"Neen, how are you?" I say calmly and hope she hasn't called for sympathy reasons after possibly coming across the article already.

"Babe, I'm great! Just finished up a chat with Victoria and wanted to see if you'd pop by around noon. I've got a favour to ask you, and it's a task that only you can carry out the way that I need it done."

Lord, this sounds like a request from a mobster or something. As long as she doesn't want me to off anyone...

"Oh, well, I'll have to check with Mireille and make sure she doesn't need me to hang around the office for any last minute items. I'm sure it will be fine though. I'll let you know if I get held up with any styling tasks or print work."

"Sure sweets! Let me know. Ciao."

◇◇◇◇◇◇◇

The pop-in to see what it was that Nina needed from me has my head spinning and I'm feeling a bit clammy all over. What I assumed to be a conversation about another hilarious dating episode and a request for me to carry out a coffee run has turned into her sending me on a personal errand to the home of Ms. Victoria Lewis herself!

"Nina, you can't be serious! She would turn me away at the very moment I arrive on her doorstep! You actually think that by showing up with the handbag she left behind at your office she will somehow forget that she absolutely detests me? Not a chance." I fire the Hermes bag onto her waiting area sofa.

"Babe, I don't think. I know! Trust me, Port. It's not simply about the bag itself. It's about what's in the bag, which is for her eyes and her eyes only. Now go!" she says sternly while collecting the luxury tote and heaving it back at me. I've learned that you never allow a Hermes anything to fall to the ground so my reflexes grab the designer accessory out of mid-air.

"She's renting a place on The Bridle Path at number eighty-seven. Now scram," she commands with a little wink and a half smile that have me even more worried. Thank god I went home to change my clothes before heading to meet Nina. It would have been horribly embarrassing to show myself on Victoria's doorstep in anything less than the very Ralph Lauren pencil skirt and button up striped shirt I'm sporting. I had to make it believable to Nina that I was meeting her on my lunch hour, after all.

After hailing a cab and giving the driver my address the nerves truly settle in at the thought of the destination awaiting my arrival.

Perhaps she'll forget who I am and believe that I'm just Nina's errand girl, take the bag from me, give me a monstrous tip and send me on my way.

I can use all the tip money I can get these days seeing as my financial future is a bit hazy and uncertain.

Within twenty minutes the cab driver pulls in to a massive circular drive and drops me near a trickling fountain. The serene setting is unfortunately juxtaposed against the storm of emotions torridly ripping through my body. I remind myself to breathe, pay the cab driver, and walk on as if I'm walking the plank.

I ring the doorbell and within moments am greeted by a well-kept woman dressed in all black.

"Oh, good afternoon, you must be Ms. Delaney. Please come on in. Ms. Lewis is expecting you."

She is? Oh god, this must be a set up! She's probably read the article and is going to ream me out for being such a poor representative of the fashion industry! I'm sunk before I ever got sailing.

"Right this way, Ms. Delaney." The pleasant and polished woman guides me into a rather sizable lounge space that is decorated almost entirely in white aside from a bright pink ottoman directly in the centre of the room. I sit on a welcoming armchair and await Victoria Lewis in suspense and terror, clinging to her Hermes bag as I do so.

"Portia, Nina told me you would come by with the bag I left behind. I appreciate you going out of your way like this. You can head home in my company car when we're done."

Victoria glides in fully garbed in a silk knee length dress that is perfectly cinched at her waist to create a lovely hourglass shape. Her heels click along the marble floor while she finds her way to the sofa adjacent to where I'm seated. She seems so sweet, yet she's set up in the perfect position to go for my jugular.

"So, let's have it. Pass it on over to its mama." Victoria gestures at the bag perched upon my lap. I hand it over and am deciding whether I should curtsy after I do so, or if this would be over the top.

"Portia, how are you feeling about the events that have transpired recently at *The Stiletto Press*?"

My heart drops.

"I did have a chance to read over the harsh article Mireille printed about you and I have to say I'm quite disheartened." Her expression becomes tight and somewhat severe.

My nerves still on overdrive, I respond as calmly as possible. "Ms. Lewis, I'm extremely torn up that Mireille has painted such an awful picture of me. I'm not any of those things she accused me of. Mireille was purposely making a fool of me based on the urgings of a certain Parisian fashion scene honcho. She despises me for turning the eyes of the one she's in love with to me. I didn't intend to gain his attention and now the career-based dream that I had is fizzling all because I've enraged such a powerful woman."

The explanation flows out of me as if I had prepared it beforehand. I'm totally caught off guard by how easily I am able to communicate my hardships and unfortunate situation.

"Dear, there is no excuse that can be made for..." Victoria begins, but I'm on such a roll with my need to be understood that I continue blabbing on.

"I'm not making excuses, Ms. Lewis! She's out to get me and all I've done is attempt to live fashion as *you* instructed me to at our first meeting. I left my boring job behind and set off to Paris in hopes of finding inspiration and gaining experience. What did I arrive home with? Nothing! Aside from a broken heart, a bitch on my tail who is attempting to undo the already undone, and a bad case of jet lag. I even got fired from my only paying job! Sure, I hated it and wanted to get out as soon as I could, but not when I was already destitute and coming off such disappointment. You can't judge me based on what you read in that horrible article. Mireille, Liv, Angelica...they all set me up!"

Victoria sighs and rolls her eyes in an overly exaggerated manner.

Shit, I've upset her! Of course she'll side with Mereille and Liv. They are some-bodies and I'm just as Liv said, a nobody.

"Are you finished with your little rant? Are you ready to let me continue now that you've gotten that unnecessary rambling out of your system?" Victoria asks, clearly unimpressed.

"Yes, my apologies…it's just that…" I stop myself and simply bite my tongue awaiting a lashing from Victoria's.

"Portia, what I was intending to say before you cut me off, is that there is no excuse to be made for Liv's behaviour. You cannot let her manipulative scheming dampen your spirit! It offends me greatly that you seem to equate my advice to you with some sort of failure. I understand that I was curt with you at our first meeting, but Nina has shared with me all of the excitement that you experienced in Paris and I have been in contact with the individuals that you have impressed so greatly. I speak with Michele regularly. *Crave* promotes his talent endlessly, and he spoke of you as if you are bursting with the same drive and innovation that he is. His opinion matters to me more than a thousand Livs!

He also said you are a dream to work with. He's so eager to partner with you in the future that he's mentioning you at every interview he gives, every dinner party he attends, and each event he is part of! "

I'm speechless and a bit awestruck by how impressed Victoria seems to be with me. Or is she simply impressed by others' opinions of me?

"Now, I've been thinking and speaking with not only Michele, but with Danielle Parent as well. Danielle is a dear friend of mine, and although we head up magazines that are in direct competition, it is a very healthy competition. She once worked under me at *Crave*, but then took over at *La Vie* when the original chief editor stepped down."

She pauses and breathes in deeply as if what she will say next is stirring up a deeply rooted nostalgia.

"I went to Paris many years ago, before I even knew Danielle. It was a life-changing experience for me. So as soon as Danielle was offered the opportunity to take on the head position at a prestigious Parisian magazine, I practically shooed her out the door and begged her to take it. Not only did it mean that she would be able to go back to her home, but it meant that I would have a reason to return to that wonderful city as often as I could." Her eyes are diverted to the swaying branches outside.

I attempt to keep the conversation on track to cause her to divulge more. "It must be wonderful to have a good friend over there! It makes the perfect excuse to head over the Atlantic as often as possible."

"It does, most certainly, Portia. Do you sometimes wish, though, that you could slow down time or even reverse it?"

I hear a vulnerability seeping out from behind her seemingly ever-present confident exterior. I nod at the inquiry. "Portia, time passes so quickly. We all have so many intentions in life and make all kinds of plans, but, well, you can't experience plans or enjoy plans or gain any kind of love of life from plans until the plans are made real. Make them real, Portia. Don't get lost in the blue prints for life's course."

She turns from me for a moment to regain composure and there is a drawn out silence until her assistant enters with a tray on which she's balancing some delicious looking hors d'oeuvres and a pot of tea.

"Thank you, Jenna. Go ahead and take a break. We'll be a little while longer."

"Yes, Ms. Lewis. I'll be in the backyard if you need me," Jenna says in a sweet tone then pads out of the room and Victoria directs her attention back to me.

"I suppose you're wondering why I'm telling you all of this. I'm getting to the crux of the matter. I assure you."

"Ms. Lewis, I'm honoured you are even shedding light on my situation and taking the time out of your busy schedule to speak with me. I did not expect it after how our last conversation ended."

She pours one cup of tea and then another while commenting on my words. "Yes, well anyone can change their mind about a person. I judged you irrationally based on one silly mistake you made. I worked extremely hard for my current position and I felt that you were making light of that with the little fib you told. I now see that you are aware of this all."

"I am, Ms. Lewis. I never meant to make you feel as though I disrespected or belittled your title. I got carried away and regret it deeply."

"Water under the bridge is how I view the whole incident. Now, as I was saying I had intended to go to Paris often, but Portia I never made those plans real. Danielle and I would meet all over the world, but a wedge was driven between me and Paris in the form of my husband. He insisted I never return and that when Paris Fashion Week came around each year I send my assistant to represent *Crave* at the event. I let him smother the flame in my heart, the flame that burned so brightly for the memory of my time there."

"Why would he insist that you never go back?" I question impulsively but am horribly aware that I am in no place to ask such personal questions regarding Ms. Lewis and her marital situation. She fails to reply and instead returns to a previous topic of discussion.

"Danielle Parent was disgusted to discover Mireille's intentions, Portia. After you contacted her she made a point of getting to the bottom of the whole scheme. She tried tirelessly to keep Mireille from printing a word, in the end Mireille caved, but only in regards to withholding the lies about Danielle herself. Danielle tried to clear your name as well, Portia, but when Mireille would not let up, Danielle contacted me knowing full well that both my opinion along with her own far outshine any negative words scribbled down by Mireille. You're not undone, Portia, because Danielle, Michele and I refuse to let that happen."

I want to jump into her arms and cry on her shoulder at these words, but realize Victoria may renege on her opinion of me if she sees me crumble and act so vulnerably, not to mention the fact that I would surely wrinkle and ruin her gorgeous silk dress in the process due to my weight and my tear stains. Instead, I speak of my appreciation in the most ineloquent way possible, stuttering and muttering while choking back tears.

Victoria looks puzzled and quite uncomfortable in the moment. She halts my attempts to display appreciation verbally by offering to stuff my mouth with the plated goodies before us.

"Portia, drink your tea and please try some of this food that has been prepared by Jenna." She pushes the tray across the ottoman as if to say "shut it, honey."

"I know you had asked me something earlier that I did not respond to, Portia. It is an issue that tugs on my heartstrings and sends me back in time. It's as if I've been conditioned to lock it away for so long that I get anxious at the thought of finally being able to revisit it."

"Oh…" I engage in her willingness to share the details I had been wondering.

"You see, Nina has been brought on board mostly because my husband and I are in the middle of a separation, which is headed toward divorce. She's helping me find my identity again that has for so long been wrapped up in my husband's. It's been so difficult over the years attempting to be at my best in the eye of the media and wear a smile as if he and I have a solid relationship. Sadly, it's been over for quite some time. Not on paper, but it has been over in our hearts for years."

She stands and wipes at her dress that has become a bit clingy due to static, takes a sip of her tea, and walks towards the garden door. I remain seated, feeling uneasy and uncertain as to whether to follow her or wait until she returns. After a moment, Victoria ambles back in through the French doors, diminishing my uncertainty.

"So here I am, a middle-aged woman, longing to revisit my plans from my early years. Portia, no matter how successful a person is in the fashion industry, or any industry for that matter, this success does not fill that void left when there is not a true love. I've never really experienced true love aside from in a relationship with one man from the time I've spoken of."

"In Paris?" I inquire, hoping that I'm not being too brazen with my question.

She sighs and nods. "Portia, this man, the one who you feel has caused these issues between you and Liv, it is clear that he adores you. I know that he must! Liv would not travel all this way to try and ruin your situation if he didn't. As crazy as she may seem, she is a woman just like you and I. We both know that we have keen instincts when it comes to matters of the heart."

"I suppose so," I reply.

"But, Portia, it's not just Liv's efforts that have made me absolutely sure of this! Michele has made me aware of this man's continuous efforts to benefit you. Even since you left him behind he has worked endlessly to promote you! I received a call…last Friday…it was him, Portia, this Mr. Boisvert. He urged me to allow you the opportunity to work under my guidance. He swore that you are the diamond in the rough that *Crave* needs."

"He did?" I whisper, feeling outside my body as I do.

"He did. I must say that I was unmoved and I simply shrugged off the request, but did look into his experience and felt that his look was so intriguing that I simply had to have him sign on for *Crave's* fall issue."

I'm reminded of the reason I was made Liv's personal punching bag and footstool. "It was you! You're the reason Guillaume is leaving for New York! Ms. Lewis, Liv hunted me down thinking that I had something to do with it!"

"This line of work toughens a girl up quickly, Portia. There are a million Livs waiting in the wings, so the more you dwell on your hurt feelings or your insecurities, the easier you make it for those others to steal the spotlight. If you get knocked down or out, you get back up and don't let it phase you," Victoria says passionately, but I'm finding it hard to believe Victoria has been knocked down by anybody.

"Believe me, I've been there. I may appear to be on top of the game. It takes playing that defensive zone constantly to keep it that way."

I'm beginning to feel the intimidation I initially was harassed by in my interactions with Victoria melting away as she reveals more and more of her true character. "I believe it, Ms. Lewis. You must have been challenged by your share of Liv's throughout your career."

"I certainly have! There was a Claire, a Paulette, an Avery and the list goes on for miles, but back to Guillaume Boisvert, you do care for him deeply. I can see it in your face when I bring his name up." Victoria lingers on the subject and my closeted vulnerability is threatening to reveal itself.

"I did, truly, but I just can't trust him. I don't think, I mean he's in Paris and soon to be New York. He'll have a thousand Americans lining up to be swept away by him with his charm and hotness. I just don't see the point in…"

"So what are you going to do? Push him out of your mind, ignore the efforts he's putting in on your behalf, settle for some business tycoon here in Toronto because it seems easy and the image you want to portray to those around you? Darling, it's not all it's cracked up to be. I won't let you make the same mistakes I did. I see a spark in you. The same spark that burned in me earlier in life."

She pauses, somewhat breathless and worked up. I even spot a tear trickling down her cheek. She suddenly rises and strides over to her Hermes bag, the very same one that I returned to her. She shuffles through it, I assume to search for a tissue. Then the unimaginable occurs… a gasp, a shriek, a perfectly primped, yet unconscious Victoria Lewis crashing to the marble floor. The scene plays out so quickly that I sit frozen gathering my wits and then finally act. I race to the garden to holler for Jenna to assist me.

"Oh my god! What did you do to her? You've sent her into shock!" Jenna yells at me while running circles around Victoria's seemingly lifeless body.

"I didn't do or say anything. She went to get something out of her bag and then something in it made her scream, and then the next thing I knew she was passed right out. Elevate her legs! I'll grab a wet cloth."

By the time I've returned to the scene from fetching the cloth, Victoria is stirring and is propped up on her elbow, slowly coming to.

"Ms. Lewis," Jenna says. "How do you feel? Is your head sore?"

"Jenna, I'm fine. I don't feel any pain," she responds. "I was so surprised by what I saw in my bag, I suppose the emotion overtook me and I passed out!"

"I see," replies Jenna. "Well, do you want me to ask your visitor to leave so you can recover in peace?"

"Not at all! I'm actually even more inclined to have her stay, to ask about what I found. It's so fateful that all the memories brought rushing back since you and I have begun our discussion, Portia, are so connected to the discovery I've just made."

Victoria directs her attention and words towards me. She sounds sweet and child-like in the moment.

I go to her side, feeling drawn to her vulnerable conduct and keen to find out what the mystery object is that shocked her to unconsciousness. "Ms. Lewis, what was it? What shocked you so severely?"

"Call me Victoria, dear."

These words have me beaming on the inside.

On a first name basis with Vicoria Lewis!

"It…well…it's a…here I'll show you. Perhaps you knew of it all along." She once again shuffles through her tote and pulls out what appears to be a black and white photograph, and I laugh heartily at the revelation.

"You did know! Didn't you?"

Victoria smiles and hands the photograph to me.

"Ms. Lew…Victoria, Nina and I just happened to converse with the very man in that photograph while at the base of the Eiffel Tower. I assure you that I had nothing to do with getting the photograph out of his grip and here now in yours."

Nina!

"You are stunning in that picture. I always believed you were a knockout, Victoria, but you are beyond gorgeous, and have a glow to you that I only see on people when they are truly head over heels."

She smiles, gently removing the photograph from my fingers, running her own along the outlines of her one true love's smiling face. She looks up at me, her expression tight.

"And I walked away from it, Portia. I turned my back because of fear. I was afraid what the world would think of me for attaching myself to a penniless musician. Was that glow and that head-over-heels bliss not fully present when you were in the arms of Guillaume?" She turns the conversation back to my situation. "Will you walk away as I did and regret it the rest of your life?"

"I…don't think it's the same, though, Victoria. My situation has another woman in the mix and Guillaume is so well known that he could have his pick of anyone."

"But he's choosing YOU, Portia! YOU. Day after day, humbly working behind the scenes to give as much of himself to you and your needs as he can from such a great distance. He's allowing you your space also, not forcing your affection for him. Those are not the actions of a player who intends to break your heart."

I frown and hang my head at her words even though I should be tickled at the thought that Guillaume cares so much for me. Guilt is replacing the excitement I should feel; yet, the distance weighs on my mind the most.

"Portia, I had no idea how pertinent this little meeting with you would become to *my* next step in life. The blueprints are taking form again!"

Victoria is so cheerful, it's as if I'm talking to a different woman all together. "I think I want to go...well...no I'm going to go! I'm going to Paris! Jenna!" She calls towards the kitchen where Jenna is tidying up. "Jenna, get me on a flight next week to Paris!"

Jenna pokes her head out from the kitchen.

"You heard me, Jenna, forget the dishes, get yourself on the phone to my travel agent and make it happen."

"Sure, Ms. Lewis. I'll get right on it," Jenna says clearly surprised by this request.

"Portia, I know I was harsh towards you and I still would like you to prove yourself before I take any steps that might result in you being employed by *Crave*, but when it comes to love and matters of the heart, I am a softy. This idea has just swooped into my mind and I had no intention of offering this before the fate of this meeting became so evident to me. You will go to New York, you will stay in my guest apartment on the Upper East Side, and you will intern at *Crave's* New York office! It will be unpaid, but it sounds as though Michele is desperate to work with you so you're sure to gain financial stability with that deal, and once you prove yourself as an intern, I will have no problem promoting you. More importantly, you will go to Guillaume, you will explore the relationship you have with him, and extricate the worry about distance from your mind so you and he can simply be. Be away from Liv, away from his Parisian life that swallowed up his time. You will both be two fish out of water and able to navigate your way in a new environment. I, on the other hand, will be in Paris because as Audrey said 'Paris is always a good idea,' darling."

She finishes listing off her majestic demands and is awaiting my response, but a response does not come. I'm gripped by emotion. My throat is tightening and my eyes are flooding due to the feeling of appreciation and relief that has come as a result of Victoria's proposal. It's not quite the form of proposal I've always dreamed of, but certainly has the makings to be even more than I could have imagined.

"Don't say a word, dear. Jenna will contact you with your departure plans and itinerary in a few days' time. You get home and start making arrangements to be a force to be reckoned with in the Empire State. How's that for *nothing*?"

CHAPTER 26

"Look at you, doll! Brimming from ear to ear, looking absolutely divine and radiant. Now what, oh, what could have happened to make you walk in here as if you've just struck gold?"

Nina welcomes me after making my way back to her office in Victoria's company car. The ride to the office is a blur. I'm still experiencing a lingering shock from Victoria's proposed future for me. Nina's inquiry and cheeky welcome only solidify my suspicions that she knows full well what the reason is for my current ecstatic state because the reason was all her doing.

I don't respond, I don't react to her greeting. I stride directly to her and wrap my arms around her. I lay my head on her shoulder and feel the anxiety and distress that have gripped me for so long now melting away.

"Port, Victoria called me a moment ago and let me in on her little secret about her plans for you. I knew of everything else that she would discuss, but that…well that I didn't know…you deserve it all, Port. You deserve to live your dreams. I'm going to miss you terribly, babe, but I'll make regular visits to you and your swanky new lifestyle in the Big Apple."

Nina speaks in a soft, sweet tone. I sigh at the thought of leaving the woman who has been my dearest companion and soul mate through all of my ups and downs, but know that the bond between us is one that can survive, no matter where life takes the two of us.

"Nina, it was all because of you. You were the inspiration behind Victoria offering me what she has. The photograph turned her from the rigid, powerful woman I've only ever known her to be, to the romantic, joyful woman she appeared as in the photograph. When did you…how did you…"

"Our final morning in Paris, doll, I didn't go to see Stefan. I intended to, but for whatever reason I couldn't stop thinking about that photograph and knew that in Victoria's depressing divorce situation, a thing like that photograph would only be of use to help her learn to love again. I knew if she saw it she would remember what real love and adventure felt like and perhaps see things more positively.

The elderly man gave it willingly hoping that when I presented it to her, the reaction would be just as it has turned out to be. It sounds as though Paris will be a hot spot for Victoria over the next little while, which means I may spend more time there as well. I do want to maintain her as a client. So I've been toying with the idea of allowing Charlie to attempt some coaching sessions so that she can hold things down here when I'm overseas. She has turned over a new leaf in her own life and I truly feel that her personable nature is starting to shine through. Sorry, sweets, I'm rambling. Back to your incredible news!"

"Nina, I'm just as excited for you. Don't apologize. You are so deserving of my attention in every way for the impact you've had on my life today. Did you know about everything at *The Stiletto Press* and Liv and…"

"I did, hon. I mean, not until you told me how you were having a tough time finding your place there. It was after that conversation that I knew you were bottling up some information. I pried. I chatted with Victoria who had already been informed about the whole article issue by Danielle Parent. I knew you'd be gutted. So I asked Victoria to give you a little pep talk and to assure you that she and Danielle would refute Mireille's words. I slipped the photo in hoping that Victoria would find it and that you may witness a softer and more compassionate Victoria. That is the Victoria I have come to know and admire over the short time I've known her. My plan went even better than I had thought!"

Nina grabs my hand and spins me around like I'm her latest success story. I engage her in her lunacy and continue twirling along with her until we both crash to the floor in a fit of laughter.

Rolling on to one side I whisper faintly, "Neen, I'm going to miss you terribly. You've been my rock through everything and mean the world to me."

"Doll, I'll be the furthest thing from your mind when you're wrapped up in Guillaume's arms living the life. But you know I'll miss you like crazy. We'll just have to become jet setters and make the most of it all."

"Promise me one thing, Neen."

"What, hon?"

"That when you're in Paris, you track Liv Pickard down, march up to her and give her one of these." I turn to Nina and make the largest raspberry, flatulence sound I can muster. We both begin laughing uncontrollably once more, and I vow to lock this moment in my most cherished memory compartment of my mind.

"So, babe, it sounds as though you'll be on your way to New York sooner than we know. I'm going to see if Paolo will host a send-off party at his place. It's so beautiful there in the summer, being right on the beach and all. Hopefully Charlie will refrain from torching his house this time." She giggles. "Let me know a guest list by tomorrow and I'll put the wheels in motion."

"Anyone but Liv and Angelica, sweetheart," I reply.

"Oh, I forgot to mention, Angelica had no choice but to move back to Edmonton! She had nothing and no prospects so she's apparently doing admin work for her dad in the oil sands office. Imagine our posh Ange up in the oil fields sporting Versace and Gucci!" Another fit of laughter ensues.

"As long as you, Victoria and our best girls are all there, it'll be the only way I'd want to be sent off."

◇◇◇◇◇◇◇◇

The party was a raging success and there were no fires or victims to speak of. Only the expected guests attended and Victoria dazzled us all with not only her attire but also her toast to both Nina and I. The heartfelt speech outlined how pivotal the two of us have been in her rebirth and new excitement for life and love. She then wished me all the success and love while I settle in her beloved New York.

The night ended with a plate of delectable cupcakes I insisted be ordered from Desmond & Beatrice Bakery after the support the attendant showed me a few short days ago. Nina made sure to fetch my preferred champagne that we toasted once more with after sending helium balloons drifting into the night.

Hugs, tears and farewells leave me somewhat emotionally drained by the party's end, but I cab home filled with an enthusiasm and elevation that far exceeds any I've experienced. Me, in New York, working at *Crave,* in the near reaches of Guillaume Boisvert, thousands of miles from Liv?

It doesn't get much better than that.

CHAPTER 27

The rush to get everything in Toronto organized for my departure in the few short days I had was a bit of a challenge. But I managed to find a couple to sublet the condo from Minnie and I until the lease runs out, pack all my belongings, mostly for storage, visit with my parents who were over the moon with joy for my exciting new venture, squeeze in one more farewell session with Lola, and drop in to Mireille's office to let her know she and Liv have failed.

Mireille directed me to exit the premises immediately. I had no problem complying. So now here I am in the Empire State, ready to begin to build my own dream empire in the form of fabulous couture design.

The wind breezes through my tousled hair as I make my way to the waiting car at JKF Airport. The friendly driver, hired by Ms. Lewis, welcomes me and helps me into a car fit for the President himself. I breathe in deeply, taking in all that compounds my present circumstance and breathe out, attempting to send the haunting thoughts of lost love, vicious manipulation, and insecurity into the welcoming sunny day. I prepare myself to be welcomed by my present. Present in more than one sense as Guillaume is just about the best gift a girl could ask for.

My usual reaction when having just arrived at a new and most certainly exciting destination, such as New York, is to hang my head out the window, bug-eyed like a child seeing snow for the first time. I don't...I am lost in thoughts attached to the unfolding of the previous month. Resonating on the recent remodelling of my life's path, fear attempts to grip me as those thoughts veer towards, *Portia, it all came together just as quickly as it may all fall apart.*

I close my eyes attempting to squint the negative from my mind. Instead, I'm harassed by visions of Liv's ferocious expression the moment before I felt her clammy palm hard against my cheek. The haunting persists and I wonder if Liv has truly been extracted from my life.

The driver indicates we're almost at the location designated by Victoria Lewis. Looking out the window and seeing the rows of buildings breezing past I'm sent back in time. My mind replays the night I spent with Guillaume over and over. The memory until now has been more like a nostalgic reminder of a love lost, but in this time and place, I let it overtake me in the most blissful way; the feeling of his moist lips running up and down my body, his muscular build heavy upon my own filling me with the most sublime sensation. Liv cannot separate me from the explosion of desires I currently have pulsing through my core. He's fully mine in this moment and this place. I'm reminded of the sweet words whispered over and over in my ear that I can finally hear so clearly again...

Portia, beautiful Portia...

"Portia, beautiful Portia." The words in real time wrench me out of my dream-like state. I turn to see the one I've been longing for relentlessly. My body is shaking and the urges stirred up from the state of fantasy are surging through me. The fantasy made real, I cannot contain my elation at the sight of him and allow a faint smile to find its way to my trembling lips.

"Guillaume," I say in a hushed tone. He reaches into the car, and helps me out. I feel like Bambi, learning to walk. He wraps his arms around me. I gaze deeply into his beautifully hypnotic eyes. Not able to look away to see even what portion of the city I've arrived in, simply transfixed, he leans in and I feel once more those tender lips against my own. My body reawakens in time with his touch.

"I made clear that my heart would not leave you. With you, Portia, is where it will stay."

The swirling, swiveling sketch of my past has become clear and obstacle free. I look around to see my new surroundings. Amongst the beauty of Central Park and Park Avenue, Guillaume takes my quivering hand in his own and we set out on a journey to explore our new home and our rekindled affection. The bitter taste of disappointment has been washed clean.

Sweetness is all that remains.

-Fin-